Eldorado, Iowa

Eldorado, Iowa

A NOVEL

Amy Weldon

Bowen Press

—— TYLER, TEXAS ——

Published 2019 by
Bowen Press
Tyler, TX 75703
BowenPressBooks.com

ISBN 978-0-9994729-6-5

Printed in the United States of America

For Elizabeth Spencer

Under the porch, nobody would find them. Footsteps might pound up and down overhead as adults muttered to themselves or called to the dogs. The boards would creak and groan. High above, the house would hum with its regular daytime life. But Sarah and Seth would be hidden down in the cool dusty dark, alone.

Through the brick foundation lattice, light fell in squares. Just above them, Father's chessboard sat on the table in front of the parlor window, ranked with creamy-white pawns and queens and kings that had been carved from the tusks of great elephants. They were not for a little girl to touch. And not for a colored boy.

In the cool dark, their breath was very loud. They tried to be quiet anyway so as not to startle the animals—snakes or possums or anything—that might be denned up under here with them. In the world up above, Seth would scoff at her: "possums live in trees." But under here he did not joke. He leaned his head next to hers into the crack of light that fell across the doodlebug tunnel, an upside-down cone in the powdery dirt. *Doodlebug, doodlebug,* they breathed. *Fly away home. Your house is on fire and your children all gone.* And sure enough the hidden doodlebug would scramble up out of the cone in a panic, clawing the crumbs of loose dirt under its feet. It would struggle up, fall back again, fleeing disaster. But this house would never catch fire. It would always be here. And they, its children, would never fly away.

They took their marbles from the sack and played if they were sure the soft click and rattle could not be heard. The ollies and aggies left round holes in the dirt, like the place down in the pasture where the meteor had hit. Or maybe it had been a falling star. *One. Two.* Hop out of the circle. Hop back in.

Mama's feet—her impatient skirt swinging from left to right—would appear suddenly in the yard. "Sarah!" she'd exclaim. "Where on earth are you? I swear, girl, you . . . "

And Sarah and Seth would draw together, hunkering close and holding their breath against the giggles rising in their chests.

Hide out, hide away, hide together. No one would ever find them. As long as they could stay right here, in the place no one else could see.

1

Alone, Sarah wanders out the front door and into the September afternoon. Her skirts brush down the porch steps and over the grass, crushing one fallen leaf, then two. A sudden breeze trembles the maple sapling in the yard, and she sets both hands on her belly. A quiver answers her, under the skin stretching tighter every day. She has to soak in as much light as possible, before the winter comes and the sun is gone here in Iowa. When her baby thinks of *home*, it will think of this little town on what is still, technically, the frontier. Not the plantation, back in Alabama. She's made sure of that.

Despite herself, her mother's voice natters in her head, approving her: *a lady, walking on her lawn.* Her lawn. That's what it would be called back home. Here it's really just the clear square of ground in front of the house, where the old doctor broke up the prairie sod before he died. There are no flower borders, no herringbone brick walks, no walls. Under her feet, the soil is deep and black, netted with tangled roots tamped down by buffalo, or by whatever large creatures walked this corner of Iowa with their milch-cow snufflings, once upon a time, as the glaciers melted and the grass grew tall. She imagines them lumbering into this tiny town, like Mr. Dickens's Megalosaurus waddling up Holborn Hill. London must be so crowded, teeming with dirt and noise and life, in its matter-of-fact foreignness. A great city. Not like this small town at the edge of the world. This place with its optimistic signpost: *Eldorado.*

"You'd better take the Dickens," Mama had urged. "God knows what else you'll have to read out there." So the red leather novels had gone into the trunks with the big blue volume of Shakespeare and the Spenser and Mrs. Wollstonecraft's *Original Stories*. With the quilts and the butter churn and the thick woolen capes and the knitting needles and the gold-rimmed teacups and the medicine chest and the anatomy texts and the forceps and the knives. With old Nero the cat in a big basket. With the blank diary at the bottom of Sarah's red morocco sewing box, latched tight, its pages swarming with silences she can't break.

But not the piano. *No.*

Sarah wanders to the dirt track running past the house—Eldorado, Iowa's main street—and looks to the north, then the south. High limestone cliffs, forested with maple and oak and black walnut, rear above the roofs. At the foot of those cliffs, the river unspools a thin silver thread. She turns her head to look up the street. She knows each building by now: Mrs. Thorson's inn, the Linsvolds' general store, the McElvains' house, Mr. Gabrielson's forge and undertaking parlor, Mrs. Thorson's house, the Johnsons' house, the church, Reverend Preus's house, the schoolhouse, the Olsons' house, the Sawyers' house, the Gundersons' house, the tiny bank with its iron-barred windows, and the square red-brick house where the four Norwegian seminary students live (the Norwegian Lutheran Church paid good money for that brick). Farther down toward the end of the valley stands the cabin the Thorson twins have built for themselves, on their own land. Almost all of them are covered with neat board siding, whitewashed or painted the pale brown Mrs. Linsvold can buy in bulk from St. Paul. The forge and the church are made of stone. How fast these Norwegians and Germans and Swedes, fresh off the boat, had worked. How quickly time seemed to accelerate as Sarah herself moved further into it. When these buildings were built, the war was just getting started back in Alabama. Indians made their camps on these prairies and the wide flat plains beside the river. Now the Indians were gone, pushed further west by the same blue-coated soldiers who had marched down the road past Sarah's own home. And Sarah's home was gone too.

At the end of the street stands old Dr. Foster's house. Now it belongs to Sarah and her husband, Galen—the new doctor has taken the old one's place, just as if he'd never left. This town seems a good place for them to be, *a going concern*, as the land agent had exclaimed. Eldorado. A place where the Lutheran Church of Norway is training young men to minister, in English, to Norwegian settlers. A little town that only needs a doctor. A place to set the pieces of a life on top of one another until they make a wall, a roof, a door.

In its round dark cask under her heart, the baby clenches and pitches: grabbing for its toes, elbowing her bladder, quickening. Four months yet to go until it's born, just over the border into the new year 1876. This child is strong. She speaks to it: *I feel you in there, honey. I'm going to see you soon.* A whim strikes her to unbutton her blouse and stretch the growing mound of her belly toward the sun, to feel her child rotate and swim face-first toward the warm world beyond her skin. Galen's anatomy books have shown her its curled shape, fed by its purple-black cord. Her blood is carrying the news of this sunlight even now, from the surface of her skin straight to the child in its dark. *I know you feel this.* In a year, she'll walk on this lawn with the baby wrapped in a shawl. She'll point out the leaves tickling down through the air to the grass, the bluejays hopping and screeching in the big maple tree. She'll turn its face toward the cluster of buildings down the street and the bluffs reared high above the river, spangled with yellow, orange, red, and green. She will show this world to her child.

She reaches for the buttons of her blouse and stops. *Silly,* she smiles at herself. *I can't walk around with my shirt hanging open.* She should be warm enough, anyway, with all the light there is. This morning, she and Rosa Lee raised all the windows in the house, including the window of Galen's study. Rosa Lee is inside the house now. Through the window, Sarah can hear the slip and slither of bread dough on the kitchen table. She should go inside to help; she's being selfish. *The true lady, the mistress of the house, assists her servants in all their tasks,* the conduct books all exhort, *never ceasing from her own calm labors; her untroubled appearance belies her weight of care.* Instead, Sarah turns away, wanders one step further, then another. Wind nudges a blonde curl out of its knot. Her footsteps rustle in the dead grass, and her skirt crackles through the red and gold maple leaves scattered there. More leaves are pasted to the dirt track that is the end of Main Street, ending at their door. Old Dr. Foster's door, Sarah corrects herself. When the baby comes, the house will be really theirs.

Every week, now, the days are shorter. The sun's leaving them, slipping over the edge of the world like Galen's tired face slips out of sight below the edge of their blankets. He curls up like a child at night, now, nestles in, breathes deeply. But then he starts to shout through the bars of his dreams, pedaling his feet against her swollen legs. If she leaves him alone in their bed, it gets worse. So she throws herself over him like a woman smothering a burning child with a blanket, stretching her arms and legs over his, as close to him as the baby-stomach will allow. This is the only thing that calls him back to her. In his sleep, he huddles downward to nest his cheek against her belly or her breast, and she shifts to accommodate him as best she can. In the mornings, she wakes without ever knowing that she fell asleep.

She could sleep out in the yard, right now. Lean against a tree in this warm sun, out of the wind, and just close her eyes—

"Sarah?" Galen is calling her. So she turns and walks back across the lawn to the house, crackling through the grass and leaves, *thump, thumping* up the steps and across the porch. Chairs stand against the wall in the foyer, where the grandfather clock reads just after two. She comes through the door and turns to the left, to the small front parlor that's now Galen's office and dispensary in one.

An old man's voice wobbles through the door: "And he always told me that the bowels are—"

"Ah, Sarah," interrupts Galen, "this is Mr. McElvain, the founding father of Eldorado. He was the first settler here and because of that the first mayor." A tall thin old man with a stained white beard sits blinking on Galen's examining table, his worn plaid vest buttoned tight. A long-tailed black frock coat like Mr. Lincoln's trails over the table, and a watch chain drapes across his stomach. One link, close to the middle button, has been replaced with a loop of string. His watery gray eyes fasten on Sarah, then slide away. "So this is your wife," he says to Galen, and smiles. "She is a lovely one for such a remote place as this, sir." He pauses. "I named it, you know. Eldorado. Such a hopeful name."

Sarah smiles, as if she's never met this man before. But she has. He appeared in Galen's office the first week they were settled in this house, asking to see *the good doctor*, and comes back every week since. He never remembers her. But he remembers her husband. Galen's fulsome introduction makes him sit straighter, wobbling his mouth as if about to make a speech. She presses down a flash of irritation. Someday she too will be old and need a patient girl to help her. Won't there always be a patient girl, sighing and setting down her knitting or her pen to rise to someone else's task, as long as there are men whose feelings must not be hurt? As long as there are mothers to flatter and satisfy, to please?

"Sarah," Galen says, "Mr. McElvain has asked that we note his symptoms, but to relate them he needs my undivided attention. So I ask that you act as our recording angel this morning. He's got entries in Dr. Foster's ledger. Do you mind?" He's trying not to laugh: the reddish-brown hair over his forehead is trembling, and his wide mouth is quirked down, his long chin twitching. She could look at him and break that laughter loose, if she wanted. But the old man is so anxious, the one string-looped link so frail.

"Of course," she says. "Good morning, Mr. McElvain." She crosses to the tall cabinet behind Galen and removes Dr. Foster's maroon-bound ledger. The pages crackle. *McElvain, Philip*, mutters Dr. Foster's handwriting, *4 April 73, Dementia of which I know not the precise Cause. As ever, record the symptoms he relates: a thickening of the Stool, a "madness in the Bowels."* Then, crammed into the margin: *Poor creature.*

She and Galen have read this whole ledger together. "What would they think if they knew we knew so much about them?" she laughed. The wart removed from Mrs. Thorson's upper lip ("he must have been really good," marveled Galen, "I never would have known, to look at her"), kidney stones, oxen kicks and broken legs and sprained wrists and kettle-scalds and babies: the Thorson twins twenty-five years ago, the little Johnson girls ten and eight, the Olsons' boys. One living, two in the tiny cemetery behind the church. *Don't think of it*, Sarah commands herself. She grips the ledger, firming up her smile.

But, thankfully, the men aren't looking at her. Galen's face is expectant, and Mr. McElvain leans close. "The thing is," he confides, "the bowels are such a delicate machine, when they go off it unhinges the rest of the body, and the mind . . . " He peers at Sarah from under his thick eyebrows. "Doctor"—he leans closer—"is it fit for her to hear this conversation?"

"Oh, Sarah often assists me," Galen says. "Please continue."

Mr. McElvain leans even closer. A sour whiff rises from his clothes. Since Sarah, poised over the ledger with her pen, can smell it, it must be even worse for Galen, but he doesn't move away. "The bowels, sir," says the old man. "They run down with age, like any machine. But one can do one's part to keep them up. Oats, sir, for breakfast! Horses have no such complaints, and thus we learn from the beasts!" He snorts with laughter. "When I perform my morning ablutions I am careful to monitor the stool. It is a valuable indicator, sir, of the state of one's inward body. As opposed to the outer one. When I was a Harvard man, I read all about this distinction. In the original Greek." Sarah scribbles, sighing, *Harvard man. Original Greek. Bowels, bowels, bowels.*

"Well, Mr. McElvain," intones Galen, "yours is a serious case." The old man straightens. "So I am going to give you a rare tincture, to be taken for a week. I've never known it to fail. Sarah, will you reach me a bottle?"

Sarah swivels behind her and selects a tiny empty glass bottle from the cabinet. She hands it to Galen with a flourish. "Thank you, dear," he says. Looking deliberately away from her, he opens the lid of his medicine chest, releasing a musty chemical wind. The box is heavy mahogany, two feet square, with a gold inlay in the lid and levered trays that rear up on smooth hinges when the lid is opened. In the worn purple velvet interior, vials are slotted, labeled in Galen's hand: *Fels.nap. Merc. Laud.* His hand moves to the back left corner: *Plac.* Carefully, he draws from its slot a slim vial full of white grains, then shakes it just enough to rustle them. Mr. McElvain watches every move. "Ah," Galen says, "how well it survived its journey West. I have to be careful; it's like to spoil."

"Indeed," Sarah adds. She grins to herself, thinking of the bin in the kitchen which she and Rosa Lee dip into for cakes, pies, or a spoonful in a cup of tea, and Galen dips into to fill this vial. "It's most valuable."

"And necessary," Galen says. Into the empty bottle he tips a pinch of the white grains, then funnels water down its neck, corks it, and shakes until the grains melt. "Guard it, sir," he warns. "Take a half a spoonful once daily until it's gone. I'll re-examine you when the dosage has run its course."

Mr. McElvain slips the bottle into his vest pocket and staggers to his feet. Through the long white beard, his lips tremble. Sudden tears spring to his eyes. "Sir," he blurts, clasping Galen's hand, "you are a very great healer. The mantle of Dr. Foster rests upon the shoulders of a suitable heir, sir. In this wilderness, healing is a rare thing."

"And necessary," Sarah adds.

Galen smiles at the old man and shakes his hand. "I'm privileged to practice it," he says. "With my lovely assistant."

Mr. McElvain turns to Sarah and bows. "Guard her, sir," he warns. "And the child she bears. It is a wilderness but, with care, not inhospitable."

"I'll remember that," says Galen gravely.

Footsteps thump up the front steps, and a tall woman—her thick hair scraped into a knot, her apron water-spotted—appears in Galen's office door. "Oh, Papa," she sighs. "Dr. Archer, I'm so sorry." Her angular face burns. "I thought he was all settled in his bedroom with his books, and here I find him, again."

"Please don't worry," Galen says. "He's no bother."

Mr. McElvain leans to Galen, frowning. "This woman," he says, in what he thinks is a low voice, "dogs my steps like the Furies. I suspect, but cannot prove"—he leans closer still—"that she steals. My Tacitus is never in its same place, let alone my Shakespeare. And my chamber pot, sir, migrates. I find myself in her house, a house of thieves and—"

On the woman's weary face, tears and anger chase each other back and forth. Sarah steps close and pats her on the shoulder.

"Lear, sir," continues Mr. McElvain, oblivious. "Only Lear knew such troubles as I. Such daughters as this."

"Bessy is doing well by you," Sarah blurts. Why is she arguing with this poor old man? But she can't ignore the pain on his daughter's face. She sees Bessy every day behind her whitewashed house up the street, hanging Mr. McElvain's clothes on the line, sees her in church, helping her father into his pew. How could you ever get used to this? To anger in your father's eyes, to impatience, to judgment, to unknowingness, to fear? Once, Bessy was the schoolteacher in Eldorado. She'd come here with her father years ago, never married, her mother long dead. Now she takes care of him, and one of the young Norwegian pastors-in-training from the red-brick seminary up the street has charge of the children's school. Mr. McElvain is healthy; his body will continue its burbling, cheerful life as his mind crumbles. And Bessy will keep on, just as she is.

Sarah reaches for Bessy's hand and squeezes it; it's long and slender, roughened with laundry and work. She leans close and murmurs a line for Bessy to recognize: "How sharper than a serpent's tooth it is to have a thankless . . . father."

Bessy smiles, blinks, and squeezes Sarah's hand back. "Never afflict yourself to know more of it," she returns another line, "but let his disposition have that scope that dotage gives it."

Mr. McElvain turns to the door. "I must leave you, for the moment, but will see you anon," he says. "My translations call." Again, he bows to Sarah and shakes Galen's hand, ignoring his daughter. Settling himself inside his coat, he shuffles across the foyer and down the steps out into the bright fall sun. But then he stops, peering side to side. The wind catches his long beard, lifting white wisps light as milkweed.

"I'll be by to see you soon," Bessy sighs, "some afternoon when he's napping." Sarah hugs her, and Bessy trudges out the door toward her father, taking him by the elbow. He leans against her as they walk away.

Sarah will make him smile, dispel the chill that settles over both of them as they watch the McElvains disappear. "Now, Galen," she pretends to scold, "what happens when we run out of sugar?"

"Nonsense," Galen says. He's smiling, but then his eyes shade over. "Dr. Pickett taught me this. You get that old and you just want somebody to look at you."

Sarah considers. It doesn't seem that she, or Galen, could ever be that old. But they will have their child, and their child's descendants, to take care of them. Will they still be here? She pictures

Eldorado grown to fifty houses, a hundred, with another church, with a milliner's and a bookshop and maybe a tea room, with the little Norwegian seminary blooming into a college, with a bigger schoolhouse full of even more children. Including theirs. But what if Galen says, again, *I can't stay here*? Where will their real home, eventually, be?

Mobile had seemed close enough to home, once, with the oyster vendors and the ships creaking and swaying down at the edge of the Gulf and the red-skirted, painted-faced ladies laughing, strolling the Rue Doloreaux—"don't go near," her mother had hissed, snatching her aside. There was Aunt Maude's house, now Mama's. And before that there was Fairibault, the plantation, lost, as Seth was lost: the memory stabs Sarah's heart closed inside, even now. But were any of these ever really hers? No, she thinks now. For a place to be yours, you need to feel that no one else in your family has been there first. You need to feel that you are building your own house, cleaning and planting and standing back to look on what your own hands have wrought. You need a world of faces and names no one else in your family knows. You need to make that world on your own, without your mama telling you where to put the highboy or how to hang the curtains, or sniff that you're over-beating those biscuits. You need to sit with your husband across your own table, your baby-stomach nudging you away from your plate so you have to stretch out your hands to eat. When the baby arrives, this house, this town, will feel like home.

Fairibault could never belong to her again, anyway. Not after her father was gone, and her brother Johnny too, killed and buried in an unknown field: Manassas.

Not after Seth stepped into his rowboat and pushed away from the riverbank. Running.

This is a fact: Sarah does not know where Seth is now.

Maybe Rosa Lee—whose light voice hums over the slip and slap of dishes and dough in the kitchen—has had another letter from him. Maybe.

Galen squeezes Sarah's shoulders with one arm, kisses her, and settles himself at his desk to write up the morning's other patients in Dr. Foster's ledger. He's reached the third-to-last page; soon, it will be time to open one of the blank ones he brought from Mobile.

Sarah should go into the kitchen and help Rosa Lee finish making bread. *Selfish. Little Missy leaving everybody else to do the work.* Instead she turns toward the door. From his spot on the worn chair in the hallway, old Nero the cat uncurls, stretches straight up—ears tightening, yellow teeth bared in a yawn—and jumps to the floor. She opens the door for him and follows him outside again. In the grass, the wind lifts a leaf and tumbles it over until it hits another leaf and stops. "Still a little too warm, even for September," Mrs. Thorson has been complaining. "But it keeps the laundry out of the attic." In every attic in Eldorado, including the attic of this house, hang clotheslines, and buckets to hold smoldering coals that steam clothes dry slowly, over days, in the winter. The alternative is to let them freeze, outside on the line. How cold must it be to freeze wet cloth all the way through?

Winter in Iowa will be so much colder than it was in Alabama. At Fairibault, in the crisp bright December, she and her father had gone quail hunting, wrapped in shawls and coats. Old Caleb drove the wagon full of hunting dogs. He was Seth's grandfather, and Rosa Lee's. Alvah was their mother. Warm hands with pink fingertips, a loud worried voice, a crisp apron that softened as the day wore on to sunset.

Seth had lifted the mockingbird's nest from the ground, a rough sphere of stick balanced on stick, and set it in her hands. She kept it on the windowsill in her room until one day it was gone. "I had Alvah throw it out," Mama said. And that was all. Mama knew Sarah couldn't, and wouldn't, say anything more. And she never had.

Not even to Rosa Lee, Seth's sister, who had come with her and Galen to Iowa after Alvah died and Fairibault had gone for good. She could not speak of Seth to anyone, couldn't even write it in the little diary with its blank pages. It's still at the bottom of her red morocco sewing box. Shut like a mouth. Latched tight as a tongue.

Mama had stood so close to handsome Tom Wainwright, pouring the words into his ear, like that assassin Claudius to Hamlet's sleeping father: *you know how hard it is to raise these girls with their father gone, how hard it is to keep them in the right, how hard it is for me, a widow woman on my own—*

And Seth had disappeared.

Only the conduct books were left, with their smug stinging words: *How precious is virtue, once lost.*

Sarah shakes her head and looks around her. Fall is revealing the shapes of the trees now: branches curve in cupped lines toward the sky, or sprawl and quiver in the wind. Birds' nests are tucked in their forks, thickened with feedsack scraps and tangles of horse hair. A hornet's nest dangles in a thorn bush, its chambers of chewed pulp light as cross-sectioned lungs. Old Caleb opened up an empty nest once for her and Seth and Rosa Lee to see the gray and brown striations in the layers, the pulp woven tight around the branch itself: nothing but a gunshot or a club could bring it down. How can hornets survive winters here? How can any beast? *The fox has his den, and the wild crows their nests,* sings a verse of Matthew in her mind, *but the Son of Man hath nowhere to lay his head.* By any measure, she has such a place. She has a solid house with a good wood stove and a good roof and thick walls. She has Galen and Rosa Lee and neighbors who have given them a stock of vegetables for the cellar. In four months, she will have a son, or a daughter, of her own. She doesn't have to think of anything else if she doesn't want to. She doesn't have to think of anything but how to make this place her home.

Against her will, in her head, Mr. McElvain speaks King Lear. *Suspend thy purpose if thou didst intend to make this creature fruitful . . . into her womb convey sterility, dry up in her the organs of increase, and from her derogate body never spring a babe to honor her . . .*

Sarah shoves the words away, welcoming a sudden flush of anger. They have nothing to do with her. *Morbid. Mad old man.* Just for an instant, she remembers the baby before this one: the thickened mass of red that slid from her as she wept, as Galen held her hand. She admits the fear: tossing on the mattress upstairs in the depth of this coming winter, her husband's and Rosa Lee's worry-twisted faces hanging over hers. "Too early for you to be taking on so," Mama would chide. "You're not six months along, girl." But Mama didn't know what she feared, and never had.

The wind tugs hair across Sarah's eyes and fingers the fringe of her shawl. She's wandered out of her own yard now, into the light-dappled edge of the woods. Nero picks his way through a little patch of mud ahead of her, stopping to shake one paw in disgust. The light softens his rusty black fur. Above her head, a young maple blazes, red and gold. It's still so warm. When will the winter fall on her?

She peers east, toward the Gundersons' house tucked under a cluster of aspen. Little Finn Gunderson—six years old, in short pants and bare feet—is picking runner beans and poking them through the willow fence at his mother's fat white geese. They wait alertly, setting up an excited squabble when he approaches, feinting and jabbing their orange bills toward his hand. Then they fall silent when he turns away. Finn pauses, grins to himself, then walks a couple steps and whirls back around to face the geese. Immediately they start clucking again: *more beans, more beans!* But then they hush, so quickly Sarah looks into the sky.

And there are wild geese there—six of them stringing across the sky overhead, their plump gray-brown bodies bobbing. The air

is so quiet she can hear the quick pant of their wings. They'll probably settle down in the river shallows past Mrs. Thorson's, where
the water will barely cover their wide black feet. Mrs. Gunderson's
geese tilt their faces to the sky, skeptical, then crane their necks to
watch little Finn, now distracted, wander through the garden, beyond their reach. The big gander sets up one experimental cackle.
No more beans.

Sarah wonders how the wild geese will keep from freezing as
they waddle through the snow to get to the river, then paddle. She
wonders how she will get along this winter. When Galen will sleep
quietly again. What she'll see when she looks into her baby's face.

☙

She, Galen, and Rosa Lee have been in Eldorado since March,
come from Alabama to forget.

It had all begun so differently than this. She was never supposed
to end up thirteen hundred miles from home, in a dead man's house
in what her mother still called Iowa Territory. It was so far from
Aunt Maude's neat little house in Mobile, which had been left to
Mama on Aunt Maude's death, and where Mama was living right
now, grand as any lady could want. In that house she had hosted
lavish receptions for Sarah and for Jane on their wedding days,
attended by the best people in Mobile. She had sold Fairibault after
the war—after Father was gone—so that she could bring her girls
to Mobile and marry them off. Every lady they knew had told her
so: "You got two pretty girls, Livia. Take them down to the city to
meet somebody civilized. There's nothing left for young folks up
here in this part of the world." Everybody said it. *Nothing left.*

It was a good thing, wasn't it, that Mr. Ferris didn't agree. Rough
Mr. Ferris with his farmer's hands bought Fairibault for a song because the fields were going back to sweetgum and scrub pine and
the house was gray where all the white paint had flaked off. Sarah

ripped the tangles of honeysuckle and trumpet vine from the columns herself—dismaying the hummingbirds that zoomed and flickered there—before he came out to see the place. He wouldn't see them poor, wouldn't see them living like white trash. But his eyes were kind. He'd looked from her and Jane to Mama and then to Rosa Lee and Alvah, the only ones left after Emancipation. "Miz Fairibault," he'd said, "I'm gonna give you a fair price for this place. And in my hands you never have to fear for it. I'll treat it well."

Mr. Ferris was the kindest of the men who had been circling for months with greedy eyes: *the land's been layin out,* Sarah could see them thinking, *and whatever we plant in it now will go like gangbusters. Now we just got to get it away from—*"A widow with two daughters," Mama mourned. "Oh, how they take advantage. All of them."

Then why'd you sell it? Why'd you not keep it, run it yourself, bring it back? Sarah snapped. *Aren't you the one who always tells us a woman must also work, not let herself run to melancholy?* But as loud as these words rang in her head, they never cracked the locked gate of her lips. This was the beginning of the time when silence overcame her speech. It was just easier. This was the time when she packed her moving trunk with as many of Father's books as she could carry, leaving aside her own clothes. "Come, now, girl," Mama scolded, "they'll have libraries in Mobile. Mr. Ferris praised the look of the library shelves. He wants these books included in the price." This was the beginning of the time when Alvah looked at Sarah worriedly, pressed on her a hot biscuit dripping with honey and butter or a sweet chunk of whipped-sugar candy. (*Divinity,* what a name, and what a wise divine God to have taken Johnny, then Father, then Fairibault away from them. So wise, wasn't He? So correct in all His ways?) This was the time of long afternoons in the parlor in Mobile, sitting absolutely still. This was the time when as proper young ladies she and Jane attended Miss Spofford's Academy, and at her graduation Miss Spofford put the small locked diary into her hands. "Sarah," she murmured, "if you can't say something out loud, write it here, where no one else can see."

This time was blurry and dim, with no clear beginning, but it did have an ending she could set her finger on: when she stood in St. Hubert's Episcopal Church next to Galen, a bundle of creamy magnolia blossoms in her hands, and promised to follow him wherever he went. "Whither thou goest I will go," Reverend Elder's voice boomed. "Whither thou lodgest I will lodge." Galen had come for her, seeking her in the dim foreign country where she had wandered after Fairibault was gone, after Seth was gone. He had brought her out. And he would keep her, safe, away from that place. He would take her to a land that was all their own. At that thought she turned to him and kissed him before the Reverend even gave her permission. A smothered giggle rippled through the crowd. Galen jumped a little, startled, but recovered himself, then grinned, put both arms around her, and kissed her back.

Then Galen carried her away from that dark silence and from Mama, out of old Aunt Maude's house that had become Mama's, to a house of their own in a different part of Mobile, with a little stable in back for Charley the fast-trotting sorrel horse and a Seven Sisters climbing rose on the garden wall and a canopied tester bed Sarah sweetened with bundles of herbs from Aunt Maude's garden. In their swift buggy, she and Galen rode down to the shore and strolled to the edge of the water to gaze at the glittering line of the horizon, way out there. She remembered the boats and the fishermen shouting, the tobacco smell and the sting of salt and fish in her nose. Sand rasped her bare feet when—wickedly—she left off her stockings and carried her boots in her hand. This ribbon of land under a blue sky, with the waves slinging themselves against it over and over, was always new, with only her to watch it change. It was a place with no story but her own, and she could make any story she wanted.

Then pretty Julia Kenner, the cotton factor's young wife, died in childbirth. Tom Kenner, her husband, was found in a ditch with his neck broken. His horse grazed nearby, trailing its reins through the weeds. "You could still smell the whiskey," everyone whispered. And Galen slid sideways toward that deep silent lake from which he had just drawn Sarah herself. "My boy," old Dr. Pickett told him, "you did all you could. A breeched child is tricky, you know that." He stood over Galen's chair, gripping his shoulder. "We all lose them, son." But Galen didn't seem to hear.

Then the time of traveling came. They traveled for so long in a haze of trains and wagons and hotel rooms where rough sheets nibbled at their skin. "Sarah," said Galen in the dark, "darling, it's a risk, but if we just keep on going—"

"Yes," she interrupted. She would say anything to get him further from Mobile, where people looked pityingly at her and where their friends stopped Galen on the street to clasp his hands and whisper, "God's will, not your fault."

Whither thou goest, I will go.

She was his wife. There was nothing for her to do but to trust him.

The words tangle in her head: *A stranger in a strange land. By the rivers of Babylon I sat down and wept. How shall we sing the Lord's song in a strange land? Jerusalem, if I forget thee—*

Her younger sister Jane had wept, thirteen hundred miles back on the train platform in Mobile, seeing them off. Jane never cried. But that morning, she'd clasped Sarah close and held on, her tears trickling onto Sarah's neck, down into her collar. Sarah's own tears spotted the veil that swathed Jane's hair.

A veil of tears. Ha. Ha.

"Such a clever girl," Miss Spofford had praised, "always reading."

"Good marriages," Mama had sighed. "That's all I ask before I die. To see you girls married well."

(After all, wasn't that why Fairibault had gone?)

"He's my husband, Mama," Sarah said to her mother's tear-puffed face. "I'm going with him." Pressing behind these words were the ones she couldn't say. *I'm going. You can't stop me. I know what you tried to do to Seth. And I will never forgive you for that.*

She set her arms around Mama's brittle shoulders, touched her cheek to Mama's cold one. Then the train pulled away.

I'll never see you again.

Settlers didn't often see the families they had left behind in the East. She and Galen were *settlers* now, no longer the handsome young doctor and his pretty wife, so prosperous, giving teas and visiting the milliner's. But then, no one was the same anymore. Fairibault was gone. Seth was gone. Alvah was gone too, her face gray and shrinking as she lay in the bed in Aunt Maude's back room, as Rosa Lee whispered, "He's safe, Mama. I know it." Sarah kept herself away from the room, trying to shut her ears to the crackle of a letter unfolding, the murmur of Rosa Lee's voice reading what she could only hope—never ask—were Seth's words. It was his mama's and his sister's private thing, now, something she could never know for sure.

When Sarah asked her to go West with them, Rosa Lee said yes. She'd been doubtful at first: "I bet they got plenty colored gals out there, what'd they need with one more?" But then her face softened and turned rueful. In her eyes, Sarah could see unspoken truths: *My Mama's gone. Seth is gone. And I won't stay here to work for her.* Surely Rosa Lee knew, too, what Sarah's mother had done.

Mama had swished into the room while Sarah was packing her trunk. "I hope you know what you're doing, filling Rosa Lee's head," she'd hissed. "Giving that girl ideas. Taking her away from all she knows. I thought she'd stay here, now Alvah's gone. Marry some nice free colored man."

Rosa Lee had snorted when Sarah relayed this statement: "Huh. How many colored free she think there are in Mobile?"

Mama said, every day, what a blessing Alvah had been all those years, and how much she missed her. But she never mentioned Seth. And she spoke to Rosa Lee as little as possible, except to snap, as she stood on the train platform, "I hope you know what you're doing, girl."

And so the three of them had gone. *In the wilderness they wandered.* But they weren't wandering, they were settling, making a home for themselves where none of her family had ever been. Up through Tennessee and Missouri and Illinois. Into Iowa, headed vaguely for St. Paul, the city where Jane's stolid banker husband Felix had connections. Far north. Far west. Mostly just far. First by train. Then wagon. "Those people are looking at us," Galen had whispered, in some dirty town near the Mississippi River. "Let's get a wagon and travel by ourselves. We'll find our way."

It was March by the time they'd reached Iowa, the air sharp as the rims of ice in the water pail. Nero the cat huddled in the nest of rags inside his basket, nosing under the blankets next to Sarah each night. She and Galen and Rosa Lee slept in a row in the wagon bed. In the daylight, they wrapped themselves in coats and shawls and still shivered. Galen's long hands calloused, reddened, and cracked.

"I never," Rosa Lee declared at sunrise, "*never* been this cold."

"Me neither," said Sarah.

"Not too late to go back home, is it?" Rosa Lee said ironically.

"Be worse," Sarah said, "back home."

Rosa Lee smiled. "Right," she said. "With your mama on our backs." She and Sarah pulled their shawls tighter, stirred the fire, and huddled closer. This was an adventure. A new life, and a new home. It would have to be.

If Sarah wasn't wary, a voice like Mama's would crackle in her head: *what a husband he is, to put you in such danger, make you wander like a tinker's child. This is no life for a woman.*

But this is my life, Sarah had answered it. *He is my husband. I trust him.* There was no other choice. And look at all she was discovering because of him. She had never seen skies so big, spaces so empty, as in this world they were riding through. Pale rosy light lay deep over the grass in the morning, which blew and moved like the sea. The wind bit the exposed knobs of their cheeks. In the middle of the day Sarah and Rosa Lee could shed a layer or two and turn their faces to the sun, bouncing on the wagon seat as Galen walked beside the oxen. From flat plains, as they went north along the Mississippi, the land seemed to tense and rise: they began to see high limestone bluffs covered with oaks and maples and shaggy cedars and fir trees, looming over clear cold rivers at the bottom. They passed little settlements with Biblical names (Gehennah, Rehoboth, Jericho), with tiny churches and their tinier cemeteries with German and Czechoslovakian and Norwegian names (Schultz, Hruska, Trondor). They stopped at inns with short dark-haired people or tall blond-and-red-haired people who spoke to Galen and Sarah in lilting voices and stared at Rosa Lee. Curiosity was heavy in their eyes. A small boy reached to touch Rosa Lee's hand, gently, with one finger. She looked at him, with a small smile. "No," she said, "it don't rub off."

And then they'd come upon Eldorado. In the inn, Mrs. Thorson in her sing-song Norwegian voice told them the old doctor had just died, and they could move into his house if they would only stay. "It's a good town," she said, "but we need a doctor." Galen's face had brightened. "Yes," Sarah said, "it must be Providence!" Mrs. Thorson laughed, and Galen smiled. She hungered to keep that look of hope in his eyes, any way she could. This could be home. It would have to be.

So she and Rosa Lee had wiped down walls and windows and hung new curtains and dusted off old Dr. Foster's furniture: his secretary stuffed with papers and ledgers in his slanting hand (*Mrs. Thorson, twins* in the "case" column, *quilt + one dozen eggs* in the "payment" column), his dining room table and chairs, his four-poster bed. "Let's move it downstairs for Rosa Lee," Sarah said. She would sleep with her husband in their own bed. She draped Jane's crocheted doily over the chest of drawers and hung her dresses in the tall wardrobe that had been the doctor's. His clothes were still there: rows of shoes and rusty black coats. What fit Galen, or what Sarah and Rosa Lee could alter, they kept, and what didn't, they set in a box by the door to give away. They opened their windows to May breezes that blew softer each morning, twirling the dust and cobwebs from the corners of the ceilings out into the world. On the roof, the doctor's bronze wind-vane—an angel with uplifted trumpet—swung back and forth, pointing into a summer that bloomed in the air around them every day.

Then the gifts had started coming, neighbor by neighbor. Seeds for tomatoes and peppers and carrots and hard-shelled squash. Seeds for rutabagas and turnips: Sarah had thought those were only food for pigs, chopped in chunks, but come winter, Mrs. Gunderson warned, she'd be glad of them. A fat ewe delivered as payment for a plaster cast on Mr. Gunderson's broken leg. A bolt of warm brown homespun cloth, a skein or two of yarn. And Minx, then an orange tabby kitten squirming in the arms of Mrs. Preus, the minister's wife. "The runt of the litter, it's true," Mrs. Preus exclaimed cheerfully, "which is why she's so small, female orange tabbies usually are the runts, but they're also the best mousers. In the winter, the mice will carry you *away*." At first, old Nero had hissed and spat at the new kitten; last month, however, Sarah had been wakened by a singsong caterwaul below the windows that went on until she heaved herself from the bed and threw open a window and flung one of Dr. Foster's old boots at them. The dark shapes of Nero and Minx disentangled and shot away across the yard. Then Minx's sides began to distend. "Kittens!" Rosa Lee exclaimed. There'd be no need to drown them here; every house, every store, and even the church needed a cat.

"Let me show you two how to set up your cellar," Mrs. Preus had offered, and so Sarah and Rosa Lee followed her through her neat parsonage parlor, with its worn horsehair chairs, bookcase with Martin Luther's works and Scripture commentaries and the same red-bound set of Dickens that Sarah had, and down into the cool root cellar cut right into the earth. Mrs. Preus opened the lids of wooden bins, rolled up her sleeves, and rooted her hands through the pale sawdust inside, then drew forth beets and turnips still plump from their long winter underground. "Getting to the end of them," she exclaimed, "at last. Just in time for spring!" She indicated the cabinet full of seed jars, neat pasted labels in her pastor's-wife hand: *Brandywine Tomato. Jacob's Cattle Bean. Yellow Squash.* So many seeds pressed like faces against the glass, waiting for the sun to let loose all they held inside.

In that sun, in May, Rosa Lee and Sarah had dug up the garden and planted their seeds, including the okra seeds they'd brought from Alabama. Galen went to taciturn Jeremiah Brown on the other side of the valley and bargained for a Guernsey cow they named Siss. ("Jeremiah, he's a little different, living out on that farm by himself," Mrs. Preus had said.) Mrs. Thorson brought them chicks that grew into five speckled hens and an irritable rooster. Now, all around the house those chickens were strutting and scuttling and quarreling, nestling their feathered bustles into their loose-dirt wallows in the yard, blissful as ladies settling into parlor chairs.

The vegetables had flourished. "I don't know whether that okra's gonna come on," Rosa Lee worried. "Will it get hot enough here?" But the seeds sprouted thumbnail-sized green leaves that sprang up on tall stalks, widening into pointy star shapes. Then came the creamy flowers with the dark purple circles at the heart, and the okra pods. At home they'd be picked twice a day, to get the small pods while they were still tender—they came on so fast, in that heat—but here once a day was enough. Sarah and Rosa Lee sliced, battered, and fried the okra in lard or boiled it whole to slurp down with butter and salt. "Better eat it now," Galen laughed, spearing a plump pod with his fork, "while we've still got it."

Now it was fall. And they had come through a summer here. In Mobile summers, the thick air had stunned Sarah flat as a lizard to lie in the sand and listen to the waves. Here the summer mornings were crisp and the dew stung her bare feet. She and Rosa Lee had waded in the shallow, slow-moving river as brown trout fled over the rocks. Wildflowers had bloomed in the ditches and tall orange lilies had sprung in a row along the side of the barn, opening their throats to the sun. The branches of the apple tree behind their house had swelled with fruit that turned green, then gold-streaked red. In the dining room, even now, a bowl of those apples stained the air with their wistful cidery smell.

A letter from Mama caught up with her in Iowa at last. Sarah has not even opened it, because, based on the last one, she can guess what it will say. *You and Jane are all that a grateful loving mother could hope for. I thank the merciful Lord that you have good husbands to provide for you long after I am gone to join your dear father, as all earthly things must pass away. I hope all is well in that godforsaken wilderness in which you find yourself and into which your child must be born. Remember the discipline of daily Scripture.*

You remember it, Mama, Sarah thinks furiously. *You.* At least once a day she climbs the stairs, planning to root that unopened letter from her trunk and rip it to pieces. But she stops herself. What kind of daughter does such a thing? What kind of woman tears to shreds her mother's words of advice, loving and well-meant even if they make her so angry sometimes she has to walk into the yard to be out from under the same roof with them? What kind of woman is so unnatural?

Unnatural woman. Unnatural girl. *You know what they say about her and that colored boy—*

Here, in Iowa, she will never hear those whispers again. Never have to fight down the words as she looked into her mother's eyes: *I know what you did. Sold Fairibault and banished us for good.*

Even after the war, Alvah and Rosa Lee and Seth did not leave. Even after Johnny and Father died and the money dried up like a spring in deep summer. Women in church cut their eyes and whispered, *so lucky you were able to keep them, Livia. They're so loyal.* But Sarah had overheard Alvah's voice, tired and definite, stinging her ears: "Where would we go?" she'd replied to Seth. "You tell me that."

Someone had brought Fairibault into being, that world in which Sarah grew as plainly and unknowingly as the wild lilies deep in the woods (those secret white stars rising next to the little stream at Easter and then gone), that world she had believed would never die. And then someone had made it disappear. Life was complicated, she was grown enough to know. But a stubborn angry child-self deep inside would not stop asking. Who banished us—who lost our home—for good? Was it you, Mama? Was it Father? Was it the men in their marble buildings in Charleston who sipped their morning coffee and scratched their signatures on papers to send her brother into the field to catch a bullet in his chest? Was it the men who had hunted down people like Seth and Alvah and Rosa Lee and chained them up and shoved them onto those auction blocks for farther back down the long ladder of years than Sarah could know, those men like sorcerers who wreaked on all of them the curse of her home (for *home* it was, would always be) without which it was now obvious to everyone of sense that the war never would have been born? Or was it God, without the tacit permission of whose eye, bright and merciless as Helios, nothing supposedly ever happened at all? In the Bible, Job had ranted and Jacob had wrestled and Moses had crept around up in the mountains asking for a sign and eventually God had deigned to show himself to all of them. *I'm gonna set this bush on fire and*

*turn my back so you can stand the sight of me, son. We're gonna
wrestle and we'll see who wins. You think you've got it bad, but let
me show you how much grander the world is than anything your
little self can see.* True, the world was grand, even at times mirac-
ulous: Galen's warm hand on her belly where their child slept, the
particular music of cottonwood trees with their million excitable
leaves, the pearly pink sunrise over the prairie. But someone had
set a canker-worm—people in bondage, people who could work
on land and maybe even care for it but never own it for themselves,
and the thick net of lies and silences that held them and everyone
around them in its grip—deep in the heart of the world Sarah had
once believed would never die, and that devouring worm tunneled
its way up into life and left wreckage in its wake. Someone had
planted the seed of that devouring thing and let it grow and Sarah
could not be sure this someone had not been God.

Galen still goes to church every few weeks, sitting in the pew
for his patients to smile and speak to him and pat him on the back.
Rosa Lee goes with him. Sarah stays at home, not quite able to say
why. She knows that Reverend Preus asks after her: "you tell Miss
Sarah, now," he says to Galen, "you tell her that we hope she's feeling better by next Sunday." She misses the hymns, the comforting
rustle in the pews, and the deep quiet that follows the words of
prayer, when the whole hidden world holds its breath. She misses
playing the piano. But she can't go through that door. God may
very well be looking down on her. But maybe He is not.

Mama had only smiled thinly when nosy ladies in Mobile had
asked how she'd come to be a widow. "Suddenly," she said. "God's
will."

God's will. Like Sarah's wild brother Johnny, lost and buried
miles away, so far north it snowed on his grave every winter. *God's
will.*

Like her father's voice downstairs, helpless: "I can't turn Eugene
away, Livia, I promised."

In human voices, *God's will* was a portal to lies. To silences. *Things known and unknown. Things done and left undone.*

God's will. Inside Sarah, these words can still upset an anger she tries to keep in its upright vessel, contained, like muscadine wine curing on a shelf. This anger deepens as her own baby grows, as the small feet kick against the skin below her left ribs, as the tiny backbone settles in sleep against her own, as her child swims up and up toward the world, toward the moment when she'll look into its eyes. *God's will.* Then that vessel in her heart overturns and the anger seeps through her, bleeding down like wine into a tablecloth, darker, reddish-purple, black. Babies like hers died every year. She had already lost the small bloody baby-that-never-was. How could you say such loss was ever called to life by God? And if this were true, how could you then settle yourself into your pew and sing to him—*A bul-wark ne-ver faiiiii-linnnnggg*—as if he deserved one iota of your praise?

They were up there in the cemetery now. Small bones turning to dust in long grass, under hidden stones, under silences.

Inside herself, Sarah laughs: *I don't believe you, God. You old deceiver. You punisher. You cheat.* In the Bible story Sarah hid inside her tent and heard God bragging to his henchman Abraham—*lo, Sarah thy wife shall have a son*—and thought of her husband's withered body and her own, of all the urgent sad nights, of all the waiting, that had already passed. *Therefore Sarah laughed within herself, saying, after I am waxed old shall I have pleasure, my lord being old also?*

The thickened blood that passed and passed, soon after her marriage in Mobile: she had named it as her first child although nobody else would. "Sarah, honey," Alvah had told her, "just be patient. Y'all are young. You'll have so many children yet." Her mother had sat on Sarah's bed and cleared her throat, not quite meeting Sarah's eyes. "It's God's will," she said. "Nature's way of taking care of something . . . wrong."

28

That girl and that colored boy, the Mobile voices had whispered gleefully. *You heard? It's just . . . against nature.*

So many lies. Here in Iowa, she would never have to hear them again. She would not have to open that envelope worn fuzzy at the edges by its passage through mailbags and trains and the Pony Express, with her mother's sharp handwriting pleading, commanding,: *Sarah Archer, The Doctor's House, Eldorado, Iowa Territory.* She could leave that letter unread in her trunk as long as she wanted, with the lid firmly shut, here in her home in a place her mother could never reach. Who knew what the letter would ask of her. Who cared. She would refuse to listen, simply because, now, she could.

In the morning's chill, Sarah climbs the back steps with her chamber pot in her hand, freshly emptied into the privy and swished out with lime-water. The sun's been up for an hour, but she couldn't drag herself above the surface of sleep until now. She'd sunk back again and again, grasping at the vanishing tails of dreams: she was netting white lace that kept coming apart in her hands; she was holding a freakishly large baby with a puffy, plaintive face; she and Seth were swimming in the lake at Fairibault, touching the tips of their fingers together underwater. The dreams trouble her. Maybe they'll fade as the day takes hold. They usually do.

Her swelling feet in their knitted socks are thrust into Dr. Foster's old boots, which are wide enough to give her ease. Her own boots are too narrow now; she's rubbed them with tallow and stashed them in the bottom of the wardrobe until after the baby is born. Her other dresses hang above them: the plain gray and brown work dresses with their waists let out, the blue-flowered one that makes her think of spring, the bottle-green one that Galen says makes her look like a mermaid. Under her clothing now—the same blouse and skirt from yesterday—she wears her Motherhood Corset from Whalen's Dry Goods in Mobile, sent by her mother. It laces up the front, with a thick elastic panel right over her stomach. "I don't know about this," Galen says, frowning, when he sees her put it on. "Dr. Pickett always told us it supported the baby, supported the spine. But it doesn't look like it can possibly feel good."

"Actually," Sarah tells him, "it does." The concern in his eyes moves her, and she kisses him to see it shade away. In the morning, when she first puts this corset on, she has to adjust her breasts carefully inside the padded canvas top. They're sore, larger now, the nipples rosy-brown. But when the corset is laced, it lifts her breasts and cradles them, and their dull ache goes away. She and Jane had always been slim enough to go without corsets if they wanted to, to get away with only a single chemise—thrillingly bare—between their skin and their dresses. But she can't do this now.

She pictures her mama's body inside its loose nightgown, pictures Alvah's body. Alvah didn't wear corsets. "For *them*," her mama explained, "it isn't needful." In Miss Spofford's Academy, she and Jane, sitting in history class, had giggled at old Miss Tanner's bosom, which sagged despite the obvious pinch of the corset under her black woolen gown. "I bet her ninnies hang down to her belly button," Jane snickered. "I bet she has to roll 'em up like stockings to get 'em inside her dress." Sarah doesn't want to look like that. She's not even thirty, yet. She imagines her body returning to its former shape after the baby is born—stomach magically deflated, breasts springing back up toward her collarbone like the balloons released over Mobile Bay on the Fourth of July. She will die if Galen doesn't want to touch her any more. If there are no more babies. If the pieces of this life in Iowa Territory—*it's a state*, she corrects herself—come apart in her hands.

She would have laughed, a year ago, if anyone had told her she'd be living here. Like fierce old Sarah in the Bible, disbelieving, taunting back at God himself: you must be funning me. *You must be wrong,* said old Sarah's laugh, right in God's face. *I don't believe you. I want a baby I will never have.*

"But it just goes to show," said her mama, "Man proposes, God disposes."

And God had disposed her here, apparently.

As the baby grows bigger and more restless, Sarah finds herself on the porch often at this time of the morning. The sun rises up and throws yellow-gold light all over the bluffs until their pale stone faces glow. The whitewashed walls of the schoolhouse shine. Sometimes, Sarah glimpses a pair of eagles hunting: one diving low to the water, the other circling higher and higher, almost out of sight. Their nest, four feet across, rests in the biggest cottonwood in the valley, halfway down the path to the Thorson twins' homestead. The light bathes her face, and she smiles. *This is the day that the Lord has made,* sings her mother's voice in her head, if she is unwary. *Let us rejoice and be glad in it.*

She brushes the lines away. There is plenty to be glad of here. But nothing that her mother has created. Nothing that has to do with her at all.

The baby tickles and Sarah lays her hand on what she knows is the top of its head, just beneath the roof of her own skin. Morbid. Too much pondering first thing in the morning.

"Kitty, kitty!" she calls. Minx dashes across the yard and leaps onto the porch, then shoves her small head into Sarah's hand, purring. "You catch anything good to eat last night?" Sarah asks her, rubbing her ears. "Sure looks that way." In their nest under the porch, the kittens stir and peep, but she fights the urge to hunker down and beckon them. She's been leaving too much to Rosa Lee these days, mooning and daydreaming. *Lazy. Get to work with you, young missy.*

Sarah opens the back door and stands, toeing off the doctor's big boots. Minx brushes past and trots to her saucer of milk. "You're up early," says Rosa Lee. She stands at the wide kitchen table in her calico dress and thick knitted socks and a shawl, the ends tied together to keep them out of the flour. Both hands in a bowl, she's mixing lard and flour for biscuits. She splashes buttermilk into the bowl, kneads, judges, splashes again. "I couldn't sleep either," she says. "Don't know why."

Heat radiates from the stove, drawing Sarah close. She hooks the stovelid up with its iron stick to see the fire crackling inside. Then, from the barrel next to the stove, she dips water into the kettle to warm it for Galen. The door to Rosa Lee's room, just off the kitchen, is cracked; Sarah can see the edge of her neat bed with the quilt she and Alvah made. From his curled-up place against her pillow, old Nero stands, stretches, and leaps down. There's her rocking chair in its corner. There's her little desk with its paper and inkwell.

Are there letters from Seth in that desk, right now?

Sarah scoops a pinch of tea leaves into a spoon-shaped strainer, then pours hot water over it into her cup, stirs the strainer around, and lets it sit. She nudges the tea canister back into the cluster of jars at the center of the table: jam pots, butter crock, salt and pepper shakers. The jar of chowchow they put up this summer is almost gone. Thankfully, there are still six jars left in the cellar.

"You know those Thorson boys," says Rosa Lee. She presses a round tin cutter straight down on the flattened biscuit dough, then pulls it straight up, like Alvah taught them both: biscuit dough won't rise if it gets pinched.

"Yes," says Sarah. Everyone knows the Thorson twins, Trygve and Oyvind, tall, red-haired twenty-five-year-olds who have broken ground on their own farmstead just beyond the edge of town. "I always thought they'd take over the inn," their mother, Linka, sighs, "but young men got to make their own way. And their father—" Linka's husband Jens, dead when the twins were small—"would be so proud." Oyvind is quiet, his shoulders a little stooped, his gaze steady. Trygve stands straight, his voice with its funny Norwegian lilt loud, his smile quick. He walks with a little swagger. Two more bachelors in a land full of them.

"Well, Trygve started talkin to me the other day," says Rosa Lee. "When I went up the street to see about the spinnin wool at Gundersons. He was out there in the wagon by the store, waitin on Oyvind."

"Talkin to you?" Sarah asks.

"Just this and that," says Rosa Lee. "You know how they do." She looks at Sarah, significantly. Sarah raises her eyebrows. Rosa Lee relents, smiling. "Well," she says, "he waved to me and grinned real big, and said it sure was a lovely morning, and even lovelier—" she pauses, blushes deeper—"now that he seen me."

"He fancies you!" Sarah exclaims, grinning. Under the table, Minx laps the last drops of milk from her saucer—"y'all spoil those cats," Galen always grumbles—and saunters over to lean against Rosa Lee's legs, purring. Sarah fetches the can of milk to tip more out for Nero. With a flush of guilt she sees the can is full; Rosa Lee's already milked Siss the cow this morning. *Lazy girl. Why don't you help?*

Rosa Lee reaches down to trail one hand along Minx's back. "I don't know," she says. "He *is* a nice fellow." She pauses, and her grin turns wicked. "And he's pretty." Both of them snicker; silly Betsy Roper at Miss Spofford's Academy had always gushed, "Girls, he surely is a pretty man!"

"And the best thing is," Sarah murmurs, "he's got a twin, just in case."

Rosa Lee widens her eyes in mock horror. "To say such a thing!" she breathes, as Sarah's mama would. "Listen at you!" Then she laughs. "Shoot," she says. "One's enough for me. No matter how pretty they are." And they giggle and try to hold it down—Galen is still asleep—but giggle harder and wipe their eyes.

Sarah straightens in her chair, poker-faced. "But Rosa Lee," she intones, "what about those poor seminary boys? If you go courting with Trygve, whatever will they do?"

Rosa Lee snorts. The Norwegian seminary students are timid as a flock of wood ducks, bunching and scuttling away with shy panicked grins whenever she and Rosa Lee draw near them on the street. Mrs. Johnson's girl, Jenny, who's almost fifteen, is pining after Nils Ericksen, the oldest of the seminary boys, who's taken over schoolmastering from Bessy McElvain. He's tall and thin, with gold-rimmed glasses and receding hair and a kind, ministerial stoop, although he can't be any older than Sarah herself. All of Eldorado has smiled at Jenny trailing Nils to school, twiddling the ends of her long braids in her fingers. She loiters in the schoolhouse door after lessons are over, hoping to follow him back to the seminary, until Mrs. Johnson strides out of her house into the street and calls her daughter, loud enough for the whole town to hear, "Jen-ny!" Of all the seminary boys, only Nils has ever mustered the nerve to look a woman, even young Jenny, in the eye.

"I won't be no preacher's wife," Rosa Lee declares. "Specially not no preacher scared of his own shadow."

"Trygve ain't scared," Sarah murmurs. She lifts her voice theatrically. "He's brave, and big, and strong, and he will take you in his arms and—"

"Sarah!" Rosa Lee pretends to be shocked. "Listen at you. Talkin like some gal from Rue Doloreaux."

"It's only cause he's such a pretty man," Sarah says, straight-faced. She and Rosa Lee giggle. "Oh, lord," Rosa Lee laughs. "We'll see."

Sarah studies her friend's narrow waist, her small square hands in the dough, her bun of long hair skewered precisely with one pin to the left, one pin to the right. Her hair has always been soft, crimpy and long. Rosa Lee was light. Lighter than Alvah, even. So was beautiful Celia with her stolen dress.

In Alabama Rosa Lee might never think of a white man, nor he her. But here, so far north, was a different place. So maybe—

The kettle wiggles on the burner, then chatters and hisses as water bubbles inside it. With a rag around the handle, Sarah sweeps it off the stove and carries it upstairs to Galen.

He's still asleep, or seems to be, his long back curved under the layers of quilts. It's taken him longer to wake these days. "Galen," Sarah says. She settles the bowl more firmly in the washstand and pours the water slowly, careful not to crack the china. "Galen."

"Mmmrrh," Galen moans. He stirs. Under the quilt, his shoulders hunch and his knees draw closer to his chest. He grinds his bottom hip deeper into the mattress.

"Galen," Sarah says, "it's past sunup."

"Mmmgrmh," Galen mumbles. Sarah smiles and keeps pouring the water until it reaches the brim of the bowl. Above it, the mirror clouds with shifting plumes of steam. She sets the empty kettle on the floor and both hands on the mattress to balance herself, then leans over. Galen turns his face upwards into her kiss.

"How's the baby this morning?" he asks. "Kicking you?" His eyes fasten on hers, then he swings his legs from under the quilts and sits up. His shoulders stretch straight up, like a cat's, and his body contracts in a shiver. "Damn," he mutters, "it's cold in here." Edging around the bed, he comes to Sarah and kisses her, then crosses to the washstand and dips his fingertips in the water. Then he drags both hands down his face, slowly, and studies himself in the mirror. "The thousand-year-old man," he groans.

"Mr. Sandpaper," Sarah agrees. She smooths out the lumpy mattress as best she can, then tugs up the sheet and blankets and the bottom quilt and plumps up the two goosedown pillows. Folding the top quilt into a long bolt, she lays it across the foot of the bed so she can see both quilts. One was made by her mother, before she was born: a Log Cabin with stripes of blue and pink and green. The other is a Star of David with blue and black and brown strips.

These were the play clothes she and Jane wore as little girls, the same play clothes Rosa Lee and Seth wore, homespun woven, cut, and sewed by her mother and Alvah. The blue and black were from pokeberry juice, the same berries Jane and Rosa Lee and Sarah would crush to paint their fingernails deep purple and wave them in the air like queens.

Mama had helped Sarah and Rosa Lee pack these quilts into a trunk to go to Iowa, alongside clothing, the churn, the box of kitchen tools, Galen's books and medicine chest, Sarah's books, their dissassembled bed. Not the piano. "But," Galen promised, "we'll be able to buy one in—what was that city Felix named? St. Paul, surely." They'd have to shift all of this from the train to a wagon eventually, so they couldn't overload. Cautionary tales had filtered from Oregon: rocking chairs and armoires and trunks of hoopskirts abandoned by the side of the trail. So many beautiful things left behind, always a woman's. *Be reasonable,* the husband would plead. *Don't you want us to get to the Territory?* And the wife would have agreed, eventually. She'd have watched as other men helped her husband heave out her marble-topped parlor table, her mother's mahogany cabinet, her china in its straw-stuffed crate. Like Lot's wife, she would have turned to watch those things out of sight. Or she would have set her face ahead as her husband half-apologized: *I'll make you another one. We wanted to start fresh, didn't we?*

Sarah shakes her head. Why is she always waking herself back up, these days, from memories, or dreams? Galen nudges his chamber pot under the bed, peels his nightshirt down, and ties it around his waist, with the long sleeves dangling.

As he turns away to the washstand, Sarah glimpses the curve of his waist, the wide bony span of his shoulders. Ribs ripple under his goosefleshed chest, dusted with red-brown hair. How thin he is. He's never been what her father would call *a big man.* Her brother Johnny, six feet two and well north of two hundred pounds, was

36

a big man, eating greedily and pushing himself back from the table, muscles jumping when he reached for the decanter of port or feinted at Sarah or Jane during hide-and-seek to make them shriek. Galen has always been just under, or just over, six feet—depending on how straight he stood—and lean, sinewy rather than fleshy, with wide shoulders from which the rest of his body hangs like a suit of clothes from a hanger. He has never been a big man, and Sarah has never wanted him different. But when have his ribs gotten quite this sharp? When has his collarbone stood out quite this much, like two shallow dishes under his skin?

Galen stands before the washstand and mirror and stares at himself. His long, square-jawed face is furred faintly with dark red beard. It's been a day or two since he shaved. In Mobile, he shaved every morning without fail. His cheeks are faintly hollowed, circles under his gray-green eyes. He has been working so hard; there was Mrs. Thorson's complaint and Mr. McElvain's visit and the new medicines to write away for from St. Paul.

Sarah is stricken; how could she not have noticed this? *Selfish.* Taken up with the baby and working on this house with Rosa Lee, walking in the yard in the sun. Maybe he is just tired. Maybe with a few more sunny afternoons in this warm snap he'll revive. But the deep winter is yet to come. "Enjoy it," Mrs. Thorson said blithely to her and Rosa Lee as they harvested tomatoes and peppers in August. "Won't be planting again till May." In that heat, Sarah had welcomed the thought of cold. Now she shivers. Galen's thinness. Sadness under his eyes. Cold nights deepening.

Galen swishes a sliver of soap and water in the bottom of his shaving mug, plumping the foam into the boar's-hair bristles of his shaving brush, his long fingers light on its nub of ivory handle. He flicks the lather over his cheekbones and upper lip and chin and jaw, then clicks his straight razor open and sets it against his throat. He always begins here. Carefully he strokes it upward against his jaw, swishes the razor clean in the basin, draws the flesh of his cheeks taut with his fingertips and shaves neat tracks down the long planes of his face, past his nose. Both sides. Swish, dab, rinse. Then a final nick of the lather on his upper lip and he towels away the thin tracks of soap on his face and neck. "Ah," he says. He catches Sarah's eyes in the mirror. "I really did need that, didn't I."

Sarah wraps both arms around his narrow waist and rests her cheek on his back. His shoulder blades jump as he sets the shaving brush down and reaches to cover her arms with his own. Shadows float in the sickle-shaped curves of the scapulae; *under his wings,* Sarah thinks. She hugs him tighter and closes her eyes.

And sees her father standing in front of his own washstand just like this on a spring morning, the air luscious with honeysuckle. Staring at himself, the razor in his hand.

She was passing the door on her way outside to play. She'll never know what stopped her there. How long had she watched him, standing so still?

Oh, where melancholy leads those who let it in. She turns her head and rests her lips on Galen's back, kisses the shadow under his wing. She will keep her husband here. No matter what.

※

When she comes back down the stairs into the kitchen, Trygve Thorson is sitting at the table, eating a biscuit that's just come out of the oven. Strawberry jam trickles down the side of his palm, and he turns his hand, lazily, to catch it with his tongue, watching Rosa Lee the whole time. Standing at the work table along the wall, she looks back at him and lowers her eyes, smiling. Minx leaps onto Trygve's lap, balancing on one of his long thighs. Trygve offers her a crumb of biscuit; she picks it from his fingers and jumps back down again.

"And so Oyvind and me, we got our own farm," Trygve continues, "not that Mama was glad we should go, but a man's grown, he should have his land. But lots of things a man should have." He shoots Rosa Lee a shrewd look, then spots Sarah. "Missis Doctor," he greets her, smiling. "I brought you a patient."

Galen follows Sarah into the kitchen, knotting his tie over his vest, waving off the biscuit Rosa Lee offers him. "So you talked him into it," he says. "Good, good. I'll feel better once I get that thing out. Where is he?"

"Out in the wagon," Trygve says. "Don't want to come in yet. Scared." He snickers, then stops himself. "But it's a scary thing, true enough."

"I'm not scared," says Oyvind. He has slipped into the kitchen so quietly that none of them have heard him. "Just didn't want to interrupt." He flicks a glance from Trygve to Rosa Lee, blushes, and nods to her. "Ma'am." Rosa Lee nods back. And then he looks at Sarah, and nods again. "I hope you're keepin well."

"Thank you," Sarah says. "I am." In her condition, she should be ashamed to be up and around. "Never let a man remark on your . . . health," her mother would scold. But in this tiny town, it doesn't seem to matter. Everyone wants to wish her well, happy for another child in Eldorado.

Oyvind straightens. "I'm ready," he says. Galen nods and turns to lead him to the front parlor. Then he pauses. "Sarah," he says, "in your state, you shouldn't. Rosa Lee, can you help?"

Rosa Lee nods, swishes her hands in the basin, and dries them on a rag. But Sarah sees a flash of panic in Oyvind's eyes. *He doesn't want her to be there*, she realizes. *Afraid he'll faint in front of her.*

"I'll be able," she says to Galen, "don't worry." She looks significantly at him, and he nods. "All right," he says. "And Trygve, I think we'll need you too."

Trygve heaves himself up reluctantly, gulps, and rests his hand on his brother's back. Supposedly, twins know each other's thoughts, feel each other's pain. In Miss Spofford's Academy, the Allston twins took each other's tests sometimes, just for fun. Each night they migrated into the same dormitory bed, to be found in the morning curled together like puppies. They'd once shared the same heart, the same common blood. When Galen cuts into Oyvind's body, what will Trygve feel?

Trygve's forehead is white under his thick red hair, and sweat films his cheekbones. But he follows his brother and Galen across the front hall and into the doctor's parlor. Sarah, carrying a kettle of hot water, shuts the door behind them all.

"Now," says Galen briskly. "Sit on the table, here, Oyvind." He pats the sheet-draped bench in the center of the room. Oyvind sits, unbuttoning his shirt. Trygve sits next to him, so close that Oyvind's arm bumps him in the ribs, but neither twin moves away.

Sarah sets her kettle on the marble counter of the tall cabinet against the wall, unhooks the big tin basin from its nail, then pours hot water into it. She fills the smaller basin, too. The soap is still in its shallow dish, within Galen's reach. From the drawers ranged above the countertop, Galen lifts a stack of soft folded cloths, then a pair of steel forceps, then a scalpel. Oyvind turns his head to look at it. "If you could fold that up," he observes, "wouldn't it make a fine pocket knife."

"Sure would," says Galen, surprised. So often patients shut their eyes, mute and miserable. Their lips move, they sweat, they grip the table-edge. They don't want to look at the knife, they just want to endure what's about to happen. No one can see to the other side of pain, or fear.

"Oyvind," Galen says, "I can offer you ether, if you would like. Puts you to sleep while I operate, so you won't feel the knife."

Oyvind considers. "How does it work?" he asks.

"I hold a cloth over your nose," says Galen, "and you continue to breathe normally, and before you know it you wake up and the operation is done."

Oyvind is silent. "Can I see, at all?" he asks. "Can I hear?"

"No," says Galen, "I've been told it feels like being in a deep sleep."

"I'd rather not," says Oyvind. "If it's not going to be a long time for you to operate. I'd rather be awake."

"Are you sure?" Galen asks.

Oyvind shivers. Then he nods.

Galen lays the forceps and the scalpel on a clean white towel at the edge of the counter. On the table, the twins huddle, their shoulders still touching. Trygve wrings Oyvind's shirt in his hands. "Now, Oyvind," Galen says, "lie down on your stomach. Trygve, come around to the front of the table and put out your hands for Oyvind to hold."

Both twins turn even paler. "Hold?" Trygve stutters. "Is it—will it be—"

"It won't last long," Galen soothes. "But it helps to have something to hold on to."

Oyvind swivels and stretches out face-down on the table. Trygve kneels next to his head, his face level with his brother's, and holds up both hands. Oyvind grips them, and his grip tightens. The back of his neck and his forearms are deeply tanned, but his wide back is pale; unlike Trygve, Sarah realizes, Oyvind always wears a shirt. On his right shoulder, just below a constellation of light-brown moles, a lump as big as Sarah's fist floats under his skin. The muscles on his long back leap and tense, and the big lump twitches with them. It's a lipoma, a big lump of fatty tissue that just grows, random and benign. She's helped Galen remove them before. She props the basin on her belly where Galen can reach it to rinse the knife.

"That's fine," Galen says, "hold onto Trygve, but try not to move the shoulder." Oyvind's head nods, once. Trygve tightens his grip and looks away. "You'll feel a dampness," says Galen, swabbing Oyvind's tumor with a small cloth soaked in iodine. The pale skin darkens. "Now the first incision. Be very, very still." Galen lifts the knife and draws it across the top of the big lump. A line of blood opens as the skin parts.

A puff of breath from Trygve: Oyvind's hands tighten. But Trygve doesn't let go. With a cloth, Sarah pats the incision on one side, then the other, to catch the blood. Galen is working faster now, still smooth and deliberate. The skin curls back like curtains, one on each side of the muddy-yellow lump that is now poking through the cut. "Not implicated in the muscle," says Galen, satisfied. "Classic lipoma. That's just a big bunch of fat cells, Oyvind, just a cluster of tissue sitting there. And we'll soon have it lifted right out. You're doing beautifully." He swishes the knife in the basin and touches the gleaming blade to the end of the incision to widen it. "Now, you'll feel a little tug as I detach—"

"Galen," Sarah warns. He pauses with the knife above the wound just as Trygve slides to the floor, unconscious. Oyvind doesn't lift his head, just makes a little snuffling noise that could be laughter, slides his hands out of his brother's, and grips the legs of the table. "Keep on, Doctor," he says. "I'm ready."

"I'm nearly finished," Galen says. He hooks his forceps into the wobbly lump, lifts, and slips the scapel underneath it, left and right. With a small wet *slurp*, the tumor loosens and Galen lifts it from the wound. Sarah blots the welling blood, and Galen drops the tumor into a bowl. He peers into the wound and nods. "Very good," he says. "Came out clean. I'm going to suture up this wound, and then we'll bandage it." He threads a length of pale silk into a curved needle and sews the lips of Oyvind's wound shut, as neatly as Sarah would mend a rip in a skirt. The needle hesitates at the surface of the skin, pushes in, dives back up. Sarah looks away, holding her gaze on a single fly butting against the bright face of the window. "Good man," Galen says at last. "We're finished."

Oyvind's grip on the table legs slackens and his whole body loosens. A sigh rushes from his mouth. Wincing, he pushes himself upright, joint by joint. Trygve's still motionless on the floor.

Oyvind glances at him, then peers into the bowl that holds the lipoma. "Well," he says. He prods it with one finger, and it wobbles like a pudding. "Look at that."

Galen swabs the wound with iodine and he and Sarah wrap lengths of gauze around Oyvind's shoulder, tying it snugly. "I can send you home with fresh dressing," Galen says. "Get Trygve to help you"—he pauses, looks down, grins—"or your mother. Or come back here and I will change it every day."

"I can come back here," says Oyvind. "Don't want to bother them."

"Mrrrmmm," moans Trygve from the floor. He sits up and shakes his head. "Did I—" He reddens violently. "Oh."

"It happens often," Galen reassures him, "to all kinds of people. More than you'd think."

Oyvind lifts his eyebrows and grins at his brother, almost too fast for Sarah to see. "I won't tell nobody," he says. "Don't worry." He hesitates. In the kitchen, Rosa Lee's steps move back and forth. Sarah registers this pause—her friend's name dangles between the two brothers, invisible—and smiles. Galen hasn't noticed a thing.

In the examining room, after Trygve and Oyvind are gone, Galen cleans the forceps and scalpel and gathers the bloody cloths for bleaching in the giant wash pot. Sarah wipes the floor around the table. She swabs up blood that dripped over the edge. There are spots of sweat, too, that dripped from Oyvind's forehead onto the floor, where no one can see.

Oyvind is like Galen himself that way. And Seth.

2

Fairibault was three hundred acres that had once been a thousand, a round knob of land set in a crook of the Chattahoochee River where it split Alabama from Georgia. "That's us," Father said, pointing at the surveyor's map, where the numbers in brown ink had soaked into the paper. "That's where the Indian camp up in the woods is. That's where the big cotton field is, and the other field. That's where the creek is. And here is our house. Right here."

Father moved in a world of invisible reckonings. But Mama's accountings were fierce and quick and based on things anyone could see: *the caterpillars have eaten the tomato leaves, so you girls have to get up earlier and be quicker to pick them off next time, do you want us to lose every one?* Everyone around Fairibault, too, fell within the comfortingly quick circle of Mama's judgment. *That Everett Sayers is just plain sorry. Look at how he leaves that corn in the field, just standing there. That Eleanora Pruitt is gifted. Look at these stitches, so fine. These teacakes are so light they might just float up off this plate on their own. Ladies*—to Mrs. Hopewell and Mrs. Jones in the parlor—*I do wish I could take credit for these, but I have to thank our Alvah. Without her, we would starve. I've honestly no doubt.* And, to general laughter, Mama would smile. Maybe when Sarah was grown, she could move in this world too. She could be confident and quick like Mama, with the same firm thump of boots on the floor, the same quick swish of skirts, the same soft purr of needle-thread through cloth. A grown woman. A lady.

Mama was not quite as tall as Father but she seemed somehow bigger. Wiry and quick, she had a proud upward tilt to her chin and a long white neck and a mass of thick-piled hair that looked walnut-brown in some lights and deep blood-bay red in others. Mama would consider it a compliment to be compared to a blood bay; she had a fine Thoroughbred mare of her own, Marie, whom no one but herself was allowed to ride. Even when she didn't have time to ride Marie, she'd go down to the pasture to the fence and wait for Marie to lift her head and amble towards her, then rub the mare's forehead and feed her an apple core and, sighing, turn back to the house. *A virtuous woman*, the Bible said. *Her works rise up and give her praise.* This meant, Sarah supposed, that a virtuous woman was always busy. This was certainly true of Mama. "No time for melancholy," she liked to say. "Sadness only waits for those who let it in."

But Father's reckoning was different. Sarah could not often read into the looks on his face. Sometimes she trailed him and Johnny on their walks to the riverbank. There they were surrounded on three sides by the river, far to the right and far to the left and gurgling quietly past at their feet. Johnny and Father stood and watched the river, their shoulders nearly touching, their boots deep in the sharp grass that edged the green-smelling mud. *What are you looking at?* Sarah nearly asked. *What do you see?* But she could never break that quiet, never touch that melancholy in Father's face. And Johnny—she saw him know this, too—couldn't either.

Father was shorter than Johnny but seemed to stand deeper into the ground, shoulders squared and settled, although the colorless hair thinning on top of his head and the thoughtful look in his eyes made him seem like he might vanish from the spot, even while you looked at him. Like Rosa Lee and Sarah and Jane laughed when playing tag. *Now you see me. Now you don't.*

Maybe, when they stood at the riverbank, they were thinking about Marcus, Alvah's husband, Rosa Lee and Seth's father, who had died on that spot. Only a blurry picture of him stayed in Sarah's mind: a big dark man lifting a tiny girl that was Rosa Lee, swinging her around and around until her laughing rang through the glass of the parlor window and touched Sarah's face where she stood watching. Marcus had been a builder: he could go into the swamp with some of the other people and cut big trees and notch and mark them to reassemble into a shed or log pen or another cabin. One day a long time ago, Father and Cassius and Marcus and Mr. Wainwright's Luke, hired for the day, had been building a landing dock at the river for Fairibault. They hauled out big logs from the swamp to the bank and cleared a path to the water. Marcus waded out chest-deep and sank the two far posts and then a nearer one. But when he struck down with his shovel near the bank, he hit a nest of cottonmouths that boiled out on him before anyone could stop them. Father and Cassius ran in and got Marcus out of the water while Luke struck with his shovel at the snakes still lunging with their white mouths open. By the time they got him back to the house, Marcus was dead.

Sarah dimly remembered standing next to Mama in the cemetery, with Jane in Mama's arms, Rosa Lee in Alvah's, and Father and the preacher and Johnny—a little boy, then—standing side by side. Seth reached out to drop a handful of dirt on the lid of Marcus's yellow pine box. "That boy gonna be a good man," Cassius said to Alvah. "Good man like his daddy." Alvah nodded. Her tears were terrifying. After that, she never went to the river and she never let Seth and Rosa Lee go, either. The dock was never finished. The posts Marcus had sunk still remained upright in the water, weathering gray, settling lower every year.

Marcus was part of Father's invisible reckoning, like the others. "Our people," Father said to Mr. Wainwright and Mr. Mott at the dinner table, "are honorable sorts. They do receive a wage." Here the other men laughed or snorted. "They do," Father continued. "One silver-dollar piece per year, plus a garden patch to work. You have to give them suitable reward."

"I imagine it's easier to be so rewarding," Mr. Wainwright drawled, "if you have so few of them." Lounging backwards in his chair with his long-fingered hands on Mama's silver knife and fork, he was big and handsome, with black hair and green eyes, like all the Wainwrights. *They're dangerous*, whispered everybody in the county. *You never know what a Wainwright would do.* His words rang hard enough for even Sarah to understand. *So few.*

"That's right," Father said evenly, letting this sharp-pointed statement lie on the floor where Mr. Wainwright had thrown it. "It is. Much easier."

Fairibault had used to be larger, comprising all the land Grandfather and Great-Grandfather had gathered up from the Indians. Great-Grandfather had once seen the Indians playing their great ball games on the ceremonial grounds by the river to honor General Lafayette and William Bartram when they traveled through investigating this rich wild land. He had built himself a square log house on the same little hill where their own house now stood. By the time Grandfather died, Fairibault was a thousand acres large. But it was nowhere near that big now. Because if you had more land, you had to have more people.

People, Sarah thinks, years later. *No one used the word* slave.

There weren't many people at Fairibault. There were Cassius and Marcus—before he died—and Old Caleb, who was Alvah's father, and Celia, who was Marcus's younger half-sister. Sometimes there were Widow Spivey's men hired in to plant and get in cotton, and Mr. Wainwright's women hired in to help all of them when it was time to pick, or Luke if there was something to build. And always there were Alvah, and Rosa Lee, and Seth.

But Sarah and Jane were not allowed to go to the fields. "Stay out from down there," Mama warned. So Sarah didn't talk to the people creeping their way down the rows. From a distance, they were just a series of bent backs, trailed by the long burlap sacks that showed in flashes between the plants. One of Mr. Wainwright's women had a baby she let sleep in a basket underneath the oak tree, near the water bucket and dipper. Every so often she'd leave her sack and step across the rows into the circle of shade and sit and open her dress to nurse it. "Can't I go down to see the baby?" Jane whined, and Mama shook her head. From her seat against the window in the upstairs hall Sarah could watch the dim shape bending, taking the smaller shape into itself and sitting, just for a few minutes, under the tree.

Even when Father summoned these people all up to the house at the end of the season, to receive one silver quarter-dollar and one dime apiece, it still felt hard to see them directly. A sudden wild mix of curiosity and shyness filled Sarah when she saw these strangers who let her eyes fall on them without looking back, who never gazed on her directly but still managed—she could feel it— to take her in: two blonde pigtails with their grubby ribbons, a smudged pinafore, feet as bare as theirs. She could only look at them in pieces, too: the shine of sweat on their cheekbones, the way they swiped their sleeves across their faces, quick, the thin patches over the men's ears where Mr. Wainwright's barbering-man had cut too close, their long toes in the dust. One by one, they held out their hands for Father to set the pieces of silver in their wide pink palms—why was it that their top skin was dark and their undersides were pink?—and nodded and smiled and stepped backwards into line again. The woman with the baby wore it in a sling, tucked so snug against her that Sarah could see only one tiny hand, resting on the woman's bosom. She longed to see the baby close. But by the time she had worked up her courage to ask, Father had dismissed the people to go down by the cabins, toting their own bucket of water and dipper, to wait until Mr. Wainwright's wagon came to collect them.

Money came, somehow, from what these people did. And only those two silver coins went back into their hands.

"It doesn't do to be sentimental about Negroes, like the Northerners," Father always said. "But it's fitting to remember their work."

And the people worked. Old Caleb braided straw hats for everyone out of long river grass. He kept the saddles clean and oiled. He shoed the horses, stooping low with the hoof in his lap, then straightening up little by little, with a painful uncurling of his spine. He hitched and unhitched the mules, rubbing their long ears with his flat pink-tipped fingers, murmuring nonsense that mules liked. In Sarah's memory he was always an old man, with white fuzzy hair and tiny round dark moles sprinkled across the lighter-brown skin under his eyes. His voice was a low comforting hum that fell on her and Seth and Jane and Rosa Lee alike: *hey, child.* She remembered looking up at him, into the sun. *It's the off hind, got a stone bruise or some such.*

And Celia—elusive in Sarah's memory, she flashed like a silver fish in and out of sight. Always she rose into sight up the stairs, the crown of her head and then her wide forehead and bright eyes dawning over the sill of the top step, down the long hall from where Sarah sat pressed against the cool window glass. "What're you lookin at down there?" Celia might ask, if she were in a fine morning mood. Or she might simply nod and turn into Mother's and Father's room, or Johnny's. She would come up the stairs with an armful of neat folded sheets or a vase of camellias or a rattling breakfast tray (*Johnny's been out late with Tommy Lee Coulter, again,* said Mama's look at his empty chair.) She would go back down the stairs with a wad of soiled shirt, teacups with brown trickles down the sides, a chamber pot.

And Sarah would sit and watch her go.

I always watched, she would think, years later. *I looked and didn't see.*

Celia in the back yard teaching Rosa Lee an intricate hand-slap game: pat and cross and pat and back again. Laughing. Lifting a damp sheet high into the air to billow like a sail, for Rosa Lee to run underneath. Chasing her in a circle and spinning around suddenly to be chased: a swirl of skirts, a laughing squeal ringing through the glass that rippled her bright shape like a minnow in a stream.

If Sarah were to go down there to try and play with them, Celia would straighten up and firm her mouth and cast her eyes just to the right or left of Sarah's own, would fold her slim arms and ask politely in her colorless house voice what Sarah might require. She had learned to say that from the teatime ladies who came to huddle with Mama over their parlor cups, to gossip and rustle. Celia had begun serving in the parlor when she was ten; now she was sixteen. She would wait, patiently, behind that small grown-woman smile until Sarah went away. And even Rosa Lee, when she was with Celia, would not help. It was a mute and miserable chill, like the feeling cruel Maisie Beauchamp could give Sarah when they were playing in the church-yard circle: "what makes you think we want you over here?" Maisie would sneer as Becky and Irene and Catherine giggled. With those girls, it was cruelty. With Celia and Rosa Lee, it was some other subtle thing, too—something like a shame put onto her, a justice Sarah could recognize as hers to bear. "It's all right," she'd mumble as she turned away. "I was only—" And she'd return to the upstairs window to watch their game or their comfortable settled talk as they hung sheets or strolled to the cookhouse and disappeared inside. Without her.

The peace of the house came, somehow, from what Celia and Alvah did, alongside and underneath Mama. They buoyed her up like undercurrents below the braiding riffles you could see carrying along your paper boat, or a leaf, on the top of a stream. Money was responsible for that too, at a deeper current-level Sarah could feel but never see. But money was hard to be certain of. There would be money after the cotton was picked and sent away to the big gin at Hurtsboro. Otherwise, it would be necessary for Mama to be what

she called *thrifty*. "Good thing I learned it," she would laugh, with
something thorny bristling up inside the laugh. "A sound skill for a
soldier's daughter." *Thrifty* meant hunting for a dropped needle in
the worn parlor carpet, and knotting loose bits of thread together
to make one string. *Thrifty* meant impatient sighs at Father: "land
sakes, Ned, haven't you got aplenty books in there by now, without
ordering more?" It was a frown at Jane: "you're going to learn not
to take too much food, if it means sitting here until you eat every
last bite on your plate." It meant turning the horses out to crop the
sides of the drive and the lawn, Seth or Old Caleb holding the ends
of their long ropes, to spare at least some of the golden hay stored
in the barn-loft. Thrift was a virtue, of course. But it was connected
in Mama to something sad that Sarah could not quite touch.

Mama's father was an Army officer who had been killed when
Mama was just a little girl. Her mother had died shortly afterward.
"Of grief," Mama smiled, with a little twist at her mouth. "Bless
her heart, she was so useless." And so Mama had been raised in
Mobile by her mama's sister, Aunt Maude, who had never married,
to whom all the money in Mama's family had come down from her
grandfather. "He tried to punish my mother for marrying," Mama
said, "and reward poor Maude for being a spinster."

Yet it was hard to think of Aunt Maude as *poor* anything. She
lived in that family house in Mobile: a tall quiet brick house on
a leafy square, behind a black wrought-iron fence. Aunt Maude
had only rarely visited Fairibault. Small and dumpling-shaped,
with hair going gray, tiny hands hidden in deep ruffled cuffs, and
a fat pink silk reticule dangling from her wrist at all times, she sat
so straight in her chair that her back never touched it, and she
carried her own silver spoon with which she sampled one tiny
dab of everything. "Good," she pronounced Alvah's catfish, wa-
termelon-rind preserves, and plump boiled okra. "I hate to admit
it. But your woman is better than my Mamie." She studied Sarah

and Jane. "However, your girls need to learn better posture, Livia. Attend to that."

Despite this criticism, at Christmas that year, Aunt Maude had sent both Sarah and Jane beautiful china dolls with long braids of real hair—Sarah's gold and Jane's brown, like their own hair—and stiff silk dresses and eyes that closed. *deer Aunt Maude,* Sarah had scratched with blotty grown-up ink, *thank You for your kind rememberance of me at this Holliday season. I love my Doll, she is Beautiful. Her name is Lucinda Victoria. Janes dolls name is Pansy Josephine.* At night, she nestled Lucinda Victoria next to her until the tiny cool body grew warm as her own skin, and she could fall asleep.

Just as Aunt Maude was Mother's only relative, Uncle Eugene was Father's: a younger brother who was all, besides Father, left of the Fairibaults now. But Uncle Eugene had never come to the house, and Sarah had never seen him. She gathered that he would never send anyone a doll at Christmas, because he lacked not only money but what Mama, out of Father's hearing, called "basic decency" and "consideration" and "common sense." Father slid the pocket doors to the parlor shut whenever Uncle Eugene's name was being tossed around between himself and Mama, trapping the words in the room with them like a blind battering bird.

("A bird in the house means somebody's going to die," Alvah always said.)

Hard as they listened, Sarah and Jane could only gather scraps: Father's mother, he explained, had "left Eugene in my care. On her deathbed, Livia. Eugene's improvident, but some people just lack that sense. He'll pay us back this money, every bit. I'm his brother. He's not on the laudanum anymore, he says it. And Grandfather was so cruel to him in the will."

"Pay us back?" Mama snapped back. "With what? I've got the record here, you know. In my little green book. Everything you've given him. Correction: *we've* given him."

"Perhaps you need to remember whose money it is," Father said.

"Perhaps you need to remember who manages it, who saves and makes do and without whom this whole place would be overrun by weeds and other people's Negroes," Mama retorted.

The little green book was Mama's ledger for household accounts, kept in a locked drawer of the secretary in her bedroom. Only once, when Mama accidentally left the little book open on her writing-desk lid, had Sarah seen the rows of figures under the impatient scratch of the name *Eugene*, running down one page and almost to the bottom of a second, off at the back of the book by themselves: 2/50. 5/. 10. 7/50. 25/. 100/. 25/. 5/. Five times two is ten. Five times five is twenty-five. Two pages of multiples of five is a lot of money gone away to Uncle Eugene.

Where was he? Where did he spend this money? Sarah wasn't sure. The cities Mama and Father tossed around when they talked about him always changed: New Orleans, Atlanta, Charleston, Savannah, Baton Rouge. "You keep him away from here, Ned," warned Mama. "You just keep him away."

Yet to Sarah, their house always felt safe against Uncle Eugene or any other danger. It was wooden, white-painted and square, with six narrow columns across the front (just thick enough that Sarah's fingers could barely touch when she reached her arms around, until she got bigger) and a screened front door left open during the day so a breeze could run down the wide front hall, all the way from front to back, past the staircase and the big grandfather clock and the Turkey carpet with the frayed edges. Three square rooms opened on each side of the halls upstairs and down; the downstairs rooms connected to one another by doors, the upstairs bedrooms were all separate. Another wide hall ran down the center of the upstairs, too, and ended in a little porch right above the front door, just big enough for Mama's rocking chair. Two small gabled windows in the roof let in light to the attic. All the windows had dark green shutters, and the downstairs windows had little doors underneath them, latched with a tiny gold hook, so you could raise the windows and open those little doors and have two extra doors right onto the porch, where only a wall had been before. It was a square, plain house, except for those little doors. Nobody else's house Sarah knew had those.

Sarah liked to sit on the window seat at the top of the stairs, squeezed comfortingly into the corner with the bubbly window glass against her cheek, and look down across the world: the cookhouse and privy at opposite corners of the yard, the woodshed, the wellhouse and pump, the chicken coop, the herb garden and the big vegetable garden, the clothesline where Celia and Rosa Lee hung the flapping white sheets. Way to the side, almost out of Sarah's view, were the magnolia trees and azalea bushes at the corners of the yard, and the scarlet camellias. Further down, to the left at the bottom of the little hill on which the house sat, were the barns and sheds, and opposite them, to the right, under the oak trees, were five small cabins, with brick chimneys and small porches with chunks of cut-up tree trunk to sit on. Each cabin was just a little bigger than Sarah's own bedroom. Each door had a white china knob, and no lock. Inside, Sarah knew, the floors were dirt, polished smooth by bare feet like the dirt in the yard in front of the cookhouse. There were mattresses made of cornshucks inside big cloth sacks and plain wooden frames for the beds, tin dippers and a place where Rosa Lee's rag doll slept at night, right beside Rosa Lee. But Sarah had never sat on those porches or gone through one of those doors. She was not allowed. And she never would be.

Mostly, she and Jane had played and ate and talked with Rosa Lee and Seth outside. And when they could, they went to the woods.

Seth.

Home.

It is hard to picture people clear, Sarah thinks, when for so long they've been a feeling in your mind you mustn't admit you've ever had. It's still that way. Every time she lets herself think of Fairibault before the war, a different picture of Seth slips up first. Seth chopping a baby copperhead in half with a hoe. Seth hunkered on an overturned bucket in the barnyard next to Old Caleb, watching him set the spokes of a new wagon wheel. Seth treading water in the lake, swimming with her and Jane and Rosa Lee, laughing as Sarah popped to the surface with a big brown hunk of water-weed stuck to her hair. Seth trudging into the pecan grove to gather mistletoe from the trees—he was terrified of those high swaying branches, but Mama wanted to decorate a proper Christmas parlor—climbing into the sky, then landing safely back on the ground, handing Sarah the sack of mistletoe, his hands still shaking. The chalky green smell from the mouth of the sack. The cold gray sky shot with chips of brilliant blue.

Once she and Seth and Jane and Rosa Lee had knelt at the edge of the stream, gathering handfuls of mud and leaves and pebbles to build castles. Seth mixed his mud with clay so his tower would stand on its own, like a crayfish house. Rosa Lee rolled the mud into little balls and set them on top of each other. Jane copied her. Sarah stacked her mud in wet handfuls until she had a heap of dirt as wide and round as a snapping turtle's shell. She pressed leaves over it in a pattern, pressed pebbles into the surface. Under her hands, the wall of her creation was bumpy, smooth, prickly, grainy, immovable. "It's a cake," she said. "A mud birthday cake."

"Look, I'm an Indian," said Rosa Lee. She lifted her muddy hands to her face and dragged them down her round cheeks. "Woo! Woo!"

"Go on," Seth scoffed, "you ain't no Indian." But Sarah and Jane laughed, then smeared their own faces with mud. It felt sticky but good, tightening the skin underneath as it dried, catching their hair and turning ashy dark gray. Rosa Lee peered at Sarah and

Jane, blinking through her mask. When they giggled, their cheeks cracked. "I despair of you children," Jane mocked, in Mama's voice.

All their faces were brown and gray except Seth's. He was too big a boy to smear mud on his face, and Sarah was almost too big a girl.

And then Seth was three, then four inches taller than Sarah, with long legs and bony knees that jutted out under his rolled-up pants cuffs and long knobby hands that seemed too big for his wrists. "You gonna be a tall man," Alvah murmured, hugging him, "like your daddy." What did Seth remember of Marcus, his daddy? When Seth stood still sometimes, staring at nothing Sarah could see, his hands showed that he was thinking: tugging at the lobe of one ear, brushing over his close-cut scalp, fingering the ragged end of his belt, picking at splinters or calluses until his fingertips were dotted with blood. What did Seth think of in the place he went, alone? What did he know?

Sarah hunkered on the forest path next to Jane and Rosa Lee, where a mockingbird's nest had fallen and smashed. "Look at that," Seth breathed. He stretched the budded end of a green stick toward the tiny pink bodies. Another boy would shove the baby birds, toppling them onto their not-even-pinfeathered chests. But Seth didn't touch them. Sarah thought of Mrs. Wollstonecraft's *Original Stories*, the small green book she loved to hold in both hands: *Do you know the meaning of the word Goodness? I will tell you. It is, first, to avoid hurting any thing.*

Seth was ten, then, and he knew more than anyone. He could hitch and unhitch the mules as quickly as a man, walk along the top of the rail fence with his hands in his pockets, and whistle on a grass blade pinched between his thumbs. He could read almost as well as Sarah. Father taught him and Rosa Lee alongside Sarah and

Jane and Johnny, although Mama still frowned and sighed when she saw them go into the parlor together. "One more year, Livia," said Father, "humor my little experiment, please." Sometimes when there was nothing else to do, Jane and Rosa Lee and Seth followed Sarah up to the big magnolia tree behind the house and they sat up under the branches, which spread all around them like a lady's dress—even if it was raining, they were safe there—and they listened to Sarah read *Nicholas Nickelby*. Together they shuddered at the cruel schoolmaster, the cold room, the squeak of chalk on slates. Their lessons took place in the sunny front parlor, where Sarah's father listened to them recite. "Maybe start you on Latin next year," he told Sarah. "How would you like that? You'd be a learned woman." And he laughed. Sarah was uncertain whether to smile back. She was eight, getting to be a big girl. She was good at lessons. Wasn't that what he wanted?

That day, though, they were all finished with their lessons and chores and were riding into the woods on the backs of the old mules, Job and Shadrach. "Given a mule's nature," Father commented, "a long-suffering name is appropriate." Like always, Rosa Lee rode behind Seth and Jane rode behind Sarah, because they were still little, just seven and six. Lately the frown lines between Mama's eyes had been getting deeper when she watched the four of them set out, and she opened her mouth but turned away before words came out. When the same look was in Alvah's eyes, she'd get snappy with all four of them, particularly Rosa Lee and Seth. "You children sit down and eat," she'd say, "and don't hassle me no more. I swear." At the table in the back kitchen, they'd catch each other's eyes and shrug. If Jane was feeling particularly spiteful she'd flip her eyelids inside out when Alvah's back was turned, which only Jane could do.

That day, they were going up to the old Indian campsite on the hill above the stream. A mulberry tree hung over the trail, and they could halt the mules there and reach up and eat mulberries until their fingers and lips were purple. They found arrowheads up at the campsite, too, near the old garden patch; Father said the great-great-great-great grandfathers of the melons and squash that Alvah still harvested were growing there when Grandaddy got this land from the Indians. (Got the land, Sarah wondered: how did he pay them? Did he get the Indians to point out their land on a map?) Once, Rosa Lee had found a grinding rock and Sarah had found the flat rock to match it, with the hole worn into it. That was too heavy to carry back on the mules, so they'd left it under a tree, where they could pretend to grind corn like little Indian girls every time they wanted.

But this was the first time they had found a fallen nest like this. In the tree over their heads the mother mockingbird bobbed and screeched, hopping foot to foot.

"Good thing we came along," Sarah volunteered.

"Ants get to 'em fore too much longer," said Rosa Lee, peering around Seth's back.

"I can't look," said Jane, wincing theatrically and turning her head to the side. "I just can't look."

"Then don't," Sarah snapped.

"Crosspatch," Jane hissed. She pinched Sarah, then slid off before Sarah could retaliate. Sarah tugged Shadrach aside to stand at the edge of the trail and tied him next to Job. The mules put their long powder-gray noses together and sighed. "Stay there," Sarah warned.

Eggshell was scattered among the twigs and leaves where the nest had fallen and smashed. Three mockingbird chicks struggled chest-down in the dirt, hunching their plucked pink shoulders, which were blue-black under the skin where feathers grew. On their stringy necks, their blind heads wobbled, and their beaks strained open. The mama bird fluttered and dove overhead, hammering a string of notes into the air.

"She's cussin us," said Jane. "We better get away."

"How do you reckon they fell?" Sarah asked. She imagined the blunt head of a snake nosing up the tree and over the lip of the nest, the mama bird stabbing its back with beak and claws, the thud of the mules' hooves on the path, then the snake pausing, hooking around backwards, and bumping the nest to the ground.

"No tellin," said Seth. He stretched forth his hand with the stick, and hesitated.

"Can we put 'em back up there?" asked Rosa Lee. Her voice wobbled. So would Sarah's, if she said anything. It was shameful, but they couldn't help it. They cried like babies at the kittens that died in the loft, the rag dolls they'd left out in the rain, the twin calves the mama cow had abandoned. "Y'all are the *cryinest* children," Alvah always said. Sarah looked away from the baby birds and swallowed hard to shut the aching gap in her throat.

"The mama won't take 'em back if we touch 'em," Jane said.

"How do *you* know?" Rosa Lee asked.

"I just do," said Jane. She snatched at Seth's hand. "We should get away from here."

"But—" Rosa Lee said.

"We can't just leave 'em," Sarah said.

Seth scooped up two big poplar leaves from the side of the path to shield his fingers. Breathing carefully, he nudged his fingertips under the biggest chick, tipping it into the leaf in his other hand. The baby bird's head flopped and twisted. "Seth," Rosa Lee warned, but Seth edged the chick neatly back into the soft center of the nest. Its small cup shape was still intact, woven of horsehair and leaves and grass and a scrap of what Sarah recognized as the old pink dress that had gone from her to Jane and then the ragbag. Seth put the second chick back into it, and the third. He tucked his hands around the nest, pressing it closer to its original shape, then lifted it and looked around. "Get Shadrach over here," he said.

Sarah untied Shadrach and tugged his long head around and kept tugging until the rest of him followed. Shadrach was the biggest mule, and the gentlest. She and Seth positioned him under the tree, and Seth stood back to look. Then he set the nest in Sarah's other hand. "Hold him still," he warned. "I mean, still." Rosa Lee and Jane took hold of the bridle too. With a running jump Seth smacked himself against Shadrach's side and hauled himself up by the mule's bristly mane, then put one foot on Shadrach's wide rump and one foot on his withers and stood up. His feet flexed and released, balancing. Shadrach's ears with their knobby tips bobbed, but he didn't move.

"Hand me the nest," said Seth. Sarah cupped it in both hands and reached up. Seth raised it slowly, stretching as high as he could, and set it in the crook of a limb, close to the trunk. The mama mockingbird dove at his head and swooped just out of reach.

"Won't do any good," said Jane. "She's gonna leave 'em now. Like chickens, you touch the eggs just once and you have to take 'em in because the hen won't—"

"No!" Sarah said. "She will!" She pictured the baby birds withering and starving, drying up unfeathered in the chilly night. *Y'all the cryinest children.* She gulped. Tears were coming. She couldn't help it.

"She will!" said Rosa Lee, and started to cry too.

"Oh, for . . . " Seth groaned and eased himself down to sit on Shadrach's back. "Y'all come on. We need to leave 'em alone."

Sarah boosted Rosa Lee up behind Seth, then walked Job over to a fallen log for herself and Jane to climb on. "I'm hungry," Jane announced. "I want to go up to the house and get something to eat."

"Me too," said Rosa Lee. "I don't want to go up to the Indian camp no more." None of them did, Sarah realized. Better to get out of the woods today.

Alvah met them at the back door with big chunks of cold cornbread in a pie tin. Rosa Lee and Seth and Sarah slid off the mules, but Jane swung both legs over to one side and tore into her cornbread right where she was, tapping her heels against Job's ribs. He ignored her and dropped his head to browse in the yard dirt, lipping up grains of chicken feed. "Mmmmm," Jane mumbled. "She put bacon drippings on it."

"Thank you, Mama," said Rosa Lee.

"Thank you, Mama," said Seth.

"Thank you, Alvah," said Sarah.

"Ain't no need to feed it to the dogs," said Alvah, "when you got children around." But she was smiling. "Y'all have a good time?"

"We found a baby bird nest that fell," said Rosa Lee, "and Seth stood up on Shadrach's back and put it back in the tree."

"That's a good thing to do, son," said Alvah. Sarah was happy, then, with her tummy full and the baby birds back in the tree. She remembered Mrs. Wollstonecraft's words: Father would be proud of her for knowing them by heart. *Look, what a fine morning it is. Insects, birds, and animals are all enjoying this sweet day. Thank God for permitting you to see it, and for giving you an understanding which teaches you that you ought, by doing good, to imitate Him.* She had been a good girl, and Seth had been a good boy. Somehow, that seemed important.

"I can do that too," Jane blurted. She put both feet underneath her and wobbled to stand upright on Job's back, then flung both her arms in the air. "Hooray!"

"Child, get down from there!" Alvah called. She set the pie tin down and started across the yard toward Jane. "Your mama's gonna—"

"Sarah! Remember the circus?" called Jane. "The lady on the horse?" And she bent over, put both hands on Job's rump, and lifted both feet into the air. Jane's dress dropped over her face and suddenly her legs in their pantalets all stained in the seat with mule sweat and hairs were kicking right up in the air for the whole Christian world to see.

"Get down from there!" Alvah called, louder. "You're gonna fall and—" She was almost to Jane, ready to yank her off, when the back door slammed open and Mama strode across the yard, her skirts kicking up so high the top bootlace showed. "Jane Narcissa Fairibault!" she shouted. Alvah snatched Jane down. As soon as her feet touched the ground, Mama grabbed her by her arm and whirled her around and smacked her bottom. Jane danced and screamed and tried to twist away, but Mama kept slapping. "Jane Narcissa Fairibault!" she growled. "Be ashamed!"

"I was being a circus lady!" Jane howled. But Mama towed Jane across the yard toward the back door, with Jane fighting and twisting. "Let go!" she shouted. "Let go! I hate you!" Without breaking stride Mama hauled up on Jane's arm again and smacked her even harder and Jane howled louder and the back door slammed and they disappeared.

Soon, Mama marched back across the yard to where Sarah and Seth and Rosa Lee had moved into the shade to finish their cornbread. Her face was still sharp and angry. "Jane is being punished," she announced, "and she is not to emerge from her room until after dinner. Bread and water for Miss Circus Lady." She snorted. "Is that clear?"

"Yes, ma'am," all three mumbled. Sarah looked into her mother's face, then looked back down. Rosa Lee and Seth didn't look up at all.

But after dinner Sarah snuck a napkin full of biscuits with jelly and ham up to the room she shared with Jane. "What did she say to you?" she asked.

Jane chewed and swallowed. "She said to be ashamed," she gulped, "to show my tee-ta to a nigra boy."

"We're not supposed to say that word," Sarah admonished. Fear rustled suddenly between her ribs. Jane had done something bad, worse than either of them knew. But what was it?

"Mama said it," Jane observed. "I hate Mama and I am going to hate Mama till I die. And I am going to be a circus lady. I am."

"Wait till she's not looking," Sarah said. "I'll help you."

She fell asleep next to Jane that night, still wondering. Mama'd never let them use that word. *Nigra*. Alvah and Rosa Lee and Seth and Marcus, before he died, and Celia and Old Caleb were *colored*. They were *our people*. Even the bent distant figures making their way down the cotton rows were other people's *people*.

It was only pantalets, after all. What was here that Seth mustn't see?

But she didn't get the nerve to ask. And she didn't mention it to Jane, who was sulky for days after the circus-lady trick. "That girl holds a grudge," Alvah smiled. Even when Mama announced on the next rainy Saturday that Sarah and Jane might help her quilt, and she and Alvah and Celia hauled the bags of rags into the back parlor and set up the big quilting frame, Jane still pouted. Even the sight of the big trunks easing down the attic ladder—Seth and Old Caleb each supporting one end—didn't banish her mood. But Sarah and Rosa Lee went to the bottom of the stairs to watch them carried down ("careful, boy," Mama warned Seth), and stood at Mama's elbow on the parlor rug as she snapped the big brass locks and lifted the lids. Old Caleb looked at the avid group of them—Alvah and Celia and Mama and Rosa Lee and Sarah and Jane—and smiled. "Y'all enjoy yourselves," he said. Seth followed him out.

Like a treasure trove, Sarah thought. Celia's eyes were as eager as her own. When the lid rose, a musty, faintly sweet smell bloomed out of the trunk, and Mama tucked aside layers of yellowed muslin to reveal stacks and stacks of gowns, folded chest-up. One by one, she and Alvah and Celia lifted and shook them out and laid them over the sofas and chairs: soft green and blue and pink silk gowns and dimity sprigged morning dresses and tailored black riding habits and one ball gown after another. White faded to yellow and sparrow-brown in its folds. Deep green rusted into black. And the last: a yellow satin gown with a wide scooped neckline and a narrow waist and a skirt shaped like the bell of a flower. Mama draped it over the settee and smiled, a little smile with something hurt tucked deep inside. She trailed her fingers down the faded fabric of the skirt, which was still supple where her fingers passed. "This was my mother's sixteenth-birthday gown," she said. "This was the gown she danced in on the night she met my father. All these gowns were hers. Funny. I could never stand to wear them."

"Your mama's," Alvah said. "A wonder how they've lasted all this time."

"Yes, well," Mama said. She met Alvah's eyes and looked away. "I hate the feeling of those unused things taking up all this space. Sitting there waiting for the mice to get at them, stored away up over my head. Sometimes I think it troubles my sleep." She tried to laugh but the laugh didn't quite come off. Then she turned away. "Two more trunks yet," she said. "I think Father's things must be in here somewhere. What we can't make over, we'll just cut up for quilts."

At these words, Sarah felt rather than saw a shiver pass up and down Celia's body, stiffening her spine. Celia reached to touch the yellow gown splayed out across the others on the pile. And then, as if she were a princess under a spell, her eyes wide and heedless—*don't touch that, girl, what ails you?* Mama would surely snap if she were looking—Celia lifted the yellow gown and held it against her body. It fit itself exactly to her shape, from collarbone to floor. She tucked one arm around its waist and held it close, her other hand smoothing its length against her calico skirt. No one saw her except Sarah. Rosa Lee and Jane had joined Alvah and Mama by then, all burrowing into a trunk full of men's shirts and long-tailed coats. Jane brandished an ivory-backed men's hairbrush and swiped it against Rosa Lee's pigtails, then grabbed a silk hat out of the pile of clothes and set it on her own head. Everyone, even

Mama, laughed. Emboldened, Jane began to tap-dance and sing: "Oooohhhhh, they call me Molly McGee! No one's half as clever as me!"

"Pretty," Sarah murmured, under cover of their laughing voices. Celia nodded, once. And then she laid the yellow gown back on the pile, just as Mama turned with a heap of swallow-tailed coats in her arms. "Lord," she said, "now where will I put these?"

"Maybe we should lay all the clothes over here," Alvah suggested, "sort through 'em different from the rags."

"Yes," said Mama, "that's a good idea. We can hang what's worth saving up in the old wardrobe on the landing, till we need them." She spread the coats on top of the yellow gown—a buttercup-colored sliver peeked out from under the black, like an ember under fireplace ash—and turned to shake the ragbags out on the worn Aubusson carpet. Sarah pounced into the pile, turning over scraps with both hands. Jane set the hat back in the trunk and knelt next to her. If her parents' clothes made Mama remember, these clothes were Sarah's memories. Here was the pinafore torn on a nail when she climbed over the fence after Seth. Here was the dress ragged at the hem and collar and patched in the middle where a spark from the kitchen fire had landed in Jane's lap and Alvah had beaten it out. Here were last summer's bonnets, lank and faded from dangling down their backs as they jounced along on Shadrach and Job: *if we leave off our bonnets,* Sarah had wondered, looking at Seth and Rosa Lee, *will we turn the same color as them?*

"Our clothes!" whined Jane.

"Don't be silly," Mama said, "they're just old rags now." With brisk motions she ripped the pinafore and petticoat and skirt into long strips, then snipped them into smaller strips to form another heap in front of her. "Come on, girls, tear them up. It's even better to make them into something new." Celia and Alvah knelt and reached for other scraps of cloth, and the second and third pairs of shears.

Ignoring Jane's glare, Sarah tore a small skirt from top to bottom—first hesitantly, then faster as the old cloth gave in. The brown homespun, thinned from being boiled and beaten in the washpot, parted with a purring noise. Mama's big scissors went *snip, snip, snip*. It was exciting. Especially since, now, Mama was leaning close to her, with one arm around her—Mama was always happiest when they were doing something she would call *useful*. "Look," she told Sarah, "make a star shape out of triangles, like this, with a square in the middle." She showed Sarah how to arrange the snips of cloth: brown, blue, homespun-rough, spotty and speckly. "Make a pattern and sew it together, just so big," she said, "then you have a block. And you keep making blocks until you have the top. And then we'll put it on the frame and—"

Jane snuggled her bottom deeper into the pile of rags. "I don't want to cut them up," she pouted.

"Fine," Mama said. "You just won't have a pretty quilt to put on your bed when you get married. Like Sarah will."

"Ain't nobody gonna marry Sarah," Jane observed. "She's mean."

Mama's hands stopped and she peered hard at Jane over Sarah's head. "You have already had one punishment this week," she snapped. "Maybe that was not enough. Maybe you want me to spank you again for being so un-Christian to your sister. For being such an evil little girl."

Jane flushed, pouted deeper, and folded both her arms. Despite herself, Sarah stifled a grin; across the heap of rags, Alvah and Celia were smiling too. She knew what Jane was thinking. *I want to be evil. Damn you, you damn old Mama.* Their big brother Johnny had taught Jane to say "damn" because it made him laugh. Sarah didn't like to say it, even though Jane called her Miss Priss and Lemon Face and Sourpuss. She didn't like that laughter on Johnny's face, that amusement at his little sisters that fell away so easily when something more interesting came along.

Suddenly the front door flung open and smacked into the little side table beside the door, where a glass bowl of gardenias floated. Big boots thumped through the foyer. "Mama!" Johnny called. His flushed face appeared in the door of the parlor. "There you are."

"Where else would I be, son?" said Mama. Her voice brightened. "How was your ride?"

"That damn horse of Father's jounced me all the way up to the Crossroads and back," Johnny complained. He raked one long hand through his hair, spreading the rain through it till it leaned back sleek as an otter's from his forehead. He was handsome, Sarah reckoned, as such things are measured—gray eyes like Father's, golden hair a shade darker than hers—but mostly, he was simply her brother, matter-of-fact and omnipresent. Alvah glanced up and looked down again, still snipping. Celia looked at him directly, with no expression on her face.

Johnny shoved his heels into the bootjack next to the hall bench, wiggled his legs out of the high boots, and let them fall. "Wipe your feet," Mama always snapped at Sarah and Jane, "dirty shoes scratch the boards." Yet she never told Johnny to wipe his feet. She let him wear his dirty boots all the way in the house, even kept the bootjack there just for him. Alvah would take the boots up to Johnny's room, after this. Or Mama would.

"Well," said Mama reasonably, "you do have your own horse."

"Hoof abcess," Johnny said. He shucked off his coat and hooked it onto the rack. Rain trickled to the floor. "Got anything in the larder for a starving man?" His eyes swept the room, stopping on Celia, then shifting back to the heap of clothes on the settee. "What's all this?"

"Some housecleaning," Mama said. "We're going to quilt."

"Oh," Johnny said. "Hey, look at that." He stepped toward the pile of gentlemen's coats. "I wonder if those'd fit me."

"No, son," Mama protested, setting aside the bundle of scraps in her hands and rising to her feet. "Those were my father's, and you're taller than he ever was. And anyway, you'll get them wet, all rainy as you are. I'll make you something to eat." Sarah started to protest—*what about our quilts?*—but she was stopped by the eagerness on Mama's face, shrouded in Mama's usual look of complaint: *I wait on these children hand and foot, just run off my feet.* "There may be a little cake left," she said, "some bread and cheese, in the dining room."

Mama followed Johnny out of the parlor. They might have to go all the way out the back door across the yard to the kitchen to find food for him between meals. Which meant Mama would sit with Johnny while he ate, draw water to wash his plate and fork, get distracted by something else to be done and make her way back into the parlor and the quilt scraps and the glorious rusty sprawl of trunks and clothes late, if at all, and by then Sarah would be bored and Jane would be bored and they'd get up and go somewhere else and Mama would scold them for leaving all the quilt scraps strewn around, for being selfish girls, didn't they know she had better things to do than wait on her children hand and foot?

Sarah stood up, out of the warm spot she and Mama had made. Johnny had sloshed the vase water out on the hall table, and someone should wipe it up or it would eat away the varnish in a big white spot. She crossed the hall, fetched a rag from the bottom drawer of the dining room sideboard, and wiped the spilled water from the floor and from around the gardenia bowl on the little hall table. She'd just picked these gardenias yesterday and already they were brown around the edges. But the smell was sweeter that way. "Don't sniff them too much," Mama always commanded, "they just spoil faster." Sarah sank her face into the flowers and breathed.

Mama was always like this when Johnny was in the house: alert and watching for what he needed before he knew it himself. Even if he was sitting sullenly in the parlor with Father, paging through Gibbon or Tacitus without reading it; even if he was toeing off his boots in the hallway with his hand on Rosa Lee's or Jane's heads for support; even if he stood at the big plantation desk in Father's study, poring over the accounts ("I *knew* you let that back thirty go too cheap—now everybody in three counties knows all they've gotta do is bring a hard-luck story to get 'em some land.") Even if he was striding to the sideboard, big as life, age fifteen, to pour himself a glass of Father's whiskey ("you girls listen to me: don't never trust a man can't hold his liquor.") Even if Sarah tried to stop him: "Johnny, you're gonna get in trouble!" Even if he turned to look at her with sardonic, judging eyes: "be careful, little sister. No man likes a naggin' woman."

Alvah stood up slowly. "Come on," she said to Celia, "we can at least tidy up a little, here."

"I'll go hang these in the wardrobe," Celia offered. She set the men's coats to the side and gathered the heap of gowns into her arms as gently as if she were lifting a sleeping baby. Cradling the yellow gown on the top of the stack, she ascended the stairs out of sight.

Behind Sarah came the soft rumpling sound of Jane gathering fabric scraps in her arms, stuffing them back into the sack. Neither of them said anything to each other. There was no need.

Until those big trunks were opened, Sarah had never seen so many clothes in one place except at Mrs. Pruitt's house. Mrs. Pruitt was the seamstress who lived with her daughter Katy down the road. Mama and all the other ladies talked so much about how bad young Katy was, how prone to talking-back and disrespect, that Sarah, in her own mind, couldn't help calling her Bad Katy, as if it were her rightful name. Bad Katy Pruitt was one year older than Sarah, a small skinny darting girl with purple circles under her eyes and tight strawberry-blond braids. "My daddy is mean," she whispered proudly to Sarah, once. "He's the meanest man in town. Don't nobody bother us, cause of him."

But Bad Katy's daddy was dead. Good thing, because he was a drunk who beat Katy and her mama until he fell off his horse one night and died. His body was found in the mud, which had molded right to his shape and stayed visible in the ditch until the next rain melted it. All the ladies went to Mrs. Pruitt for their dresses and mantuas and bonnets; she smiled politely and peered at them through little round spectacles clamped to her nose, their lenses a quarter of an inch thick. She had a colored girl, Nellie, to help her, and she had Bad Katy, and as a widow she had enough new business to hire on a second girl, Mrs. Wilkins' Lou, two days a week. Because her dead bad husband had broken her leg once, she carried a slim gold-headed cane. Her hands were the size of a man's; her long fingers, nervous and deft, roamed, always seeking. When Mama went for a fitting and Nellie draped the cloth, Sarah couldn't take her eyes off those hands roaming and touching and tucking, smoothing the wrinkles and pinning the seams, while Mrs. Pruitt's pleasant voice spooled on and on.

"It's a wonder," gossiped Mama's lady friends. "She makes the finest seams, has the deftest touch. I'm still wearing that gown she made me for Arthur's christening, you remember that gown? The peau de soie, pink. So easy to ruin a fabric like that. But Eleanora Pruitt is . . . " The lady paused, sighed, and smiled with satisfaction, while all the other ladies looked rueful and supportive. "With all she's been through, she's just a wonder."

On Palm Sunday, just after Sarah's tenth birthday, Bad Katy became Bad in everybody's mind for good. All the smallest children were to carry sheaves of green palmetto branches from the swamp down the aisle to lay at the feet of smiling young Reverend White. Even the colored children were to come down from their balcony and carry the branches too, bringing up the rear of the line. "Reverend White said it, suffer the little children," the ladies whispered doubtfully, "and it *is* Eastertide." Jane and Rosa Lee would join that line. Seth and Sarah would not. "That's for the little ones," Mama had said, firmly. "You're a big girl now."

So, in their usual pew—right side, five rows back—Mama and Sarah waited for the procession. Jane had scooted down the aisle to huddle in the vestibule with Miss Hartnett, the sweet Sunday-school teacher, and the other children. Now there were only giggles, and the swishing of palms. At the organ, Mrs. Sprague struck up a hymn: "Tell me the sto-ries of Je-sus, I love, to heaaaar-rrr." In the front of the church, Reverend White stood, smiling.

And then Bad Katy—squirming in her mama's usual pew, left side of the church, two rows back—started to scream. "I want a palm!" she wailed. "I want to march!" Her whole face squinched shut around her tears. "Mama, let me go! Let me go!" She thrashed like a pup on a leash. "Let me go!"

Mrs. Sprague peered over the top of the organ. Her eyes widened, and she pulled out an extra stop. The music got louder, but not loud enough. Bad Katy hammered her feet against the floorboards. "I want to walk with a palm!" she screeched. She kicked the kneeling bench, slewing it out in front of the pulpit. "Mama! You *said!*"

"Hush," Mrs. Pruitt hissed. Her jaw clenched and her lips firmed. "You're too big for this carryin on. You got to stay here with me."

The rustling at the back of the church died below the swell of the music and Bad Katy's screams. But Reverend White, hovering, smiling irresolutely, beckoned the children and they inched forward, appearing one by one in Sarah's field of vision: little Nancy and Ray and Christina and Nelson and Victoria and finally Jane. "Tell me the sto-ries of Jeee-sussss," they warbled, eyes trained nervously on Bad Katy, "I looove, to heeaaarrr." Jane held her palm straight up in both hands, stepping ceremonially as a queen. "Things I would ask him to tell me," they sang, "if he were here."

The children passed the pew—edging to the right, far away from Bad Katy, who was sobbing—and laid their palms at Reverend White's feet. The colored children were last, feet bare and whispery on the smooth boards. The girls had pigtails bound in scraps of bright ribbon or cloth. All their clothes had been washed and washed, crackling with clothesline stiffness in the sun. Rosa Lee came last, in a blue-flowered dress that had once been Sarah's but that Jane didn't like, because it itched. "Isn't it nice," a lady murmured behind Sarah, "how they want so much to be decent."

Reverend White beamed down at them. "Suffer the little children, our Savior said," he mused, "to come unto me." With a nod, he released them, and the children scattered back into their parents' pews. The colored children filed in a line to the back of the church, to the loft where they were re-welcomed with soft scufflings and murmurings. It sounded a bit like the owls in the rafters of the barn over Sarah's head, if she was there at the right time of evening to hear it. *He who has ears to hear, let him hear.* The colored people were up there every Sunday, but she only heard them if she listened specially. Alvah was up there, and Seth, and Celia. But they would not look at her and smile, like they normally did. Here in church with everyone watching, they wouldn't smile at her or anyone.

She peered into the pew where Bad Katy sat, quiet now. Mrs. Pruitt's hand clutched her daughter's arm, gripping it so tightly the flesh pulsed out above and below her fingers. As Sarah watched, Mrs. Pruitt's hand twisted, slowly. And then Sarah heard her mumbling, below the burble of the organ in its last chords before the Invocation. "You better behave," she whispered. "You better behave." She let go. Her fingers left a white band on Katy's arm. An Indian burn: nothing hurt more than that.

When it was time for Communion, Mrs. Pruitt bent and groped for her cane. As Sarah watched, Bad Katy kicked the cane just out of reach. She paused. And then she dove for it. "Here, Mama," she said, sweet as a grown lady. "Let me help you."

"Thank you, baby," Mrs. Pruitt said. Leaning on her cane and on her daughter's shoulder, she stood, tugged her wide skirts out of the pew and into the aisle, and approached the altar with firm, small steps. She elbowed Katy into position next to her at the rail as Reverend White approached with the silver chalice, murmuring, "The blood of Christ, the cup of salvation." Sarah, standing in the aisle behind her mother and Jane, heard the *whoosh* of wind from their skirts as they knelt. He set the cup to Katy's lips, wiped it, gave a half-turn, then held it to her mother's mouth. Obediently, they sipped. *Thanks be to God.*

And everyone obeyed the rules, despite what they—or maybe it was only Sarah—had just seen.

Children, obey your parents, that your days may be long upon the earth.

The wife's desire shall be for her husband, her pain in childbirth greatly increased, and he shall rule over her.

Slaves, submit yourselves to your masters, so your reward may be great in Heaven.

It was easier to obey the rules if you weren't looking too close. And easier, too, if you never asked.

Sarah wanted to ask Mama whether she had seen Bad Katy kick the cane away. It already seemed like something Sarah had imagined. But by the time they got back from church and dished up the Sunday dinner and sat down, the urgency had rubbed off a little, and Sarah decided to hold it close inside to look at and think about a little more, like she did with the pictures left over from her dreams.

Mama was already onto something else anyway, her back straight, her voice scornful: "Children, your Uncle Eugene has had another in his endless series of—reversals." She lifted the catfish with the point of the silver server and dropped it onto Father's plate without looking at him. "He'll be staying with us. Again."

"I'd go jump off a cliff if I couldn't support myself any better than that," Johnny said.

"Be mindful of your elders, son," Father said.

"Yeah, he's my elder, all right," Johnny sneered. "A forty-two-year-old man."

"That's enough, both of you," Mama said, nudging smaller pieces of fish onto Sarah's plate, then Jane's. "I see no need for Eugene to poison this family's dinners any more than he inevitably will once he's here. Let's not hasten that moment. Girls, some sauce for you?"

"Yes," Jane said. Sarah dipped herself a spoonful and passed the dish to Jane, then Mama.

It was obvious: Uncle Eugene would be coming here, despite what Johnny said. Yet sometimes things didn't happen in the house if Johnny didn't think they should: *we had that spicy chicken* last week. *We shouldn't sell off that bottom thirty acres, not yet.*

"Be a good girl," Mama, and then Daddy, told Sarah and Jane. "You mind your brother, now."

When Johnny had turned fifteen, he'd made Rosa Lee and Seth call him Mister, until Father overheard and raised his eyebrows at Johnny, just once, firmly, and Johnny flushed. He never made them call him Mister after that.

For a long time after he died, it was hard for Sarah to remember anything but bad things about Johnny. That one time he told Sarah to take his boots upstairs and she said, "do it yourself," and Mama frowned at her until she did it. That one time Johnny shouted angrily at their father, "you'll sell off all this land, won't you? I'll get back from the war, there won't be nothin left." The time Johnny stole the thunder of her gift for Mama, at Christmas, like Abel to Cain.

That day the bare dogwood tree between the main house and the kitchen had been full of winter birds: knife-crested cardinals, red and rosy brown. A little nuthatch clung to the bark, stitching

74

up and down. Wrens came, then one sassy mockingbird, flicking his tail, then another one. They were pecking at something Alvah had hung in the tree for them: a blob of bacon fat or one of the sunflower heads she cut from the patch behind the cabins, dried, then tied face-up to a branch.

It was three days till Christmas and the only gifts anyone would give would be camellias from the tall bush grown against the wall, deep pink with fringed golden centers against a spray of glossy green leaves. War was coming, Father said. Things were getting scarce that never were before. Except there was a gift in Sarah's lap: knitted gloves, one finished, the other still missing its bottom two rows. She'd gone back into the trunks of old clothes and found a baby sweater that might have been hers or Jane's. She dimly remembered it rucked up around her chest as she struggled in a carriage pushed down the driveway, from the dim time when she was a baby too. Brown hands, a voice lifting, calming: "Child, hush." She'd dug this sweater out to unravel it into gloves for Mama, and now she was almost done.

With no wind, Sarah's chair in the sun was warm, its cane bottom sprung to a comfortable rump-shaped sag. She hooked both heels over the edge of the seat—"you so skinny," Alvah always said, "you can twist all up like a little garter snake"—and pecked with her needles at the palm of the glove. A gray lizard scuttled through the dust and stopped for a pushup, two, then three. The birds fluttered, squabbled, dashed back and forth with a purring blurt of wings in the air. Tod the old setter came and laid his long fine skull on Sarah's foot, blinking his pouchy eyes as his feathered tail swung slowly. She set the knitting underneath her tucked-up knees and picked at the knotted cockleburs in his long black ears. "If you'd only let your nails grow," Mama always scolded. "Stop picking." Tod whined but shivered and stood, stoic. "Good dog," she told him. "I'm gonna have these out in a minute." She pulled a tick, nudged it under the lifted leg of her chair, and sat down again with a *splat*. Hair-snarled cockleburs dropped around her feet. It felt good to have an animal counting on her. Like the boy in Aesop who drew a thorn from a lion's paw, earning a beast's rare and precious gratitude.

Mama complained so much about her cold hands that Sarah couldn't wait until Christmas Day. That night she fetched the mittens—just finished—from inside her old summer bonnet in the wardrobe and presented them. "Hold out your hands and close your eyes," she intoned, and a smile pushed aside Mama's now-usual irritated frown and she obeyed. Sarah slipped a mitten over each of Mama's hands: so rough, so dry. "Oh, Sarah!" Mama breathed, before she even opened her eyes. "I've never received such a wonderful gift!" She studied the mittens, smoothed them over her hands, and then pulled Sarah against her and hugged her, her face bright. "I love them!" Sarah surrendered to it: the rush of pure, uncomplicated happiness.

Then Johnny strode in—door smacking the foyer table again, sloshing the bowl of winter-blooming camellias—swinging two dead wood ducks by the necks. Their heads were jeweled with panes of color bright as church windows. "Oh," Mama breathed, rising from her chair. She peeled off Sarah's mittens and laid them down and went forward, hands outstretched.

Father paused on his way past the door, peered at the ducks, then into Johnny's face. "Beautiful creatures," he said quietly, and passed on by. Johnny's eyes dropped, catching Sarah's. His face was red. He lifted his head suddenly and glared at her. "What are you staring at?" he sneered. "Little milktoast." And he strode on through the house to the kitchen shed in the back, taking Alvah the ducks for plucking. They'd be on the table that night. Yet Sarah would not eat them. *Jacob and Esau,* rang furious words in her head. *Cain and Abel. Whose sacrifice is more pleasing to the Lord?*

When Johnny appears in Sarah's dreams, now, she answers him in Bad Katy Pruitt's voice, savage and fine: *Run off to war and leave us. Get yourself killed. Easier than staying here to be a girl. To be good. Be good.* His face is bloody, sad, regretful. She swings at his face but the air itself, thick as molasses, restrains her arm so that her hand comes to rest against his cheek as soft as a caress, as soft as love.

❧

In the early afternoons, in the heat of the day, Sarah practiced the piano. Aunt Maude had sent Mama an old upright from Mobile when she first came to Fairibault after her marriage. It hunkered permanently between the front windows in the parlor, sun-faded and lid-shut, jingling deep in its innards whenever someone walked past. Mama had taught her and Jane their fingerings and left them to it—"there, now, any child of sense ought to be able to work out the rest"—and Jane whined when Mama scolded her to practice. But Sarah relished the soft cradle of the velvet piano stool, holding her upright like a daffodil stem in its vase. She loved the quiet order of the eighty-eight keys, the octaves, the white and the black, the elegant tangle of the treble clef, the promise of the key signature memory-trick: *Every Good Boy Does Fine.* The smooth cool keys were the only things that didn't break or turn grubby in her hands. They unfolded music in her head like words on the page unfolded pictures in her mind. The sounds they made had never been heard before quite the way she made them now, for no one's ears but hers. She dreamed of playing the Schumann *Kinderszenen,* the Songs from Childhood, especially her favorite: *About Foreign Lands and People.* Sometimes she and Jane could convince Mama to sit down and play it, and then they would twirl across the carpet like grown ladies. In her head, she would sing her own words: *Come a-way with me. And go wan-dering. Come a-way with me. My fair la-dy.* She could sink into music as into water, letting it close over her head and shut everyone else away.

᪾

On one warm afternoon, Sarah and Jane rode with Mama in the little buggy, behind her mare Marie, to the cemetery to bathe their people: Great-Grandfather, Great-Grandmother, Grandmother, Grandfather, Great-Aunt, Young Aunt, and Cousin Tree. "Do y'all remember Cousin Tree?" Mama always asked. "Cousin Tremaine? You were little bitty girls last time he saw you, lifted you up and let you swing on his arms, he was so strong." Cousin Tree had died in an *affair of honor* in Mobile and been brought up near Fairibault for burying because nobody in Mama's family down there would have him. How bad would you have to be for your mama and your daddy to turn you away even after you were dead? What was so bad about dying for honor? Sarah could barely stir the memory of Cousin Tree up to the top of her mind: the ropy flesh of his crossed arms under her own hands as she swung from them, giggling, as Father laughed, "you've sure got a strong grip, boy!" There were so many questions no one would answer. Sometimes it made Sarah scared. Sometimes it made her simply tired.

Mama stepped nimbly out of the buggy and looped Marie's reins around the spiked black iron of the cemetery fence. Her homespun dress—for dirty work like this—rippled in the wind. Marie dropped her head and cropped the long grass at the base of the fence, where Enneas had missed a spot. Enneas always came over from Mr. Wainwright's plantation and cut this grass with his wobbly scythe. His eyes were milky, half-blind, his skin deep coppery-brown. Sarah and Jane had seen him here before, stooped inside a heavy green coat with cotton stuffing peeking out at the shoulders and buttons dangling from unraveling threads. "Evenin," he always murmured, even if it was still afternoon.

But Enneas wasn't here today. The wind rustled up the hill and thrashed the big cedars at the cemetery fence, blowing their thick branches apart down to the root like cats' fur. From the back of the buggy, Sarah and Jane fetched the bucket of lye soap and rags, then struggled to lift the jugs of water down into the dirt.

"Y'all go play," Mama said. Jane dashed away through the grass, Sarah following. She doubled back at Cousin Tree's stone, a modest spike of marble: *Tremaine Bellefleur, died July 15, 1850.* Eight years ago, when Sarah herself was four. She hunkered to peer at the stone—dusty, a little mildewy—and realized she was standing right on Cousin Tree's grave. Cautiously, she hopped up and down. Could Cousin Tree feel her, under that six feet of earth? What was left of him, down in that box? She wanted to know. But no one would ever tell.

Jane stole up behind her and smacked her on the bottom, then whirled away, and Sarah sprinted after her. "I'm gonna catch you!" she shouted. Jane darted toward the big trees, straight toward the wrought-iron fence, and tripped and sprawled face-first in the grass. "Ouuuww!" she hollered. By the time Sarah caught up to her, she was sitting upright, rubbing her toe.

"Let's see what it is," Sarah said. They knelt together and brushed the long grass aside. Enneas had missed this corner of the cemetery, and the grass was long enough to speckle black seeds over their sweaty forearms.

Almost flush with the ground was a tiny white stone, the size of four bricks laid side by side. And on it was Sarah's own name.

Sarah Anne Fairibault. June 3—August 2, 1845.

This stone bore her name. But her birthday was February the third. And she was alive.

"Mama!" Jane shouted. Mama straightened up from Great-Grandmother's stone. "What's the matter?" she called. Panic spiked her voice. "Y'all get snakebit over there?" She started to run to where Sarah still knelt, her bonnet slipping off her head, but slowed as she saw Sarah stand, and then came slower still as she realized what Sarah was looking at. Her long skirts whisked through the grass until she stood looking down at the little white stone. She pulled her bonnet back over her head and tied it tight. Sarah peered toward the sky. The sun was so bright, the hood of Mama's bonnet so dim, that she could barely see Mama's face. One long strand of Mama's brown hair lifted from her cheek, teasing back and forth in the wind.

Jane flung herself down next to the stone. "It's Sarah's name," she blurted. "But Sarah ain't dead."

"Isn't," said Mama automatically.

"If Sarah isn't dead," Jane prodded, "what's this?"

"Well, ours is a big family," Mama said, "you all know that. Through the Mobile connections in particular. And Sarah is a very popular name. Because it's from the Bible." She nudged back the bonnet and forced a smile onto her face.

"Who's the dead Sarah?" Jane's blue eyes were still skeptical. Sarah watched. *Keep asking, Jane.*

"Well," Mama said, "some little children die when they are babies. God takes some little children to Heaven with him to be his special angels, when they are very, very small."

"But we're God's special angels too," Jane pointed out. "And we're not dead."

"Certainly," Mama said, quickly. "You and Sarah and Johnny, and Rosa Lee and Seth, too, all children are God's—"

"Johnny's too big to be an angel," Jane interrupted. "Angels are little."

Sarah frowned; like always, Jane was going to lead herself away from the first question into a whole nother kind of argument. "Who is this?" she blurted into her mother's face. "Why is this my name?" She held her mother's eyes tight in her own. So impertinent. But something inside nudged her. *Go on.*

Mama blinked, hesitating. She dropped her lye-water rag in the grass, swiped her hands across her stained skirt, and bent her knees deeper, almost ready to sit in the grass next to them. "You and Jane had a little—" Then she stopped. She pushed herself up with her hands. "You and Jane had a little cousin, from the same side as Cousin Tree," she said, "another little cousin named Sarah, from a part of the family you don't know. And this is when she died."

"So now she's in heaven," said Jane tentatively, "a little cousin Sarah."

"That's right," said Mama. "With all the other angels." She stood straighter. "Y'all run and play somewhere else," she said, "get out of all this long grass. Snakes back in here." Without looking back, she strode away.

Jane watched Mama, then turned to Sarah, her face uncertain. Sarah knelt in the grass and brushed it away from the white brow of the stone. Her own name was cut there in curling script. A birthday. A dying day. She did the sum in her head: this Sarah would be almost two years older than herself. Almost four years older than Jane.

This Sarah had been dead for thirteen years, and she never knew.

Little cousin Sarah, who are you?

We would play with you, if you were here.

She squeezed Mama's dropped rag over the white stone and scrubbed. Dirty water trickled into the grass. The film of dirt and mildew cleared. She polished the marble with the hem of her dress. Etched underneath her name, a baby lamb curled on a bed of palms, just like the lamb in the stained-glass window at church.

A lamb for little cousin Sarah.

First she, then Jane, drew their fingers across the name. The clean stone squeaked.

In the buggy, on the way back to the house, Sarah fought to clear the confusion in her head. If this was their cousin, why didn't Mama tell stories about her the way she did about Cousin Tree? If this was one of their people, why didn't Mama come to this side of the cemetery, too, with her bucket and her lye-water rag? Why didn't she scold Enneas about cutting the grass on this side of the cemetery, as she had that one Sunday she came out and caught him limping through the gate? "I bid you good evenin, ma'am," he'd mumbled, bending to his scythe, and she'd caught him by the arm: "look here, this grass is much too long, you mustn't let it grow so much." Why had this little girl been forgotten?

Sarah opened her mouth to ask at least one of these questions. But Mama got there first. "What would you girls like for dinner tonight?" she asked. "We've still got that Lane cake from the other day. Alvah's been sayin she needs to kill that old hen."

"Country Captain!" Jane blurted. This was her favorite dish, one Mama and Alvah didn't usually make except on very special occasions. They cut up a chicken and laid it out in a bath of tomatoes from the garden, chopped up peppers, mixed in a batch of rich sweet-smelling spices and baked everything in a big dish till it was bubbly, then sprinkled crumbly peanuts over it and spooned it onto plates over rice. Daddy first, then Johnny, then Mama, then Sarah, then Jane.

"We don't have any peanuts left, honey," Mama said. "Although we do have all those good tomatoes Alvah put up last summer."

"I want fried chicken," Sarah said. "With boiled okra. And biscuits." She wouldn't ask that question after all. Inside, she quailed at the thought of Mama's frown, directed at her.

Mama smiled at her. "That would be delicious," she said. "It surely would."

By the time dinner was over and they were helping Alvah and Celia clear the plates, it was too late to ask Mama about the little dead Sarah. And by the next day, and the next, there would be no possibility at all. But maybe Father would tell her.

So when Mama and Jane had settled in the parlor lamplight with embroidery and dolls, Sarah went to Father's study, tapped on the doorjamb, and waited for him, barricaded behind his writing desk, in front of his glass-fronted bookcases, to look up at her. He lifted his head from the book on his lap (Mr. Melville, she recognized it) and smiled at her. Papers covered his desk, but he had pushed them aside to read. "There's my girl," he said.

She wanted to fling herself across the room into his arms, but she was too big. So she walked to him and bent her forehead into his kiss. "Did you have a good day?" he asked.

"Went with Mama to the cemetery," she said.

"The way your Mama cleans those stones," he smiled, "she'll wear the writing off."

Sarah smiled, too. It felt good to be with Father in his study, nestling into one of the big chairs deep enough for her to tuck her feet into and read. Glass-fronted bookcases stretched higher than her head, full of books ordered from Boston and Philadelphia and other such places. "Don't know why you got to keep buying from the Yankees," Johnny always chastised. "There've got to be some books down here."

"Ever try to get blood from a turnip, son?" Father shot back. Then Johnny sulked. Johnny'd gone off to school once and come right back home. "I should just send you instead," Father grumbled to Sarah, "you wouldn't waste my money." But every year since, when Sarah had asked him about when she could go to school too, he'd just smiled. "We'll see," he said. "Don't you want to stay here with me instead?"

Sarah ruffled her thumb up and down the deckled pages of the top book in the stack on the table next to his armchair, suddenly shy. "Father," she asked, "we found another stone in the cemetery, a little bitty stone over in the long grass that—"

"That has the same name as you," he interrupted. "I know."

Sarah was amazed, grateful. She should have guessed Father would tell her the truth. She should have known he would know what she wanted before she even asked it. She waited for his answer.

But Father just leaned his cheek against one hand and looked at her. Then he stretched his bad leg out in front of him and rubbed the shin where it broke and set wrong, back when he was Johnny's age. "What did your mama tell you about that stone?" he asked.

"A baby cousin Sarah," she replied, "who died, with the same name cause we have such a large family."

He smiled to himself. "Well," he murmured, "if that's what your Mama told you, then that's what you should know." Something in his face closed up. He was done telling her, and she still hadn't gotten the truth. And she wouldn't.

She looked at the stack of books under her hand, lifted the top one, and took it to the armchair, where she hiked herself into the seat and tucked both feet underneath herself. It didn't matter what the book was, because whatever it was, Father would notice her reading it and compliment her on her choice. He'd tell her it was too difficult for most girls but not for her.

Even if he wouldn't tell her who the little dead Sarah really was, he would praise her for this.

He watched her settle with the book, turn to the first page, and study the illustration under the title: *Uncle Tom's Cabin; or, Life Among the Lowly.* In the picture, a woman in a white head rag like Alvah's stood at the door of a cabin, with a baby at her feet. Two larger boys peered around the corner of the cabin, where a white man in a top hat strode toward their door. Over his shoulder he carried a long stick like a carriage whip. The children looked tense. The woman's hands were clenched.

Shoot, echoed Johnny's jeering voice, *no colored on this place got to fear. Father don't believe in the whip, ain't they heard?*

The man with the stick looked like Father. The woman looked like Alvah. The tallest boy—nimble, poised to run away—looked like Seth.

"So," Father's voice tickled around the high wing back of the chair, "you're reading Mrs. Stowe."

Confused at the mingled laughter and scorn in his voice, Sarah
raised her head. This was a name she'd heard in her mama's mouth,
in the voices of the ladies at their sewing: *Mrs. Stowe would have us
turn them all loose tomorrow on the roads, unfriended. Mrs. Stowe
would have us all submit to Pennsylvanians and Abolitionists. Mrs.
Stowe never even came South, did you hear? Only relied on the worst
tales and rumors. Sheer rumors, my dear.*

"Read on," Father said. "That's why I sent for it. We have to
know what they're saying about us, don't we?"

Sarah nodded, puzzled, intrigued. Is this a book Mama wouldn't
want her to read? Probably. But if Father gave her permission,
surely it was all right.

By the end of the next week, Sarah had read both volumes, as
greedily as she and Jane swiped frosting from Alvah's cakes in the
kitchen. And as with every book she read, even the ones she didn't
quite understand all of yet, like those pleasantly chilling novels by
Currer and Ellis Bell about starving girls in orphan-schools and
ghosts on wild moors, she imagined who she would be. Was she
the kind lady on the boat as Uncle Tom is sold down to New Orleans? *The most dreadful part of slavery, to my mind, is its outrages on
the feelings and affections—the separating of families, for example.*
Was she brave Eliza leaping over the ice with her baby? (Sarah
couldn't imagine a place so cold that whole rivers froze; she could
imagine only something like the logs she'd seen being floated down
the river to the sawmill, the great longleaf pines with their deep,
bitter-smelling hearts.) No, she was angelic Eva with golden hair,
gently schooling Topsy.

But who was Topsy?

*There stood the two children representatives of the two extremes
of society. The fair, high-bred child, with her golden head, her deep
eyes, her spiritual, noble brow, and prince-like movements; and her
black, keen, subtle, cringing, yet acute neighbor.*

Eva was so sweet she became an angel and appeared to poor suffering Tom in a dream: *Who shall say that the sweet young spirit, which in life so yearned to comfort and console the distressed, was forbidden of God to assume this ministry after death?*

Little dead Sarah in the cemetery was one of God's special angels. Had she had golden hair, too, like Eva? Like Sarah herself? She imagined herself, then, dead and sainted. A pleasurable tear squeezed from her eye. Seth and Rosa Lee and Alvah would mourn. Jane would mourn. Mama and Father would mourn, even Johnny. And she and the first Sarah, up in heaven together, would teach them all how to be angels.

Gradually the words seemed to melt and fade, as in a divine music; the child raised her deep eyes, and fixed them lovingly on him, and rays of warmth and comfort seemed to go from them to his heart; and, as if wafted on the music, she seemed to rise on shining wings, from which flakes and spangles of gold fell off like stars, and she was gone.

Next morning Sarah mooned around the kitchen-house, trying to catch Alvah's eye. The kitchen-house was not like Dinah's kitchen in the book, all frowsty and cluttered, full of things stuck everywhere so that Miss Ophelia despaired of Dinah's tidiness: a drawer full of *a Methodist hymn-book, a couple of soiled Madras handkerchiefs, some yarn and knitting-work, a paper of tobacco and a pipe, a few crackers, one or two gilded china-saucers with some pomade in them, one or two thin old shoes, a piece of flannel carefully pinned up enclosing some small white onions.* Sarah blinked. Alvah's scoured pots hung on the wall above the stove, ranged large to small; her spoons and whisks rested in a crock ready to grab; her flour and sugar sat in neat tin-lined bins the mice couldn't raid. If she had seen Alvah's kitchen, would Mrs. Stowe have written differently? *For a lady storyteller,* Mama's voice blistered in Sarah's head, *the truth is just one more inconvenience.*

Underneath her row of shining pots, Alvah was plucking a chicken, holding it down efficiently with one hand and stripping feathers with another, so that not a feather was left in the skin. "Alvah," Sarah breathed, in Little Eva's voice, "God is the Rewarder of them that diligently seek Him."

Alvah paused and stared at Sarah, puzzled. "Yes, child," she said, "I know." She bent closer and set the back of her hand against Sarah's forehead. "You feelin all right? You look a little pale." Sarah fled before Alvah could reach down the bottle of castor oil. When Little Eva looked pale, people called her beautiful. When Sarah looked pale, people thought she was sick.

Sarah wandered outside to where Rosa Lee and Jane were playing pick-up sticks in the dirt. They had stacked straight golden straws in a pile and were taking turns drawing them out, one by one, without upsetting the others. The first one to do that would lose.

"Here, Topsy . . . give us a song, now, and show us some of your dancing."

The black, glassy eyes glittered with a kind of wicked drollery, and the thing struck up, in a clear shrill voice, an odd negro melody, to which she kept time with her hands and feet, spinning round, clapping her hands, knocking her knees together, in a wild, fantastic sort of time, and producing in her throat all those odd guttural sounds which distinguish the native music of her race.

Jane's pink dirty hands, and Rosa Lee's brown dirty hands, darted in and out at the pile of sticks. Their pigtails, knotted with scraps of bright cloth at the ends, twitched as their heads bent to study the straws in the dirt.

Mama, piped Little Eva's voice, *you believe, don't you, that Topsy could become an angel, as well as any of us, if she were a Christian?*

Miss Ophelia approached Topsy very much as a person might be supposed to approach a black spider.

Mrs. Stowe must not have known Rosa Lee and Seth and Alvah. Or she never would have written so. They were nothing like spiders at all.

Maybe there were bad little colored girls like Topsy out there, on other plantations, in the North. There must have been, or Mrs. Stowe would not have written it. In a book, everything had to be true. But Rosa Lee was not a bad girl. Jane had been spanked more than Rosa Lee and Sarah put together.

"Come play straws," Jane invited, and Sarah plopped down in the dirt. The sun beat down on their heads. Sarah's mind calmed. The familiar smell of her sister's and of Rosa Lee's skin, and of her own, ebbed around her: coppery with sweat and sun, a whisper of lye soap caught in the cloth of their dresses. She drew a straw from the stack, carefully. Last time she'd played this game, she'd won.

"Hey, y'all, I know how babies come," Jane said conversationally. "The man lays down next to you and tinkles on you."

Rosa Lee and Sarah shrieked. Jane grinned. She'd been talking about this over and over, when their mama was out of hearing. This was another secret they were supposed to learn when they get older and until then, not even wonder about. But Jane wondered about everything, out loud.

"Jane Narcissa Fairibault!" Sarah mocked their mother. "How'd you ever hear of such a thing?"

"I saw it," Jane said. "I saw Johnny and Celia, down in the field. Just the other day."

"You did not," Rosa Lee said. She sat up straighter and peered at Jane. "Celia wouldn't go with no white man."

"Go with?" Sarah asked.

"Go down and lay down with him," said Rosa Lee. "That's how it happens. And you get a baby from that if you ain't careful."

"How do you know?" Jane pouted.

"Mama told me," Rosa Lee said. "He puts his thing in your tee-ta and you get a baby if you ain't careful. That's why you got to not go with a man unless you really want a baby. But Mama says most women got enough babies to think about already."

"I don't want a baby," Jane said. "I don't want a man to put his thing in me."

"Way you headed," Rosa Lee said, "you ain't got to worry."

Jane smacked her on the arm. Rosa Lee gripped Jane's upper arm and twisted. "Indian burn!" she exulted.

"Ow!" Jane shrieked. "I'm gonna—"

"Y'all cut that out," said Sarah. She paused. "So Johnny—went with Celia?"

"Down in the field," Jane declared. "In the high grass."

"How'd you know?" Sarah asked. "You ain't supposed to spy."

"She spy on anything," snorted Rosa Lee. "But don't nobody want to spy on her."

Jane reached out to smack Rosa Lee again and Rosa Lee twisted out of her way and snatched a pinch of plump skin from under Jane's arm. "Ouuuuwwww!" Jane wailed. "You damn, mean as a polecat, you goddamn—"

"Jane!" Sarah reproved, and Jane slumped backwards, sulking. "Johnny says it," she observed. "Johnny thinks it's funny when I say it."

"It ain't funny," Sarah said. "And if I tell Mama, she won't think it's funny either."

Jane paused, and collected herself. "But I still ain't told you," she informed them, "what I saw."

"You ain't supposed to talk about it," said Rosa Lee primly. "I ain't supposed to hear it."

"You been talkin all about it," Jane shot back. "You're the one tellin us. And Sarah wants to hear."

"No, she don't," said Rosa Lee. Both girls looked at Sarah, and she hesitated.

"See, she does want to know," said Jane. "So I saw them walkin down by the creek, holdin hands and everything. It was right as it was getting dark, and the grass was high up to their waists. And then they laid down in it and I didn't see 'em any more. I couldn't go up closer or they'd know I was there."

Jane looked around, triumphantly, but Rosa Lee's face was solemn, and Sarah felt the same expression on her own. It was like when the big male tomcat climbed on top of the female at the barn and they looked stubborn and somehow pleased. An image of her brother's face like that, of Celia's face like that, came into her mind, and she shut her eyes and shook her head to break it to pieces against the inside of her skull. When she imagined the picture shattering, like glass, it went away.

Mama wouldn't like them talking about this, or even thinking about it. This was just one of those things little girls were not supposed to know if they wanted to be good. Something not to talk about, to not show anyone.

Mama said I ought to be ashamed, showing my tee-ta to a nigra boy.

You and Jane had a little—cousin. In heaven. With all the other angels.

When Sarah got back to the house and found Mama in the parlor, she summoned all her nerve. "Mama," she asked, "how do babies come?"

Mama put down her sewing—a rip in Father's shirtsleeve—and peered at Sarah over the spectacles she used for close work. With a fine shudder all over, like a horse with flies, she lifted her needle again. "Never you mind about that now," she said. "Sakes, you're not even twelve. I'll tell you and Jane about it before you get married. Never fear."

"But what if I don't get married?" Sarah blurted. "What if I get a baby by mistake?" Fear rising, she imagined some horrible error that would yield an accidental baby: a strange fumbling, walking through the same patch of air too soon after a boy, being tinkled on by mistake. How could that even happen? But anything scary or bad could happen, under the right circumstances. Freakish horrible things could result in the mysterious, inevitable swelling: *woman's lot, woman's cross to bear. Eve's curse.*

Mama closed her eyes. Then, slowly, she opened her eyes, pinched her needle between her fingers, and pointed it straight at Sarah's heart. "You," she pronounced, "will not get a baby by mistake, before you are married. Because you will not do what married people do until you are married. I know you won't. Married people do something that makes them have babies together because God has blessed them because they are married. And if you aren't married, you won't do it. So you needn't be concerned."

"But—" Sarah floundered in a sudden ocean of silences breached, of waters dark and watchful all around her. Something was in this water that could grab her ankle and pull her down. Not like the lake, with Seth and Rosa Lee and Jane; this was a murky place she was swimming alone, as Mama watched from the shore, arms folded. She could drown in plain sight, as Mama watched her, judging out the punishment Sarah surely deserved. If she were a bad girl, she could drown; it would be her own fault.

"It's our inheritance from our first mother, Eve," Mama said wryly. "Remember what it says in the Bible?" Sarah nodded, confused by the remembered babble of words: *suffering in childbirth, desire for husband, rule over her.* "All because a fool woman didn't have enough sense to kill a snake. We tempt them, the men. They're simple creatures." Then Mama repositioned her fingers on the needle and bent to Father's shirt again. She was done talking.

So, Sarah tried to add it up. Women could tempt men without even trying. Little babies could die. And they could come into the world at any time, unasked for, unwished. Anything could happen, and if it did, it would probably be the woman's fault. *Our inheritance from our first mother, Eve. That fool.*

I know you won't do that till you get married, Mama warned. I won't, then, Sarah vowed. I won't. She floundered, then felt the silt under her feet, lake water sluicing off her dress, Mama reaching for her hand to pull her back onto solid ground.

In their shared room that night, she and Jane lay in their bed, pressed flat by the heat; a thunderstorm must be coming, it was way too hot for this early in the summer. But her body was prickly and suspicious all around the cloudy nub of her thoughts, mulish and unreadable. *Inheritance from your first mother. Our curse.* It was like itching without a specific place to scratch. It was like wanting to leap up from bed and go wandering around outside even as you feared the night snatching at you with talons like an owl's, pinning you down into some unknown danger.

On the mattress, Jane twitched and flinched at the edge of sleep. "It's too damn hot," she finally announced, in Johnny's hectoring voice. She scrambled to the floor and peeled her nightgown off over her head, wadded it up, and threw it on the carpet. Then she grabbed her pillow and the quilt right off the bed. "I'm sleeping on the floor." With the windows flung open and the night breeze moving through, the floor was the coolest place to be. Sarah and Jane had often peeled their nightgowns away and made a nest there, stretched out naked to whatever wind came through. But that night Sarah wanted to hold onto her nightgown, to the familiar bed with its stuffy heat, to anything that would get between her and her mutinous, questioning body. She turned over and pretended to be asleep until Jane's snuffles and rustlings quieted down and she was asleep too. Now they were both good girls. Until they woke up and everything began all over again.

3

A strange feeling began to build in Sarah after that, fine-grained and heavy in her blood and her bones. In the months before Johnny went to war, it accumulated in her like the cowbelly silt in a bend of the creek where the current kept twisting back to touch that spot. Sometimes, though, this feeling was light, like the gray river fog that came right up to her bedroom window. Fog was really the same thing as a cloud, Father would say, only close to earth. *Look*, a laughing voice inside her head would sing. *All these invisible things, all these clouds in which you have been walking, all this time. You can see them now. At least in part. And that's what's different.*

The world seemed full of intent, secret meaning. The touch of the air when she walked now was supple, insinuating. Now sometimes between her legs, too, there was the wad of cloth to catch the blood, part of *woman's curse*. Whenever Celia and Alvah were boiling laundry, that was the first thing she saw now, those long strips that could be folded and folded again, fluttering like unrolled bandages from the line. Celia and Alvah had to wear these cloth strips too. Was their blood, then, mingling in the wash pot with her own? Soaking into the ground at the same rate when the water was flung away and they set the big tubs up on their sides to dry?

This blood meant her body was getting ready to have a baby, to take its chance if that chance ever came along. She still didn't know exactly how she would be able to tell when a boy had done to her what a boy would need to do to make her have a baby. It was a cold danger lodged deep inside her, but it was also a kind of hope, with no way to name or separate the two.

In Father's library she lifted books and put them down: the familiar red Dickens, the Bells, still-mysterious Mr. Melville. She pored over the great book of art etchings that was spread open like the dictionary on its own little stand, turning the pages slowly. "Are your hands clean?" Father always asked, looking up from his desk. "Yes," she said obediently. But usually she came to look at the book when he was not in that room. It didn't feel right to turn these pages with his eyes on her back: the furious tangle of plump lolling limbs as women were thrown onto the backs of horses ("The Rape of the Sabines," a blushing shameful thrill of alarm), women with their plump foldy crotches exposed, staring dreamily up at the ceiling (Danae waiting for her shower of gold), David with his thing dangling right out there in front of him (*did it really look like that?*) and his long hand folded back over his shoulder, holding the edge of that lion skin with the tender matter-of-factness of a real hand. And all those ladies in elaborate gowns with their little dogs on their laps. One lady was holding an ermine, which looked a little like a dog and a little, with its twisty body, like one of the big rats you could scare up in the barn if you moved grain barrels around and exposed them to the light. Those ladies had had to fold these cloths between their legs as well, to wait for that time to come around each month. They had had mothers warning them of what they should and shouldn't do. After all, they were women, weren't they? But the little dogs looked so peaceful on their laps. Even the lady with the ermine was so calm, letting her eyes fall on something just out of the frame, her fingertips stroking the restless animal in her lap, her expression asking *Well?*

The caption under the painting said *Cecilia Gallerani*. Painted in the year 1488.

Cecilia was like Celia, as a name. Sometimes Celia had this same look, her graceful hands paused at whatever they were doing if you spoke to her and she looked at you: *Well?*

Could Celia have been a lady, too, if she had been given the chance? Was being a lady only a matter of the rich clothes you wore, the choice of animal to snuggle onto your lap, the presence of money enough behind you to make an artist say *yes* when your daddy asked him to paint your picture?

There was no question in Sarah's mind that Celia was as beautiful as the lady with the ermine. Or as the runaway Eliza in Mrs. Stowe's story: *The brown of her complexion gave way on the cheek to a perceptible flush . . . A delicately formed hand and a trim foot and ankle were items of appearance that did not escape the quick eye of the trader, well used to run up at a glance the points of a fine female article.* Celia's skin was a light warm brown too, and her hair made a puffy bun underneath the head scarf she wore sometimes, dyed purple with pokeberries. Underneath her wide forehead, her slim eyebrows arched when she talked. Celia did not often meet Sarah's eyes these days, but when she did, Sarah was struck by something down inside them: she was thinking about something secret, and there was no way of telling what.

Sarah began taking old Tod the setter for walks around the yard on a leash she had found hanging in the saddle room. She set her face in the calm, faintly bemused expression of Cecelia Gallerani with her ermine and tried to pace evenly past the azalea bushes, down the little brick walk through the herb bed. She would be a lady accompanied by her dog, like in a painting. Except old Tod was not a delicate little dog with silky ears; his eyes were red and pouchy as an old person's, his feathery tail and legs burr-matted no matter how often she went after them with scissors and her fingers. And he didn't know how to walk on a leash. When she tugged him forward he shivered and whined; when she tugged again he yelped and lay down with all four legs in the air.

Sarah went to fetch the yellow dress from the upstairs wardrobe so she would be dressed like a lady too. And the yellow dress was gone.

Maybe Mama was working on that dress after all. She turned to go downstairs and ask, but stopped. Mama would never let her wear that dress, especially not outdoors. Below that knowledge, some other voice stirred and woke. *Wait,* it whispered. *Wait.*

After dinner that night, amid the usual clatter of plates and silver being cleared away, Father kissed Mama on the cheek, went into his study, and shut the door. Johnny wandered out of the dining room, raking his hand through his hair. A moment later Sarah heard the door by the kitchen open and close.

"I'll fetch you some more water, Alvah," Sarah offered. Out in the yard with the dishpan, in the soft oncoming dark, she stood at the pump and strained her eyes to see. A tall straight figure was striding down into the belt of shadow under the big oak trees below the house: Johnny. And as she watched, a second figure came from the direction of the cabins to meet him. Celia. Wearing a pale dress: yellow, even in the dimness, like a firefly.

They came together and they kissed. Then they turned and walked into the deepening blue-purple dusk, farther out into the field.

Johnny went down in the field with her.

A fugitive voice in Sarah's brain whispered back, *and why wouldn't he? She's beautiful.*

And if she went with him, then she must want him too. Mustn't she?

Celia and Johnny were both seventeen. What was a terrible dim yearning, still, in Sarah herself must be even sharper in them, struggling in and up and out like the green nubs of new leaves in the spring, right up out of the plain bare branches that had been there all the time.

To go to him and kiss him like that, to have taken the yellow dress—She must want him too. Mustn't she?

If she was one of the—people, did she have to do what Johnny told her? No matter what it was? No matter whether she wanted to or not? Even if it was—that?

Celia had reached for Johnny's hand and kissed him. In her yellow dress she was as beautiful as any other lady.

When everyone else had gone downstairs for breakfast the next morning—all their voices mingled around the table, including Johnny's—Sarah lingered on the landing and opened the door of the wardrobe. The yellow gown hung there again, just as if it had never left. Except there was one damp spot near the hem where it had been sponged and was not quite dry. Sarah bent and ran her fingers over it, a faint clovery smell rising to her nose: soapwort mixture, which Alvah and Mama made by crushing the roots of those little white flowers. It would get out any stain, gently and carefully, which was important for very fine things. Like a long-dead lady's yellow satin gown, which a girl like Celia was never even supposed to touch.

Twenty years later, Sarah reaches for Celia's lost face in her mind, drawing it up like a bright coin from the bottom of a stream. *She really was beautiful. How could we not have seen?*

Because there's no profit in seeing what is not supposed to be, and what you can never say.

Sarah peeked into the wardrobe every evening after that. For four nights the yellow gown would be there, and on the fifth it would not. Like a gown worn by one of the twelve dancing princesses, whom only the poor but clever tailor could catch in their midnight journeys, slipping down through the door in the floor to be rowed across the river to the glittering ball. To fail to solve the mystery was to die. Sarah knew the mystery but wished that she did not.

"Sarah, what ails you?" Mama asked when she saw Sarah pacing up and down the yard with the old setter on his leash. "What'd you want to drag old Tod around for? Aren't you a little old to play pretend?"

At these words Sarah's eyes burned and swelled with tears. Suddenly her own hands looked stubby and foolish on the worn leather leash with its big knot in the middle. The old dog looked tired, and foolish too. Mama had taken the spell away without even knowing there was a spell. And soon there would be nowhere left to go outside of Mama's sight, where Sarah could keep her own spells safe inside. Mama was watching her now ever more sharply as Sarah's legs grew longer and her wrists began to dangle from her sleeves. "Time for you to wear a corset, soon," Mama encouraged. "Won't that be nice? You'll be a grown-up lady, then." The bright note in her voice was not meant to mock, but it did, just like Father remarking, "you'll know Latin, then, be a learned lady. And stay here with me." A terrible anger scorched through Sarah. Mama and Father both wanted to pack her into some girl-sized box meant to fit some other girl, like she had packed Lucinda Victoria, her doll from Aunt Maude, back into her little wooden crate to keep her safe. Fold in arms and legs, one by one. And shut the lid.

She bent and unclipped the leash from Tod's collar and he wagged his tail apologetically and trotted away. Even Tod didn't want her. She lowered her head and blinked and walked faster to keep herself from crying.

She came upon Seth and Johnny standing down in the hidden side of the hill, behind the cabins, well out of sight of the house. Johnny stood on one side of a rough square scratched in the dirt with a boot-toe, Seth on the other. "Now the rules are," Johnny was saying, "you have to come out with your hands up. That's the rule. And no shirts. Cause you can't be grabbin em." Johnny's shirt was already off, bunched up and thrown on the smooth-swept dirt beyond the edges of the square. His chest was bulgy and his nipples prickled, pink. He held himself straighter to keep from shivering in the little breeze. With both arms stretched straight in front of him, he flexed his fingers and wrists, balled up his hands, and then curled them back toward the middle of his chest. He stared at Seth, and Seth stared back. "Now you."

Without moving, Seth seemed to draw himself taller, his body dense and angry, tightening down around his spine. He unbuttoned the top button of his shirt—an old one of Father's, Sarah recognized the pipe-tobacco burns on the sleeves—and jerked it off suddenly over his head and wadded it up in one hand and flung it behind him. "Come on," he said. He curled his fists. "I'm ready."

Johnny jumped forward and swiped at Seth with his right arm. Seth blocked it with his left fist and hit Johnny in the jaw with his right: a deep wet *crack*. Never had Sarah seen anyone get hit before. It was exciting but scary. Should she yell out? Both Johnny and Seth would have to listen to Mama or Father or Alvah or whoever came flying down that hill, shouting *You boys!* But they wouldn't stop for her.

Johnny reeled back so far Sarah thought he might fall. And then he lunged forward and caught Seth in the side of the head with one fist, and then in the chest with the other. Seth slewed sideways and dropped in the dirt, half over the toe-scratched line. His arms flung out and uncurled against the ground. Johnny strode toward him and kicked him in the ribs. Seth grunted and snatched Johnny's foot in both his arms and jerked and Johnny staggered back on one leg. "Sonofabitch," he puffed, and hopped and twisted to snatch his leg away. Seth rolled and jumped to his feet. "Goddammit," Johnny shouted, "hold still!"

Seth crouched, feet planted apart. Through a powdering of dirt, his cheek was bleeding. His eyes were completely dark. "You come on if you're comin," he growled. "I ain't holdin still."

Johnny lunged forward again, faster this time, and Sarah shrieked. She couldn't help it. "Stop!" she yelled as she hurtled down the hill. "Both of y'all, stop!"

"What the hell, Sarah?" Johnny snarled. He drew himself up, dirty and scratched, and glared at her. Seth glared at her too. And he didn't drop his eyes.

"I'm going to tell," she blurted, more like a little girl than a grown one. But she couldn't help the panic that hit her at the sight of Seth's body knocked down and flying, and kicked. She looked at him. He lowered his eyes, then raised his head again and glared at Johnny.

Oh, she had been so wrong to run down that hill. To interrupt the boys and the thing they were trying to say with no words.

"How bout you stay the hell away from what ain't your business?" Johnny snapped. He snatched up his shirt and thrust his arms into the sleeves. And, buttoning his cuffs, he strode away.

"Seth," Sarah blurted. She turned to him, Tod's leash slipping to the ground. That strange fear still shook her—the wet crack of bone, the weakness in her own bones that was and was not alarm. Seth's chest heaved, air coming ragged into his lungs. Johnny's kick had bruised him. The smooth-swept ground had powdered him with dirt and a million tiny scratches, all over. Sarah hurled herself against him and threw her arms around him. She did not know why, or know she was going to do it until it was real. Seth quivered, astonished and very straight. And then he twisted in her arms like a fish and leapt away. "I don't need you to take up for me," he said. "Don't need—a girl."

He was gone. Sarah ran to the magnolia tree and hid under its wide lemony-smelling skirts and cried astonishing, unstoppable sobs she did not even try to name. She was such a foolish girl, trapped in this body that shoved her back and forth between ladyhood and fear. Why had she kept looking for the yellow dress? Why had she reached for Seth this way?

Eventually the crying stopped and she wandered down to the barn to see the horses. Not even riding made her feel as calm as sitting under one of the big pecan trees while the horses nudged methodically through the grass, crunching and swishing their tails and wandering near for her to rub their solemn faces with the flat of her hand. It was like being Gulliver in the country of the Houhynnms, looking up at the unexpectedly foreign curves of their bellies from below, the slim knobby legs like the trunks of trees. It was good to feel the gentle matter-of-fact horse lives going on around her own, just barely touching and not beholden to it.

Yet when she reached the pasture, she saw that Wainwright's Jim was there inside the fence, grazing along next to Mama's mare Marie. *Oh, no,* she thought. *Mama will be furious.* Fifteen hands high at the withers with a big crooked blaze that gave him a sly, startled look, Jim looked like a patchwork horse, solid red in some places and splattery roan in others. He had one eye blue and one eye brown, and a big dimply scar on his shoulder where he'd gotten caught in old wire. But he won every race he started in, from Rehoboth Town to Coweta, with one of Mr. Wainwright's skinny brown boys clinging to his neck. He could jump any fence he wanted, and if there was a mare in heat within twenty-five miles, he did. Sarah had heard the grownups laughing about it around the dinner table, especially when Mr. Wainwright was dining: Wainwright's Jim had been found with a mare over by Fort Mitchell, another one upriver. "Well"—Mr. Wainwright's laugh was booming, huge—"we keep puttin another board on, and when he wants to, he goes right over anyway. You got to say, little sumbitch has initiative."

"I will never understand why Tom Wainwright keeps that scrub horse in the first place," Mama always said. "After all, he's not a *stupid* man. Just a careless one." For Mama, the two things were often equivalent. *Sarah, don't stare as if you're struck stupid. Sarah, don't drop that, foolish girl, why are you always so careless?* Apparently Mr. Wainwright was an exception. Men usually were.

But here was Jim now, grazing next to Marie, reaching out every so often to bite her on the neck. His one blue eye gleamed.

"Oh, no," Mama groaned when she stood at the fence to see for herself. "The deed is done. I can tell. I knew I should have locked her up." She folded her lips tight. "I am going to tell Tom Wainwright to go to hell."

Of course, Mama couldn't be mad at Mr. Wainwright once his buggy was hitched to the post in front of the house, with Jim tied firmly to the back, and he was sipping tea in the parlor, his shining boots on the worn Turkey rug. "Now, Livia," he crooned, stretching out his legs and crossing them with a flourish at the knee, "you know I wouldn't interfere with your good mare for anything. I regret this every bit as much as you. But you've got to say, whatever you get *is* going to have some speed. Marie's a Mayflower filly, isn't she?"

"Don't confuse the issue, Tom," Mama countered, smiling. "Of course she is. But—"

Mr. Wainwright stuck his thick fingers into his black hair and ruffled it where his hat had mashed it down. He grinned at Mama. "Perhaps we should both thank old Jim, actually," he said. "Because he has given me the opportunity of being in your debt. What can I do, Livia, to rectify this wrong?" He paused. His green eyes darkened.

Sarah's hands froze, the needle pausing halfway through her embroidery cloth. Something in Mr. Wainwright's voice prickled, insinuated, for Mama to hear, just as if no one else was there. What did he mean? He couldn't mean a wrong thing or Mama would not listen. Father would forbid Mr. Wainwright the house if he were a bad man.

"You can serve me for the moment, Tom"—Mama's voice was clear, amused—"by getting your little scrub horse out of here." Both of them laughed, Mr. Wainwright throwing his head back so his white teeth showed. "But never fear. The day will come when

I'll be glad to call on you." She rose to her feet and held out her hand to him, smiling. The sun on it made it look long and white as Cecilia Gallerani's in the painting with the ermine, hid the calluses and little brown spots and dry patches where she washed her hands again and again.

"Well," said Mr. Wainwright, "until that time, I shall possess my soul in patience." He bent very low over Mama's hand and straightened up again, grinning. "Livia," he said, nodding. "Miss Sarah. Ladies." And he settled his hat back onto his head and strode out the door, whistling. Mama paused at the window to watch his buggy roll away down the drive, Jim trotting behind. "Until I see it with my own eyes," she remarked, "I won't believe that horse is off this place."

Sarah came to stand beside her. She was nearly as tall as Mama now. "Mama," she said, "whatever happened to Mr. Wainwright's wife?"

Mama kept watching as the buggy went into the shade of the oak trees and around the curve, out of sight. "Well," she said, "nobody really knows. There are a lot of theories." She looked at Sarah. "She was always a fragile little thing, that I remember. Like a moth. Like she'd cry if you looked at her wrong. Afraid of horses, which, for Tom, is strange. But he adored her, in his way. He gave her those two fine boys—" Mr. Wainwright's sons had been away at boarding school for as long as Sarah could remember—"and that house. Lord knows where his money comes from; he's been here as long as your father and I have."

"Is she in an asylum?" Sarah blurted. Pictures from Mrs. Radcliffe's novels swam in her head: a fragile lady in white, trapped in a damp-walled dungeon, with white wings like a moth, beating against the walls.

"Lord, no, child. You can't take novels for the truth, remember? She's dead." But Mama's voice was rueful. "I remember when he brought her here. Little old bitty thing. It's funny, a man like that—

" Mama straightened and shook her head, an ironic smile coming back to her face. "With such a little milktoast of a wife. Surprising what he prefers in women, although perhaps it shouldn't be. Just remember, Sarah, it's all too easy to intimidate a man. Just be more than three feet tall, and remotely competent. At anything."

Sarah went away wondering at a vague prickliness inside herself that came with the memory of Mr. Wainwright's bold smile. Of the feel—so brief it might as well not have been real—of Seth's body inside her arms before he twisted and leapt away. Soon she would get up the courage to ask Mama to tell her the secret of babies. *I want to be a woman too*, she would say. *I want to know for sure.* And she would fasten her eyes on Mama's just as Seth had stared at Johnny, and she would not look away until Mama told her the secret. Like Jacob wrestling with the angel. *I will not let you go until you bless me.* Like Eve, taking a deep breath as the serpent smiled, expectant. *Go ahead,* she would say. *I want to know.*

A month or so farther along into the summer, Uncle Eugene came.

Walking out to draw hopscotch grids in the dirt driveway in front of the house, Sarah and Jane found a garter snake, no more than nine inches long. Snakes liked the road because it held heat from the day into the night and even the next day. Normally Sarah and Jane would be scared of snakes, but not ones like this: slim as a hair ribbon, with long gold and green stripes. They stood as close as they dared to see its blunt head tilt up, its black pinpoint eyes watching them. And then they walked a little ways away and took their sticks and began to draw lines in the dirt: their names, and a hopscotch grid, and a mythical beast Sarah said was the gryphon from their mythology book but Jane said was just a lion with wings.

Then they heard the rattle of wheels, and a man came rolling around the bend of the driveway in a buggy pulled by a skinny lit-

tle mouse-colored mare with long muley ears and a dangling lower
lip. The buggy was dusty, its wheel hubs loose. A short, bony man
sat in the driver's seat, with wispy blondish-gray hair receding over
a round forehead like a baby's and a black coat with sleeves that
were too long. He gazed around him at the house, the yard, then
at Sarah and Jane, and smiled. They smiled back, uncertain. Some
adults thought you had to be extra nice to win children over. There
was something sinister about that effort, though. And something
embarrassing.

The buggy approached. "Watch the snake!" blurted Jane. But
the wheels ran right over the little garter snake anyway. It bowed
up into an agonized hoop and flopped sideways and twisted and
then stopped moving. Father had always said, "be watchful for
creatures in the road. If you can't slow up for it to get out of the
way, and can't tell by looking whether it's good or bad, you're too
fast. Pay attention." Obviously, this man never did.

The man yanked the reins and the little mare stopped and
coughed. "Morning, girls," he said, as grandly as if this were his
house. "You know who I am? I'm your father's brother. Do you
know my name?"

"Uncle Eugene," Jane mumbled. "I reckon."

"Don't you know better grammar than that, little girl?" Uncle
Eugene asked. Here was something else the wrong kind of adults
did: seize any chance to correct you while still pretending they
were your friend.

"That's a white-trash-lookin horse you got there," Jane remarked. "Did you steal her?"

Uncle Eugene's eyes narrowed, and he took a deep breath,
forcing a laugh back out between his teeth. "Ha," he said. "Ha.
Ha. You have every bit of your esteemed mother's wit, I see." He
looked around and spotted Seth trimming azaleas by the side of
the porch. "Hey, boy," he called, "take my horse to the barn and put
her up. I'm staying here for a while." He grinned at Sarah and Jane,

climbed stiffly down from the buggy, and took a flabby brown carpetbag from the back. Something inside it sloshed. He went up the steps and through the front door. "I'm here!" he called. "The prodigal has returned!"

The little gray horse rubbed her face against Seth's hand where her bridle was itching behind her ears. "I think I know this horse," he remarked. "She looks kind of familiar." He frowned, craning backwards to look at the buggy. "But then, a lot of horses look familiar." He shrugged and led the horse down the hill toward the barn, the empty buggy bumping across the yard behind him.

And Uncle Eugene stayed on. Sarah took to sitting in her own room at night to read, because Uncle Eugene sat with Father in the parlor, talking, his voice low and laughing and sometimes rising to a whine, as if he were going to cry. There was a rumble in response, through the doors, that had to be Father, although it was not a voice of Father's Sarah recognized. Something about him was different around Uncle Eugene—yielding, sad, hearkening to some other version of himself—as if the Father he was with her and Jane and Johnny and Mama was only a disguise.

Maybe adults were always in disguise, even when they didn't know it themselves.

There had to be some way to be a grownup without putting on that mask.

When the Decoration Day picnic came around, Mama complained, as always, that it was morbid. But she rallied Sarah and Jane into fresh dresses and into the buggy anyway, next to her. Uncle Eugene and Father rode ahead, not in the buggy. Father rode Marie—"a little exercise will do her good, Livia, and won't harm the foal"— and Uncle Eugene rode Speedwell, who pranced and jounced as Uncle Eugene wedged his fingers under the pommel and clung like a baby, the reins gripped awkwardly in his other hand and the stirrups raised high to fit his short legs. Tom Wainwright and Mr. and Mrs. Spurgeon and Reverend White and a flock of ladies from the church with their husbands had already gathered there, putting flowers on their people's graves and eating fried chicken and cake out of baskets. Enneas the caretaker, accepting a heaping plate with a nod of his head, carried it over to the church steps and sat and ate, staring out over the grassy hillside where they sat on their picnic rugs, among the stones. "We never do this enough," someone remarked, as always, "just gather like this as a community."

"Too bad it takes grief to bring us here," Mama responded. "Or something like it." People laughed uncertainly, then, and Mama had to be extra charming to smooth out the worried looks on their faces, helping them sponge and dust their stones. "I've been here already," she said. "Let me do yours."

After lunch was over, Jane and Sarah ran down the hill to the little stream in its band of trees. Narrow enough for them to jump across, the stream was spotted gently with sunlight through the leaves; the water turning golden brown and clear, like a cat's eyes. Beavers had cut some of the young trees and begun to pile them up. "Running water drives a beaver crazy," Father said. "Literally, crazy. Makes them want to do whatever they can to stop it." He and Seth and Johnny had to walk the creeks at Fairibault to make sure beavers weren't building dams. One time they had trapped a whole family of beavers and tossed them on the bank and blew up the dam with gunpowder. Sarah remembered the pile of brown furry bodies, softening and loosening in the sun, the flies walking and rubbing their hands.

There were no beavers here today. But there were fresh crawfish towers, made of mud piled up and up with a hole at the top just narrow enough to be the crawfish's door. If they crept up very carefully, Sarah and Jane could see the tips of its claws where it was sitting on its porch in the sun, just enjoying. The crawfish always scuttled backwards into its tower anyway. It couldn't know they meant no harm.

Sarah and Jane took off their shoes and stockings and set them in the grass at the top of the bank, then hunkered in the thick clay mud near the water and began gathering handfuls for their pottery. A swish and thump of footsteps came down the hill toward them. It was Uncle Eugene. The sun shone at an angle through the colorless hair thinning on the top of his head. His elbows stuck out, his hands in his pockets. Trying to be jaunty. Trying to come and play with them. But they were girls. He was a grown man.

"Hello," Sarah said reluctantly. Jane looked up, glared, and looked back down. She mashed her thumb into the center of a daub of clay, as hard as it would go.

"Can I play with you?" Uncle Eugene asked, in that joking voice adults thought children liked. "I remember when your father and I used to make clay pots. We liked to press rocks in ours. You know, up the sides of the pot. So it looks like jewels." He swept his gaze up and down the stream. "But I don't see any rocks here."

"There are some up there around the bend," Sarah said. Something dull and obedient was taking hold of her, although a second thing inside her felt queasy. *Run away*, it said, *something is strange here.* But the dull and obedient thing said *Don't be silly. Wicked girl.* She looked away from him at the little footbridge, trying to see into the dark space underneath. It was dark enough for the troll in the Three Billy Goats Gruff story. The brave big goat saved his brothers by challenging the troll: *Well, come along! I've got two spears, and I'll poke your eyeballs out at your ears; I've got besides two curling-stones, and I'll crush you to bits, body and bones.* She and Jane used to sing this part aloud when Mama or Father read them the story, when they were very little girls. But Sarah was thirteen now, a big girl. And Uncle Eugene was too big to crush. He was the troll, come out from the dark. He was real.

Uncle Eugene hunkered low, right next to Sarah. Through her dress she felt his pants leg brush her thigh. "Why don't you go fetch us some pretty stones, Janey?" he asked.

Jane scowled. "Go fetch your own," she blurted.

"Now that's not nice," said Uncle Eugene. His eyes under his bald forehead gleamed cold. "Your father and particularly your mother will not like to hear about your rudeness." He paused, and sighed, theatrically. "When all I'm trying to do is be nice to y'all." He scooped up a palmful of clay and began to work it in his bony fingers.

Jane rolled her eyes and shut her mouth, tight, and scrambled up around the little bend. *Wait,* shouted both the voices in Sarah's head at the same time. *Don't go.*

"Do you like pretty things?" asked Uncle Eugene. His face was so close to Sarah's she had to look at him piece by piece, up and down, to see it all. Troll nose, troll red eyes, troll breath with a sharp keen stink. "I bet you do. I have always found you a very precocious girl."

He stretched out his fingers and touched the inside of Sarah's knee, where her dress was hiked up and tucked behind her calves. Just the tips of his fingers landed there, first, and then his hand settled and wrapped all the way around her leg. He did not look her in the face. He looked at that spot on her leg. So did she. His hand looked knobby and hairy. *Troll claw.* He moved his hand higher. Fingerprint smears of mud stayed. If they dried there, they would crack. They would pull the tiny hairs in Sarah's skin when she picked at them. In her bath, in her very own room. Her very own, so very safe room. So far away. One corner of her dress was trailing in the water. The chill wicked up closer to her skin. She was the smallest goat in the troll-king's grasp. She was captured and she could not move.

Uncle Eugene's breathing did not change. His hand rubbed up and down the inside of her thigh. "Still," he rasped. "Be still." Sarah could not move. She could only stare at his stomach under his vest, at the watch-chain looped across it, tapping against the buttons. Gold paint flaked off the dull tin underneath. *Oh, Mama. Come help me. Please.*

Mama did not come. Father did not come. This was happening and it was bad, although Sarah could not have named it. Inside her everything was numb and quiet, with Eugene's fingers on the private inside of her leg, moving.

Something worse would happen next. The troll would seize her in the hairy hand moving higher and higher on her leg and he would open his jaws and gobble her up and she would be dead forever. And she could not move.

Then suddenly a hiss and plop and Eugene's hand was gone. "Goddammit!" he exclaimed. He stood, wildly scanning the bank up and down. "Little bitch!"

Sarah leaped up and scrambled away from the creek and ran up the hill as fast as she could go. Jane burst from the trees, pebbles falling from her hands. "Sarah!" she called, and Sarah paused just enough for Jane to catch and grab her hand and hold on. They ran together up the hill, bare feet slipping in the grass. Their shoes and stockings were left behind. Mama would be mad. But their hands clung tight together and did not let go. Away from that hollow in the creek they ran and ran, up the hill, gasping and crying. They couldn't breathe. They would not stop.

At the top of the hill among the stones Mama stood at little Sarah's grave, teasing a handful of bachelor's buttons and Queen Anne's lace into shape in a vase. They ran to her and seized her so hard she nearly fell. "Girls, my land!" she exclaimed. Their crying wiped the wonderment from her voice. "Girls, Sarah, Jane, what's the matter?" She held them tight, one arm around each of them, and they wrapped their arms around her and each other as hard as they could. Their wet faces smeared Mama's blouse and their noses ran all over her, but that was all right because Mama knew that they were scared and Mama would find out what was wrong. And then Uncle Eugene would be punished. Mama would lift her sword and kill the troll, crush him between grinding stones like the biggest Billy Goat. And then the story would be over, because Mama was brave. *Snip, snap, snout. This tale's told out.*

Mama held them, stroking their heads. Slowly she stood—one hand still curved against each of their backs—and scanned up and down the hill. They could feel by a sudden tense twang all through her that she had spotted Uncle Eugene. Sarah peeked around and saw him striding up the hill, one hand zipping up his pants zipper. He did not look at Sarah or Jane. Instead, he looked right at Mama and grinned. "Call of nature, Livia," he announced as he drew nearer.

"What happened here, Eugene?" Mama's voice lashed him.

Uncle Eugene paused and decided to smile. "Can't a man go take a piss?"

"Spare me," Mama spat. She thrust Sarah and Jane behind her and stepped closer to Uncle Eugene. "What did you do to my girls?"

His smile faded, then brightened. "I don't know what you mean," he said.

Mrs. Spurgeon and Reverend White were drawing closer now, worried looks on their faces. Then Father and Mr. Wainwright walked over, too. Mr. Wainwright looked at Uncle Eugene and Sarah, and then at Mama, carefully. "Livia?" Father said. "My dear, what is it?"

"You'd better get the truth out of your degenerate brother, right now," Mama hissed. "What," Uncle Eugene mocked, "in front of all these people?"

Quicker than a snake Mama struck out and slapped his face. Sarah burrowed deeper against Mama and shut her eyes and held on. "You son of a bitch," Mama growled. "You worthless—"

Adult voices roared above her, howling and crackling. Sarah could feel everyone staring but she could not open her eyes. Mama's whole body shook; it was like the time Sarah had been climbing a tree and a thunderstorm came, and she felt the wind take her and swing her back and forth. Then she felt Mama straighten up and tug at her shoulder and Jane's, gently. "Come, girls," she said. "Go get in the buggy and I'll take you home." She nudged them ahead of her and turned back to look at Uncle Eugene, her face white. "Don't you *ever*," she spat, "ever trifle with them. Don't you ever trifle with me."

Sarah and Jane huddled against each other in the back seat of the buggy, still holding hands. At home they went straight upstairs and climbed into their big bed. "Sick, Alvah," Mama's voice trailed them up the stairs, "a bad egg, I've no doubt." They went to sleep, still curled together, and woke blinking and disoriented in the dark, to the sound of more voices: Mama and Father, in the parlor. Without lighting a candle they slid out of the sheets and tiptoed to the top of the stairs and listened.

"Livia," Father said, "I can't turn out my brother." A long pause. "He's my blood."

"Your daughters, Ned," Mama hissed. "Your growing daughters. What are *they*?"

Sarah and Jane leaned closer as they peered through the banister down into the foyer at the dim light and the voices through the open parlor door. A sudden swish of Mama's dress: she'd leapt up, pacing. Her feet thumped, thumped, thumped, the floor creaked, creaked. "I'm going to tell you something, Ned, that you've never understood." Her voice scorched the air. "Just because somebody's your *blood* doesn't give them the right to, to—" She gasped. "Doesn't mean they act with *impunity* and you just have to *accept* their actions because of who they *are*. People *earn* respect. They have to *earn* it. *Every*one. In any decent world, a man like your brother gets tossed out of the family to make his own way. If Eugene weren't your blood, you wouldn't let him in the house. And why on *earth*—" a sob ripped at Mama's voice, from underneath—"why on *earth* are you allowing him to even breathe another drop of *air* after what he did to Sarah?"

"You don't know." Father's voice wobbled. "You weren't down at that creek."

"So you are telling me our daughter *lies*?" Mama's voice broke. "You didn't see her face when she came running up to me."

Jane reached her arm underneath Sarah's and pulled it close, against her own small ribs. Sarah leaned closer to her sister. She couldn't breathe.

"Why would she lie?" Mama's voice was spitting now. "Good God, the child barely knows how hens lay eggs. You actually believe she has the spitefulness to—"

Father's desk chair creaked and his steps approached Mama across the parlor floor. "No, Livia," he said, "no, I know our Sarah, it's just—Mother told me, Livia, she told me to look after him, she made me promise. He's always been—well, weak."

"Just like your father," Mama snapped. "And just like you."

"Livia," Father said. "Imagine turning Johnny out. Imagine if this were *your* precious boy."

A pause, a gasp from Mama. Before Jane and Sarah could move, Mama came striding across the foyer, skirts swishing, and jerked open the front door and stepped through into the night and slammed it behind her. Although they waited at the top of the stairs, hunkered low, until their feet tingled and Jane's head started to droop, Mama didn't come back, and Father didn't come out of his study. In a wavery square of light through the parlor door, that dim candle burned on and on.

Sometime in the dark—was Sarah waking or dreaming?—Mama's voice hissed through the wall: "Don't you touch me, Ned. Don't you ever touch me again."

❧

At the breakfast table, Mama and Father were both smiling at Uncle Eugene as if nothing had happened. Eugene would not look anyone in the eye.

Had it really happened?

If it had been real, surely Mama and Father would not let him still be sitting here.

But he was here. They were not yelling at him or putting him back in the buggy with the skinny little gray mare and sending him on his way.

She could still feel his hand spidering up the inside of her leg. Still hear the little creek running. She closed her eyes, hard. A sick cold bolt went down inside her stomach like she was going to throw up.

Prove it was real. She fetched a piece of paper and her ink and pen and sat scrunched into the corner of the upstairs windowsill. On the other side of the glass, the sun on the roof shingles turned the morning dew to smoke. She dipped the pen and dropped a blot of ink, then tried to draw it out into words. *Uncle Eugene—Uncle Eugene touched—Uncle Eugene touched my leg.*

Put like that it seemed innocent. A casual brush of her shoe-top, an accidental bump to get her attention or shoo away a grasshopper.

She knew what it meant. But would anyone else?

Would anyone else believe that she was telling the truth?

Good girls tell the truth. Be a good girl, Sarah.

But a good girl would never have been touched on the private inside of her leg, up under her skirt, and get this sick bad feeling all down her stomach when she thought about it. A good girl would not be wondering if—oh, horrible—she would be in danger of having a baby now. But Uncle Eugene had not peed on her. He had waited to pee until she and Jane had grabbed hands and run up the hill, away from the creek. Surely she was safe.

But to stay safe, and to stay a good girl, she could not ask Mama anything else about how babies come, or what had happened with Uncle Eugene. Because obviously Mama had decided that it was not real or it was not real enough to do anything about it. Despite her voice in the parlor, and in the dark—*Don't you ever touch me again*—today she had looked at Sarah, and at Uncle Eugene, as if nothing had happened. She was back behind her adult mask, which hid what even Sarah was now beginning to doubt was the truth.

She folded the paper in her hand over and over and ripped the pieces in half. She would burn them in the kitchen fire, when Alvah wasn't looking.

Maybe—oh, sudden surge of risk, and hope—Johnny could help her. Johnny was part of a different world. He was way up ahead of her and Jane, nudging around the edges of the man's world, which would close around him and draw him in like the fringes of the Venus flytrap in the big mauve-colored *Book of Exotic Flora and Fauna*. But he seemed to want it that way. And now, with the shadowy thing between him and Celia, the yellow dress appearing and disappearing from the wardrobe, he was more a mystery than ever. Sarah had heard him arguing with Father in the library about money: "I just need it. Never you mind what I need it for. I think that's my own goddamn business." But Johnny knew something she wanted to know, something that had happened before she was even born, when only he had been there to see.

She found her older brother at the barn, sitting on an overturned bucket, tugging bridle straps through a dirty rag in his hands. "Johnny," Sarah blurted, "when do you think Uncle Eugene is going away?"

Johnny's face darkened. "Not soon enough," he said. "I don't know why Father tolerates that son of a bitch."

She should tell him what had happened at the creek. Maybe then he would make Uncle Eugene go away, or make Father and Mama do it. But the words wouldn't come out of her mouth. Johnny would think she was a bad girl too. *Touch—on my leg—*Johnny would scowl and look dark but the darkness in his face would be directed at her. Johnny would think she was a bad girl too.

"Seems to me," he murmured, looking at the bridle in his hands, "like little Sarah would have been enough."

At first Sarah thought he had read her mind. But he couldn't have. "Sarah?" She couldn't breathe. The tombstone with her name, the little cousin.

"Our sister," Johnny said. "She came in between me and you." Something sad and lost welled up in his eyes and pushed him forward. "She died. I don't remember much about her. Except she got sick, after Uncle Eugene came here one time." He paused. "He was sick when he came here. He got better. She didn't." He looked down at the rag in his hands. "He came here with a cough. I just remember him coughing. And then the doctor came, and Sarah died."

"Is she the one buried out there at the church?" Sarah asked. "The stone with my name."

Johnny sighed. "Yes," he said. "I don't remember going to a burying. I don't remember anything except Mama crying." His face closed and he turned away, tightening his hands around the straps. A clean rag to polish the grass-foam off the bit lay over his other knee. But suddenly he wasn't moving anymore. He was just sitting still, his wide back frozen. He was a grown man now. But suddenly he looked so small.

Sarah set her hand on Johnny's shoulder. Maybe he would scoff and call her a stupid girl and tell her to get away. Maybe, like Mama, he would twist his mouth and tell her to stop being sentimental. But she kept her hand there, and she felt her brother lean against it. And then she took her hand down and walked away. Behind her she heard the clink of the bit, Johnny's hands working and working the metal, bringing up a shine.

If the dead Sarah were not enough to keep Uncle Eugene away from the house, then what had happened down by the creek probably wouldn't be enough, either.

That night Johnny rode over to Mr. Wainwright's house to play cards with him and the Rehobeth Militia. But they weren't called that then. Not until the war, and what came after it. Not until Bad Katy Pruitt and Mrs. Simmes' Robert and the Yankee House. Not until Alvah's face, strained, leaning toward Seth in the light of the candle. Not until everything was gone.

4

The only Yankee Sarah ever met was Mr. Lowell, from Massachusetts, who came to Rehobeth before the war and built the Yankee House. The Yankee House stood on land that had once been theirs: five hundred acres of cotton fields, separated from Fairibault by a long finger of woods. This land had been part of Fairibault since Grandaddy got it from the Indians, but then Father sold it to Mr. Lowell from Massachusetts, three years before the war broke out for good. "What do I need with it?" Father had asked, as if to himself.

"That's right," said Mama sarcastically. "What do we need with cotton money, we who live on air?"

"Livia," Father asked, "you want me to buy more negroes? Is that really what you want?"

Over the dinner table at Fairibault, Mr. Lowell had told Mother and Father that he had "long cherished the ambition to run a cotton farm" to supply his mills in Massachusetts. "And better yet," he boomed in his loud Yankee voice, "supply an escape from Massachusetts winters. No kind of weather for a man in my condition. Rheumatism, sir"—and he looked meaningfully across the dining table at Sarah's father—"is a hindrance to an active man, a heathen curse."

"Don't worry," Mama assured Mrs. Lowell at the other end of the table, "the winters here are lovely, such bright blue days and clement weather. Perfect for riding, for hunting."

"Mr. Lowell hunts," said Mrs. Lowell, blinking. "But I believe I've never tried." Tiny and slender as a girl, Mrs. Lowell had frail, rounded shoulders and a head that sat a little forward on her neck,

118

like an old hen's, and three ropes of pearls around her neck. Mama said Mrs. Lowell had money in her family ("from as far back as the *Mayflower*, to judge from the hints she drops") and Mr. Lowell had married her to help him make even more. Mrs. Lowell's eyes followed her husband all evening, a hopeful smile on her face. "Mr. Lowell loves to entertain," she continued, "and we'll be having balls and parties in the house." Her voice faltered, and she coughed and kept talking. "A ballroom built specially, under the dome."

"You all remember what a dome is," Father told Sarah and Jane, "like on the capital in Montgomery." Sarah imagined it as a giant white egg perched on top of a red brick house surrounded by barns and sheds to hold all the cotton Mr. Lowell would grow. Every month the house grew a little more, and every summer more slaves—more *people,* bought in from somewhere—worked up and down the fields, plowing and planting cotton for Mr. Lowell's Massachusetts mill. "Girls no older than you work in those mills," Mama told Sarah and Jane. "Imagine. And they chastise *us* for inhumanity."

"They?" Jane asked.

"Yankees," Mama replied. "Abolitionists." At Jane's puzzled look, she shook her head. "Never mind, child," she said. "Ten-year-old girls working looms in a factory. Just remember that. A house built on the backs of little girls."

Sarah imagined hunched and creeping children carrying the red brick house on their backs like a snail shell, like the people working down in the cotton rows. Were the girls, then, like the *people* in Mr. Lowell's fields, then, or their own? But a sharpness in Mama's face kept her from asking Mama this question. Mama watched Sarah more sharply than usual these days, in general. She was fourteen by then, old enough to go calling like a young lady. When they rode over to the Lowells' house to welcome them back to Alabama, Mama put a coat on Seth and set him up high to drive them, just like a real coachman. Sarah tried to catch his eye and make him laugh, but he wouldn't look at her. Sometimes she wondered if he had imagined him in the half-second she held him, after Johnny's boxing match: the single faint, astonished quiver before he twisted away. It didn't seem real, now. Increasingly, neither did what had happened by the creek. Uncle Eugene had gone away, driving out in the rickety buggy with his sickly gray mare, as suddenly as he had come. Sarah had opened her mouth a hundred times since then to raise the issue with Mama, but something in Mama's eyes always stopped her: *don't speak of it. Just let it lie.* And so she did.

"I'll say one thing for Ebenezer Lowell," mused Mama as the buggy creaked up the drive, "he knows how to situate a house. He's done more with this property than your father ever would have. But it does seem odd, with these political rumors in the wind, that he'd—" She paused, and shrugged. "Oh, well," she mused. "'Twas ever thus, I reckon. Men make what they think's a brilliant decision although any woman with a grain of sense could have told them no. Perhaps that's why they prefer not to listen in the first place."

On the top of the little hill near the woods sat the big house, with at least fifty men, white and colored, swarming all over it. "This is the year," Mr. Lowell had trumpeted to Father, "that I finish this house!" So he had hired everyone he could hire or get the loan of. "It's going to be an octagon, with that horrible dome on top," Mama said, squinting in the bright light. "As if the two of them need so much space." She sighed. "An Oriental villa, she calls it. A Turkish palace. She saw it in a travel book and ordered the plans from some other enterprising Yankee. I call it one big tacky mess." But to Sarah it looked like a birdcage, a raw airy structure of light and bone, floating on top of the hill. God could put a hook in the tip of the dome and hang it from the sky, with Mr. and Mrs. Lowell suspended inside like canaries. A skin of red brick had crept upward from the ground, over the first story and halfway up the second. But near the sky—still—the planks of what would be the dome were open to the air.

"Welcome to my home," said Mrs. Lowell, meeting them on the front steps. She cocked her head like a little bird, and smiled. "At least what will be my home."

Sarah and Jane trotted ahead of Mama and Mrs. Lowell, into the round center hall, and looked up. Higher than the roof of their own house, higher than even birds flew on their own, a colored man clung to the bare blonde scaffolding of the dome. When Sarah raised her hand to shield the sun, her hand blotted him out completely. He peered down at her and kept working, inching sideways along the boards neat as a woodpecker along the trunk of a tree. The shots of his hammer rattled down to them, out of time with his swinging arm.

"Mr. Lowell said the dome should be the last to go up, not the first," Mrs. Lowell explained, leading Mama into the hall, "but I insisted. I said, my dear, if I have to live in the cellar of my own home like a little mouse until it's finished, well, at least I can have something to aspire to."

"Or rather not a spire," said Mama, "but a dome." She laughed, and Mrs. Lowell looked puzzled, then laughed too. "Ah," she said. "A pun."

"Live in the cellar?" Jane asked. Mrs. Lowell bent to look at her and smiled. "Yes," she said, "we're finishing the bottom floor first, so we'll have living quarters until the rest is done."

She led them down a small flight of steps and into a square, low-ceilinged room with four other rooms jutting off it at each corner. In one of the doorways, Harlan Hogg squatted on his heels, smoothing a flat wooden tool over fresh plaster. He spotted Mama and nodded his head. His sunburned face flushed brighter red, down his neck and into his collar. "Missus Fairibault," he said, and nodded at Sarah and Jane too.

"Good day," said Mama, "what lovely work." Her voice brightened up from underneath, in an encouraging way Sarah recognized. *Why, Sarah, you look so nice when you hold still and don't wrinkle your dress. Why Jane, you read this whole long book by yourself.* Mrs. Lowell raised her eyebrows at Mama. "Five children," Mama whispered when they were in the next room. "Moonshiner. Went to drink, and fighting with it still. He used to help my husband train his hunting dogs."

"Ah," Mrs. Lowell whispered back, nodding.

"So you've done a kindness," Mama said. "Especially to that wife of his. Poor thing."

"This will be the parlor," Mrs. Lowell continued in her normal voice, "and I think we'll set the dining table in the central room, right there where Mr. Hogg is working. Bedrooms here and here. And the kitchen, now being completed, out behind the house, will serve for both." She went to the window—fresh glass, still smeared with dust and plaster—and looked out. "Oh, look, they've started it."

Sarah went to the window, too. Paul and Silas knelt in the dust, laying brick in arrow-shaped patterns that overlapped, like a fish's scales. Paul and Silas were old; they went to everyone's house whenever there was a good stone wall to build or bricks to lay or something fine to build that needed care. They had built Mama the red brick sidewalk winding through the knot garden in the side yard at Fairibault, with a pattern of circles in the center that looked just like a knot someone had started to untie. Mama had clapped her hands and jumped up in the air when she saw it. "Oh, Ned," she said, "how beautiful!" She hugged Father tight and started planting her herbs the very next day, with a hedge of boxwood all around to keep the chickens out. And as Paul and Silas packed their tools to go, she had walked to them and looked them right in their faces. "The two of you," she said, "are true craftsmen. This is lovely. I thank you both." They had smiled back and murmured, "thank you, ma'am." But they didn't raise their eyes.

"Herringbone," Mrs. Lowell said with satisfaction, watching Paul and Silas work. "A nice straight line, for the whistling walk."

"What's that?" Mama asked.

Mrs. Lowell paused. "I thought all the Southern houses had one," she said. "That's what my neighbor said, back home in Boston. She went to a great plantation in Virginia and was told they called this little walk from the kitchen to the house the whistling walk, so the—" She looked at Jane and Sarah. "So the servants whistle when they carry in the dinner, and you know they aren't tasting it."

"Well, maybe in Virginia," Mama said. "But here, we trust our people more than that."

Mrs. Lowell's face flushed. "I'm not mocking," Mama said, setting one hand on Mrs. Lowell's arm. "It's a lovely name. It's just not one I've ever heard."

"Well," stumbled Mrs. Lowell, "that's what she called it, even so."

Mama turned, tactfully, and led Mrs. Lowell and Mama and Sarah back up the stairs. They wandered again around the echoing wooden floor of the center hall, under the dome. "Niches for statuary here, and here," Mrs. Lowell explained, her little voice swallowed by the churchy soar of the air, "Greek, you know, something tasteful. And the piano will go here, at least for now."

"Piano?" Mama asked, and Mrs. Lowell pointed to a hulking wooden crate with *Steinway, Boston* stenciled on the side. "Not unpacking it yet, not fully," she explained. "Got to leave the cover on. Protected from the elements. But I really should crack the cover over the keys at least, make sure it's in tune."

"How long have you played?" Mama asked.

"I'm learning," Mrs. Lowell explained. "Mr. Lowell thinks it lends such an air of taste, but I confess I've never been quite musical."

"Everyone has to learn," Mama said kindly. "Sarah, here, is learning too."

"How long have you been playing, dear?" Mrs. Lowell asked.

"Since I was little," Sarah said, suddenly shy. *Steinway, Boston.* A big city, so far away. What did that piano look like under its shell of hard lumber packing-crate? Longing flooded her. If she could pry up the board covering the keys and reach inside, into the dark mouth of that giant benevolent beast, she could bring forth any sound she liked, as long as no one else was there to hear.

Mama led Sarah and Jane down the steps and into the carriage. Seth glanced at them and Sarah rolled her eyes. He smiled back, quickly, and looked down.

Mama turned to wave at Mrs. Lowell as they drove away, then resettled herself. "Yes," she said, "it'll be impressive, if he ever finishes it. And in the meantime, she'll live in that cellar like a mouse. Doubtless, some Virginia lady told her that it's all the rage."

Mr. Lowell kept traveling back and forth between Alabama and Massachusetts: "he's trying to maintain his factory," Mrs. Lowell explained to Mama, "in these . . . political times, it's difficult." Red brick climbed up and up the outside walls of the house until it closed in and the whole skeleton was hidden. Men climbed all over it to paint the dome and the roof-trim and the railings of the upper galleries and the front steps a sparkling white. "We're finishing the outside first," Mrs. Lowell explained. "Oh, still so much plaster-work to do." More and more, when Mr. Lowell was gone, she sat at the dining room table at Fairibault with Mama and dithered: "Now, what is a suitable name? Yours is so lovely, just your family's name."

"What about yours, or a variation?" suggested Mama, wearily. "Lowell . . . " But even Sarah could tell the only possibility would be something with *low* in the name.

"Shadows," Mrs. Lowell said, dreamily. "My dear friend May spent a week at a glorious home in Louisiana, with such a lovely name, Shadows-on-the-Teche. That's the name of the river that it's on." Mama nodded. "But our river's name is not French, which seems needful. Shadows-on-the-Chattahoochee? I doubt that would suit."

The Lowells eventually decided to name their house Lowood— like the bad orphan school in *Jane Eyre,* although they didn't seem to know that—although after the war started and the Lowells moved back to Massachusetts, everyone in Rehobeth called it the Yankee House. Before she left, Mrs. Lowell had the doors and windows boarded shut, inside and out. And she and her husband never came back. The great house stood alone, a hollow cage. Nettles and dogfennel sprang up in the yard and the white paint of the trim flaked away and the heavy silver chain across the driveway rusted brown. The cotton fields returned to blackberries and sweetgum and seedling pine. No part of it beyond the cellar, the kitchen building, and the whistling walk was ever finished. And no one—almost no one—ever went inside.

One day, Sarah saw Alvah and Rosa Lee and Celia sitting on the porch of Alvah's cabin. Even at a distance there was something in the tilt of their heads, the angle of their bodies, that tingled worriedly in her mind. Something worried was in Alvah's face too. Celia spoke, too softly to hear. And she set both hands on her stomach and held them there.

Then, one morning, Celia was gone. Nobody said *run away,* just *gone.* Sarah and Jane heard only confused angry flusterings, voices blurred and arguing behind doors, Father and Johnny shouting. Would Celia be like Liza in Mrs. Stowe's book, jumping over chunks of river ice with the baby *strained to her heaving bosom?* No one would tell her. And to ask, amid that clamor of anger, was unthinkable.

Father's weary voice twisted through his study door as Mama's feet clicked back and forth on the floorboards: "I'm not going to advertise. Let the poor child go. She's obviously got a pass and money in her purse." He paused. Mama's anger burned white, palpable even in silence. "Listen to me, Livia. Do you really want to keep her here, seeing her and the baby, every day?" He paused. "I doubt it."

Mama did not speak directly to Father for a week. "Could you ask your father to hand me the biscuits, please," she said to Sarah. "Ask your father if he'd like the last of the port. Perhaps he'd prefer to enjoy what the work of his hands, and, more importantly, his father's hands, built before every last servant runs away to the land of Mrs. Stowe."

"Save the port," Father said. "I have a separate reserve."

"Ah, a reserve in the study," Mama concurred bitterly. "The gentleman's prerogative."

After dinner, Sarah opened the wardrobe at the top of the stairs. The yellow dress was gone.

The war was a distant and hazy thing to Sarah and to Jane. Johnny hurtled toward it in a blur of Mama's arguments and tears and Father's exhausted, resigned looks. "It'll grow that boy up," he says. "Teach him to do his duty." These words brought a particular fury into Mama's face that Sarah didn't understand. But *duty* was a normal word, a good word even, and Johnny nodded when he heard Father say it. "I ain't a child, Mama," he said. "I've got to go." He looked at Father, and Sarah understood. Father's bad leg kept him from volunteering. So Johnny wanted to go, for both Father and himself. What would soldiers have to do, anyway? Confused images swirled in her mind, like leaves disturbed at the bottom of a stream: Napoleon meeting his Waterloo, the sleek gray cavalry coat Tommy Lee Coulter's mama down the road had begun sewing for him last month ("I'd advise you," she told Mama, sitting importantly in the parlor with her needle flashing, "order some for your boy, it's good quality"), George Washington's troops shivering in the snow at Valley Forge with bleeding feet. But George Washington was not in Johnny's army. George Washington was technically the Union now. A Yankee. Could what had once been *our* side now be *theirs?*

Johnny and Tommy Lee Coulter—his best friend since Sarah could remember—practiced drills on the lawn, turning and trotting their big horses, as the mules watched curiously over the fence. Their saddles creaked; their bits and stirrups jingled and flashed. They galloped forward and jabbed their bayonets into a straw-stuffed cloth sack dangling from the big sycamore in the yard. They raced, whooping and laughing, down the driveway out of sight. At night, their voices rang through the dining room, swooping over each other like hawks in flight. Johnny poured whiskey for himself and Tommy Lee and Father and they clinked their glasses and took a drink, solemn and exalted.

And then one morning, Johnny saddled his roan, gathered his blanket-roll and knapsack, hugged her and Jane and Mama and shook Father's hand, and rode away. And Sarah never saw her brother again.

Your gallant son was killed in action at Manassas Junction, Virginia, said the letter. Sarah studied the signature at the bottom, curling like the plume in a cavalier's hat: *your obedient servant, Major Gen. J. E. B. Stuart. July 22, 1861.*

"You're a big girl now, near a woman," Father said, holding Sarah close as she sniffled against his shirt. "You and your sister have to be good to your poor mother."

Mama wept. Mama shouted. Her face acquired a set white tautness, with permanent bruised smudges under her eyes. And ever afterward, she kept the letter announcing Johnny's death in the bottom of her red morocco sewing case. Until the day Sarah left Mobile for Iowa, as a married lady, she saw that letter whenever she opened that case, looking for extra thread or needles. The gray-white corner of the envelope peeked from under skeins of silk and scraps of embroidery cloth, its edges fraying and softening more and more. Mama took it out to read again and again, as if, this time, it would be bearing different news.

That red morocco sewing case, with that letter inside, was resting on Mama's lap when Galen and Sarah came to her years later to tell her they were leaving Mobile. "Well," she said finally. "It's in the nature of children to leave their homes, leave their mothers behind. Especially the nature of daughters."

The weeping that wrenched Sarah's body that night, as Galen huddled close to her, murmuring, was wrung from deeper sorrow and deeper anger than she ever knew she could feel. On the day of their leaving, she looked her mother in the eyes, kissed her mother's taut white cheek, and told herself she didn't feel anything like that sorrow or that anger anymore. But she knew then, and she knows now, that this is a lie.

"Men real good at makin plans and leavin us to do the work," Alvah said when she thought no one was listening. Men were also good at leaving women behind. So many men—her brother— gone. So many women left to mourn and wait.

They went to fight for this land, they said. For the land that was frozen in its winter shapes and colors in Sarah's mind, as she remembered what to her was its most beautiful season: the bare brown trees against the blue winter sky, the peeps of hedgerow quail, the startling glossy greens of cedar and pine. Their high square house, secure on its little hill, surrounded by the sycamore trees. It was worth fighting for, this land. Truly.

But look at it now, Sarah thought after Johnny's death. *Look at it.* Growing up in sweetgum and blackberry vines. Wisteria and honeysuckle fingering the columns of the house. Paint peeling off the house, the sheds, the barns. Fencerails splintering and falling. Why go off to war at all? Why not stay, make this a place where people want to stay and work? Where Celia and Seth and Alvah and Rosa Lee might want to stay, too, to raise up a place within this land for themselves?

Schoolmistress Spofford in Mobile would have said, "folly, human folly," in her history-class voice, clear, rueful, quiet. "Will we never learn. Will men never learn. Over and over they go to war and leave us women to salvage what we can. How are we as a people ever to make peace if women—who know peace best, who carry it within our bodies, in our hearts—refuse to ever, ever tell these men *enough*?"

War was a strange way to solve problems started with words on paper, with loud angry voices, with speeches about honor and about *insults that gentlemen could never tolerate*. The gap from words to the smashing of bodies and bones and the spilling of blood was so wide, but those same gentlemen leapt it smoothly as hunting-horses over a ditch. They sent boys they'd never even met out onto fields to stare at each others' campfires all night, listening to the soft sounds of deer stepping close, of raccoons washing their hands in the little streams at the edge of the woods. Then, when the sun rose, a man on horseback rode back and forth and raised his saber and shouted at those same boys to shoulder their guns and form a line. All the while, those gentlemen slept at home in their feather beds in Charleston. Then they rose from sleep to peer across the harbor at the fort out in the bay, sipping coffee from their china cups, handed to them by the dark hands they as *gentlemen* had enlisted those boys to help them keep. It was strange. Johnny was her brother. He'd been carried, like her, in the warm cave of her mama's body. And she would never see him again. Because men in marble buildings miles away had marched him off and told him to look across the field at the distant shape of a stranger's head, just visible over the bristling line of wagons and gun barrels and horses tugging at their traces, their nostrils flaring red in fear. And then they'd told him to pull the trigger.

5

In Eldorado, October settles around the old doctor's house. Sunny warmth gives way to a chill that bites deep in the mornings and the evenings. Maples reach a peak of brightness and then drop their leaves, as a flame flares just before it's doused. Wind rattles a loose window in the parlor; Galen stuffs the cracks between sill and frame with scraps of cloth to hold it tight. Sarah counts the jars of preserves and tomatoes, then opens the lid of the bin where potatoes and carrots sleep in sawdust. She rechecks the woolen capes she and Rosa Lee have been keeping in their trunks, then shakes out the folds of the blankets for moths before adding them to the weight of quilts on each bed. Minx the cat leaps under the lifted sail of the blanket, then curls up to nap.

The children of Eldorado come in from their summertime and trudge into the whitewashed schoolhouse up the street. Nils Ericksen, the oldest of the Norwegian Lutheran seminary boys, waits for them. His glasses flash as he opens the door in the morning, then releases the children at midday. While they eat their lunch and chase each other in circles, Nils perches on the steps, paging through a small red book. Sarah recognizes it: one of the Athanaeum Classical Library series, like her father's.

The days are still warm by midafternoon as the fall retreats into winter. Despite the rueful undertone to the light—amber-colored and sad—the sky can still turn bright china blue, the wind soft. So one afternoon Sarah grips the mending-basket by its handle and carries it outside, turning sideways to get both it and her stomach through the door. She crosses the trodden dirt yard and sits in one of the wooden chairs she and Rosa Lee have parked near the chicken coop. She'll get the mending done, and some more rows knitted in the baby's sweater too. She isn't idle. But she can't stay inside the house another minute.

Clouds churn and pass, gathering and swirling against the blue. Wind snatches a handkerchief from the top of the mending pile and smacks it against a fence post. Sarah sighs, defiant. She'll get it when she's good and ready. And if one handkerchief is lost, it's no irreparable mistake. *We're not so poor,* rings Mama's voice in her mind, *that we need descend to that.*

So Mama sold Fairibault instead, so there would be no descent at all. They would move up in the world. Her daughters would marry well and live a lady's life, a life of leisure. The words tickle obscenely in Sarah's mouth. Feathers on wide hats and stiff skirts that rustle into parlor after parlor and teacups that clink and clatter as voices stop and start again. Always, it was there. No telling how the Mobile ladies had all heard the rumors about her and Seth. But they had.

That's her. That older girl. The one who—That colored boy—

A shame, when the second girl's—Jane? Yes—so pleasant, and young Felix Dalton so attentive—

Isn't it a shame when sisters spoil each other's chances.

But that was over now. No need to think of it. She tilts her sewing box. The blank diary inside it tilts too.

Sarah tucks her shawl around her. As long as she's sitting in full sun, it's warm enough to stay out here. The house seems so dark these days: the ceilings lower, the backs of the parlor chairs and sofa arched higher to cut out the light. She reaches for the baby's tiny sweater, delighting in the softness of the fine gray wool that Mrs. Thorson spun for her. With the needles lightly but firmly between her fingertips, she lets her hands take up the familiar dance. Left hand hooks a loop of wool and drops it on the right and right darts underneath to loop and lift and clear the way for the loop the left hand's just prepared, again. The needle tips nudge each other as cosily as two birds pecking seed out of the same flower. One whole sleeve is finished now, and she's worked her way across the shoulders to the collar and halfway down the other sleeve. Then, when that is finished, she'll go back and begin the long circling loops down and down around the baby's back and stomach until she reaches the bottom row and binds it off, with a nice sturdy edge that won't unravel.

Old Nero the cat curls under her chair, flipping his tail. Minx is out hunting. All their kittens are gone, to the church and the general store and eager families. Little Finn Gunderson got the white kitten for his own. White like his mama's fat geese.

Under her skin, the baby's quiet. What furious intent blooming must be going on inside this cask where her child rides, inside that small curled body with the feet tucked together instep over arch. The blood is circling, silting its minerals into her child's bones. The fine white fibers of the bones themselves are knitting and binding to one another, thread on thread as bark binds to a tree, as a stalk unfurls its flower into the sky.

You didn't care about babies that much until you held one, and then suddenly you did.

The first baby she ever held was her cousin Mattie Lea's. Mattie Lea had come to visit from Macon County, just after the war, when women could move around on the roads again as long as they had a man with them. Mattie Lea's husband Ronald had had half his leg shot off at Vicksburg and was hard of hearing, even though he was only a few years older than Johnny—than Johnny would have been. Ronald either sat as close to Mattie Lea as he could get, whispering, "what's that? what'd she say?" or in a kitchen chair at the end of the porch, propping his feet against the column, smoking and staring out into the yard. Ash and cigars piled up like a little anthill next to him. When he got that way, Mattie Lea would set the baby in his lap, straddling the stump where the leg had been.

"It's the only thing," she confided to Mama, "that gets him back, in such a state."

Mattie Lea had a little colored girl, Phinzy, to help her, but Phinzy was so shy she'd hardly speak to anybody, even Rosa Lee. If you tried to talk to her, she'd stare at you with huge wide eyes and clutch the baby tighter and scurry away. When Ronald was sitting and smoking and Mama and Mattie Lea were talking and doing embroidery in the parlor—Sarah was supposed to be with them but it bored her to distraction—Phinzy spread a quilt on the porch and laid the baby on his back and dangled a little soft ball of cloth on a string, or a flower, or her own pigtail ribbon, over the baby's face. His blue eyes went in and out of focus as he frowned and reached, flexing his fingers. "Baby," Phinzy crooned, "you a good baby, ain't you." Strictly speaking, the baby's name was Ronald Clarence Nevelson, Jr. "But that's too long-handled a name just yet," Mattie Lea said. Especially, Sarah thought, for something that looks like a little grubworm.

Mama and Mattie Lea came out of the parlor and stood in the door, watching Phinzy and the baby. Mama smiled. "Mattie Lea, why don't you give that child some rest," she announced. "Phinzy, you go on in the kitchen and Alvah will give you somethin sweet. Sarah will take this baby. She's fifteen, she needs to learn."

"Mama!" Sarah protested. Phinzy looked up in fear. "Go ahead," Mattie Lea nodded, and Phinzy stood up slowly, then trudged into the kitchen.

"Now, Sarah," Mama said, "you pick him up and walk with him. See how he's fussin?" Mattie Lea smiled. "Go on," she said, teasingly, "it's fine. He likes it when you dandle him a little." And the two of them turned and walked, laughing, skirts swishing, back into the parlor.

Sarah peered at Ronald, smoking at the far end of the porch; what if she just scooped up the baby and plopped it down astraddle of his leg? "Go to your papa!" she could say, like Mattie Lea.

Or she could sneak back to the kitchen and summon Phinzy. But that would be cheating. Mama was right. Once she was married, although who knew when that would be, she'd have one like this herself, and so she'd better get used to it.

She stood over the baby and looked down. He furled one arm thoughtfully, stuck all his knuckles in his mouth, and looked back at her. Now his little fat hand was shiny. Sarah shuddered. How did Mattie Lea keep from being disgusted by her own baby? Especially the diaper. Thank goodness he was clean now, or seemed to be. No smell.

She knelt and thrust one arm under the baby's neck and shoulders and one arm under his knees and heaved until he came up off the blanket and flopped against her chest. His head wobbled– so heavy, it seemed like it might just break off, like a big sunflower— and his wet mouth fell on her shoulder. Quickly she turned him around until his back lay against her chest, and she held him with one arm under his bottom and one arm across his ribs. Now he could see out in front of him, like a person. His fat thighs squished against her forearms. The soft fluffy top of his head lay right under her nose. She breathed in the smell of it and closed her eyes.

"Look at you!" Mattie Lea exclaimed when they walked into the parlor. "How well you're doing!" Sarah grinned, and Mama smiled. "That's it," she said. "Just walk around and talk to him like folks. That's what babies like."

So Sarah walked back outside and around the house with the baby. "Those are chickens," she said, "and when you get big enough to handle a knife and fork, you can eat one." The weight of him made a warm sweaty spot against her dress. She held him out in front of her to look at him, and his eyes wobbled to the left and right before they fastened on hers and a thoughtful smile came over his face. Bubbles popped on his lips, between his plump jowls. "You're laughin at me," she told him, pleased. She patted his cheek with her fingertips. The wobble was satisfying, like tapping tomato aspic to see it quiver. She turned him around so that his head was underneath her chin and breathed his baby smell and counted the veins: one, two, three.

She carried him back around to the front of the house and sat on the front steps. Ronald's chair was empty, and she heard his voice from the parlor, then Mattie Lea's laughter. Her hair trailed down on either side of the baby's face, and he peered out from beneath it. "Long-haired baby," she giggled. "You're a little long-haired baby."

Seth came around the corner of the house and crossed the yard, with old Tod the dog trotting behind him. He smiled, then veered toward them. "Hey, big 'un," he said to the baby. Quickly he reached out to tickle the bottom of the baby's foot, then smiled at Sarah and continued on across the yard.

Something below Sarah's heart bloomed and quivered, and she froze. She closed her eyes. The warm weight against her chest. Seth's smile. His long hand reaching toward her, and his long strides carrying him on and past her, out of sight. His shoulders moving, wide and supple as wings, under his shirt—

Violently, she blushed, as if she had actually touched him. She could not move. It was here inside her, suddenly, all one thing, and nothing she could understand.

It had appeared in her again, with Galen. But Seth was first.

Now, sitting in her small wooden chair, chickens pecking around her feet, she drops her eyes to the round moon of her belly, filling her lap, nudging the dangling rows of her knitting every time she breathes. She thinks of her child. She thinks of Galen. His face against her neck as he moves and he murmurs to her and she arches and cries out until she's like to fly apart. Such happiness. To know and carry inside her, staining all through her in a rich and secret red—*Mary kept all these things, and pondered them in her heart.* Galen's thick hair, shifting in the light from brown to copper-red to bronze, that she slides her hand into to clutch the slim, thoughtful cap of his skull. Galen's troubled eyes, with the dent between them that she sets her thumb onto and smooths, gently, till it goes away.

And layered underneath those dreams are the dreams of Seth. The hesitant intentness in his face, the pressure in the air between them, like a storm coming on. In the Yankee House, alone—

You shouldn't. You shouldn't. But you do.

The back door bangs and Rosa Lee strides across the yard. "Sarah?" she demands. "I saw you, all slumped over. Are you all right?"

"Was I?" Sarah says. She straightens and looks at Rosa Lee's worried face and blushes, so bright there's no way to hide it. "I was just—"

"You took a little nap," says Rosa Lee, smiling, "that's what you did."

"I reckon I did." Sarah smiles too. "I was dreaming."

"Well," Rosa Lee says, "I think I'll stay out here a little while too. Those things still got to soak." She nods at the tub full of small-clothes, floating in blueing to whiten them. Then she settles in the chair next to Sarah's and reaches over to hook a sock from the top of the mending pile. "You got your darning egg out here?" she asks.

"It's in there somewhere," Sarah says. Rosa Lee rummages, then pulls out the little red morocco sewing box, just like Mama's—Sarah's twelfth birthday present. She unlatches it, threads a needle with stout thread, and wiggles the darning egg down into the sock. Then she begins to weave the thread across the smooth wooden surface of the egg, from side to side of the ragged heel. First left to right; Alvah taught them both. Then top to bottom.

"Do you ever think about home?" Sarah blurts.

Rosa Lee pauses. "Home," she says. "Well. Not so much as I expected. I do think about Mama."

"I think about her too," says Sarah. She reaches for Rosa Lee and rests her hand on her sleeve.

Rosa Lee looks at Sarah and smiles, just a little. There's something tender behind it, hurt and secret, and a ghost of Alvah's smile. "I wish we could've taken her back home from Mobile," she says. "Laid her in the ground up by the old church."

"I know," says Sarah. "I do too."

"But that land ain't ours no more," says Rosa Lee. She corrects herself. "Ain't yours."

"It was yours too," says Sarah. "We couldn't have stayed there as long as we did without y'all. With the war. If you'd gone, we'd—"

If they'd gone. What if Alvah and Rosa Lee and Seth had joined that rumored throng, *all the colored going north*? In the days after the war Sarah went downstairs every morning, as soon as she woke up, to make sure Alvah was still in the kitchen, or coming across the yard from the cluster of cabins down in the trees. Before sleep, when the spent day ran itself in pictures across the inside of her head, Rosa Lee was always there: swinging with her in the big board swing, climbing up the low branches of the magnolia, settling there in the flickering light through the leaves to listen, with Jane and Seth, as Sarah read *Nicholas Nickelby*. There was no such thing as home without her.

But there was no such thing as home without Seth, then, too. And yet one morning Seth was gone.

Sarah teeters suddenly on the edge of tears. She's closer than she's ever been to asking Rosa Lee directly: *why didn't you go? Why did Seth go? Where? Do you have letters from him? Could I see?* Rosa Lee watches her with guarded eyes, intent, resolute. In that gaze is a door half-open to a place Sarah has never quite dared to look into.

Where did Seth go? Why did you stay? If she asks, right now, Rosa Lee might tell her. Or she might shut that door and Sarah will never be able to go near it again. She hesitates. Too chancy. So she drops her head. Pregnant women are subject to whims. She can pretend it's only that. She wants to ask. But she cannot.

Silence is a killing frost but there is safety in it too. Sometimes, the wrong word breaks something apart in friendships, or in your own heart, that can never be put back together. And this is true even if you want to say that word more than anything: fear settles in your throat and in your stomach, curled around your voice like a hand around the base of a weed, ready to tug it out by the root, with only a torn place left.

Even people who love you cannot be told everything. Even Galen, who brought her out of her dark place after Fairibault was sold and they moved to Mobile. Who watched her across the room on that January night at a Euterpean Society musical evening in Miss Spofford's parlor. Miss Spofford's Sybilline smile: "like Voltaire, I do what I can to cultivate my garden, even here." Sweet cakes and punch in china cups, fingernail-thin.

"It was during the Bach," Galen said later, "that Mr. Eckhart was playing, remember? You looked so sad. And I wondered why."

Four years after that night, when he took out his wallet in St. Louis to pay the hotel keeper, a smudged scrap of paper fluttered out. Sarah picked it up from the dirty carpet. *Bach's Aria*, read Galen's scribbly handwriting. *From Goldberg Variations.* She turned to him, and he took the paper from her hand and smiled. "I wrote it down," he whispered, shyly, right there at the hotel desk. "I wrote it down, so I would never forget." And he turned to pay the bored clerk, and Sarah hooked her arm through his and pressed it against her ribs.

That was then. Now, with the shadow under his shoulder-wing, the dent in his forehead growing deeper—

Rosa Lee is saying something. "What?" Sarah asks. "Oh . . . I was . . . "

"It must be true," says Rosa Lee. "You have a baby and you lose your mind." She laughs. "But I ain't like to lose mine anytime real soon."

"Why'd you say that?" Sarah asks. "The way Trygve's been talkin to you. You've been acting like it's nothing, but I think he's got intentions." Since the morning of Oyvind's operation, Trygve has returned to their house as often as he can find a pretext. He brings potatoes and carrots from the big crop the twins raised. He consults with Galen about a twinge in his knee or a speck of grit lodged in his eye. He slows his oxen so his wagon takes as long as possible to roll past their windows, and he waves. On the seat next to him, Oyvind waves too, turning his eyes shyly away. Let his brother shine. Let his brother draw the eye of the beautiful young woman in the doctor's house.

"I don't know," Rosa Lee muses. "He told me he wants to go walking, some night. That he'd come for me and we'd walk."

"Oh, Rosa Lee," Sarah says, "he's a good man."

"I know," says Rosa Lee. Her face brightens, but a shadow flickers underneath. "I just don't—I mean, what would Mama say?" She pauses, turning the lump of the darning egg inside the sock.

"Out here it's different," Sarah says, finally. "It's got to be. He's not even from this country, not really. And he truly fancies you. He's got good land, and Oyvind to help him. You could add on to the house, and you'd have babies too." She grins at Rosa Lee, relieved to see her friend's face soften. "And he's such a pretty man." Rosa Lee snickers. "And," Sarah continues, "you'll be here with me. We can still be together."

Rosa Lee's still smiling, but a different kind of light is underneath her smile now, rueful and secret. Behind her eyes, the door blows open a little further, and then eases shut. "Maybe we can," she says. "Maybe so." She bends again to her darning, and Sarah takes up her knitting. Then there's no more sound but the click and rustle of needles and thread and the rumple of their skirts' edges as a little wind kicks its heels, whistling, all around the yard. Hens peck and scratch and nestle their feather-bustled bottoms in the dust, idiotically content. Sarah finally clears her throat. "Your mama would like Trygve, too," she stumbles. "I know she would, she—" The grief of it presses against her, the whole lost world of faces and voices too thick to lift into words. Rosa Lee leans close, brushing her shoulder against Sarah's. And they settle in their chairs and work.

Trygve comes calling for Rosa Lee a week later, just as the warm snap is ending and Sarah can smell the thin, cold edge of true November in the air. He's sent a letter by his mother, blotched letters straggling over a neatly folded page: *To Miss Rosa Lee Lincoln. I ask you for the Honor of Walken wit me one Eveneng. Please to Reply. Mange takk. Tusen takk. Trygve Thorson.* And Rosa Lee, after showing the letter to Sarah—grins flashing across their faces—

goes into her room and writes a note back, folding it into neat quarters: *Dear Mr. Thorson, I accept. Please call tomorrow at half past six.* Rosa Lee puts the note into Mrs. Thorson's hand, and Mrs. Thorson searches her face, then smiles at her. "My Trygve is a real good boy," she says. "You'll be glad you told him yes, I think."

Along about three o'clock, Sarah sets the iron on the stove so it will be hot enough to press whatever dress they pick. She helps Rosa Lee open her trunk and spread the contents over her bed, inspecting for weak seams and worn spots, sorting through the neat gray serge, the homespun skirts, the lilac frock that had been Jane's until the girls at Miss Spofford's said it made her skin look green. They go through Sarah's trunks too, and the wardrobe. "No," Rosa Lee keeps saying, "not exactly." If either one of them thinks of Celia in her stolen yellow dress, they do not mention it.

Along about five o'clock, they have some hoecakes and cold ham; Rosa Lee says she can't think of eating, and Sarah doesn't want to stop to cook. "Some husbands would complain at a cold dinner," Galen says theatrically, "but not me." He gathers the plates from the table and sets them in the dishpan. "I'll read for a while," he says, "you girls keep on." Sarah kisses the top of his head and follows Rosa Lee into her room.

"What am I going to wear," Rosa Lee moans. She peers at the white dimity, sprigged with pink flowers, that she'd made herself back in Mobile. "I thought I'd wear this one, but it's too summery." She flips at the skirt with her hand. "I just don't know."

"I know," Sarah says. All day she's been thinking it, and hesitating—only she has ever worn this dress, the bottle-green dress she wore when Galen first kissed her on the lips, and then when she saw him next, wearing it again, he kissed her throat and her shoulders too before she pushed him away, blushing. Its neck is high enough to be ladylike, low enough to nudge aside. "A mermaid," he'd whispered. "All in green."

When she comes back, carrying the green dress, Rosa Lee's eyes widen. "Oh, Sarah," she says. "Are you sure?"

"I've got a baby," Sarah says, grinning, "I've already lost my mind."

When Trygve knocks on the door at just a shade before half past six, Rosa Lee answers it, wearing the mermaid-green dress, her hair swept up. Sarah, fussing purposefully in the back parlor, sees Trygve's eyes widen and his face flush underneath the tan he still carries from summer. Rosa Lee puts out her hand, and he holds it until she gently takes it away.

"Oh, Trygve," says Galen, emerging from his office as if by accident, "how nice to see you."

Trygve shakes his hand and smiles. "Doctor," he says, grinning. "Oyvind sends his greetings to you and Missus Doctor and Miss Rosa Lee. He says tell you that he's doing well." He pauses and leans closer, comically. "I'm sorry I made such a big dent in your floor." The story is easeful to him, although he's apologized to Galen before, and Galen knows that Oyvind's shoulder has completely healed. They have to talk about something besides the shy thing shimmering in this room.

Galen grins back. "Don't worry," he says. "Happens to a lot of folks."

Sarah comes forward, then, and shakes Trygve's hand. "Tell Oyvind that we're glad he's so improved," she says. "And have a lovely walk. It should be a beautiful evening. I'll have some tea for you when you get back." She hands Rosa Lee her cape, the twin of Sarah's own—thick, warm boiled wool, the heaviest capes her mother could find. Rosa Lee drapes it around her shoulders. Trygve watches the gray folds settle as if he's watching a candle-snuffer bell descend over a flame.

"Goodbye," Trygve says formally, and he opens the door and ushers Rosa Lee out ahead of him. The wind catches the edge of her skirt and flares it bright green in the light, and they are gone.

Sarah nudges the latch shut and stands for an instant with both hands on the worn brass knob, smiling. Then she feels Galen's lips on her neck, his arms around her, resting on the round lump of her belly, and she leans backwards into his warmth. "I remember that dress," he murmurs, shaping the words against her skin.

"It brought me luck," Sarah murmurs back. "I hope it'll do the same for her."

Galen kisses her neck. "Come sit down," he says, "you've been bustling around all day." He follows her to the parlor, where a fire is burning, and settles next to her on the low sofa, draping his arm across the carved back. She leans into him and he wraps his arm around her. His smell ebbs into her nose, soft: the sun-dried cotton of his shirt, a tang of iodine and chemicals, the familiar salt of his skin. She nestles into the hollow of his neck. He rests one hand on her belly and they sit quiet for a while.

"It's good that case went so well," Galen says finally. "Oyvind's shoulder."

"I know," Sarah says. "But then, it wouldn't be likely to go otherwise. You did good clean work on him. And he's young."

"That doesn't always matter," Galen says.

Sarah stiffens. "Galen," she says. "You know that's done with." The radiant, quiet warmth of his hands on her belly, of the quiet drift of time on the sofa in front of the fire, begins to leak away. Why does he have to bring this up again?

"I know," says Galen. "I just—sometimes I can't stop thinking about it."

"Remember what Dr. Pickett said?" Sarah asks. She pushes back and looks at him. "We talked about it, he talked about it with you. Remember?" Dr. Pickett had told Galen, back in his little office in Mobile, "son, there's no such thing, in medicine, as certainty. You work and learn and take care of your patients as best you can. You always take the risk. Sometimes you lose a patient. So do we all." And he had reached out and put his hand on Galen's shoulder, and Galen had sobbed. It wrenched at Sarah, this wound opening onto a place she reached for but could not heal.

"Yes," Galen says. "Yes, I know."

"I'd better get the tea started," Sarah says. She struggles up from the sofa, pretending she doesn't feel Galen's hand on her elbow. Anger leaks into the place where the warmth has been. With the baby coming, with winter coming, there is enough to worry about without one lost patient from two years ago coming back. Again. She shouts silently at him: *We need you too. I need you, now.*

My girl, rings Mama's voice, *melancholy waits for those who choose to let it in.*

Everybody got a dog inside, echoes Alvah. *You feed it, and it grows.*[1]

Why can't Galen stop hearkening to that melancholy? Stop feeding that beast, kennelled too deep in his heart for her to reach, and be with her, right now?

In the kitchen, Sarah boils water for tea and begins to gather cups and saucers. She breathes in, deeply, trying to calm the bewildering rage that has swept aside the warmth of her husband's hands, his kiss. *I'm frightened, too,* she shouts inside her head. *I'm frightened too.* Twisting on a mattress, bleeding, screaming—every picture she's ever imagined flashes behind her eyes. Four more months. Her body broken open—the dark head, pushing—

Mama's voice: *Eve's curse. It's how God blesses married people when they're married.*

She reaches for the last teacup, and it slips through her fingers and shatters on the floor. "Goddamn it!" Sarah shouts. Now there are only eleven teacups. Not the even dozen that came with them in their straw-stuffed crate from Mobile. On the trail to Iowa they'd passed a scatter of things beside the road—a chest of drawers, a horsehair armchair with deep slashes in the back and sides (*birds will find that for nests,* she'd thought, *if they haven't already*) and a crate of china just like hers. On top of the ripped-off, skewed-open lid, under the darkening sky, one teacup nested in one saucer. "Want it?" Galen had asked, nodding at the crate, "maybe we could find room," but Sarah shivered and shook her head. They rode on and left that teacup there, to fill with rain, to empty with the sun. To bleach, like bones, until some other woman came along. If any woman ever did.

Morbid. Sarah shakes her head and stoops awkwardly, gathering the pieces into her hand and dropping them in the waste bin. Then she fills the tea strainer and sets it in the pot, pouring the hot water carefully. Sugar bowl and four cups and saucers on a tray. It helps, to put even one small thing right.

The front door opens; Rosa Lee and Trygve have returned, in a rumple of capes and scuffling of boots. "Cold enough out there?" Galen asks.

"Yah," says Trygve. "I bet there's a snow coming on."

"Snow?" Galen says. "With all that warm weather just a few weeks ago?"

"Warm to you, maybe," Rosa Lee adds, and they all laugh.

"It ain't so cold," says Trygve, "once you get used to it."

Sarah enters with her tray and greets them, looking carefully at Rosa Lee, whose face is bright with cold. She catches her eye: *And?* Rosa Lee smiles: *I'll tell you later.*

"Seems like it's been too warm to snow," Trygve is telling Galen, "but Iowa ain't like Norway that way, weather changes quicker."

"This summer was so beautiful," Sarah adds. "Is it always like that?"

"This was a good summer," Trygve says judiciously, "nice and warm, a little late starting, but the wheat come in good. And the corn. Mama's vegetables done real good. She's got a lot of them put up, down cellar."

"I don't know what we would have done without her," Rosa Lee says. "Those seeds she gave us came right on. And we've got 'em all saved for next year, with the things we put up too."

"Mama likes to give vegetables away," says Trygve. "Especially when she likes people." He pauses. "And she likes you."

They sit in the parlor and drink their tea until Trygve finally stands. "Thank you for the pleasure of your company," he says formally. Sarah stifles a grin: is there a book to teach English courting language to Norwegian bachelors? "If I might call again?"

"Of course," says Rosa Lee. "Please do."

Trygve bows, and bows at Galen and Sarah, and nods again at Rosa Lee, and goes through the door and back into the night. "It'll be a cold walk back down the valley," Galen observes.

"But he won't be feeling the cold," Sarah says, grinning at Rosa Lee. "Will he?"

Rosa Lee grins too. "I reckon not," she says. "Depends how fast he walks."

Sarah follows Rosa Lee into her bedroom and sits in the little rocker while Rosa Lee takes off her cape and unbuttons the mermaid-green dress and drapes it over the foot of the bed. "I'll sponge this off tomorrow," she says.

"No bother," says Sarah. "How did he like it? You should have seen him look at you. Just like he was under a spell."

"It must have been the dress," says Rosa Lee. "It's powerful." She and Sarah giggle. "But, yes," she says, "I saw it too."

"Did he—" Sarah asks.

"He held my arm while we were walking," Rosa Lee says, "he took my hand, and it felt—" She pauses and her eyes drift to the window. "Safe. He's a good man. Likes to talk." She smiles. "He was talkin about what all he and Oyvind done to that farm, what they're gonna do this year. Plow it up all the way to the foot of the bluff in the spring. Bustin sod like no tomorrow." Her smile deepens. "If it was anybody else, I'd say he was conceited."

"He's showing off, all right," Sarah agrees. "For you." Rosa Lee nods. Galen had described his practice, his patients, and Dr. Pickett's praise to Sarah herself this way, as if to say *This is my work. This is my life. And this is all you'll never lack.* A man holds open the door of his life, Sarah realized, and lets you look through. You investigate the roof, the walls, the hesitant, warm light shining from inside. And—hoping—you follow him through that door.

Rosa Lee unties the top bow of her corset and hooks her fingers through the laces and tugs them loose, one by one. "Lord, I'm tired," she says. "Don't quite know why."

"You've got things to think about," Sarah says. She hugs Rosa Lee and climbs the stairs to her own room. Galen's asleep already, curled on his side of the mattress, the feather pillow doubled up and shoved into the crook of his neck and shoulder. Sarah undresses as quietly as she can without waking him and slides, shivering, into the circle of heat around her husband, under the layers of quilts. It is cold outside, colder than she knows: thirty degrees? Twenty? Probably even less. She lies on her back, but the baby's weight presses uncomfortably and she shifts onto her side, closing her eyes. But although her body loosens and sinks deeper into the mattress, her mind doesn't quite settle, floating, drifting.

Trygve has told Rosa Lee something important, she knows it. Something good. Even if he didn't speak it. There was no getting inside of words, sometimes, when everything inside you expanded outward into a heat and light that was just too much for your ordinary life to hold. When there was a man for you to love, and who loved you.

In the mornings just after her wedding, before Galen was up, she'd sat in their back garden in Mobile, on the little iron bench under the crape myrtle trees, with a lead pencil and a little school exercise book. Hummingbirds laced in and out of the honeysuckle. She wrote, experimentally, *My happiness at life with my dear Husband is such . . .*

My happiness. Two small words that pinned her feeling down, deflating it. That soaring in her chest wouldn't funnel down onto this page. But she should write it. How else would she remember?

When Mary Wright, the oldest girl at Miss Spofford's Academy, got married and came back for a visit, and in the school's little garden, she'd shown them all her diary. Lindy and Jane exclaimed over her sweeping silk gown, her fringed parasol, her sleek small carriage with its pair of ponies. Sarah studied her: wouldn't something show on you once you had done that thing that married people did? But Mary looked exactly the same: plump, bored, her neck still too short, her fingers stubby. But Francis had chosen her, and so she was not their classmate, Mary, anymore. It was a mystery.

"Tell us." Lindy leaned forward, eyes gleaming. "What is it like"—she arched her eyebrows—"being married?"

"Heaven!" Mary murmured back. "When he holds you . . . Remember *The Duke's Daughter?*"

"He clasped her to him," quoted Jane, giggling, "and she swooned at his inescapable mastery."

"Like that?" Lindy asked hopefully. "Oh, Mary!"

"Better," Mary said, shooting a sly look at them. "Better!" Her face turned pink and she rolled her eyes skyward and giggled. "I wrote about it, want to see? I take my diary *everywhere* now." She drew a little shagreen-bound book from her reticule and opened it to a page halfway through. It fell open there easily: *who else has she showed this to?* wondered Sarah, cynically. *But maybe she's just happy.* Envy flooded her. She forced her eyes onto the thin pale-gray pages, the color of a quail's egg, scratched over with Mary's excitable handwriting, the tails of g's and y's reaching down to tangle in the tops of the letters below. Mary lifted the book and read. "It is needless to dwell on the many and conflicting emotions of my wedding day," she intoned, "since no time can obliterate their freshness—the mixture of joy and sorrow, the pain of adieus and separation from my home and kindred, the happiness of loving and being loved, the natural and inevitable regret over a spent girlhood, the grave responsibility of the future, the fear of unworthiness, the overflowing gratitude to God for the wisdom and happiness of my choice. These and a thousand other feelings make that day one ever to be remembered."[2]

"Oh, Mary," Lindy moaned, "that's beautiful." The girls sat silently. Mary tucked the little diary back into her bag. "You are so lucky," said Jane. "Oh, that is just the most *elevated* thing I have ever heard."

"I know," admitted Mary, smoothing her skirts. "I know how fortunate I am. I believe it's the will of God. Like I wrote. *Overflowing gratitude.*"

"But what about—" Sarah asked, and stopped herself. *What about, you know, how it actually feels to—?* Shame scorched her.

Her face had been so close to Seth's in the ringing dim air of the Yankee House, ragged with cackling and cooing and the flapping of wings. *I could kiss him. He could kiss me.*

It could happen.

She had lifted her hands from the piano, the last notes of Bach melting like smoke, and knew he was behind her. She stood, and turned. Seth. His lower lip, smooth as a pillow. Sweat clinging to the line of his hair. His eyes. And a fire in her chest that flared as the minutes ticked past in the bright day beyond this wall.

Had Mary felt that, with her prim Francis in his mercantile suit? In her elegant tester bed with printed curtains where she lay back, swooning, closing her eyes, waiting for him to lift the hem of her gown and touch that place only a husband could touch, where—

"Congratulations on your happiness, Mary," Sarah stuttered, and she got up from the grass and hurried over the lawn into the house and sat in Miss Spofford's red velvet chair and reached blindly for the *Iliad* from the marble-topped table and forced her eyes over the lines, but here too was a man's body, broken and dragged bumping through the dust behind chariots, soft flesh torn, Hector's hands and arms and wide chest slashed by rocks—

"We tempt men," Mama had snorted. "They're simple creatures." But what if women could be tempted, too? By men?

After her wedding, in her own garden, she lifted her pencil to her diary page and reached for her husband, in her mind. The smooth sweating weight of his chest. Gasps, shouts as something inside her body shuddered, and he shuddered too. His long hands, unbracing to lace their fingers with hers. The sleep that dropped over her after she straightened her nightgown and nestled her back against his front. It made her want to go to him again. There was no way to name it.

"If you can't say it anywhere else," Miss Spofford had urged, pressing the small book into her hands, "you can say it here."

She turned the pencil wrong-side up, then right-side up. *I am most grateful to God for the blessing of my husband,* she wrote. *How many memories flood me when I think of . . .* But these were Mary's words, not hers. Stupid bland words big as the hulls of giant boats, too smooth and high and far away for her to climb into. She could not climb into words, onto them, and sail away, out into the space inside her right now. Where the heat, and Galen's hands, and that deep shuddering, were now. This desire. Mary's words wouldn't capture it. And she didn't know what would.

She closed the exercise book, then went upstairs and put the book in her drawer and slid into bed, again, next to her husband. For a while she thought about the little book every few days. Then a month went by, and she hadn't thought of it at all. The details of the first mornings with Galen blurred as new mornings and new nights were laid over them like leaves on a forest floor, until what was underneath started to dissolve into the ground on which she stood, every day, in one year, and then another year, of her marriage. Packing for Iowa, she stuffed the book into the bottom of her red morocco sewing box, its empty pages promising silently: *if you need me, I'll be here. If you can't tell anybody else, tell me.*

That little book is still in the bottom of her trunk, still empty. She closes her eyes and feels sleep swirling up in her, delicious and deep. She does not need to write about Galen to keep him in her mind, to keep him here with her. Surely, she does not.

Seth she will remember with no words at all.

6

Just before Thanksgiving comes the first snow in Iowa. In the morning, Sarah and Rosa Lee and Galen put on their boots and cloaks and mittens and go walking through the bright sparkle of the changed world, white and crisp. Sarah and Rosa Lee wad up snowballs and shatter them harmlessly on each other's backs, shrieking like girls. Galen tries to build a snowman, but the light powder won't hold together. "But I will make a man!" he bellows like Victor Frankenstein. He shovels the snow into a loose tower with his hands. He sets his hat on top of it, sticks a carrot about where the nose would be, and stands back to admire it. Then the snow tower collapses. "Oh, well," Sarah says, still laughing, "this isn't the last chance you'll get."

"No," Galen says. His smile flickers. "Unfortunately, it's not." He peers into the bright sky, squinting at the sun, then digs the carrot nose out of the snow and takes a bite.

How quickly this cold affects Sarah. How quickly her delight at crunching through the snow turns to a shivering desire to huddle back through her own front door, heat up the warm vegetable soup she made, settle with *Bleak House* or *David Copperfield* or *Barnaby Rudge*. She sinks into Mr. Dickens' vivacious, knowing voice as she sinks into her mattress at night, for sleep that never seems quite enough no matter whether she's had eight hours, nine, even ten. "I'm just tired these days," she apologizes to Galen, to Rosa Lee. "I don't know why."

You can't just mope, child, scolds Mama's voice inside her. *You've got to go outside.* It's true. Melancholy waits for those who let it in. So does oblivion, sleep rich with dreams. Or just soundless and deep, a space where she and her child float, alone. Like music used to feel. When was the last time she played the piano? Miss Spofford's school? Aunt Maude's house? It all seems a blur, these days. Except for the anger that burns and leaps, without warning, when she thinks of her mother.

On a sparkling day, she swathes herself in her cloak and long scarves and shawls and edges down the steps Galen has shoveled clear and steps into the trodden road that leads up into the center of the town. Her body is heavy and uncertain, but although she's frightened of falling, the stillness in the house is worse. The bright blue sky is intense, but with a forlorn quality underneath, the daylight itself aware that it won't last long. She tips her head back to the sun and closes her eyes, letting the light saturate the bright red space of her vision. This must be what it looks like to her baby: a veil of flesh made rosy with a light half-seen.

The wind sands the tip of her nose. She could freeze solid and smooth in such cold, into a woman of marble. Yet Mrs. Thorson, Mrs. Gunderson, even Mrs. Preus, the busy minister's wife, at her indoor work of prayer circles and knitting bees all day, have been roughened by the wind, not smoothed. Mama would scold: *your face is your fortune, girl.* She tucks the scarf around her face again, adjusting it so it laps high on her cheeks and leaves a slit to breathe through. Breath in a scarf makes a cold place that freezes, itself, if you stay outside long enough. And she walks on. There's really nowhere to go. Just outside.

On the low stone wall of the cemetery sits Mr. McElvain, gazing at the small cluster of stones. The single maple tree at the top of the hill, bare as a burned-out torch, flings its branches back and forth in the wind. Only the tip of the old man's nose peeks out, shiny red, from between the layers of a red knit muffler. Bessy has wrapped him up well and turned him loose, like a child. Like Sarah herself. *Just go outside, you need fresh air.*

"Hello, Mr. McElvain," Sarah says. He cranks his torso around slowly to face her. His eyes swim with tears which could be grief or could just be the bright cold day. He blinks and looks at Sarah, then turns away to stare back up the hill.

Sarah follows his gaze but sees only the low stones swathed in snow, the single bare tree. There's no stonemason in Eldorado yet, although surely that will come in time. One has to go all the way to St. Paul to get a gravestone, Sarah's been told; she hasn't been here long enough to see what happens when somebody dies.

There are no more than ten or twelve stones in this cemetery; Eldorado is just not that old a town. Who remembers the faces of the people buried here, how they stretched in a smile or crumpled in a frown? If someone loved you, are you still remembered, somehow, under the high ceiling of heaven? Shakespeare trickles into Sarah's brain: *But you shall shine more bright in these contents / than unswept stone, besmeared with sluttish time.* Surely people here came with lye rags and buckets to clean the stones as Mama always had, back in the cemetery in Alabama where that little Sarah still lay under her white stone, flush with the earth. Mrs. Olson must come to clean the stones of her small twins, pointed east into the rising sun. She would not leave those stones to be forgotten. As the little Sarah was forgotten. Not forgotten: hidden.

Mrs. Olson, unlike Mama, would not lie.

"I remember a child." The wind snatches Mr. McElvain's words out of his mouth and tumbles them like leaves up the hill. "I remember a girl." He pauses. His pale blue eyes swim with tears. He swallows, dabs at the raw pink skin around his eyes. "This wind is so cold, so hard."

Poor houseless wanderer... Only when Mr. McElvain turns to look at her does Sarah realize she's said the words aloud. "Nor rain, wind, thunder, fire, are my daughters," he intones. "I tax not you, you elements, with unkindness." He smiles at her. "But I believe, my girl, that you misquote."

"Mr. McElvain," Sarah asks, "did you have another daughter? Besides Bessy, I mean?" It is too bold a question for this old man she hardly knows, shaking in his warm knit muffler as the wind licks the edges of his coat, lifting the tips of the collar, the tails. She doesn't know why she asked it, or what truth he could possibly remember to tell.

But the old man nods. "I remember a child," he repeats. "I remember a girl." He pauses. "Maybe she was real."

Sarah's eyes prickle. She imagines Cordelia, draped over her father's arms, his grieving face lifted to the hollow ceiling of the castle that was once his. A dead child. A dead girl.

How would it feel not to remember such a loss? To teeter back and forth on the edge of a grief that might be grief, or might only be a troublesome memory? To wander in it, lost?

And to spurn your living daughter, to accuse her of thievery and ruin—

She'd rather die than come to such a state herself.

Everyone here on this hill had thought the same thing. *I'll never die. I'll never be so old.*

And yet—

How shall your houseless heads and unfed sides, your loop'd and window'd raggedness, defend you from seasons such as these?

The fugitive thought flashes across her mind: if she died in this town, and was buried here, would anyone know who she had actually been? That she had come from Alabama, not Norway? That she had loved Galen? That she had loved—

"Come along, Mr. McElvain," Sarah says, looping her hand around the old man's arm. Automatically his elbow bends and he straightens to accommodate her. "Let's not sit in this cold. It's a beautiful day, even if it is so windy. We can walk."

They tack slowly up the street, the wind belling Sarah's skirts sideways, stinging her eyes. But even so, it is good to be out here; Sarah feels a lifting of the wintry sleepiness that never quite leaves her now. *Melancholy waits for those who let it in.* They pass the school, its windows shining in the morning sun. Mrs. Linsvold opens the door of the general store to sweep a puff of dust out into the air; she looks curiously, then understandingly, at Sarah and at the old man. "Tell Bessy I said hello," she calls after them.

At the McElvains' front door, Bessy reaches for them—"come in here, you must be freezing"—and unwinds her father's muffler from around his sharp, reddened face. He stands as patiently as a child before nodding at them both and wobbling to the foot of the stairs. "I feel the need for a rest," he declares. Bessy and Sarah watch him climb to his bedroom and wait for the soft closing of the door.

"Thank you for bringing him back," Bessy sighs. "Where did you find him today?"

"On the cemetery wall," Sarah says. "Just sitting there."

"Visiting Cordelia," Bessy says. "That's what he says. When he remembers that Cordelia ever existed." At Sarah's questioning look, she nods. "My sister. I barely remember her." She leads Sarah into the parlor and they settle into two horsehair chairs before the tea table, where a pot is already steaming. An open book lies face-down on the sofa. This is a treat for Bessy, Sarah realizes, to have her father out of the house, or quieted in sleep, so she can read without listening for him. Sarah feels guilty at her own weariness of reading, the long evenings of letting her eyes skim the page, half-checking at the familiar words: *There was no possibility of going for a walk that day* . . . Bessy doesn't have anything like her opportunities to sit and read, anymore. She should be grateful, as her mother would urge. *Not everyone's so fortunate, my girl, as you.*

She sips her tea and looks around her: two carved horsehair chairs and the little sofa, three glass-fronted bookcases full of books, more in the room beyond, an elegant walnut secretary with delicate legs and a folding desk with a gold lock inset in the lid, shining from use. This room reminds Sarah of Miss Spofford's parlor, back at the Academy for Young Ladies in Mobile. Naturally: until her father began to fail so much, and Nils Erickson took over the school, Bessy had been the Miss Spofford for this town.

"It's as absorbing as a child, to care for him. At least, that's what those with children say," Bessy remarks. She looks at Sarah's shawl-draped stomach and smiles. "But you'll find this out, soon enough."

"Do you miss the school very much?" Sarah asks.

Bessy blinks and smiles, a small, hurt smile. "I do," she confesses. "But how could I teach. Now. Father showed up at the school one day calling for me. Walked right into the classroom as Jenny Johnson was reciting Keats. Walked up to me and asked if I had seen Cordelia."

Sarah shivers. Her vision of Mr. McElvain with a dead girl draped over his arms, eyes lifted like Lear's to heaven, returns to her. Bessy's hands, long and finely shaped, are worn; three deep lines curve outward from the corner of each eye. Some women get those lines from smiling, others simply from the weight of care. Bessy would be one of the latter ones. Her hair is still thick but threaded with gray under the mix of light brown and gold. *Washed out,* rings Mama's voice, pitless, factual. *Old maid.*

"I reminded him Cordelia had the whooping cough and died these twenty years ago," Bessy continues, calm, "and he started to cry. The children were so confused. I knew, then, that I would have to stay with him." Sarah nods. She's heard of old people doing all kinds of things at such an age: scorching the kettle dry on the stove; wandering outside, confusing the night with the day; allowing pet cats to breed until the house was rank with battling toms. "It's a good thing Nils was available, and willing," Bessy continues. "The children adore him." She refills Sarah's teacup and tips the last of the tea, including the dregs, into her own.

"But I know they remember you," Sarah assures. "You could always go back to teaching. Someday. They'll send Nils on to a church somewhere, that's why he's here."

Bessy smiles. "Maybe," she says. Through the ceiling, they hear the rustling, faint as an owl in the rafters of a barn, as the old man stirs in his midday sleep.

౬

When Sarah walks back past the school, the children have been released for recess. Shouting, they dart and plunge through the snow, shattering the blue shadows at the edges of the schoolyard. Nils perches on the steps with the red Athenaeum volume in his hand. "Anders!" he calls. "Remember the golden rule, Anders!" The smallest Olson boy, stalking his brother with a handful of snow to shove down his collar, straightens, blinks, and, with elaborate unconcern, molds the snow into a ball and tosses it in the air.

Sarah grins. Nils sets his book on the schoolhouse steps and stands. "I find," he observes, coming to lean on the gate, "that children can govern themselves. With a little help, no?" His smile widens. "No more than anyone needs."

Bessy is right: the children would be fond of Nils. Atop his thin neck, his round face is as open as one of theirs, his smile as bright, with a sneaking wit below that makes Sarah smile too: he can't be any older than twenty-two, which makes him younger than Sarah herself. He's as tall and thin as Mr. Irving's Ichabod Crane, with thick round spectacles in gold frames that grip his long nose. Resting on the schoolyard gate, his bony-knuckled hand is large, his wrist wiry and strong. A blue anchor—inked directly into the skin, Sarah realizes, she's never seen such a thing before—floats below the knob of his wrist, in the gap between his coat sleeve and his glove.

Nils sees her looking. "From my sailing days," he says.

"Sailing?" Sarah asks. She tries to keep the skepticism out of her eyes: this pale thin boy with his thick spectacles, sailing?

"Well," Nils confesses, "I call them sailing days, anyway. My village, Haugesund, is just a little place, a little port right by the ocean, and from when I was a boy I wanted to sail. But—" he gestures at himself comically, ruefully—"I'm not much for sailing. I learn languages, I read. My father is a minister and so he tells me I can still be useful, I can go on ships as pastor. I can have church for sailors, at the dock. And I went on a voyage, once. Fishing sloop to Iceland. One night there was a storm, and the cabin boy was terrified. I prayed with him. We turned back, the storm was just too bad, and when we came back in sight of shore and I saw his eyes. I saw that he was . . . different. And I thought—" He wrings his hands in the air, stricken shy. "This is what my life should be. There are so many big wilderness in the world. Compared to this, Norway is all settled. I want to travel where they need me. So." He smiles. "My father tells me the church is building a seminary here to minister to our people here, our settlers, in English, and I can be a pastor in the new country. I come here and study and I like it here, and then they need me for the school. So I am a teacher who will be a pastor. But I hope—" He blushes. "I hope Miss McElvain will be able to return. She loves her teaching so. I see it when I first arrive. The children, they are good children. And they miss her."

"I think you're right," Sarah says. "She misses them too."

"Martin Luther, he wrote that we serve God where we are," Nils says, "in our stations in life where He has chosen to place us. But I believe those places can change even as they keep us serving God. I believe we are not always in the same place. Miss McElvain's father, he needs her. But—" He looks at his shoes. Sarah knows what he's thinking: her father is an old man. Soon, Bessy will be free. And what then?

After Nils has smiled and turned to ring the bell and call the children in, after Sarah has returned to her house and hung her cloak on its hook by the door, she thinks of Nils' words. Of Mama's familiar saying: *Man proposes, God disposes.* Anger returns, sudden and bewildering. Oh, certainly, Mama. It must be God's plan for Bessy McElvain to wear out what's left of her youth and energy on a father who can't keep fixed in his mind who she even is. It must be God's plan for Sarah herself to lose her first child before the third month, then to follow Galen to Eldorado and give birth to the second child in a strange land.

God's plan: Alvah's slow wasting, her brown skin fading to gray. Mama lifting Alvah in bed to rub her back with the special cocoa-butter unguent from New Orleans. Rosa Lee murmuring to her at night in their small room, words Sarah was not meant to hear: "he'll come back someday, Mama, gonna try his luck in California first."

Rosa Lee would have gone to Seth, after Alvah died, if Seth had been somewhere it was safe for her to follow him.

California was as far as you could get from Alabama without falling off the edge of the world. A sickle-shaped slice of land on a map, an Eden of a place, violent and seductive, with gold trickling from the earth and men planting knives in each others' backs. The Spaniards who first came to the South had looked for this; so had the French with their Vine and Olive Company settling Mobile. Seth would never have let Rosa Lee follow him to California until he had made a safe place for them both. Somewhere, Seth was working on that plan, right now. But where?

God's plan. Seth made plans too. *Man proposes, God—*

Sarah shakes herself upright and goes out to gather laundry from the line. The shirts and skirts and trousers have frozen, damp-dry, and she stacks them under her arm in flat sheets and totes them into the house, rigid as unwilling children. In front of the stove, she sets the ironing-cloth on the table, sets the flatiron to heat, and once it sizzles at a damp finger-touch, begins smoothing it back and forth on the damp fabric. Under her hands the clothes hiss and go limp, then dry in upward clouds of steam. *Like departing souls.* How fanciful. How foolish.

Sarah lays one of Galen's shirts flat, hooking the corner of the table into the shoulder and tugging the button-placket straight. The iron noses against each buttonhole, smoothing, smoothing. "Don't worry about ironing my shirts," Galen always tells her, "it's a Sisyphean task." Then he pauses, quirks his mouth up at the corner, then down. "Like housework in general, I reckon. Like medicine." On a good day, he'll laugh at his own rueful joke. Lately, he just looks down and frowns, then turns away.

But she'll make this effort no matter how quickly Galen's shirts get rumpled or stained or even, once, burned with the tip of the nail he uses to cauterize the places where he snips warts away. It's dangerous to send a man loose into the world without the mark of your care on him. Other women will look at him and wonder whether you're doing all you should be doing to keep him fed and clothed and loved. *Poor thing*, they'll murmur as he passes. *Looks just like a scarecrow. No telling what she does with her time.* And if he sees pity in enough people's eyes, he'll start to wonder this himself.

Bad wife. Bad woman. Bad girl.

Sarah's thoughts roam back and forth over the iron. Nils smiled so secretly, turned so red at Bessy's name. Does he fancy her? Maybe when her father dies, he'll—Mr. McElvain is so old. Old people can endure; they're used to it. But everybody has to die, sometime. Mr. McElvain is older, even, than Aunt Maude in Mobile.

❧

"You needn't think I'll leave you with this house before my time," Aunt Maude had declared to Mama, sipping tea in the parlor, Sarah and Jane bracing their feet to keep from sliding off the horsehair chairs. "You're my only living relative, as you know. But I'm living, too."

But then Aunt Maude went to bed with her last illness, and she didn't get up.

"Girls, go say goodbye," Mama had murmured. Despite all the times Aunt Maude had joshed her—"I'm still alive, Livia!" she'd announce at breakfast—her face was damp, her handkerchief crumpled in her hand. "Aunt Maude has been very good to us, and it's a comfort to her to know how grateful we are. And to see you girls, just before she goes."

So Sarah went into Aunt Maude's bedroom, alone. It was dim and cool in there, although it was bright May outside, beginning to warm and steam with the heat of summer. The heavy silk draperies sagged together over the high windows, cutting out most of the light. On top of the heavy mahogany dresser hunched Aunt Maude's jewelry case, the size of a large hatbox, with a gold lock. A small lantern glowed on the side table; Aunt Maude's maid Hattie kept it there, burning all night, as if Aunt Maude were afraid of the dark. Maybe she was.

"Shut that door," Aunt Maude said. Sarah pushed it almost closed, with a crack in case she needed to call for help. Silly. She was twenty-three years old then, a grown woman. But there was something scary about the short plump body in the high tester bed with its ivory rosettes of silk in the canopy, something sad about the high white bun of hair flattened at the back from lying on the pillow, about the bright filmy brown eyes sunk deep in the skull, something odd about the small hands resting on the coverlet. Something scary, like Bad Katy Pruitt's mama's hands, roaming and grasping.

"So," Aunt Maude rasped, "you've come to say goodbye."

"Yes," Sarah admitted. Aunt Maude could always tell when you were fibbing, even if you were fibbing for a good reason.

"It's only proper," Aunt Maude observed. "Respect." She sighed. "I know it's commonplace to belabor the ingratitude of your relatives at such a time, but I've got to say, you girls and your mother have"—she coughed, her face reddening—"been good companions. And you never asked for more than your share. Unlike some."

Sarah looked down at Aunt Maude's hands, lying loosely on the coverlet. A pale small finger with its own little nail jutted out from the side of her wrist, below the heel of her hand. It jumped, just slightly, up and down, as Aunt Maude's heart beat: *too fast*, Mama had worried. *She's always had too much blood.* Extra fingers. Sarah has heard of such things but never seen them. Aunt Maude has always worn gloves, even in the house. But dying must make her reckless; why, now, would she care what anyone thought?

"Yes," Maude continued, "you've been good girls, all three of you. And I'm not unaware of how you have suffered, with the loss of Ned and your home. So I am leaving your mother this house, which she knows and has, admirably, not belabored, and I want you girls to pick out something from my jewelry chest. You've been good." With another cough she fumbled between her breasts, under the foamy ruffled nightgown, and drew out a tiny gold key on a dirty string. "Your faces are your fortunes. And nothing sets off a pretty face like good jewelry." Aunt Maude spread both hands on the coverlet. The little spare fingers twitched. "Take this key, child, and open the chest."

Sarah took the small gold key between her fingers, flinching at its slippery warmth, and walked to the big chest on the dresser. The lock was stiff; she had to turn the key back and forth several times before the small tumblers gave and she raised the lid. Inside it was lined with purple velvet, the nap worn a smooth paler purple where these pieces had been lying for years. Trays held rings topheavy with rubies, big moonstone pendants, brooches, a diamond collar. But the jewels lay tangled together, as if Maude had just tossed them in there, tired, after a party.

Sarah tugged open the bottom drawer of the chest, breathing in the old velvet's musty smell. She saw an envelope in her own childish handwriting tucked into the bottom: her letter of thanks, she realized, for Lucinda Victoria, the doll. Draped over and tangled in a nest of old bracelets and brooches was a slender rope of pale ivory-gray pearls, narrow at the top near the clasp, larger at the bottom.

"What have you got there?" Aunt Maude called, craning up from her pillows. "Bring it over here. All of it."

Sarah nudged the bottom drawer shut and lifted the heavy chest in both arms, walked carefully to the bed, and set it on the silk coverlet. Then she tilted it backwards, just a little, until she could open the chest's drawer again. The pearls lay tangled, shining quietly. "There," Aunt Maude said with satisfaction. "That's just what I thought of for you. My own debutante pearls. You'll be wanting them in a few months."

"I haven't thought of it," Sarah said, truthfully. She dreaded the debutante balls, dreaded the dress fittings and the stares and the whispers. *That colored boy. That scandalous girl.*

"You'd better start," declared Aunt Maude. "Most important time for a girl. Of course, you're a little old to be a debutante. But that can be blamed on the war." She coughed, and her six-fingered hands picked at the heap of jewelry in the drawer until they disentangled the pearls and held them out. "Here," she rasped. "Come here, child."

Sarah bent her head and Aunt Maude clasped the pearls nimbly together at the back of her neck. The vestigial thumbs brushed her skin, and Sarah flinched. She straightened and felt the pearls drop against her collarbones, light and definite. "Beautiful," Aunt Maude proclaimed, "just right for a young girl's complexion. Old women like me should wear diamonds. Not pearls."

"You'll be wearing your diamonds again any day now," Sarah said obediently.

Aunt Maude laughed, then coughed. "Not I," she said. "Go look at them."

Sarah crossed to the mirror. The graduated weight of the pearls did make them pool prettily at the base of her neck. They were pretty things. But their weight felt cold.

"Pearls need to be worn," Aunt Maude continued. "They need to touch skin to stay lustrous, I don't know why."

Sarah came back to the bed and bent to kiss the old woman's forehead, sticky with sweat and powder, strangely chilled. "Thank you, Aunt Maude," she said.

Aunt Maude looked up, straight into her eyes. She reached up with her chilly plump six-fingered hands and gripped Sarah's wrists. "You know you were the first child I ever held, ever really saw and talked to?" she asked. "Do you know that? I held you, when you were but a baby. The only one. The only one." Then she smiled, lay back, and closed her eyes. "Go on," she said, "and tell your sister to come up."

In another month Aunt Maude had died and Mama had inherited the house on the quiet street in Mobile and the seamstresses had begun circling around to fit Sarah for her white debutante gown. And in another year Sarah had married Galen. And in another two years beyond that, Aunt Maude's pearls, along with Galen's wedding diamonds, had gone to the jeweler's shop. She had set them on the counter and looked her husband in the eye. "I don't mind," she'd said. "We'll need the money out there."

It is hard to believe, sometimes, that she has ever owned the pearls, or the diamonds. When she goes for weeks, now, wearing nothing but her sturdy homespun skirt and muslin blouse under layers of shawls, when she labors to knit up a sweater for the baby rather than to net a fichu of lace to wear over a morning gown. When she walks around town in two layers of socks and Dr. Foster's old boots. But she would not take those pearls back, now, if she could.

The past and the present seem to hook together this way, more and more, these days.

West and west again, Sarah had slipped away with Galen and with Rosa Lee, to Eldorado, Iowa. To anywhere, to make the voices stop. But the voices wouldn't stop. They never had.

꙰

In Mobile, the neighbors whispered. *What's the matter with that oldest girl? Pretty child, seems smart enough, but I've never heard her talk. Maybe she's dumb, poor thing.* And then an answering whisper always came: *You know, they say that she and a colored boy* . . . In Miss Spofford's classroom, Sarah gripped the book with both hands and stared at the page: *Elle dit que . . . Elle ne peut pas dire que . . . Elle ne dira pas que . . .* [3] "Sarah"—Miss Spofford's voice floated over her head, heard from the bottom of a gray-green well—"recite, please." And out of her own throat, out of that depth, nothing would come.

Seth was gone. Fairibault was gone. Neither one would come back. That was all there was to say or to know, in the whole world: a fact crushing her underneath its indifferent weight, and she without even the words to name it.

To open her mouth now was to open a door into that place again, where the silence clutched itself tight inside her. Too tight for her to sleep and rest, or to eat. "Sarah, child," Alvah said, "you know you love my biscuits, now why don't you put a little slice of ham on here, and make you one with honey too?" She had taken a bite obediently—*just flour and lard, just smoky flesh*, wondered her brain distantly, *how had anyone ever decided this was food?*— and smiled at Alvah to see her face relax. So many times she had opened her mouth to say to Alvah, *it isn't true.* Or, *it wasn't like they say.* Or, *please tell me where he is.* And she never had. A warning silence gripped the roots of her tongue, ready to pull it out for good. Worse than anything was the thought that Alvah might be taken in by Mama's lie, and might lie to Sarah, too.

Under Miss Spofford's worried eyes she huddled over her books, turning and turning the pen in her fingers. All the other girls around her scribbled busily, paper curling gently in the wake of their words like soil behind a plough. She wrote one word, another word, and stopped. She loosened her grip on the pen, lifted her hand to her mouth, bit her fingernails. Edge to center. Head craned sideways, she let herself get taken by the little red bursts of pain. Suddenly Miss Spofford was behind her, one hand on her shoulder. "Try this conjugation," she suggested, touching the back of Sarah's bitten hand with her fingertips. "Etre. Etre." Obediently Sarah wrote over the red sprinkles soaked into the paper: To be. To be.

"Women's lives, Sarah," Miss Spofford said, later, "are deformed enough by stories. No need to give a lie more power than it needs to have." Sarah blinked, could not answer her teacher, could not look into those kind worried eyes. *I'm too far down. I can't reach your hands. I can't grab on. Leave me here.*

At twenty-three, she stood in a line of younger girls in white dresses on the raised platform in the St. Athenasius Hall and blinked at a gaslit sea of faces raised to look at her. The mamas simpered, the young men smirked. Or they simply stared. A young man or two, or maybe three, folded her gloved hand into his and set the other hand on her corseted waist and turned her in circles as the music sawed and sawed away. Mama and Alvah had laced her corset ("you're so thin," Mama mused, "we really needn't bother, but a man can tell if you go without, and if you do, he'll think you belong down on Rue Doloreaux") and twirled her like this in front of the mirror. "Turn around, let me see, you look beautiful. That hem even in back? Hand me a pin." They uncrimped her curls from the papers, let them fall: "And your hair can hold the curl, God knows, unlike your sister's. We need to put some lemon juice on it, set you in the sun, it's gotten so dull this year." Sarah let their hands nudge and move her, sweep each curl up onto her head, let the young men turn her in stiff circles, curtsied to them as they bowed and turned her loose. Next to Mama, Jane pouted, her thoughts plain on her face: Felix Dalton had already come around to call on her, and she didn't see why she had to wait on old skinny Sarah to get married, why did she always have to be second, ever since they were little. From the platform Sarah could see Mama whispering: "Hush, just give your sister one more chance."

That winter Sarah began attending the Euterpean Society musical evenings in Miss Spofford's parlor. And there, on a January night, Galen saw her.

"It was during the Bach," he said, "that Mr. Eckhart was playing, remember? You looked so sad. And I wondered why."

She had told him, gradually. But in the short dark days of winter, it came to her again. All of it. Especially the parts that Galen did not know.

7

The war meant life without Johnny and without Father. Without anyone but Mama and Alvah and Jane and Seth and Rosa Lee in the house that only grew taller, thinner, more rickety and forlorn.

She can begin the story anywhere. All the pictures lead to the same place.

"Every bit of this would have been different," said Mama bitterly, "if your father had had enough sense to leave at least part of the Fairibault money in dollars. Not this Confederate trash." She wadded it up and flung it onto the floor, where she stepped on it as she paced. When she got like this, Sarah and Jane wanted to leave, but they couldn't, because she would only snatch them back to sit again on the slick horsehair chair and the low needlepointed footstool she had made when she was a young lady. "My girls," Mama keened, "I need my girls around me. To help me gather my resources. Oh, if only your father . . . ."

This sentence ended variously, depending on the day. If only your father had had more ambition. Had been more attentive to his rich uncle Edward. Had not been content with a hundred acres of cotton and birddogs and horses and Thucydides. Never did her mother say what all three of them were thinking: if only your father hadn't—

Yes, Sarah railed to herself, *that made quite a bit of trouble, didn't it? That was a decision with some consequences.*

But when she felt this expression cross her face, she wiped it off. No one else must see it.

Actions have consequences, Mama and Father always said. And what was around Fairibault, then, was nothing but consequences, results of actions by people and in places too far away to fathom: Mr. Lee, Mr. Grant, Mr. Lincoln, Mr. Calhoun. Fort Sumter. Manassas, Gettysburg, Vicksburg, and now, last year, Appamattox Courthouse. The war had blown around them like a summer tornado, receding and then touching down. Johnny's death. The slow pinch of worn-out clothes and worn-out shoes and hunger. Maybe this was God's doing too. Mama didn't talk too much about God, didn't make a stir on Sunday mornings anymore to go to the little church at Rehobeth. The house had escaped, and Job, one of the two old mules, and some chickens. Mama strode around the house and barn, carrying the pistol from the bottom of the big cherrywood gun cabinet, whose key dangled from a string around her neck. She watched Seth more narrowly these days, fingering the spot where the key lay under her dress, against her skin.

"Think of it this way, Mama," blurted Jane sarcastically in the parlor one day. "Had Father more ambition, we'd have lost more than we did."

Mama would smack her, surely. But instead, Mama turned, considered her, and laughed. "Well," she said, "another county heard from. When did you get so bold?" Jane grinned, and Mama grinned back. She continued pacing. "At least they haven't run away," she said. "And not likely to."

They were Alvah and Seth and Rosa Lee. Sarah had heard the rumors too, clashing like swords. One, the Yankee soldiers would take any slave who asked back to the North with them. Two, the Yankee soldiers would hurt and kill anybody they ran across. Especially women, white or black.

Mama had explained this in the parlor, too. "When you see a soldier, especially a Yankee," she hissed, "you've always, always got to run and hide. They know no decency, no mercy, and they hurt a woman in a way she never recovers from even if she does not have the luck to die. I pray to Jesus you girls never look on such a fate. You promise me"—and she gripped them tightly—"you promise me you run and hide the second you ever see a Yankee soldier, ever." Alvah must have heard these rumors too, because flickers of fear crossed her face when she looked at Rosa Lee. And at Seth.

One morning, early, slipping back into the house from the privy, Sarah was arrested by the sound of Seth's voice through the open cookhouse window. "But Mama," he said, "what if all that's just a lie?"

"Where would we go?" Alvah's voice stung. "You tell me that."

Sarah slipped away, stunned. What if Alvah and Rosa Lee and Seth joined that rumored throng, *all the colored going North?* What if, like Celia, they just disappeared? If Alvah and Rosa Lee and Seth could walk away, then everything was a lie, and always had been. Including home. Including love. Including the touch of Alvah's hands tucking Sarah into bed, including her smile and her voice as she came out to see them sitting on the mules, in the yard: *y'all have a good time?* If Alvah, like Mama, concealed and half-told and even lied—*you and Jane had a little cousin—I know you won't do what grown men and women do until you get married*—then nothing was real at all.

"They're perfectly happy," Mama snorted. "And anyway, without us, where would they be? Look at the ones I saw last week, on the road. Just wandering. If we turn out Alvah and the children, where do they go?"

"Nowhere, Mama," said Jane. "We've got to take care of them. It's our responsibility."

People had always asked Father, "I don't understand it, Ned. How do you keep that place, with just those few men and those women?"

Well, Sarah thought, *we didn't. That's the answer. We didn't.*

When Grandfather got it from the Cherokees, Fairibault was one thousand acres. When their father died, it was less than five hundred, including the house, the woods, and the flat bottomland by the river with the cotton picked by Mr. Wainwright's rented people. Eventually, all but Alvah and her children were gone. "I'm going to give them papers," Father said to himself in the library late one night, with Sarah reading in the opposite chair, "give them their papers and let them go where they will." But he never had. No point in doing so, then, Sarah's defended him in her mind. The fields going fallow and the war deepening and Johnny gone. It wasn't given to girls to know the details of such things. But if Father had not freed them it must have been for the right reasons.

But then Father—

It is burned into Sarah's mind in a single picture:

Late in the first year of the war, after the letter about Johnny's death. Heat, white and still as a dream. The light in the sky is heavy, platinum and strange. In the wind, the leaves on the big oak turn silvery bellies to the sky. "Storm's coming," Alvah murmurs. And from the barn: a single shot.

The echo rings and dies. They run. Seth gets there first. He stops at the door, his body still flung forward into that dark space. He pulls himself out and turns around. Mama is right behind him. "Miss," he stumbles, "Miss, you oughtn't see."

"I'll see, I will," Mama says. "Move, Seth."

Still he pauses. "Move, boy," Mama growls. "Let me see him."

And she is into that dark open door too. Her cry through that door, then, is a dark black hole of a wail. A dark open door through which anything might writhe into the light.

"Y'all come on," Seth mumbles to her and Rosa Lee and Jane. They follow him around the other side of the barn and back to the house.

It must be Seth who goes to the Acres two miles west and gets Mr. Hopewell, who must get Mr. Wainwright and Mr. Mott, because soon there they all are, galloping to the barn. "Sit back down, honey," says Alvah. Her hands smooth Sarah's hair, then Jane's, behind their ears. Her fingers shake. "See now, look at these wild plums Rosa Lee found, what a treat . . . One at a time, real slow, now." Alvah won't tell her what's really happening. Alvah is soothing her as if she is so much younger than her actual fifteen years. Alvah isn't looking at her because she doesn't want to break a question loose in Sarah, doesn't want to wake the sound of that shot in the air again. Nobody looks down the lane at the barn. "A treat," Alvah repeats. "Why don't y'all be good girls and just set right here. Set right down here and stay."

Sarah cranes her neck. Their long wagon with Mr. Mott's horse hitched to it trundles away down the drive with a ragged cloth fluttering out the back. That's the old horse blanket that's always thrown over the stall door. It's covering something lying still in the back of the wagon. The horses are trotting quietly, not galloping anymore. Mr. Wainwright follows on his own horse, fast little Jim. Where is Seth?

Out in the yard the pump goes *chunk, chunk, splash.* The cook-house door bangs and here is Mama. Her hair stands up all fuzzy from its bun, with a big chunk hanging down. Mama's eyes are bright white and dry. Sarah can't look at Mama. Can't touch her.

Where is Mama's dress? She's walked all the way up from the barn in her shimmy and her petticoat, or she has just taken off that dress right out in the yard, where anyone can see—

Down Mama's front there's a wet place, a big pink stain. Her petticoat hem is wet and red. Her hands are still dripping wet from the pump. She swoops them over her head and all the frazzly little hairs smash right down. "Alvah." Her voice is low and crackly. "Alvah, I need a tub." And Alvah takes her hand away from Sarah's hair and turns to set the big kettle on, then the little one. Then out into the yard for a bucket.

Through the door, Sarah watches. Old Tod the setter sidles up to Alvah, dragging a long rope of brown cloth, dark and sticky, in the dirt. Wagging his tail.

Alvah gasps, then moves between the door and Tod so Sarah can't see. She gathers up the long cloth thing and stuffs it in her bucket and smacks Tod on the head and hisses at him and he yowls away across the yard. Alvah plops the bucket under the pump and sluices water over it and flings the water out again. It's reddish-brownish-clear, like tea.

"Mama," Jane's whimpering, "Mama," so Sarah and Rosa Lee haul her off the chair and run behind her across the yard and up the stairs to Mama's room where Mama sits stark naked in her dry tin tub in the center of the carpet. Bony knees drawn up, arms looped around them, hands clasped. Just waiting. "Mama." Jane runs right to her, but Mama's just sitting there. Her eyes are open. "Mama, Mama." They reach out one by one, even Rosa Lee, and pet her hair down flat like Alvah pets theirs and whisper to her, "Mama, it's me, look at me," but Mama doesn't look at anything at all.

Outside the leaves rustle and shout and the wind comes up and the rain comes down.

Father is dead. This is where the picture usually ends.

❧

Sarah sits under the skirt of the big magnolia tree. Inside her head is only a blank white place with no words in it. It hurts although there is also no way to make the words come to fill it up.

Seth ducks under the cover of branches with *Nicholas Nickleby* in his hand. Sitting on an opposite branch, he opens the book and begins to read aloud.

There once lived in a sequestered part of the county of Devonshire, one Mr. Godfrey Nickleby, a worthy gentleman, who taking it into his head rather late in life that he must get married, and not being young enough or rich enough to aspire to the hand of a lady of fortune, had wedded an old flame out of mere attachment, who in her turn had taken him for the same reason: thus two people who cannot afford to play cards for money, sometimes sit down to a quiet game for love.

Seth keeps his eyes fixed on the page and reads, in a low, clear voice. He does not look to see that she is crying, although surely he can hear.

Nobody in Mobile ever asks how they survived at Fairibault until they came to live in Aunt Maude's house. No need for anyone to dig up the bones of those days. Sarah, Jane, Mama, Rosa Lee, and Alvah came to the city to live as ladies and ladies' servants. That's all anyone needs to know.

And Seth escaped to live on his own, somewhere else. No one needs to know exactly where. Aside from Rosa Lee and Alvah, no one does.

How had they all survived?

A picture rises to the grasping fingers of Sarah's memory: the glass jars crowded with dried black beans, on the shelf of the cookhouse pantry, on the shelf of Alvah's own cabin. The Indian beans. A trip up the hill to the campsite, Sarah and Jane trailing behind Rosa Lee and Alvah, each with a basket and a flour sack. The sun toasting the triangle of bare neck between Sarah's braids and her collar, the hum of grasshoppers, long weeds scratching her legs and snagging her hem as she trudged toward the edge of the woods. Ahead of her, Alvah climbing the path through the trees. "Y'all need to keep up," she called, "snakes hear us comin and get out the way."

How long ago was it that Indians had really lived here in this camp? They were here when Grandfather got ahold of it. And the government had helped him and Father move them off the land, although Father wouldn't tell Sarah exactly how this had been done. Twenty years before her birth, fifteen? But although the cleared campsite had grown back in scrub pines and high grass, she could still tell where it had been, could still see the trodden trace of a footpath down the side of the hill to the stream below, could still see the line where the big trees hesitated, not quite ready to reclaim the circle of space. Shallow bowls of campfire sites in the dirt. The edge of a quartz arrowhead glinting from the dirt. The grinding stones at the edge of the clearing, where Sarah and Jane and Rosa Lee had left them to play with. The lines and circles where other people had written on this land. Above the saplings and grass, a clear blue ring of sky.

And, in a still-sunny spot at the edge of camp, the garden. For years now Alvah had collected seeds from the beans and squash and melons that the Indians had left behind. In Alvah's own patch, they grew on frames of wood scraps, in neat hills and rows, weeded and hoed. Here they sprawled in tangles through the grass, their wide leaves shockingly domestic in these woods, their fruit mealy-pale on the bottom where it rested in the grass; Alvah's own squash and melons were evenly ripe all over, since she turned them every night. No Indians were left to harvest this garden anymore. Of all the people who had ever lived on this land, only Sarah and Seth and Mama and Rosa Lee and Jane remained.

"Y'all help me pick," Alvah sighed, dropping her basket in the high grass. "Got a lot to do once we get back down there." She bent to the hard orange-and-green squash; a waxy *thump, thump, thump* came to Sarah's ears as the pile in the basket got higher and the grass flattened under its weight. Her hands moved among the tangles of vines and vegetables sprouting from each others' shriveled, sunken hearts. Rosa Lee struggled to wrench a huge squash off its vine. Sarah started on the bean vines that had tangled up the trunk of one tree and over to the next one. Some pods had dried light brown and rattled to pieces as she twisted them into her sack, scattering the small black beans against the cloth; some pods were still moist and plump, dark green with a blush of black and pink under their skin.

Seth would eat these beans, too. She would help to feed him, and to feed them all. A timid image of his body came to her. Food makes flesh, makes bodies out of what had passed through someone else's hands. A funny thing. Or, depending on who the people were, a loving one.

Love. How to know what that even might be. Was it the way the image of him hovered in her mind, close and distant, how the feeling of the single time she had reached out to hold him still lingered on the skin inside her arms. How it was like she was looking at him even when her eyes were turned away.

Without asking she knew she could not make any indication of this. If she touched this picture in her head—like touching a finger to the surface of a pond—it would shatter. *Forwardness*. It was unwomanly. It was a sin.

It was an in-between feeling, for a waiting time.

How had they survived?

The Indian camp gave them squash and beans and melons every year to eat from the top of the hill and the garden patches behind the house, then replant, the seeds scattered on cloths in the sun to dry and then saved in envelopes from Mama's old letters and Father's old bills. The girls picked blackberries from the tangled fencerows and mulberries from the trees full of shrieking crows. "Y'all go on," Jane hollered back at them. "These are *ours*." Mama and Alvah shared okra, tomatoes, corn, potatoes. There were the jagged, bitter leaves of dandelions and the pecans that fell crackling into the leaves each fall, the wild shoats Seth trapped, squealing and lunging, by the legs—

And Seth's trap gave them the possum.

Only once were they hungry enough for that. The six of them were beginning their third week without meat, Seth's snares and slingshots empty on a spell of bad luck. But there were wood scraps to build a cage he rigged with a piece of string and baited with a rotting Indian-camp melon. And so, one morning, there was a possum: an old fat one with grimy-white fur and a ratlike tail that slithered against the bars. It blinked in the light when Seth dragged the cage out of the bushes around the garbage pile. Normally possums played dead. This one looked them right in the eye, one by one, curled its pink claws into fists, and snarled.

They stood around the cage, staring down. Sarah could feel everyone thinking the same thing she was: *we're hungry . . . but.*

The possum peered into Mama's face, and spat.

"We've got to cleanse him," Alvah insisted, her face horrified. "Y'all *know* what he's been eatin."

So for another week—"normally you go six," Alvah worried, "but we've got to have meat"—they dropped melon rinds and cornbread chunks and collard-leaf ribs into the possum's cage. He snouted up the scraps, shoving them in with his little pink hands and licking his teeth. "What should we name him?" Jane asked.

"You don't name somethin fore you eat it," Alvah observed, "if you still want to eat it."

Finally, Seth went out to the yard and came back with the dead possum dangling upside down by the tail. With the big knife he slit the belly skin and peeled it back. "Euuuhhhh," Jane and Rosa Lee groaned, squinching up their faces, but Sarah watched the skin peel back in layers, over the meat they would soon roast in a stove stoked as hot as it could go. She watched the delicate veins and cords roping along the undersides of Seth's arms. His hands were as big as a man's. "Big as your daddy," Alvah often said to him, proudly. "Lord, if he could see you."

She was sixteen and a half. Seth was eighteen. Technically, he was a man.

And it felt different to look at him than when they were children, swimming in the lake in their undershifts, balancing on the backs of the mules. She turned away, reluctantly, when he approached the pump and unbuttoned his shirt and sloshed the water over the long planes of his shoulders and back. She was not supposed to look at him, was not supposed to feel the back of her neck and her scalp tingle, alert, when he was close by, was not supposed to feel her face get helplessly warm. *Women tempt men. Our inheritance from our first mother.* Seth was a colored boy. Some danger lurked here, for both of them; if it broke loose, it would be all her fault. But what if the tempting wasn't something anybody did? What if the tempting simply *was*?

❧

On a baking-hot August day, Sarah and Jane and Rosa Lee went swishing through the brush at the edge of the woods behind Mama and Alvah, wrapped in long shawls and sleeves. "Now there's a reason why I made y'all bundle up," Mama warned. "My little cousin Eustace got bit by a swarm of bees and swelled up twice his size and never did come back to himself, completely. Lived in his mama's house the rest of his days." Seth, walking ahead of all of them, wore an old coat that had been his father's and carried a bundle of damp crumbly wood under his arm. He was the man, and bee-robbing was now his job. Soon all of them heard the swarming, an intent busy whirring of wings. Sarah could see them in the flickers of sunlight through the trees: one tiny circling dot, then another and another and another. And then she spotted the tree itself, a big rotten pine snag leaning at an angle to the ground, with a shifting, golden mass of bees rippling over the bark around one wide gash about halfway up the trunk. The hum in the air was the exact temperature and noise of the thoughts in her head, just before sleep, when they sped up ready to tip her directly into dreams. She'd never seen so many of one living creature.

"Okay, y'all," Seth called back, "get ready." He pulled a pair of gloves from his pocket and drew them on, then tightened pieces of twine around his pants legs and his jacket sleeves. Alvah handed him two tin pails. "Be ready," he warned, "to come in and drag me out."

"We'll come get you, son," Alvah reassured. "But you know they're not gonna hurt you. That's what you have to go in there thinking about. Remember?"

Seth nodded and struck a match, lighting one of the chunks of old wood till it smoked. The smoke grew thicker as he hoisted the torch in the air and approached the bee tree. "Calms 'em right down," Alvah whispered, "his daddy did it the exact same way."

"I hope Seth doesn't end up like Mama's cousin," Jane observed. Sarah shushed her and Rosa Lee pinched her and Jane subsided. Even she had the sense not to howl. Who knew what a sudden noise would do to bees?

Seth brandished the smoking chunk of wood, approaching the tree. The wriggling mass of bees on the trunk softened and scattered and began to drop bee by bee into the grass. "Look at that," Mama marveled. "Just like they're drunk."

"They are," Alvah smiled, a crack in her worried expression. "Something like it."

Seth stood still, letting the smoke seep into and around the hole in the tree. Then he tugged his coat sleeve further down toward his wrist, straightened his glove, and reached into the hole, brushing past the last few lazy, circling bees around its mouth. Carefully, he drew his hand back out. Dripping from his fist was a chunk of waxy honeycomb he dropped in the tin bucket at his feet. Then he reached for more. It was as dark as the cherrywood table in the dining room. Soon Seth was walking back toward them with a bucket of honey, stubbing out his torch in the dirt. Alvah reached for him and held him close for a long time, letting all her worry out in one big squeeze. "Not even one sting," she marveled, pushing him away to arm's length. "Taking on the hive of wild bees. Just like Samson in the Bible."

"It ain't nothing," he scoffed, "anybody could do it." But he smiled and dropped his eyes to the sticky bucket. "I reckon this will be enough for a while."

And it did take them a while to use up that honey, even in those hungry days. "Let's have a treat," Alvah declared, "now that we seen him safe back out of that swarm." Mama agreed: "we have enough flour in that second bin," she said. Sarah and Jane and Rosa Lee picked blackberries from all the best spots along the hedgerows and the fringes of the lake—"you girls watch for moccasins!" Mama warned—and Sarah brought them to Alvah in a tin bucket mounded high, glossy black and sweet. Then she loitered in the cookhouse despite the heat, watching Alvah prepare Seth's cake. She liked the cookhouse, with its sweet smell of heated heart-pine wood and stone. The whitewashed wall over the stove was filmed with the smoke of every meal eaten since the last coat, a thin gray stain like the one left by tired hands opening a door in the same place, over and over.

"Looks like you ate enough berries to make a whole nother cake," Alvah observed, glancing at Sarah's purple hands. She stirred the flour together with eggs and a dollop of honey, then folded the berries in carefully, to keep as many as possible from getting squashed. She poured the batter into her black skillet, tapped hard on the counter, and slid the pan into the stove and shut the door. "There you go," she said. "Won't take long." And she turned to move around the kitchen, wiping up the little hills of spilled flour with a damp rag, wringing it out cloudy-white into the basin, flinging the basin of water in a dark arc over the sandy yard outside. Then she came back in, sat down at the table in the center of the room, and reached for the bowl of beans there. "Help me shell," she said, and Sarah cracked the tip of the first bean with her fingernail, unstringing it slowly. Bean strings were tough, like the fine strings at the treble end of a piano. Way up on the inside, to produce the finest sounds.

"How did Seth learn to do the bees like that?" she asked.

Alvah smiled, her eyes on her fingers. "His daddy used to take him," she said. "Marcus. You remember Marcus?"

Sarah frowned. Marcus was a tall shape in her memory, moving about the yard with Alvah, carrying something for her, for Mama, for Father. Swinging Rosa Lee to make her laugh. Before the water moccasins. "Yes," she said. "I do."

"Marcus's daddy taught him to do this too," Alvah said, "and he made me go watch him, and took Seth, so Seth could learn. First time he did it by himself. Ain't had a real good tree in a long time."

Sarah waited, wanting only for Alvah to keep talking. She wanted to hear Seth's name in his mama's voice. But Alvah smiled, holding a story close to her, still. "I remember Marcus used to talk to em," she mused. "If I was listenin. He used to go up there to em, whispering, 'you little bees, you pretty little bees.'" She smiled, deeper. "He used to brag to me he could move a rattlesnake out of his path just like she was a woman. Tell her she was beautiful." Her smile dropped out of sight as quickly as a stone into a well. Sarah thought of what Alvah must also be thinking of: the water moccasins twisting through the muddy water at the dock, fastening their fangs in Marcus's leg. This was a part of the story that was Alvah's own, a sad part braided with the happy one. Sarah looked into her face and hesitated. No more of this story was going to come today.

They sat quietly, shelling beans. The golden smell of cake deepened in the air until finally Alvah rose from her chair and took it out of the stove. "Well," she said. "Look at that." Heat and sweet cake smell billowed into their faces.

"Let me turn it out on the platter, Alvah," Sarah begged. "I can do it."

"Better wait for it to cool," Alvah suggested, "just a little bit." But then she relented and handed Sarah a plate. "Go on," she said, "I reckon it ain't goin to stick."

Sarah flipped the cake upside down, then pried the pan off. The brown crust was even all the way around except for a jagged hole in the center, where a chunk of cake still clung to the pan. "Oh, no!" Sarah moaned. "I ruined Seth's cake!"

"It's all right, honey," Alvah said. "See?" She scraped the stuck cake off the inside of the pan and fit it back over the hole. "Can't hardly tell." She paused. "You know," she mused, "you could call this honesty cake now. Cause now you can see what's inside." She paused. "And you know, we need some honesty in this world."

In Sarah's memory, those days were precarious as the drop of nectar at the end of a honeysuckle stamen, nipped with a fingernail and drawn slowly, slowly to bring the sweetness out to the tongue. Honeysuckle. She and Jane and Rosa Lee had stood at the fence so long, plucking, sipping, swallowing, the white and yellow triangles of discarded petals at their feet. "Enough flowers," Rosa Lee mused, "we could have a whole jar of this."

"Just hold it right up and drink it," Jane agreed. "Like water," Sarah said. "Imagine."

But they had only that touch of sweetness, a taste that made the hunger ebb back and then return, sharper. Beans in their watery broth. Collards gritty with sand. Always the hunger, a deep itch in her bones.

And yet they lived. The war ended. Then, so did their lives in that house.

When Mama told them Fairibault was to be sold—"it's useless to argue with me," she declared, although none of them had said a word, "any of you"—Sarah and Jane and even Rosa Lee had snuck upstairs to the big window in the front bedroom, the company room, where no one ever went. In her fist, Jane grasped Mama's diamond ring; Jane was as good as a mockingbird at thievery. "We'll write our names," she declared, her pointy face fierce. "Then nobody will ever forget this house is ours."

Sarah set her arm around her sister's shoulders and the three of them leaned close, their breath pressing in clouds against the glass. "You first," Rosa Lee said generously. "You the one done the stealin'." Jane chortled and etched a sweeping J into the glass, followed by a crookeder *a, n, e*. Then she handed the ring to Rosa Lee, who carved her name in two neat blocks, smaller than Sarah would have thought possible given the awkward angle and the way you had to scrunch your fingers around the ring to get it to screak across the glass. "Now you," Rosa Lee said. Sarah set the ring against the glass and tugged. With a tiny squeal it tugged down, then up, then down again until she had one tall *S. A. R. A. H*, with a stiff tail over its back like a nervous cat's.

"Good," Jane approved.

"We need to put this ring back fore your mama finds out," Rosa Lee said.

"Wait," Sarah said. The diamond's cutting edge felt firm in her grip. She bent closer and, between her name and Rosa Lee's, cut into the glass four small letters: *s e t h*.

The sweetness that she felt looking at Seth's name against the light, like touching her tongue to the honeysuckle drops—that fugitive sweetness lingered. Like walking out with him on the day they found the mockingbird nest. Sarah had been going toward the trees, Seth back toward the house from the barn. They fell into step together up the path into the woods without admitting that was what they were doing. Surely there was no need to admit it, was there? They were just two people walking, who happened to be going in the same direction. Up into the woods, on the road that would eventually take them to the Indian camp, the same road on which they had found—

"Remember the mockingbirds?" Seth asked. "When I stood up on old Shad's back?" He smiled. "Didn't ever think I could do a trick like that. Like somebody in the circus." Sarah smiled too, and then she felt the smile leave her face as it was leaving Seth's. Both of them remembered Mama shouting, snatching Jane down from the mule's back. *Mama said she should be ashamed, showing her—*

Sarah pushed the image aside. A white fog of anger rose in its place. Why was this Mama's business, anyway? What was wrong with just walking with Seth, whom she had never not known in all her life? What was wrong with feeling his hand swinging next to hers, almost but not quite touching?

You know quite well, my girl, rang Mama's voice in her head. *Shall I elaborate?* Mama had never uttered these words to Sarah but Sarah could imagine them, perfectly. A flush of shame ran over her body at how exactly Mama's voice fit into the shape of questioning and doubt inside her. Mama inhabited her. Mama filled her up and left Sarah herself to fit into only as much room as was left. Mama scolded. Mama pressed her toward what Mama thought was right or wrong without regard to whether Sarah herself might even be beginning to feel differently.

The light deepened around them, mixed with shadow. Leaves crunched under Seth's feet. Sarah's skirts swished against a stand of buckeyes lining the path. Seth did not look at her and she did not look at him but she could feel the air next to her displaced, softly, a pressure against her skin in exactly his tall, limber shape. She turned her head slightly toward him—not meeting his eyes—to catch the salty tang of skin from his open shirt collar in her nose.

They were just walking, without going anywhere. Weren't they? *Go away, Mama,* she thought, sudden and furious. *Go away.*

"Hey, look," Seth remarked, stooping to the path. "I guess it fell." He lifted a mockingbird's nest out of the leaves, a rough sphere of twig balanced on twig, with a soft circle of horsehair and feathers still tucked into its heart, and placed it in Sarah's hands. A shard of pale speckled eggshell still clung inside. His fingers brushed hers and lingered, just half a second, then were gone, leaving her own skin suddenly cool where they had been. Both of them bent over her outstretched palms to study the nest. Her heart beat harder, up into her throat. If Seth wanted to, he would raise both his hands right up under hers, cradling them and covering them, holding up the nest along with her. And he would tip his face just that one small bit closer and he would kiss her.

And she wanted him to kiss her. Her blood urged and urged, everywhere.

She stole a look upward at him. His skin stretched over his cheekbones, his dark eyes flickering at her and away and back again. Something in his face wanted to reach for her too. But then he stepped back and turned away. "Come on," he murmured. "I reckon . . . "

He didn't finish that sentence. He never did.

When they came out of the woods, they stepped right into Mama's path. She had brought Marie out for a ride, leaving the colt back at the barn—they could hear him whinnying, bolting back and forth inside the paddock fence. Sarah went to Marie and rubbed her nose but it was no use. "Well," Mama said. Her face was impossible to read. "Looks like you are having a pleasant walk."

"Yes," Sarah said, looking down.

"Be sure you fix that board in the fence where it's fallen, in the big pasture," Mama addressed Seth. "You can hear that colt down there. He'll tear himself to pieces. Damn fool."

"Yes, ma'am," mumbled Seth.

Mama swept a scalding, cool gaze over Sarah and lifted Marie's reins and nudged with her heel and rode up into the woods. Seth looked at Sarah, nodded just a little, and turned away to walk toward the barn. And Sarah stood still on the path, where she was, the mockingbird's nest in her hands.

The next day at breakfast, Mama announced it was time to cut Marie's colt. He was a yearling now, grown out of his round-fore-headed baby shape, his tail long and swishy like Marie's. He had a big white patch across his face, just like his father, Wainwright's Jim. "If you let 'em go too long," Mama remarked, "they start think-ing they can get away with anything." She looked at Sarah and Seth. "You two are biggest. I need you to help."

At the barn, Mama rigged a rope around the colt's leg and back and toppled him. Sarah and Seth scrambled to sit on his neck and on his haunches while Mama tied his front legs together. She hand-ed Seth the end of the rope around his back foot, crouched down, and began to cut. The colt strained his head back and pedaled his legs, but the ropes around his fetlocks held. Sarah settled hard-er onto his neck. His nostrils flared red—breath whistling—and when he tilted his nose toward the sky, the knob of hair and bone over his bottom eye was rubbed white with dirt. "Dammit, girl!" Mama growled. "Hold him still!"

Sarah couldn't look at where Mama was hunkered between the colt's back legs with her knife. Instead, she looked at Seth. He sat hard on the colt's haunches, straining the top leg up and away with his rope. And he couldn't help looking at what Mama was doing. His face went ashy underneath the brown, as if he might vomit. But if he looked away he might let the colt's leg fall and he might get in trouble. Mama had explained it: if she cut in the wrong place, or if Sarah or Seth let him wriggle at the wrong time, the colt would bleed to death.

"Just one more little cut—" Mama grunted from between her teeth. And then she drew away a big bloody handful of flesh and sat back on her heels and tossed the flesh aside. Old Tod the setter dashed to it and snatched it up and trotted away. She uncorked the big jug of Mr. Hogg's moonshine from the cellar and splashed it over the wound, waited a second, then splashed again. Seth's eyes watered, but he didn't take his hands off the rope to wipe them.

"You see what I'm doing here," Mama told him. "He needs this twice a day, do you understand?" Seth nodded.

"Good," Mama said. "Let him up." Sarah scooted off the colt's neck and Seth untied the ropes from his back legs while Mama untied the rope around the front. With a big heave and scramble the colt stood and staggered to the other side of the pen, where he stood, swaying uncertainly. Red and black blood, dried and fresh, streaked the inside of his back legs. Mama's face softened. "I know," she murmured. "I know, baby. I know. But we had to."

She turned away and caught sight of Seth's face where he still stood, gathering up the bloody ropes with shaky hands. A strange smile flickered over her mouth. "Don't worry, boy," she told him. "You behave yourself and you'll be fine." And she strode to the stable pump and sluiced her hands clean.

⁂

The soldiers came on a dusty, hot day. Mama, Sarah, Alvah, Jane, and Rosa Lee were all sitting in the parlor, mending, with the windows to the east and south open to catch the breeze. Mama looked up, over Sarah's head, and flung her mending to the floor. The needle popped out of the cloth and bounced at the end of its string. She strode to the big bureau with the ivory inlays and opened the top drawer. Then she turned, sweeping her eyes over Sarah and Jane and Rosa Lee, stopping when she met Alvah's eyes. "Y'all go hide!" she snapped, snatching her pistol from the drawer. This was the plan they had made. This must mean—Sarah looked past Mama through the open window. Yes. A line of blue-coated men on horseback was coming down their driveway. The man in front was almost to the stream.

Alvah froze. "Come here, girls," she hissed. She snatched at Rosa Lee's shoulder and herded her and Sarah and Jane up the stairs. Jane stumbled and tripped, scrambling herself back up with

188

both hands. "Come on," Alvah breathed, "y'all hurry." She followed them into the upstairs hallway, jerked down the cord for the attic trapdoor, then hustled them up the rickety ladder and climbed up and pulled it after herself. Their feet thumped on the boards. In the dark, panicked mice rustled away.

"Where's Seth?" Rosa Lee wailed, and started to cry. The thick air swaddled her voice in dust and heat.

"I don't know, honey," said Alvah quickly. "But I know you girls need to stay—" She firmed up her lips. "You girls come over here with me." Stealthily they threaded through the trunks and dress forms to the small ventilation window that overlooked the front yard and cranked it open and huddled underneath. If they were very careful, they could see. But in any case, they'd hear. Maybe it would be bad. But it was better than huddling in the silent dark, straining their ears toward the little bright rectangle of light they daren't approach.

"Seth can look after himself," Sarah whispered, and patted Rosa Lee.

"That's right," Alvah said quickly. "Seth will be all right."

Mama had told them it would happen just like this. "Run and hide in the attic if soldiers come," she'd warned, "no matter what else you're doing. I'll stay behind—if they see the house looking empty, they'll burn it to the ground. Maybe they'll take pity on a lone woman." Maybe.

Why did we believe her? Sarah wonders, years later. *Why did we scurry up there like fools when they could have lit a match and burned the whole house down with us inside, no matter what Mama said? When they could have come inside and gone roaming around until they found us? When they could have—hurt Mama? Right there as we watched? But they didn't.* She shivers. *They didn't.* Maybe the soldiers wouldn't have hurt anyone. Maybe they would have been happy to take Rosa Lee and Alvah and Seth back to the North with them. *Pillagers. Liberators.* There was no way to know which of the stories was true.

Alvah and Sarah and Rosa Lee and Jane settled underneath the window, waiting. Sarah tried to raise up and look, but Alvah snatched her back. "Y'all stay down," hissed Alvah, "so help me, you stay here." Her hands pressed them down, her fingers gripping like claws.

Mama's voice rose suddenly over a blur of men's voices and a scuffle of hooves. "Well," she called, "you take that horse if you think you can handle her. But I'm warning you, the last man to ride her is a dead man. A dead man, but a gentleman. Yes, a gentlemen. Who learned how to ride by choice. Not jerked out of some Yankee slum and plopped onto some cow-hocked nag."

What was Mama doing? Slowly, Sarah raised up to peer through the window. Just below the slate-shingled pitch of the roof stood a ring of blue-coated soldiers, sweating through the cloth under their arms and at the brims of their caps. They slouched on the backs of their horses, who lowered their heads to graze, switching their tails and stomping their feet against the flies. One of the soldiers chewed something slowly in his mouth and spit into the dust, his eyes fixed on Mama. At the front of the group stood a tall soldier with more gold braid on his coat than the rest, holding Marie and Marie's colt by their halters. The colt fidgeted, but the man held him tight. *Thank goodness he's all healed up,* Sarah thought idiotically, *they won't keep putting moonshine on that cut.* From the direction of the man's stare, Sarah knew that Mama was standing on the porch, staring back at him. He peered at her sharply. "Your husband, ma'am?" he asked.

"My husband. Yes," snapped Mama's voice, from under the pitch of the roof, "my husband died." She stepped off the porch, into Sarah's view. The big soldier edged backward. "We lost our son, we lost our daughter, we lost our money, and he shot himself. And as you can see, he left me here. With all the riches you survey."

She flung one arm theatrically around her. And Sarah saw the familiar yard and house through the soldier's eyes: paint flaking off from the brown boards underneath, the overgrown azaleas and the dead rose thorns on the fence, the bare porch where the rocking chairs had been chopped up for kindling, the vines tangling up the columns and poking through the porch ceiling, the holes broken in the lattices where raccoons had rooted in the cool foundation dirt. No wonder Mama wouldn't let them clean it up. Sarah looked closer at her mother—streamers of hair twitching loose from its bun, worn brown homespun dress belted tighter around her waist with a rope, bony raw hands flung open and quivering in anger—and she shivered. *They think Mama's stranded here, alone. They think she's mad.*

It was a lie to let them think so. But nothing Mama had said was a lie.

Mama's skirt drooped where the pistol hung in her pocket.

"These horses look well enough," grumbled the big soldier, his eyes still on Mama.

"Our grass, although you may not credit me," Mama snapped, "is still Confederate property. Like Nebuchadnezzar, I may yet descend to eating it."

The tall soldier shifted from one foot to the other. "We're taking these horses, Ma'am," he said. Mama started to speak, but he held up his hand. "We're taking these horses," he said, louder, peering even closer at her, "and I'm marking your gate to indicate we've been here, do you understand? That we've been here and—"

"There's nothing left," said Mama bitterly. "Nothing left for you to steal."

The tall soldier nodded and tied Marie's rope around his saddle horn, handing the colt's rope to another. "You men attend to me," he shouted. "We're finished here." He turned his horse and led the soldiers down the drive, trotting in a neat line between the stands of sycamore, away from the house. The big soldier was last to go, spitting in the dust again, turning his horse and riding away at the back of the line. Mama stood, watching them. In the attic Sarah and Alvah and Rosa Lee stood, watching too. Marie lagged, stretching her leadrope across the tall soldier's thigh. The colt trotted to catch up.

At the distant front gate, the tall soldier swung from his saddle and the blue-coated group milled around the big cedar gate posts. Then he remounted and all the other soldiers followed him and Marie and the colt down the road and out of sight. Their gate was marked now. Like the Israelites' doors in the Old Testament. *Let the angel of death go right on by me, Lord. I've got the sign.*

Mama dropped to the ground and lay still.

Sarah rushed to the trapdoor and scrambled down the ladder, then bolted down the stairs and out the front door. "Mama!" she called, kneeling and scooping her mother's body against hers. Her face was pale as a dead woman's, her lips stringy over her teeth. "Mama, wake up!"

"Just wait a little while," Alvah said. She and Sarah dragged Mama up onto the porch and laid her down on the boards. Alvah touched her hand to Mama's forehead, then straightened up to look down the drive in the direction of the soldiers. "Maybe I done right, to run and hide like that," she murmured to herself. "Maybe not."

Sarah looked at her. She'd heard what all of them had heard: *Mr. Lincoln's set you free, and the soldiers will take you on with them if you will go.* Alvah looked back, her mouth twisting slightly. "We'll go, someday," she said to Rosa Lee, just as if Sarah were not there. "But we ain't followin a soldier's camp." She looked sternly at them both. "You heard it. What they do to womenfolk."

Then Alvah caught sight of something over her shoulder, and turned. Seth stood on the porch behind them, sprung from God knows where. He stared at them, then spun away on one heel. They watched him stride through the open front door and out the back, opening a passage of bright light across the whole house. Rosa Lee started to follow him, and Alvah touched her arm. "Let him go, baby," she said. "I hope I done right. I truly hope."

꙳

The mockingbird nest sat on Sarah's bedroom windowsill until after her seventeenth birthday, which was celebrated with a new patch in the underarm of her dress and a stew of dandelion greens and Alvah's dried Cherokee beans. Sarah looked at it every night— the rough globe of stick balanced on stick, with the single eggshell shard inside, still holding onto the shape of what had broken it apart from within. It sat in a bright spot of sun on the windowsill that made the eggshell glow, as the thin edge of skin between her own thumb and finger glowed when she held it up to the light.

But Mama didn't know, yet, that she thought of Seth and of walking with him when she looked at that nest. There was this tiny glowing space inside of Sarah that was free of Mama, where only she and Seth were. And when she looked at that nest she felt as if she were bent over it as over a small fire, coaxing a tiny, flickering spark that burned and burned and was growing, quiet and definite. The fire might warm. The fire might destroy.

꙳

Sarah wandered back up the forest path, alone. Voices came from up ahead, and the snuffle and stamp of horses. She edged closer and ducked behind a big oak tree. There was Mr. Wainwright's big black horse, Achilles, that somehow he had managed to keep although the Yankees had stolen Marie, tied by the reins to a sapling, scratching his neck against the bark. Standing just beyond him were Mr. Wainwright and Mama. From their comfortable looks, they'd been talking for a while already.

"So you see the difficulty," Mama said. Her voice was full, rueful, just a little gleeful and light. "We have to do something about him while we can."

Mr. Wainwright shook his dark head, his green eyes fixed on Mama. "I can't believe it," he rumbled. "That Ned would tolerate such behavior." He dipped his head respectfully at Mama: Ned, of course, was Father, and Father, of course, was gone.

Mama's mouth twisted. She lowered her head and shook it, slowly. Mr. Wainwright gazed at her. Then something in his face shifted suddenly and he snatched her against him and kissed her. He locked both arms around Mama's slender back, cupping her head in one palm. Mama strained backwards a little but not very much. And then she lifted both her own arms and twined them around Mr. Wainwright's neck and kissed him back. He moaned and strained Mama against him, with one arm against her waist and one hand still deep into her hair, his fingers working and working up underneath the heavy knot at the back of her skull. He would undo it and all her hair would fall. But Mama did not seem to notice this. Her face was swallowed up in his, her body bending and stretching like a tree in a very high wind.

Your servant, Madam. That was what Mr. Wainwright had said to Mama in the parlor, when he came to fetch his little horse Jim. Servant was the proper word for Alvah and Rosa Lee and Seth, if speaking of them to anyone outside the family. Why was she thinking about this now, with Mama swaying in front of her, locked in Mr. Wainwright's grip, as she had never been locked in Father's? Sarah remembered her voice hissing through the bedroom wall, after the day of Uncle Eugene and the creek: *Don't you touch me, Ned. Don't ever touch me again.*

With an effort Mama untangled her arms and pushed herself back away from Mr. Wainwright, whose hands trailed down along her waist and her hips. "Tom," she breathed. "We can't—" She ran both hands over her hair, tucking the pins deeper where Mr. Wainwright had loosened them.

"We can perfectly well," Mr. Wainwright growled. A smile flickered on his face. "I'm a free man. And you're a widow. You can't tell me Ned ever gave you this kind of—"

"You're a rogue," Mama said firmly. A smile leaped under the surface of her voice but she was fighting to keep it off her face. "That's what you are. A rogue."

"Didn't I explain that to you?" Mr. Wainwright asked. "I bought a substitute for the fighting. One of the cousinry." He stepped close to Mama and slipped his hands around her waist. "But I'm sending money to the Cause. Thank God, there's some money left."

"That's not what I mean," Mama said.

"Somebody had to stay here, after all," Mr. Wainwright continued, "to look after you." He lowered his face to her neck and Mama's head fell back and she closed her eyes. "Tom," she muttered. Her voice shook. "Tom." His mouth moved slowly on her skin. And Sarah could see that her mama was lost.

Sarah pushed herself to her feet and stumbled away. Then she broke into a run and didn't stop until she was back in the yard, under the wide skirts of the big magnolia tree, huddled against the trunk. Thank God no one else was around. She did not want to look another person in the eye, knowing what she'd seen. Mama's head thrown back, Mama overtaken by what must be the same bright glowing feeling that lit her own body when she looked at Seth, except that Mama wasn't supposed to feel that about any man but Father. Father had shot himself and here was Mama letting Mr. Wainwright set his brutal mouth all over her face and his hands on her body where only Father was supposed to touch. Father was dead and here was Mama acting like it did not matter one bit. Mama was tempting Mr. Wainwright more than Sarah had ever thought about tempting Seth, or anyone. She was sinning. She was doing wrong, worse than she had ever warned Sarah not to do. Worse than the Yankee soldiers would have done if they had caught her and Jane and Rosa Lee. *Hurt a woman until she prays to die.* Mama wanted Mr. Wainwright to hurt her like that. And that had to be a sin.

Sarah gathered herself up and slid off the magnolia-tree branch and strode into the house. She was not only hungry now but angry. She let that anger rise in her, fanning and fanning it. She would confront Mama. She would be like a heroine in Mrs. Radcliffe's novels, seeking justice for her father. Her dead father, who needed her to speak for him against the treachery of Mama.

When she burst into her room, the first thing she noticed was that the mockingbird's nest was gone from its spot on her windowsill. She looked all around but it wasn't anywhere. Turning to rush back into the hall again, she ran directly into Mama, who was brushing her freshly dampened hair back with one hand, carrying an envelope in the other. Her face had fallen back into its habitual keen, irritated half-frown, so thoroughly that Sarah wondered in spite of herself if she had imagined Mr. Wainwright's lips on Mama's in the woods.

"I'm going to run this over to the post," Mama announced. "Your father's wastrel brother Eugene, having heard belatedly of his death, has written to ask—although of course those weren't his words—whether there's any money to be had. I'm attempting to warn him off, although I doubt it will do any good. Prepare yourself." And she turned away, but Sarah stopped her. "Mama," she asked, "what happened to my nest?"

"Your nest?" Mama frowned. "Oh, that frowsty thing on your windowsill. I had Alvah throw it out." And she passed by Sarah and continued down the stairs.

❧

At church next Sunday the word snaked through the congregation: Mrs. Simmes' Robert, a colored boy, had disappeared. Mrs. Pruitt's name, and Katy's, were tangled among the whispers. Mr. Wainwright stood in a cluster of other men, their voices low. "We keep order," he rumbled to them, smiling, as Sarah passed behind him. "No more than that."

Sarah had only seen Mrs. Simmes' Robert a few times that she could remember. Mrs. Simmes was a widow lady who lived in at the Rehobeth crossroads, near the general store, in a white clapboard house with a single white rocking chair on the porch. Because her husband had left Robert to her as what she called *a source of income* but she herself had only the house and yard now, she hired him everywhere and collected the money. Robert had been one of the line of *people* standing on Fairibault's lawn to collect their silver quarter-dollar and dime apiece from Father. He was the boy, sturdy and short although he must be about as old as Seth, who loaded sacks of grain or cotton seed into wagons at the general store, wiping his face with a red neckerchief, or climbed up a ladder to wipe the church windows with rags and vinegar. Where did he sleep at night? Where did he keep what surely must be the few things that were his own? Sarah couldn't tell. When she went by Mrs. Simmes' house, she could never see Robert there, only widowed Mrs. Simmes with her perfect upswept gray bun, rocking and rocking in her immaculate chair.

After church Mama took Sarah by the arm and led her into the parlor and closed the doors. "I need you to understand what happened to Katy Pruitt," she said. "She's going to have a baby because she and Mrs. Simmes' Robert did wrong. I thought not to even tell you. But you will hear of it. You're a woman and you need to know. Robert is gone, though. He's not ever coming back. And"—something tender and flinty at the same time flickered in her expression—"he'll never bother you. Or Jane."

Speaking fought with silence in Mama's face; a part of her obviously didn't want to tell Sarah, but another part did. And Sarah felt a reluctant interest, despite the anger still turning over and over inside her at Mama for throwing the nest away. She felt grown, and trusted. "Was it like—" She paused. "Was it like Eugene? What happened at the creek?" Had Mrs. Simmes' Robert touched Bad Katy like that, up on her leg? Like Mr. Wainwright touched Mama, kissed her? Or was there more? There had to be. The old sick dread rose, mixed with a curiosity that wouldn't let her be silent.

"Eugene?" Mama stopped. She peered at Sarah, and swallowed. "Eugene is of no interest. You don't need to be concerned with him again."

"But—" Sarah's voice faltered, struggled inside her throat. "It was, it—He—"

Mama set both hands flat on the tea table. She did not reach for Sarah, or touch her. "Stop it, girl," she said. "Don't be hysterical. It won't do any good." Her face looked taut. She stood up and walked out of the room before Sarah could fling any of the words swarming in her like Seth's tree-stump bees: *I hate you. You don't know what I saw. You lie. I know it. You let Johnny do whatever he wanted with Celia and you never told. And you, and Mr. Wainwright. I saw you. You lie.*

Now she would never know for sure what had happened to Mrs. Simmes' Robert. But if Bad Katy was going to have a baby, it could not be anything too good. He was gone, and he was never coming back. That was one way people disappeared for good. Stories about them ebbed into the air you breathed without realizing it—your mama's meaningful looks, the hum of voices that stopped when you walked into the room, the knowledge that existed only in tiny fragments: *Well, that boy's gone now. Thank goodness.* And another lady would look shocked; you weren't supposed to be thankful when someone was gone, only relieved. Quietly. *Don't know what Eleanora Pruitt's going to do about—*And the words washed and washed at the pictures you might still be carrying of people's living faces until they were simply gone.

Or, like Celia, they ran away. Off and gone, never seen again. Alvah and Seth and Rosa Lee could have gone, too. But they didn't. Why?

Johnny would have said, "Let 'em go. We can always get more." Johnny would have said, "No sister of mine."

But you can say nothing against me, she growled at him, inside her head. *You went down in the field with Celia.*

No good girl, no good woman, was supposed to know of these things. *No sister of mine.*

No one knew what she knew. Would they still call her good, if they could see the knowledge she carried in the center of her brain, too deep for words to reach?

In Mama's words to the soldiers, she'd heard the truth.

Little Sarah was not my cousin. She was my sister.

No one knew that she had guessed. No one knew that she had seen underneath the words thrown like dustsheets over that little white stone in the grass, over Father's death. And over Celia's disappearance, even though no one had said anything about that.

Her pain in childbirth shall be greatly increased. The Bible words, in Mama's voice, rang reasonlessly in Sarah's head. *Her desire shall be for her husband, and he shall rule over her.* But Celia didn't have a husband. If Johnny had gone to the field with her—but they weren't married, so how could—

But they had done it anyway, and then, one morning, Celia was gone.

Maybe she would meet Celia's daughter on some street, in some future yet unseen. A girl as tall as she or Jane, with Johnny's roguish tilt to her eyes and creamy, pale-brown skin. She wondered if that girl would pass right by, or if she would stop, she and Sarah tugged to look at each other by something they couldn't name.

The feeling that rose in Sarah when she looked at Seth had no name, either. Inside herself was the only safe place for it. To tell anyone about this feeling was to kill it, and, even worse, it was to make Seth, like Mrs. Simmes' Robert, disappear.

We keep order. It was what could happen to a colored boy.

☙

"Go over to Eleanora Pruitt's and take her this," said Mama, shoving a basket into Sarah's hands. Sarah nudged the cloth aside to see a nest of warm biscuits, with a jar of strawberry jam at the center. "Tell her I sent it. Tell her we're beside her in her trouble." She peered at Sarah. "You be polite if you see Katy. But you probably won't."

Would Bad Katy be captive in that house, like a princess in a fairy tale? What if Sarah had to take her away, help her escape, like Eliza in Mrs. Stowe's novel? What if Bad Katy asked her what had happened to Mrs. Simmes' Robert? "I don't know," Sarah would say, truthfully. Because no one had put words to what Mr. Wainwright and the other men had done, only Mr. Wainwright himself: *We keep order. No more than that.*

Big handsome green-eyed Mr. Wainwright with his hands on Mama's body.

The ditches rustled and snapped as Sarah walked by, full of hummings and chirpings and stems breaking under some small creature's weight. It was goldenrod time, wistful September, with nothing new of the summer left to come into bloom. There would be the pink and white Confederate roses bowing on their tall stalks, waving their wide pointy leaves, but not until October. There would be the ruffly red camellias, but not until nigh Christmas.

When would Katy have her baby? Sarah let her thoughts funnel ahead toward Mrs. Pruitt's small house in its cluster of cedars. Just around the bend in the road and across the creek bridge. With

Mrs. Simmes' Robert, Katy had done what you were not supposed to do until you were married. With Robert. A colored boy. And she had gotten a baby. Sarah's brain jumped and spun, shying away from the picture that lay at the bottom of her thoughts like a stone: Seth's long back turned away from her, sluiced over with water thrown out in long bright sheets like blades. She imagined her arms around him, drawing him close to her, like Mama and Mr. Wainwright. She shut her eyes. Her body loosened and prickled in a way that was thrilling. And terrifying.

Katy had gotten a baby that way. With Robert. And Mr. Wainwright had made Robert disappear.

What if Katy didn't want Sarah to rescue her? What if she was waiting, like a bad fairy, like a troll under the bridge, to haul down an unwilling companion, so she would not have to be alone? It came to Sarah sudden and vivid as a dream, stopping her feet in the dust of the road: a vision of Bad Katy grasping her arm, saying, *come on, now, stay with me a while.* Saying *don't you have some things you want to ask me?* Saying *you know you want to know—*

Saying *well, now. Aren't we cozy here together. Just like sisters. And I know you'll never leave me.*

Sarah shivered and blinked to wake herself out of her cold fear. *Calm yourself,* she commanded in Mama's voice. *You're acting like a madwoman. These biscuits are getting cold. Take them on. A nice little treat for a neighbor. Just to show her she's in our thoughts—*

And in our dreams, Sarah's own thoughts continued. *In our fears. Curled under the quilt. Close as a sister, held tight by secrets against our own skin. We can twist and thrash but we can never wake up. We walk up and knock on that door anyway, because we have to.*

The colored girl, Nellie, opened the front door of Mrs. Pruitt's house and blinked at the bright afternoon. "'Mon in," she murmured. "Miz Pruitt workin back there." Nellie's face seemed sleepy, shaded, hollowed. Around her eyes were lines like Mama's, lines cut deep, too, from her nose to the corners of her mouth. Nellie had always seemed like a girl. But here—Blind panic spurted up under Sarah's heart, beating its wings like a trapped bird. *Trapped. Trapped in this house.* Under the usual smell of new cloth was a different smell, now: salty and not quite clean, of dishes or clothes not washed, of a body—

"I can't stay," Sarah offered, "I just brought—"

"Miss Sarah," Nellie murmured to the air behind her, "from over Fairibault."

"Well, now." Mrs. Pruitt's spectacled face floated up toward Sarah out of the dark hall. "Look how kind." Sarah fought to put a smile on her face, to hold out the basket in steady hands. Mrs. Pruitt's long needle-pricked fingers darted forth and grasped it. Then she held it close to her face to breathe in the fresh biscuit smell, although she didn't tilt her head down but remained looking right at Sarah. Her pink-rimmed eyes behind their spectacles did not move.

"Mama asked me to bring them," Sarah said. "Asked to be remembered to y'all."

"Tell your mama we're keeping well," Mrs. Pruitt said. "And we thank her."

Next to Mrs. Pruitt, Nellie stood, calm and fixed, peering dreamily over Sarah's shoulder into the yard. Sarah shot a glance down the hall. Only the usual things were there: the mahogany bench on which ladies could set their reticules, the rumpled threadbare rug, the big severe daguerrotype of Mr. Pruitt before he got drunk and fell off his horse and died, the bright sunroom where Nellie and Mrs. Pruitt worked. A bolt of black serge was unrolled across the work table. No sign of Bad Katy anywhere, or of anything having to do with a baby.

"Katy's out in the yard, I reckon," Mrs. Pruitt mused. "Don't know where she got off to."

"Can't go far," Nellie agreed.

"Well," Sarah said, "tell her I said hello. Enjoy the biscuits." She turned and hurried down the walk as fast as she dared until the door shut behind her. She would be away from this house—*the witch's cottage*—in an instant, and then—

"Sarah." Bad Katy's voice came from the privet hedge. "Sarah, wait."

Sarah stopped her feet and shut her eyes. This was the point in the story where she, or Jane more likely, would also shut their eyes and whimper deliriously to the heroine, *don't look! Don't turn back!* But the heroine had to keep right on. And Sarah opened her eyes.

Bad Katy huddled under the privet hedge, looking up, like a little girl in a hideout. Except Katy was not a little girl. She was almost eighteen, just a little older than Sarah herself. She was tired and feverish-looking, her eyes dark-circled. Her strawberry-blond hair was muddier now. And as she struggled to unfold her legs and stand, the shelf of her belly poked out from under her worn gray dress, firm and defiant, as if all the life in the rest of her body had drained toward it like water. *No one wants to look at me*, it said. *But I am here.*

Katy reached a hand up to Sarah.

And Sarah turned away. Fear broke loose and pushed her away. She hurried up the September-dusty road almost fast enough to run. Keep walking, and she would be out of sight. Otherwise the touch of Katy's hand would drag her down. *Here with me, stay here.*

After that day, Sarah never saw Katy again. Some said she had gone to Mrs. Pruitt's cousins in Augusta. Some said she had gone to the maiden sister of dead, mean Mr. Pruitt, a lady who lived in Charleston and was quite a fine person, considering. "We need to get that basket back," Mama said sometimes, "but I just keep forgetting." And as simply as that, Bad Katy Pruitt became a ghost. A story with no ending. A figure walking out beyond the edges of the map, in unimaginable space: *Here be Dragons.* Alone.

How the memory stings Sarah now. *She was just a girl, without a friend in the world. She called to me and I ran away. Because—I was afraid? Not exactly. I was curious, but I knew I shouldn't—Not exactly. Because—because—*

I ran away, supplies Sarah's brain now, firm and rueful, *because I could not imagine her. I couldn't look. I couldn't see. Because everything*—everything—*said to me,* It's easier if you don't. Pretending not to see. Participating in a lie. It's easier that way, for everyone.

A ghost.

No sister of mine.

What Sarah never told Mama, or anyone, was that she slipped back later and left her doll, Lucinda Victoria, in a basket underneath that bush.

"Whatever happened to Lucinda Victoria?" Aunt Maude would ask, years later.

"I gave her," Sarah would reply, "to another little girl."

※

Before their wedding, Sarah sat with Galen in the back garden of Aunt Maude's house in Mobile. "My father," Sarah said, "he—" She waited. "He—" In the trees, a baby wren rasped over and over *Come find me. Come find me.*

"Why don't you tell me what happened?" Galen said. "Just tell it."

So she let the story come back, in pieces, as much as would come. The shot, the coppery edge of thunderstorm in the air. Mama in her dry bath, sitting, waiting, staring straight ahead, unseeing.

"That's all I remember, Galen," she said. Something inside her was tearing open, steadily as ripping out a seam. "That's how I remember it."

She bowed her head so she wouldn't have to look at him and he wouldn't have to see her cry. She fought and gulped down the tangle of achy tears in her throat. She had been knowing this for so long: why was she crying now, in front of him?

"They'll want to pity you," Mama had hissed, fixing Sarah's and Jane's bonnet ribbons tight around their chins on the way to church, "they'll want to feel sorry for you. Schadenfreude is a deep delight to little minds. But don't you let them see you cry." She jerked the ribbon tighter and snapped each loop into a perfect curve. "That's what they want."

What if Galen saw her cry? What would that do? Surely no man really wanted to see—

She felt him shift toward her, just a little, and then his cool hand rested on the back of her bowed neck, right above the collar of her dress. It warmed her, just sitting there. In that moment, it was all that held her to this spinning world. Without it, she would fall. Spin off into a darkness deep and howling as that open barn door. "Oh, Sarah," he said, his voice quiet as breath. He sat beside her, and he did not take his hand away.

Outside the parlor, she had hovered behind the closed pocket doors as he talked to her mother, his voice steady. "I've got a good practice here," he said, "going to be a partner and then assume the whole practice when Dr. Pickett passes on. He's told me so."

Mama's voice was a blurred mumble then. Only a couple words: *position, expectations.*

"I know what you expect," Galen said—he wanted her to hear, even through the doors—"and I know what Sarah wants. I promise you, I will endeavor, every way"—He paused. "Her happiness," he said, "is all that I want in this world."

Leaning against the carved wooden doorframe, Sarah closed her eyes. Rosa Lee and Jane, hovering nearby, squeezed her hands.

By going into that room and asking Mama if he might marry her, Galen was telling her that the rumors about her and Seth didn't matter. He had heard them, everyone had. "The Yankee House," she told him, "we went there so I could play the big piano Mrs.

Lowell left. We didn't do anything wrong." But she had never told him the rest of it.

❧

Mrs. Lowell had lived in the half-finished rooms on the ground floor of the Yankee House for longer than anyone thought she would, telling Mama that Mr. Lowell would be moving down to join her very soon. She hunkered down there like a chipmunk under a rock, climbing up into the grand entryway to play the piano that had come all the way from Boston—upside down on a mattress, she told Sarah, in a wagon jolting up the driveway. "It was never in tune after that," she complained. She broke off the pieces of board and had her colored men sew her a canvas shroud to fit over the piano. But she never played it well, in tune or not.

Maybe that was why it was so easy for her to leave the piano in the empty vaulted hall. "Next season, we'll return," she promised Mama, kissing her cheek dryly, "we'll see you then, Livia dear." But they never did return, and for a while no one saw the piano except the rats and squirrels and pigeons that managed to make their way inside. Then Rosa Lee and Jane and Sarah and Seth wandered over across the fields that had once been part of Fairibault and let themselves in through an unlatched window that opened onto the sturdy baking table, down in the cellar. The Lowells had so much money stashed away in Massachusetts that they could leave this perfectly good baking table right here. They jumped down and fumbled with the latch of the kitchen door until they could tug it open and walk back out again. The whistling walk that had been Mrs. Lowell's pride stretched from this door to the cookhouse across the yard, its red bricks warm in the sun. Sarah trotted up the steps into the sun and turned to look back into the cellar. If the path from cookshed to cellar was all you ever saw of this house, it wasn't so grand at all.

Sarah, Seth, Jane, and Rosa Lee left that door unlocked, although they knew they shouldn't. Whenever they felt like it, they could come to the house and cross the cellar floor, eyeing the rolled-up mattress on Mrs. Lowell's makeshift bed and giving a tug to the pull-rope of the ceiling fan. The fan was one wide wooden blade that swung on a hinge from the ceiling; one of the *people* who were supposed to whistle, obedient and loud, as they brought Mrs. Lowell her dinner could stand in the corner and tug the rope to swish that blade back and forth over the table, shooing away the flies.

Up the stairs and they were in the house's main hall, an empty vaulted space three stories high, which was sweet with sun and dust and the indescribable sadness of places left behind. Bare wood beams still sent forth their warm piney smell, all the way up inside the dome. Seth tossed the scratchy folds of the canvas piano cover against the wall, and Sarah drew up the bench and played, first the *Kinderszenen*—"About Foreign Lands and People," she had memorized it at last—and then Bach, the *Aria from Goldberg Variations*. That was harder, more stumbles still. Seth sat on the canvas, loose wrists propped on his knees, his long hands quiet. Over their heads in the rafters of the dome, doves rustled and nested by twos. In the sculpture niches all around the walls, Jane and Rosa Lee placed small offerings: a cluster of golden-brown sycamore balls, their soft fibers shedding and drifting to the floor; a pinecone; a snakeskin they curled neatly as a necklace on a lady's dressing table.

Slowly, as the fall days went on, something rueful and sad deepened under the sunlight, the way it always did—a smell in the air, intimate and familiar, that Sarah sometimes thought she could catch if she turned her head. It was an actual smell in the air and a memory of smells; fallen leaves drying on the forest floor; Father's warm remembered cheek above his stiff collar when Sarah hugged him before bed; the grassy tang in the air of the Yankee House hall as Seth passed by her to investigate the pile of siding board or a workman's empty tobacco pouch left on the mantel, or to peer up at a hammer hooked and dangling from a rafter seventy-five feet in the air. It was the color of piano chords as they rang and rippled and faded. It was the taste that memories could have, memories of people you did not realize until it was too late were already on the way to being lost.

Rosa Lee and Jane went back to Fairibault ahead of them one evening, and Sarah remained at the piano, taking one more run at the Bach. The notes were wine-colored inside her, exalted and sad in a way that felt right for the dusty warm dome of air suspended above her and for the rustle of the dusk outside. She and Seth were here alone. *I sit here at the piano,* hummed a cool voice deep in her brain, shivering down her spine like a soft hammer on a treble string. In a novel the hero would come to her and set his lips on the back of her neck. He would run his fingers along the underside of her arm, bearing the weight of her hands invisibly in his own. Images beat like trapped birds in her head: Seth's long hands, his smooth back turned away, silvery with water, his worried and quizzical smile, his feet with their wide toes in the summer dust. Herself setting those feet, like the woman with Christ's, in a basin of cool water. Lifting them out to nestle them in her own lap. Unbinding her hair, slowly, letting it rush over her shoulders. Closing her eyes so she could feel rather than see him reach for it, fan it around her face. Bending her head to let it fall, let it fall.

She lifted her wrists from the last hanging note and turned. Seth stood behind her, almost but not quite, out of reach. Between them, something waited for one of them to say *yes.*

She stretched up from the bench and he stepped forward and leaned down and they kissed.

It was the smell of him that surprised her and warmed her with what she would later recognize as tenderness, and regret. It was the smell of her own skin after she'd been outside, pulling weeds, picking tomatoes: warmed by blood and sun, tangy with the soil she'd worked her fingers through so deeply she still smelled it. Slipping water over pulses, wrists, the backs of each finger. Even after she washed, the smell of his skin was her own.

Carefully she stood up. Inside her arms his shoulders and back flexed like water, lifting, carrying, moved by its own force. His mouth was very soft. He was afraid. She did not know the name for this. She was afraid. She was a bad girl. Like Bad Katy Pruitt. Maybe worse. *You won't do what married people do until you get married. I know it. Tempt him. Women's sin. Our inheritance—A colored boy—*She wanted this thing she could not name. She wanted Seth.

She kissed deeper into him, then, pressing herself close and standing on her toes. The pressure opened her mouth and Seth flinched, sighed, hesitated, even as his body jolted a wave of heat up both of them, riding in their blood. His hands went to her hair, her waist. Then she couldn't feel him touching her. His mouth was gone. The air was damp there, cold.

"Hey," he mumbled, uselessly. "We—" He took a step back, into a square of sun on the boards, and looked at her. "I—"

They stood. Sarah couldn't speak although the words chased themselves in her head, all up and down her veins. Seth wouldn't look at her until she dropped her eyes and then she felt his eyes on her. She kept hers down and let his stay; their clear brownish-gray was something she'd never finish seeing into if she lived a million years. Her brain was strangely becalmed. Nothing seemed important enough to break the surface of this instant.

"Got to be getting back," Seth finally said.

Sarah looked at the piano. He nodded and left her there. And until the sun was almost down, she played every song she knew, letting them ring and shake the empty dome of noise and light and heat. She wasn't ready to take this flush all through her body, this buzzing in her veins, out into the world that had never seen it. That was the world of Mama and Jane and Alvah and Rosa Lee and the mules and chickens and cats, the world that wouldn't want to know this kiss had ever been. She would be here, alone with the piano and the ringing in her veins that no living person had ever, ever felt and no one ever would again.

At sundown she left the Yankee House and walked home and climbed the stairs to her own room. Ignoring Jane's questioning look, she carried the bathing tub from their room out to Alvah's cookhouse, filled it with buckets of water heated on the stove, and locked the door. From her sponge the water ran down, trapping seed-pearl bubbles against her skin. Skin. It was a mystery and a fact. It was familiar and strange in the way your own face grew strange if you stared at yourself in the mirror without blinking. What was it that made up someone else's body, or your own? Pink curves of shoulder and breast. A mouth with the faint olive taste of any mouth that ate the same things you did: greens and scrounged meat and vegetables that sprawled from each other's hearts in a deserted Indian camp. The urgent salty boy-smell, same as her brother's when she'd passed close to him. Familiar, like that, and yet entirely something else.

Mr. Wainwright and the Rehobeth Militia would take Seth away and kill him if they knew of this. And she would be responsible.

Once you had looked and seen this way, there was no way not to see it, ever again. Pass that barrier of skin and you are up against another person's inside self in a way you could never describe, and never could have forseen or understood.

Remembering Seth's kiss does not make her cry anymore, as it did in the long silent time in Mobile. Maybe that is a good thing. Galen is her husband, the man she loves, the man she huddles under the warm quilts with and kisses in the sickle-shaped shadow of his shoulder blade, his wing. Desire can sleep for so long and then flare up at the oddest thing, hidden deep in the body like the ambergris in one of Mr. Melville's fantastical whales: a rare and precious substance to anoint the heads of kings. If Sarah sometimes sees her husband slumped in his chair and thinks briefly of sliding her palm down his belly, then thinks of Seth, leaning against a tree to eat the sandwiches they had slapped together themselves—well, maybe that is only natural, if not to be dwelt on now. Seth was the first boy who kissed her. The first boy she kissed.

And if she dreams one night in snowfall and wakes with her body clutching itself, rapturously, deep inside—a clutching she at first mistakes for labor—maybe this too is inevitable, as dreams always are. In her dream she's lying with Seth after all, on the rumpled canvas piano cover. In her dream, she has been the first to step toward that wall, feeling his eyes on her back. Feeling, before she even hears his feet on the boards, that he has followed her.

꽃

Uncle Eugene came back to Fairibault late in the night, walking. The blur of his voice and Mama's rose in the hall. "How dare you come here? Expecting us to feed you?" Mama hissed. "I warned you not to come back here. You do realize your brother is dead. You do realize you have no more of a claim on me than any stranger."

"Nowhere else," Uncle Eugene moaned. He coughed. He sounded close to tears. "I've got nowhere else to go."

Mama was quiet for a long time. "Very well," she finally said. "There are spare cabins in the quarters. I'm sorry to ask Alvah and her family to tolerate you. But you will not be under the same roof with my girls. Your brother never forbade you anything. But I will."

The next morning, there was Uncle Eugene at breakfast, thin and ashen. Seth passed the dining room door, carrying a single shabby bag and a pair of shoes with holes in the soles. Eugene did not look Sarah or Jane directly in the eye, eating modest dabs of scrambled eggs and pushing his plate straight back after four bites. "Thank you for your hospitality, Livia," he murmured, and Mama nodded, curtly. She looked at Jane, and at Sarah. A tension in her face would not slacken.

Maybe Mama knows, somehow, what happened in the Yankee House. Can I hide in plain sight of her? Just keep calm, just—never let her see?

※

Two days later, Mr. Wainwright came to dine.

Mama went out in the yard to greet him. He swung down from his big black horse Achilles to stand very close to her. Through the glass Sarah heard their voices, then a sudden burst of laughter: first his, then Mama's. Mama's thin smile was strained yet confident. Sarah knew that smile. Something had gone wrong and would be put right. That smile came when Jane broke the china shepherdess and had to sit, even on a sunny afternoon, clamping the tiny arm to the tiny body until the glue set and the shepherdess was good enough to pass for new. Or when Rosa Lee had let the biscuits burn on their bottoms and would slice off the round black discs of crust, toss them to the chickens, and pile the biscuits in the basket for dinner anyway, their fluffy white hearts exposed. *No waste in this house. What do you girls think, that money grows on trees?*

Actions have consequences. Someone always has to pay. And Mama always seemed to know when Jane or Sarah or Rosa Lee or even Seth had done something wrong.

Why was Mr. Wainwright here? What was that look, so intent and confidential, on Mama's face? That yearning in the upward curve of her throat?

Behind Sarah, Alvah and Rosa Lee bustled, softly, setting the table. Seth was upstairs valeting—that was what Uncle Eugene called helping him put on his coat, shine his shoes and brush his thin hair over the top of his head. Make him presentable. As if anybody could.

Sarah turned away from the window and started to the door. Maybe she could wander out into the yard and linger there, pulling weeds from around the boxwoods at the house's foundation, sweeping off the front gallery, close enough to eavesdrop. But Mama would stop her. *Eavesdroppers never hear any good. Go back in the house.*

And a sudden conviction seized Sarah: Mama was talking to Mr. Wainwright about her.

"We keep order," Mr. Wainwright had said after Robert disappeared and Bad Katy's stomach had begun to swell. "No more than that."

The fear grew in Sarah's chest. Mama was talking to Mr. Wainwright about her and Seth. Mama had seen them coming back from the Yankee House, not quite far enough apart. Mama had asked Jane or Rosa Lee where her sister was, where her brother was, and been told—how careless, how fatal—*Oh, they'll be along in a minute.* She must have found out. Mama knew everything. Now Mr. Wainwright and the other men would do to Seth what they had done to Robert.

Sarah heard a step behind her on the carpet. Alvah stood, looking through the window over Sarah's shoulder, her eyes fixed on Mr. Wainwright. There was nothing in her face for Sarah to read. She turned away and went out of the dining room, back to the kitchen house.

Mr. Wainwright sat at their table, big as life, talking and laughing through dinner, just as he had when Father was alive. Once or twice his gaze bent to Sarah, then to Jane—with something like sadness in his look—then back to Uncle Eugene, who had helped himself to the port three times already. "More for you?" Mama offered ironically, filling his glass again. Uncle Eugene looked surprised, but drank it. "Thank you, Livia," he slurred. Mr. Wainwright smiled. Mama watched them both, smiling too.

"I've got a horse you'd like to see," Mr. Wainwright announced at the end of dinner, setting one hand on Uncle Eugene's shoulder. "Back at my barn, only a little ride away. The night is fine." He lifted his eyebrows and smiled. Sarah watched him. Why was he offering to look at horses in the dark?

Uncle Eugene wobbled to his feet. "Well," he murmured, "reckon I could look, it never hurts to look."

"That's right," Mr. Wainwright encouraged, clapping him on the back. "A nice little ride after dinner does a man's digestion good." He grinned, ushering Eugene toward the door. "But wait." He strode back to Mama, who rose from her chair to meet him, and bent low over her outstretched hand. "Thank you as ever for your hospitality. Ladies." He smiled. Sarah blinked and bobbed her head. Something in Mr. Wainwright's smile chilled her bones.

Out the front door and down the steps went Mr. Wainwright's firm steps and Uncle Eugene's wobbly ones. Mama sat back down and sipped her wine. Alvah stepped forward to lift the empty plates from the table. Her gaze went over Mama's head, through the window, and stopped on Mr. Wainwright, who was helping Uncle Eugene up onto the back of old Job the mule. Mr. Wainwright himself rode his patchwork Jim, the little stallion who could jump any fence if a mare was on the other side. A blur of voices, a jingle of coins, Seth's surprised "thank you, sir," and the hooves rustled up and away from the house.

After dinner Sarah slipped through the back door and made for Alvah's cabin, into which she had never set foot; neither Father nor Mama would allow it. "Not fitting," Mama said. "Leave them privacy," Father said. But Father was dead. Mama was in charge. And Sarah had to know what Alvah had seen when she paused, her hands on Mama's dirty plate, and stared out that window. Through a crack in the curtain the oil lamp glowed. Not letting herself think

what she was doing—*leave them their privacy! Eavesdroppers never
hear any good!*—she huddled under the window like Bad Katy under the privet hedge, straining to hear.

Their voices were urgent and weary, quick and uncertain.
They'd been talking about this for a while.

"It's probably nothin," Seth said uncertainly.

"It ain't nothin," Rosa Lee burst out. "You know what happened
to Robert."

Alvah was quiet. "I've got to say," she said finally, "your sister's
right. That man don't come around for nothing." Tears ripped her
voice into rags. "My boy," she said, "I don't want to say it, I don't
want to know it, but—You're gonna have to go. Just for a little
while."

"Seth? Go?" Rosa Lee started crying too. "But he didn't do
nothin. He ain't—"

"That don't matter, baby," Alvah said. Her voice went flat inside.
"You know it. Both of y'all grown enough to know that."

Another silence, broken by Seth. "How will I go, then, Mama?"
he asked. "Where?" Sarah shivered at the raw anger in his voice.
"Where am I supposed to go that they won't string me up?"

Under the window, Sarah flinched backwards and wobbled
against the forsythia bush Alvah had planted there. It crackled and
Seth's voice paused. Sarah caught her breath and leaped up and
ran, tucking her skirts against her legs to keep them quiet, until
she was under the big magnolia tree at the edge of the lawn. And
on the lowest branch, where Seth and Rosa Lee and Jane had sat
on rainy days to listen to her read *Nicholas Nickelby*, she sat and
wrapped her arms tight around her knees and let the shame shrivel
her until she could hardly breathe. *String me up.* The words swayed
in front of her, inescapable. That was what Mr. Wainwright and
the Rehobeth Militia had done to Mrs. Simmes' Robert because a
girl had tempted him. And she had turned away from Bad Katy's
upstretched hand, as if she was any different. The inheritance of

Eve: it was in her, and it made her a deadly thing to Seth or to any boy. It would stretch her open on a bed, screaming, as a baby pushed out of her. It would beat in her blood as she kissed Seth although she knew she was not supposed to. It would trap Sarah as it had trapped Katy in their mamas' houses for good, bad girls in their own purpose-built prisons. Only what she deserved.

She had put Seth at risk of death, because he was a colored boy.

Uncle Eugene didn't come back to the house that night. Neither did Mr. Wainwright. One of his skinny brown boys rode up on Jim, bearing a note Mama snatched and read and threw into the fire. The next night, Sarah was nudged out of sleep by the sound of the front door closing and Mama's feet slipping up the stairs, almost too soft to hear. Then under Mama's closed bedroom door came the scratch of a match to light the lamp, the subtle scurry of a pen across a page.

On a sunny morning oddly soon after that Mr. Wainwright appeared in his buggy in their drive with a strange woman in the seat next to him. "This is Caroline," he announced. "My new bride. No, we can't stay. We're off to New Orleans for a honeymoon. But I did want her to meet my dear neighbors." He grinned at Mama. "My friends." In a pale yellow dress with a beige traveling cape over it—tied with a wide white silk ribbon at the neck, although the sun was warm—and a white lace-trimmed bonnet, Caroline sat with both hands folded in her lap, blinking and smiling. Her face was a perfect oval, a little too stretched at top and bottom, her lips too pale. Caroline's eyes were wide pale blue with no expression, eyelashes and eyebrows the same pale color as the hair swooping in two tight bands down across her forehead. She turned her head slowly and obediently—mouth pursed open, just a little, palest pink—to look at Sarah and Jane blinking in the sun next to the buggy. And then she lifted one hand—white glove still perfectly unwrinkled in the palm—and waved. Up and down, an obedient little crinkle of the fingers as if Mr. Wainwright had just taught her how.

"Caroline's aunt was my own dear mother's sister," Mr. Wainwright said. "It would have made her so happy to see this." His words were thick and oily in Sarah's ears, pleased with himself as a hero in a novel. What would Mama say? What would she do? What could she do but watch him, and smile her same little smile, ironic and undisturbed, with something hardening in her eyes. Sarah could see it. She doubted whether Mr. Wainwright could. "Fetched out of the convent," he continued, "just for me. To ease the life of a poor old widower."

"I didn't know any of your people were Catholics, Tom," Mama said.

"Just the Savannah branch," Mr. Wainwright replied, "the genteel ones."

"Up here at Rehobeth," Mama observed, "gentility's in short supply. Except in words. And words are cheap. But not as cheap as promises."

Mr. Wainwright's grin retreated and his jaw tensed. His eyes and Mama's locked. A mockingbird flashed in a tumble of gray and black and white through the air to perch on the back of a porch chair, flicking his tail. Caroline's gaze followed him, dreamy, as if she had forgotten Mr. Wainwright was there at all.

"I'll say farewell," Mama continued. "Y'all will be wanting to embark." She stepped forward to the buggy and closed one hand over Caroline's where they lay folded in her lap, and squeezed. Mama's face went into the shade of Caroline's bonnet, her dark hair blotting out Caroline's pale skin, and she set her cheek against Caroline's and closed her eyes. Then she stepped away from the buggy and turned with a swirl of skirts and went into the house and closed the door.

Mr. Wainwright stood in the sun, looking after her, his confident smile completely gone. After a moment, he straightened his shoulders, tipped his hat to Sarah and Jane, climbed back in the buggy, and drove away. Sarah and Jane waved at Caroline, but, her face still set blankly ahead, Caroline did not wave back.

When Sarah went in the house, she saw Mama standing at the window watching the buggy out of sight. "Poor girl," she murmured, and she turned away. She never mentioned Mr. Wainwright or Caroline again. They were part of Fairibault now. And Fairibault was soon to be gone, locked up for Mr. Ferris. All of it would be left behind.

❧

A stubborn heart keeps beating, and beating, even when a stubborn brain wishes everything would stop.

Tomorrow, Sarah and Jane and Mama and Alvah and Rosa Lee would drive away from Fairibault for good. Humble Mr. Ferris with his kind eyes had come and signed the papers and Fairibault was gone, in a whir of packing and sorting and dropping exhausted into bed. Tomorrow they would go to old Aunt Maude's house in Mobile. They'd leave Father and ghost Sarah under their white stones in the cemetery, under the grass that grew longer and longer now that Old Enneas with his scythe was dead. Alvah and Rosa Lee would come with them.

Seven days ago, Seth had disappeared. The knowledge was lodged in Sarah, fine as a nettle spine, Because of what Mama said to Mr. Wainwright. A slow nod, a slump of his shoulders. A confidential tilt of her head. And Seth was gone.

He left no note for Sarah. Only this: when she woke up, a finch's nest rested on her bureau, smaller than a mockingbird's but woven tighter. The finches could nest anywhere, in the trees in the woods with the other birds but also in the foamy ferns in their baskets on the veranda. You wouldn't see them– the blink of brilliant reddish-purple on their heads, the drab brown bodies—until they wanted to be seen. They could go anywhere. And did.

Seth had slipped into her room—while she was downstairs? While she was asleep?—and left this nest for her to find.

Mama had had Alvah throw away the mockingbird's nest she and Seth had found. Never would she get this one. Never would she even touch it.

So Sarah left the house as the night came down, cupping the small prickly nest in her palms. She walked across the fields that had once been theirs, past the finger of woods and the Yankee House to the bank of the river. She sat there by herself, not thinking, only seeing. The brown water gurgled and snatched at itself as it spun a long line past Fairibault to—where? Spinning a thread, like Alvah at the wheel. Like Ariadne in the Labyrinth: holding her thin silver line in her hands, following it to the dark warm place at the center of the world where he would be, not a beast but a boy who was waiting there, alone. For her. His breath would be warm in that darkness, against no one else's skin but hers.

The posts Seth's father Marcus had sunk for that imaginary dock still stood, lonely, in the water.

She imagined it, because there was nothing else to do: Seth stepped carefully through the deep mud and the thick grass and the willow seedlings down the bank. He dropped his bundle of clothes and food into the bottom of a narrow wooden boat, then set one foot and the other down. He stood, then, on a chancy wooden floor above a flood, rocked and tipped by water that would take him—where? He set one hand on his father's post and pushed off. He sat down and squared his long hands on the oars and curled them in a circle, through the water. A line of drops flung, flashing, back into the current. And Seth was gone.

Sarah bent forward, with the finch's nest cradled in her hands. The river crept up her knuckles, the backs of her hands, her fingertips, her wrists. And then it lifted the small firm knot of straw and twigs out of her hands. The nest was woven so tightly the water didn't seep through the bottom; it bobbed away from shore, bouncing gently off a sunken twig and then a log and then spinning out, away. It twirled in the current, smaller and smaller, until it blended with the dark and it was gone.

A sleepy fat mockingbird on a branch blinked at her. Maybe this was the great-grandbird or the great-great-grandbird of the chicks she and Seth had saved from the forest path. He'd stood on old Shadrach the mule's back and she had handed him the naked pink babies in their circle of twigs. Surely those chicks had lived because she and Seth were in the same place at the right moment, together.

A big turtle on a log—the last one still awake this evening, of all the turtles in the world—peered at the floating speck, then cranked its head slowly around to stare at her. The air was so quiet she could hear the scrape of its belly-shell on wood as it heaved itself off the log and plunged away. River creatures peeped and hissed and sang, rustling past her through the grass and leaping at mosquitoes with a sudden rush and snap. Tree frogs buzzed and chimed in a rising hum that separated itself into waves: *see see see see.* Deer eased down the opposite bank and dipped their noses in the water and swung their heads up to look at her. *Drip, drip, drip* splashed back into the river from their slim muzzles, and they quivered and wheeled and scrambled off. She flicked a twig into the current, and then another one. Entering the river, they became things she'd never touched, swirling on down to Eufaula and Apalachicola and the Gulf of Mexico: water, water, wider than the sky.

Seth was gone. Now there would simply be his absence to live with as one day became the next, and the next, for more days than she could imagine.

The little nest would melt, breaking apart in the water. But the pieces might remember they had once been knit together, holding something that was once alive.

You can't sit here forever, said Mama's voice in her head. *Come on, my girl. We've got an early start. And we'll come back to visit. Mr. Ferris said we could.*

I never will, Sarah knew. *I never will.*

Her own feet didn't seem to make a sound as she walked through the fields back up to the house. Beside the back door, the fire bucket still smoldered. Mama had been burning papers. One charred half-curling ledger-spine was left. *Accounts.* It was all that was left of Mama's little green book, in which she'd recorded all the household figures and all the money ever given to Uncle Eugene. Mama must have decided not to reckon on any of it, anymore.

8

In Iowa, the winter deepens, slowly. A big wagon brings more flour and cornmeal and sugar and coffee to the little Eldorado General Store. Sarah has knit down to the stomach of the baby's sweater by now. Only three or four more rows to go. The baby wriggles in Sarah's belly, then falls silent when Rosa Lee speaks to it, smiling: "All right, then, come on out if you want to." They bake and they wash, hauling water till they think their backs will crack in two. Nils Erickson and Bessy MacElvain meet in the street, pause and speak, and walk away again. Nils turns to look back at her. Trygve and Rosa Lee walk in the late afternoons as the light goes down, brilliant orange-pink and blue over the smooth hills of snow. The days go by.

One night, in Sarah's dreams, Galen rises from his pillow and comes apart. The matted curls at the back of his head lift and dissolve into air. His arms and legs float up from his torso like the ropes that tie a balloon to the ground. His chest shimmers. Through his skin she begins to see the curtained half-light of the window; between the sickle-curves of his shoulder blades, the moon. He will join the moon, float up to it in pieces, float away. "Galen!" she calls to him. "Galen!" But he doesn't hear. He can't hear. Because drifting over it are the melancholy notes of the *Goldberg Variations* aria, plum-colored and somber and sweet, with the little stumble right where she always misses the note, herself. *I lost my piano,* she howls in a voice only she can hear. *No piano. You took it. It's gone.*

She wakes, heart hammering. Under her breasts and her arms and all along her belly, she's sweating. She heaves herself up against her pillows and stares down at Galen, not quite believing what she sees: still pressed into the pillow, his face is creased in sleep, his curls mashed flat. But her shifting against the mattress has stirred him, and he opens his eyes as she watches. Like a baby, it takes a few seconds for him to focus. "What?" he mutters.

Sarah shakes, still, rattled by this dream's strange residue of fear and anger. "Look," she says. "It's snowing again." She leans far out over the cold floor and tugs back the calico curtain against the night. Even in the dark, the snow lights the world on its own, with an eerie, quieter grayer light than the moon. She holds her breath. If she listens, she might even hear it fall.

"Mmmgh," mutters Galen, and closes his eyes again.

Sarah swishes her legs out from under the quilts and sets both feet on the floor. "I'm going out," she announces, stooping awkwardly to snatch the doctor's old boots and shove her feet in their thick socks down into the toes. Like Orpheus, she has to leave this room without turning back. The dream's odd conviction lingers, cold and certain over her hammering heart: if she does not keep going, up and out of this room, her husband will dissolve, will come apart and leave her here. But she will be first. With their baby under her heart, bumping like a moored boat at her ribs, she will be the first to walk away from him.

Galen shifts. "Going out?" he mumbles. "Still snowing?"

"Of course," Sarah says. She tosses the quilts all the way back with a satisfying whoosh and cold air rushes underneath it; Galen winces and curls tighter. Outside, a wind whirls snowflakes into the air and dies; a loose windowpane rattles. There's a cold faint light in the sky from somewhere she can't see. "I want to walk." Nothing will please her more than to feel the chalky scuff of fresh powdery snow under her boots, to look back and see the trail of her skirts in the snow like a peacock's-tail track in the dust. To hug her layers of sweater and cape against herself and let them go, feeling the air between the layers warmed by her own body. To look straight up into the sky, right into the million tiny wet taps of flakes on her eyelids and hair and tongue. To be out alone, in the deep night silence that rings on and on like the last note, even after she lifts her fingers from the piano keys.

Galen stirs again and sighs. "Sarah," he says.

"What," Sarah says. She's already into her skirt and blouse, not bothering with her Motherhood Corset, and twining her shawl around her shoulders and her neck. Her cape will go over that.

"My darling, you can't go out there in this snow at this time of night," Galen says. The patience in his voice infuriates her. "You'll slip and fall."

"I can too," Sarah says. She lets this cold anger boil up in her voice. "I've got to get out of here. Can't lie here and just—"

Galen sighs. He swings his feet down and sits up. "I'm coming too," he says.

"No, you're not," Sarah snaps. She thumps down the stairs in the doctor's old boots and steps out into the night. The air teems with a soft roar, millions of tiny flakes falling and striking, and under that a deeper silence than anything. She turns her back to the house and starts walking. The snow almost covers the tops of her boots already. In her belly, the baby is quiet, wondering. *Good boy*, she murmurs. *Good girl.* She keeps walking. *I'll just go to the end of the street and see how I feel.*

She passes the inn and the schoolhouse and the church. Behind the big tree at the little cemetery gate, she stops and lowers herself down, with one hand on the gate, to pee—snickering at the steaming pit she makes in the snow, but it comes on too suddenly to fight—and kicks snow over it and keeps walking. She brushes snow off her shoulders, surprised to see how much is there. Something inside her is easing now, and she knows that when she goes back in, she'll be able to sleep. But there's just a little more to go, to the place where the road runs out and the fence ends and the wild part of the valley begins. All the cattle and horses are in their barns. What do deer do on a night like this? *The foxes have holes, and the birds of the air have nests, but the Son of man hath nowhere to lay his head.* She shivers and stares up at the bare tree branches over the narrow path of the street until she can distinguish them from the night. The snowflakes on her face intensify their sting. She lowers her head.

And there is Mama's voice: *Men forgive themselves everything and women nothing.*

Yet Mama also said, *in a marriage, you must forgive. More than you ever thought you could.*

Forgive. Forgive. Sarah fights the bewildering anger that rises in her now, surely as the acid in her baby-compressed stomach after eating turnips. Every time she thinks of her mother now, the anger comes. In her mind she paces and shouts, driven back and forth by its force: *why couldn't you see that I—You sent for Mr. Wainwright and Seth ran away in fear for his life. You drove him off. And I'll never see him any more.*

Why can't she stop thinking about Seth? Why can't she stop reaching for her mother in her mind, clawing, clawing, reaching for that remembered face to draw blood? Even though it only opened scratches in her own chest, the mirror of that heart she reached for over and over? Reverend Preus would say she needed to forgive, that a lack of forgiveness left you open from the inside to anything else that wanted to hurt you, and to everything that person had ever said or done to wrong you. "Unforgiveness leaves you vulnerable," he said. "Only feels like it makes you strong."

Maybe, Sarah, the person you really need to forgive is yourself.

Forgive herself? For what? What had she ever done? It was Mama who had mourned for Johnny and sold the land and carted them off to Mobile. Mama who had turned Sarah in front of the mirror and dressed her and sent her off to market. Mama who had held Alvah's hands, weeping, as she died in her neat back room in Aunt Maude's house. Mama who had somehow learned about Sarah's kiss with Seth in the Yankee House, under the great unfinished dome, and punished her for it without ever saying a word. Was punishing her still. *You'll never know where Seth is,* a voice like Mama's mocks inside her head. *He saw Tom Wainwright at our table and knew it was best to run. From you.*

That night Mama had been drinking from Father's leftover port, going over accounts, late, in the study. Sarah, awake, got out of bed to see if she couldn't walk herself sleepy again, came across the lamp burning in the study. She could curl up right here in the big wing chair and tuck her feet under her. Sit here with Mama for a while. As she had done with Father.

"Men forgive themselves everything and women nothing," Mama said suddenly. She was tipsier than Sarah knew. "Nothing." She lifted the square-bottomed glass and slurped the last pool of port. "A gentleman's prerogative." She smirked.

"Forgive?" Sarah murmured. Why? But she doubted Mama would answer. This would be one of those gates Mama swung shut as Sarah clambered over it, turning away even as Sarah stretched out an arm, calling *Wait*—

"Us in our corsets and furbelows," Mama mused. Her eyes were blurry. "Us in our hoops. Like fools. Toting around our own goddamn cages. Like the goddamn Man in the Iron Mask in one of your father's goddamn books."

"Father was good to us," Sarah volunteered. Her voice shook.

"Father was—" Mama paused, sighed. She sloshed a wave of port out of the decanter. Most of it landed in the belly of the glass. "Your father was right. This Madeira is very fine." She sipped. "Unfortunately, he wasn't right about too much else, it seems."

Sarah sat, gasping like a hooked fish on the riverbank. There was literally nothing she could say, except in her head—begging or angry words that wouldn't spin themselves out in a neat thread through her lips. Begging words: *won't you listen to what I*—Angry words. And the anger, most of all, must not come forth. *Oh,* she thought, *you say this now. After you let Johnny—It was all your*

fault. After you let Johnny do what he wanted, say what he wanted.
When we said 'go to hell' just like him you shouted. Called us little
hussies, slapped our bottoms and sent us to bed. Bad girls. Johnny
said it and you smiled. He lamed his horse, got Celia pregnant. He
took you away from me. The warm place at my side getting cold. Our
quilt forgotten. And Uncle Eugene, you let him—You knew. Even as
you yelled at Father let him keep breathing air? you let him live.
You let him come back. Even though you knew what he did to
me. You knew and nothing changed. Because you wanted to meet
Mr. Wainwright in the woods, hold him up tight against you and
kiss him just like Father had never existed. You didn't care about
anything else. You wanted to feel that and you didn't want anyone
else to feel it. Not even me. Just because Seth was colored. Just
because he was a man. Did you know, Mama? Did you ever know?
You had to. Right under your nose. Nothing in this house, you
brag, escapes you. Well, it does. It does. Johnny escaped you. Seth
escaped you too. And so will I.

"Son, I don't know why you had to be so wild." Mama's voice
interrupted Sarah's thoughts. She leaned all the way back in Father's chair to stare at the ceiling. There was a meandering crack
in the plaster there, branching like a blue vein in Sarah's wrist. "But
oh, you were my proud boy, my good proud boy." And suddenly
Mama was crying, as harsh and ragged as if Sarah wasn't there.

Sarah went to her mother, set her hand on her mother's back,
and felt it jump and shudder with her sobs. She would wait here
while grief for her brother possessed her mother's body, wait for
it to pass. *Cast it out,* the preacher would shout. *Cast this evil out!*

It was so strange to touch her mother's body. To know that she
herself had been in that dark warm world, bathed in unthinking,
unimaginable love. Even in the quick touches of Mama's hand on
her elbow, the stiff hugs of going and coming and going, the impatient swish of the hairbrush or the scuttle of fingers up dress-back

buttons, there had never been that type of love. Even in Mama's face bending close over the bed at night, before sleep.

It's Johnny she loves. Not me.

The knowledge spread though Sarah, a dismal stain of blood under bruised skin.

It's Johnny she longs for. Even though I'm right here. I am here only to bring honor. Or shame. I am bad or I am good. I'm a daughter. Nothing more. If no one but me saw Uncle Eugene's hand on my thigh at the creek, it could not have been real. Right? But Seth must be chased away because I kissed him. That is the thing that no one can forgive.

She kept her hand on her mother's shoulder, waiting for the hitching and jerking and crying to stop. Her own eyes were dry, the sockets sandy in her skull. It was as if she watched her mother there at her dead father's desk, in the house of women swimming alone in this night, from a great distance, impossible to bridge with tears. King Lear's voice thundered at her: *So young, and so untender?*

Her own voice answered: *So young, my lord, and true.* A daughter who could not hearken to the lies. Not anymore.

Mama sniffled, slowly pushed herself upright, and, finally, reached and patted Sarah's hand. She swiped the back of her palm under her nose. "Such a comfort," she said, looking straight at Sarah. A small wet smile crimped her face. "You are such a comfort." If Sarah said what she were really thinking, Mama would never speak to her again. Yet there is no time, she knew, especially with your mama, to say the words you really think. For they are never the words she wants to hear.

Mama turned her face further up into the light and opened her mouth slowly. Her eyes were still fixed on Sarah's face. "You know what happened, don't you?" she asked. "You know I . . . sent him away because of you. *Had* him sent. Made sure he would never ever come back to put you in that sort of danger."

Sarah's chest was full of something heavy and inexpressibly cold. Him? Mama was talking of Seth. She had to be. *You did this for me. Really? You never thought to ask me, did you. Never thought to say. And—oh, more than anything—never even seemed to know that my life is not your own and has no similarities to your own. Not even close. Doesn't even share a border. I have grown up inside my own head and you never even saw. You never wanted to see. Seth is gone because you scared him away and you call yourself protecting me from danger. And then you cling to Tom Wainwright and kiss him as you never kissed Father, as you hissed at him <u>Don't touch me</u> when you thought no one could hear—*

But this heavy cold thing would never melt. *Thaw, and dissolve itself into a dew.* Or into speech.

You hypocrite. You murderer. Most foul.

You liar.

"Goodnight, Mama," Sarah said, kissing her mother's forehead. She walked slowly until she was out of the room, then ran before the tears could catch her there, back to her room, to cram a pillow against her face, to lie facedown and quiet as the sobs tore out of her one by one, until she slept.

She remembers those sobs, can feel them shaking in her chest right now. In the deep stillness of the snowy Iowa night, she clutches the round mound of her belly to make them stop. *My child won't know that world. I'll never lie to her like that. I never will.*

She doesn't hear the muffled crunch of Galen's steps until he's right behind her. "Here you are," he murmurs.

"I am," she says. Her back is to him. She won't turn around until she can stop these sobs threatening to break out of her body. He sets one hand on each of her shoulders, and when she turns around, she turns directly into his embrace. His coat is sticky with snow that melts against her cheek. When she raises her face to look at him, he brushes the dampness away. His hands are bare, still faintly warm from where he's shoved them in his pockets. He's come out after her without his gloves.

They turn and walk quietly home in the tracks they've made. In the dark, they undress and crawl back under the quilts, mashing the lumps in the mattress ticking aside with shoulder and hip, settling together until their shared heat warms the bed and they fall asleep.

"You're like a woodstove," Galen says as they wake, drowsy, in the morning. He nestles closer. "Feels good." But now one simple fact bites into Sarah's mind like ink into thick paper: Tom Wainwright smiled and rose to his feet and led Uncle Eugene out of the dining room, while her mama watched. And no one ever saw him after that. No one saw Seth, either.

Mrs. Simmes' Robert had been found hanged and burned.

"That frowsty thing on your windowsill?" Mama said. "I had Alvah throw it out."

These things are connected in her brain, strung in a straight line sagging from their weight. But she cannot make them come clearer yet.

Eventually, Sarah climbs out of her nest and draws with her finger on the window, burning the shape of hearts, diamonds, her own name into its skin of ice. The heat her finger trails keeps melting it even after she steps away. For the first waking hour of the day the words burn like that, too, inside her mind. Uncle Eugene. Seth. Tom Wainwright. Oh, Mama.

At midday Oyvind gallops down the street in his wagon and jerks the big horses to a stop at their front steps and storms into the foyer, shouting for Galen. "Up in the woods, cutting logs for the new barn," Oyvind blurts as Sarah and Rosa Lee rush out of the kitchen, wiping bread dough from their hands. "A big log rolls.

On Trygve, hits him to the ground. I push it off, but Trygve don't move."

"You were right to leave him there," says Galen, snatching his bag. Sarah can see the initial diagnosis forming behind his eyes. Her stomach sinks.

"Trygve," cries Rosa Lee. "Can I come with you?"

"Best if you don't," says Galen, and he hugs Rosa Lee, quickly, before following Oyvind out the door.

Sarah and Rosa Lee grab their shawls and hurry down the street to the inn. But Mrs. Thorson is already gone. The door's swinging open. The four big room keys on their tiny hooks behind the counter scrape back and forth in the wind, and the lead pencil on the counter rolls to the left. Calendar pages flutter: *try Mrs. Murphy's Patent Bluing, the Laundry Day Delight!* On the stove in the small room behind the counter, a kettle is shrieking itself dry. Sarah hurries back there to move it off the stove and returns to Rosa Lee, who stands in the middle of the room with both hands over her eyes. She's crumpled, suddenly, after hurrying to get here, declaring she will go on up to the woods, she will see what's happened to Trygve. She stands in the inn and sobs, and Sarah holds her. "He'll be all right, Rosa Lee," she keeps saying, "he'll be all right, Galen and Oyvind and his mama will take care of him."

Without Trygve, her friend will be—a widow? Without ever having been a wife. Big Trygve, his eyes alight at Rosa Lee in the green dress, walking at night with her in the wind -- what will she be, now, if he is gone? "Rosa Lee," she says, "if you want to go to him, we will. No matter what Galen says."

"I do," Rosa Lee sobs. "I'm just—so scared."

Two wagon ruts stretch down the valley to the twins' farmstead. Sarah and Rosa Lee hurry on in the wind. "Go ahead without me," Sarah urges, "I'm so slow," but Rosa Lee shakes her head, "I need you there too," she says. A woman's boot tracks rip the snow ahead of them: Linka Thorson, running.

Outside the cabin, the twins' big Percheron, hooked to a wagon, stomps his back leg uncertainly. One of his reins has slipped from its hook on the driver's seat and trails over his back into the mud. The cabin door is closed, and they can't hear anything inside. Rosa Lee is first to open it and step inside. There's a quick burst of voices. On the threshold, Sarah hesitates. And she steps inside as well.

On one of two beds in the cabin's single open room, Trygve lies peculiarly rigid under a quilt, his eyes open. He's hissing Norwegian, and Linka kneels at his head. "Pain," she translates, "he just keeps saying, it hurts, it hurts." She's crying, and wringing out a rag in warm water to wipe her son's forehead. She turns as Rosa Lee enters, and Trygve's eyes, and Oyvind's, follow hers as well. Oyvind startles, Trygve's eyes widen and close, slowly. He's not glad to see Rosa Lee, Sarah realizes. He doesn't want her to see him.

Rosa Lee dips her head but comes forward to the bed and bends and reaches for him. He blinks at her, his eyes brightening with tears. "I couldn't not come," she tells him. Linka hands her the rag and she smooths it over Trygve's forehead, his cheeks. "I had to see you."

Trygve closes his eyes, pressing tears out of the corners, down his temples into the pillow. Rosa Lee touches a corner of the rag to them. Oyvind turns away to hide his own tears.

"Rosa Lee," Galen says. "Trygve's in a lot of pain. It's best now if you and Sarah go—"

"I'm staying," Rosa Lee snaps. "I'm not going anywhere."

"You need her, Galen," Sarah says. "She can help."

Galen looks carefully at Trygve's face. His eyes are still closed, with an expression underneath the pain that makes Sarah's stomach clench. "All right," Galen says. "But Sarah, you go home."

"I'll take her," Oyvind blurts. He steps quickly outside, and Sarah follows him. Trygve doesn't want Rosa Lee to see him like this. He wants her with him. But in one way, it's worse if she stays. Because even though Galen hasn't told her, she knows what's happened to Trygve, what the diagnosis will be. So does Oyvind. So does his mother. So does Trygve himself.

Oyvind helps Sarah onto the wagon seat and scrambles up and snatches the reins and jolts the big horse into a trot. Then he gulps and gives way to sobs. His whole body jerks and hitches like a child's. "I couldn't stop the log," he gasps, clutching the reins in one hand and clenching the other over his face. "I couldn't stop it, and it rolled—"

"Oyvind," Sarah murmurs, "Oyvind, it was not your fault." She sets one arm around Oyvind's shoulders. "It was an accident. Nothing you could have done."

"I told him we should build the new barn," Oyvind gulps, "so I could make myself a house out of the old one and he and Miss Rosa Lee could have the cabin." A fresh wave of tears crumples his face, and Sarah pats his back, suffused with a strange, tender sorrow. This is a twenty-five-year-old man, only four years younger than herself. She should know what to say to him. But she doesn't.

"But I'm sure he thought this was a good idea," Sarah says, "and wanted to do it himself. Maybe he'd been thinking of it already?" Certainly Trygve had been thinking of it. Standing in the door of hers and Galen's house, helping Rosa Lee on with her cloak. Taking her walking in the green dress. Certainly he had been thinking of the home, the wife, he would have at last, here in Eldorado. But where will that light in his eyes go? What will he say to Rosa Lee? What will they do?

Sarah remembers her cousin Mattie Lea's husband Ronald propped in his chair on the porch at Fairibault, his half-leg jutting. Mattie Lea sweeping up behind him to set the baby astraddle of his leg, kiss the top of his head. "It ain't every woman," Ronald had said to Mama proudly, ruefully, "can be married to a cripple." Mama had nodded, patting Mattie Lea's arm: "yes, she's a girl of character." So was Rosa Lee. She would not desert Trygve for this. But how could they marry, now?

Oyvind draws up in front of Sarah's house and helps her out of the wagon. "I'll be right here," she says uselessly. Oyvind nods and slaps the reins on the Percheron's back and gallops back up the street, out of sight.

⁂

Galen doesn't come back to the house until after dark. Sarah meets him at the door with a cup of tea he accepts and sips from once before collapsing onto the parlor sofa. He closes his eyes and pushes the skin of his face up and down against his skull with both hands. "God, I'm tired," he says. "So tired."

Sarah leans into him. A tense weariness ebbs into her body from his. He drops both hands in his lap and stretches his legs out in front of him and tips his head back onto the carved wooden frame of the sofa; it must be uncomfortable, cutting into his neck, but he doesn't stir. His gray-green eyes are open, staring, dark. "Broken," he declares, finally. "He can't move."

"Oh, Galen," Sarah whispers. She squeezes her eyes shut against the picture of Trygve in the bed, hissing in Norwegian *it hurts, it hurts.* But it doesn't help. When she opens them, Galen is still staring at the ceiling. "What will you do?" she asks him.

"Hell, Sarah," Galen snaps, "I don't know. What can you do for a paralytic?" He flings both hands into the air, so suddenly it seems he will strike her face, and drops them in his lap. "What can you do except make them comfortable and wait for them to die?"

"I'm sorry," Sarah murmurs. "I'm sorry."

He's drawing away from her, deep into himself: she feels him leaving, like a physical coolness. Like an empty space in bed. She heaves her baby-thick body up from the sofa and climbs the stairs to their room and undresses and huddles between the quilts until her own warmth makes a place in which she can fall asleep. Everything in her head seems to have swollen shut, tight and miserable with pain. Nothing will come. Just as she closes her eyes, she remembers that Rosa Lee didn't come back in the house this evening. Maybe she is still at the cabin with Trygve. Maybe she's walking back on that road, all by herself. "Galen," she starts to call, "where is Rosa Lee?" But the delicious upward-swirling tendrils of sleep twine around her wrists and ankles and draw her down.

If Galen comes to bed that night, she doesn't know it. He's not there when she falls asleep. And he's not there when she wakes up. Neither is Rosa Lee. When she goes downstairs in the morning, she pauses in the office door: splayed-open medical books cover the long table, dogeared and pencil-scribbled in Galen's handwriting. There is a woodcut of a young man in an upright sling that looks like a torture device: *the frame of Hippocrates,* the caption reads. *In the earliest medical texts of ancient Egypt, spinal cord injury is called "an ailment not to be treated."* The words leap to her eyes: *severed axon. Wallerian degeneration. Eighty days bedridden before death. Progonosis: poor.*

Sarah turns to another book—*Foundations of Surgery*, reads the gold-lettered spine. What if Galen could cut into Trygve's spine to scoop out the shattered cell and nerve matter as gently as Sarah herself would scoop a rotten place from a peach? *Laying a patient upon his belly and by incisions laying bare the bones of the spine,* Sarah reads the flat words on the page, *breaking up these bones and exposing the spinal marrow itself, exceeds all belief*. Maybe this doctor is referring to a miracle; a surgery like this done to make a patient walk again. *Lazarus, take up your bed and walk. Trygve, rise.* But she doesn't think that's what this doctor means. *Exceeding all belief. It won't happen. He'll never walk again. And Galen can't save him.*

Sarah makes some oatmeal on the stove and eats it, thinking. The twins' cabin, that's where they are. That's where she'll go. She casts about the kitchen but finds only a bundle of cold hoecakes, a pot of jam; it can't be helped, they'll need something to eat, this is better than nothing, she'll make everyone a big meal later. She bundles the food into a basket and wraps her cape around herself and sets out into the bright winter day, down the long path to the cabin.

Four houses down and she reaches Linka Thorson's inn. A window on the first floor, near the back, is cracked open, just a little. Why would Linka have a window open in the winter? Then she realizes: fresh air. For invalids. Trygve's in that room. In the bright sun, the window seems dark; she can't see anything inside through the glare on the glass.

In the yard between the privy and the kitchen door, Linka stands at her laundry kettle, a waist-high iron cauldron that swings on its hooks over the fire pit, between two cedar posts. Jens built this wash-place for her when they first came here, when Trygve and Oyvind were babies small enough to swaddle in their baskets and plant a safe distance away, under the tree, while she built the fire and heated the water. Jens is fifteen years dead but the great cauldron still hangs here, an orange bloom of rust on its belly, big bubbles of air trapped in cloth and soap floating inside. The snow has retreated in a ring from the fire, from the fury of Linka's effort. *Beat it back. Melancholy waits for those who let it in.*

With both hands, Linka grips a stout stick and stirs, then jabs it deep into the water to punch the cloth all the way down. Her forehead and her bare arms shine with sweat despite the cold; her hair straggles like a witch's from its bun. Pound, swish, lift: sympathetically, Sarah's own arms ache.

"Mornin, Sarah," Linka says. Her eyes are shadowed, bruise-dark underneath. Quickly, she shifts to hide the heap of quilts and linens in the laundry basket at her feet, but not before Sarah sees the stains. "What you doin out?"

"Come to see you," Sarah says, "I thought you might need some food. I'm going to make more, but this is all I had. Nobody's at my house so I thought they must be—"

"In Trygve's room," Linka confirms with a nod at the window. "Your husband and Rosa Lee. We brought him here this morning."

Sarah looks at the washpot. "Let me help you," she offers, but Linka shakes her head, "no," she says, "not with your baby. When the boys were comin, Jens did the wash." A smile chases itself away across her face and her lips tighten. Sarah steps toward her and stops. Linka's head dips lower. If she comes closer, Linka will cry. *Please,* says the grip of her wide reddened hands on the wash stick, *don't.*

"This is beautiful," Sarah says instead, peering into the pot. Swirling slowly in the warm water is a quilt with faded wagon-wheel shapes of blue and yellow and red. Once the blue must have been the color of the river in October, an hour before sunset, the red the same red as the inside of a rose. But this quilt has been in and out of the washpot many times. She looks at Linka's roughened hands on the washing stick. Iowa is a hard place. It wears away so many lovely things.

"These were my mama's dresses from Norway," Linka says, "too old to use anymore, but Mama, could she wear out a dress. I tell you. I took up all the scraps, made this quilt for the trunk when we came. Can't think but the colors will cheer him up." She looks at Trygve's window and looks away. She stops stirring, and her voice shakes. "Something pretty in there," she says, "he always liked this quilt, he just needs something pretty."

Sarah steps forward and circles Linka's shoulder with one arm and Linka leans against her neck and cries. The water settles and the soap film thickens and grays. From under the surface, bubbles rise and pop one by one.

"I shouldn't," Linka finally says, "he'll hear me." She straightens and shoves the stick into the pot, then lifts it, leaning heavily on the end, to lever the sopping quilt up to the rim. "Hot," she says, "don't touch it." Sarah can see the faded rainbow-shaped wheels, the uncertain stitches—she was making this in Norway, she thinks, when me and Jane were making ours in Alabama—and the lumps of cotton stuffing clumped together under the white muslin backing, and the ghosts of stains. *He always liked this quilt.* That boy in his dark room. How many times will this quilt be boiled and swished and washed and rinsed before the stitches pop, and the last shadow of these colors is gone for good? How many times before the scraps of Linka's mother's dresses fall apart, again? Against her will, Sarah hears her mother's voice: *Why does she keep putting that beautiful thing on that poor boy's bed?*

"Rinse," says Linka to herself and swivels to drop the wet, bunched quilt into a nearby tub of cold water. A swirl with the stick, a careful twist back and forth through the water, and then she lifts the quilt up out of its bath with both arms and carries it to a clothesline stretched tight between two bare trees. Sarah grabs one end of the quilt to keep it from dropping in the dirty snow and they spread it over the line neatly, then stand back. The wheels of color march left to right, one by one.

"It's nice and sunny today," says Sarah. "This might get almost dry."

"What does the doctor say about Trygve?" Linka asks suddenly, not looking at Sarah. In her apron pocket, her hand twists and twists. "What does he really say?"

Sarah hesitates, a second too long. How to describe the look on Galen's face, the stacks of books splayed helplessly all over the surgery table, the anger and fear in his outburst: *wait for him to die.*

Linka pauses, too, and trails her fingers over the quilt. "Rest, he says," she murmurs. "We'll try it. And we'll see."

※

Snow streams past the parlor window, blowing horizontally, smooth as a river. She must stay here. *Hold down the fort. Rest yourself. Take care of your baby, now.*

Sarah sits to take up her knitting, then stops. A listening silence in the house tells her she's alone. Maybe Rosa Lee is out in the barn milking Siss. If so, she'll be there a while; milking holds you in a kind of half-sleep in your very spot, forehead against the leathery sag of flank, manure and dust and hair warm in your nose, hands kneading and pulling as if you're a kitten working milk from Minx's belly. Knead, pull, stroke, listen to the *hiss, splash, hiss.* Feel Siss prop her back leg and drowse, settling into the relief. Sarah will feel this in her own breasts, with the baby. How soon?

She can't get distracted. She has to move quickly before Rosa Lee comes back. She will never be forgiven if she's found. Pregnant women take strange notions, Mama would say. But even that is no excuse.

The air in Rosa Lee's room is still and cool, faintly scented with the herb sachets they made this fall. Lavender and rosemary and mint, tucked all over the room: in the quilt chest, under each of the plump pillows propped at the head of the bed. In the wardrobe where Rosa Lee's seven dresses hang. In the drawer of the little writing desk which rattles as Sarah pulls it open with shaking hands. First thing she sees: Seth and Rosa Lee together, in a photograph of warm tans and whites and browns, stamped in one corner with *M. Gilmartin, Rehobeth, Alabama* and fastened on a dove-gray rectangle of cardboard. Alvah had their picture made, before Seth went away. Sarah's never seen this picture. Never knew it existed.

Seth sits prim and straight on a chair in the old black trousers and shoes of Johnny's that Mama gave to him, in the white linen shirt Alvah had cut and sewed with her own hands. Rosa Lee stands behind him, one hand on his shoulder, wearing the gingham frock she sewed in the parlor as Sarah and Jane sewed—their quilts? Other dresses? Rosa Lee must be twelve here, maybe thirteen. Which would make Seth seventeen. Which would mean that in another three years, he would be gone.

In their eyes is a knowing that Sarah sees clearly for the first time; it's taken the camera to show it. Something both sharp and soft, wary and resigned, hopeful.

Alvah had this picture made of them, because they were a family on their own. Without Sarah and Jane and Mama. Without anybody but themselves. Sarah remembers Alvah's voice: "The two of you, look after each other when I'm gone." Alvah's skin was gray, her touch reaching, grasping, sliding away.

Sarah reaches for the ribbon-wrapped bundle of letters in the back corner of the drawer. The handwriting on the envelope is Seth's; she recognizes it from the school notebooks in Father's study, slanting capitals and careful square lowercases that march sturdily across the paper. *Miss Rosa Lee Lincoln. The Doctor's House. Eldorado, Iowa.*

The first letter crackles open in her hands, although it is also softened with rereading, like the letter announcing Johnny's death, carried deep in Mama's sewing box. The date June 1875, a little more than five months ago.

Rosa Lee. Seth's voice is plain in her ears. *I didn't see fit to write you for this last long while because I was not in range of a post box. They say California is the place to make your fortune like Dick Whitingdon but I dont know. They are killers here over gold and whatever else they think is worth anything. Mama wd despair of them. But Ive got work. Our crew still builds this road out up out of this valley. Weve got good mules and the foreman he is fair. Put money aside each month and someday I hope as Mr. Douglass wrote to earn a living for us and the families we might build. I think of our Mother and our Father often and I know you do the same.*

Sarah cannot help herself; she skims ahead looking for her own name, for some sign of herself, although this too is trespass. (Mr. Douglass? What author is this?) She has no right to pry into Seth's words and seek herself. But among the march of neat square words she sees only a single postscript: *A baby, you say—*

A rustle from the doorway: when she turns around, Rosa Lee is standing there.

"I wasn't—" Sarah stammers. "I didn't—I mean, I—I'm sorry."

Rosa Lee glares back. "This is my room," she snaps. "My private things. You know that."

"I'm sorry," Sarah says again. Rosa Lee stands still, barely moving aside as Sarah brushes past on her way out of the room. She has pried. She has meddled. She has betrayed. She will never be forgiven, or deserve to be.

In her own room she stands still before the window despite the urge to pace, to fling herself out into the snow and walk and walk. She wants to be out of this house. But that means this is precisely where she should be. She must be punished for prying. She must punish herself.

Or maybe—it comes to her as cold and factual as the gray light against the glass—maybe she already has. She stands very still as the question grips her and holds her in place: What if it was all for nothing? What if she and Alvah and Seth and Rosa Lee were all wrong about what Mama intended with that confidential tilt of the head, wrong about what Mr. Wainwright was after? What if their mistake had driven Seth away? What if fear had spoken through her, and she had let it, by not stopping him, by not daring to ask what Mama really knew, by being silent? And what if, now, the distance from home had let her see it clear?

What if her silence was assent, and her assent itself, a lie?

Seth, gone. All for nothing.

The image of Trygve's face bent from within itself in pain rises up in front of her.

Mama would say *God has a reason. Man proposes, God disposes—*

For nothing. All for nothing. What if it really is?

A week goes by. Rosa Lee goes to the inn to read to Trygve, to pass a damp rag over his forehead, to help Linka haul dirty quilts outside and clean ones in, every day. Oyvind walks her home. When he leaves her at the door, they nod and trade a look that is troubled, and deepening.

In their own house, Rosa Lee wraps the ends of her shawl around her arms and draws it closer to herself, hugging her elbows to disappear. Tighter and tighter. Sarah reaches for her and Rosa Lee accepts an arm around her shoulders, a squeeze, a look, before disappearing into her small room with its neat quilted bed, its small desk, its cold winter morning light. Before she goes upstairs Sarah hears Rosa Lee's rocker creaking, back and forth, back and forth. Or her pen scratches out words Sarah will never know, now.

Sarah takes out the small blank diary again, sits with the pen poised over the page. The words boil and swirl, too many to force their way out through her fingers and down into an orderly line. *Baby. Trygve. Rosa Lee.* Why, why. Yes, she wondered where Seth had gone but foolishly did not ask, did not simply make an inquiry of her friend, but spied, pried, meddled. In this winter, winter, winter where everything is going wrong with no way to set it right.

At meals, Galen eats one bite of everything on his plate before pushing it away. The shadows under his wings deepen. He lets Sarah hold him, still, wrap her arms around his waist and kiss him. But in their bed at night he curls tighter into himself, sinking lower into the mattress, into a place Sarah can't touch. In his dreams, he's still, his long face twitched by fears and voices she can't see. She used to fling her arms and legs over him, to rescue him as if he were a drowning man, a child on fire. Now she edges closer and closer and never touches him. *Zeno's paradox,* Headmistress Spofford would say, *it seems simpler than it is. Run and run, but you never can reduce the distance. It's infinite regression; the goal is always receding.*

Mrs. Preus comes by to cheer them up and does the opposite. "Well," she offers, after fifteen awkward minutes, "if Trygve passes on, Rosa Lee, you won't have to be alone, there is still Oyvind, and he obviously cares for—"

"For heaven's sake." Rosa Lee stands and slams her teacup on the table. "They're not like bookends. Can't just trade them for one another." She glares at Mrs. Preus, frozen in her chair. "How dare you. You don't know." Sarah reaches out a hand but Rosa Lee rushes out of the parlor into her room and slams the door.

"She's right." Mrs. Preus's eyes are fixed on her lap. "It was tactless of me. The Reverend always says I need to learn to judge my silences. You'd think that I'd be old enough to know better." Sarah murmurs consolation, pressing back her own anger. All the women in town are gossiping, surely, in frontier calculation: *well, at least that girl will still have the other twin. She won't end up a spinster, God forbid.* What kind of place was this where women totted up the balances of life so coolly?

December tenth is Galen's birthday, three months before Sarah's own, five months before Rosa Lee's. They bake him a cake and Sarah presents him with the new muffler she's knitted, tucking it carefully around his neck and kissing him. He smiles thoughtfully. Above the thick folds, his face is gaunt, the hollows of his cheeks deeper.

"My birthday," he says, "What a thing to celebrate." His eyes grow horribly bright. "Isn't the world a better place because I am here. Aren't my patients better off." He shoves his chair back and stands, the cake forgotten, at the window. "Oh, look. It's snowing again in Eldorado. Yes, this must be the promised land. How providential for us all." With the muffler still wrapped around his throat, he strides to the door and snatches his coat from the coat-tree and steps out into the snow and slams the door behind him.

Sarah is still, speared to her chair. Rosa Lee sits next to her and sets one arm, then the other, around her shoulders and Sarah leans against her. "We need some sleep," says Rosa Lee finally, and they go to their rooms and crawl into their beds, leaving Galen's cake on the table. The drop into sleep is fluid as the fall of a stone into a well.

As Sarah wakes the next morning, the knowledge hovers over and her and lands with a flutter of wings, like a bird on a fence: she has reason to fear what's happening to Galen. His father was also a physician who drank himself to death: this is the reason Galen has never touched so much as a drop of wine at Christmastime. Galen's father disappeared while still a living man, leaving only a body to sit at the table, to prop itself up with a ghastly smile, to arrange its tools and its books: *now, son, you take these, they'll set you up right.*

In their courtship, Galen had spoken of his father for the first time. She was rooted to the spot by the pain in his face. By the shoulders tipped forward by its weight. By the eyes, blue shifting to gray and then darker blue, and the words of self-reproach that darkened them: *I shouldn't have told her, I shouldn't have said—*

Her blood had risen toward him in one wave. *Oh, my darling. I see.* She cupped her hands around his face, drew it to her own, and kissed him. *I see you. I will take it away.* His jaw had tensed against her palms, the back of his neck stiffening, even as his body slumped forward, even as his mouth loosened. Between her fingers, inside his skull, his thoughts were raving, even now: roaming, shouting, hammering their fists against their prison walls. *She'll be frightened, she'll—What there is in me to fear. What I fear. If I show it to her, will she—*

She'd let her fingers slide to the back of his neck, kissing him, kissing him. Circling his slim anxious skull in her own hands. Pressing her body against his. Still not close enough. Oh, to climb inside. To pass directly through the skin, to join. *I'm holding you. Right now. I will not run away.*

When the beast comes to you, shy, wild, and lays his head in your lap, you breathe softly, you stroke him lightly, so as not to startle that mystery, that rarity: a man tipping his bare heart into your two cupped hands.

Against her neck, Galen had huddled, and kept speaking: "I thought I could—correct it somehow, if I used the same tools, turn it back good."

He had sobbed and sobbed, just before they left Mobile, for Mrs. Kenner, the patient who had died, with her baby, under his care. "It's not like your father," she'd told him. "Those women died because he—" Because he was drunk. But she couldn't say that word to Galen. He had lost only Mrs. Kenner, but his father had lost several. The first one was a colored girl with no name. The second was a poor-white half-French girl down by the docks: "Rue Doloreaux," everybody said, knowingly, "or heading there. He shouldn't take on so about a girl like that." But the third was just like Julia Kenner. Wife of a young cotton factor, first baby. By that time her pains came, late at night, Galen's father was settled into his whiskey bottle. But when they called him, he went.

"Retained placenta, it had to have been," Galen said. "She died in a fever a week later. They wet-nursed the baby and it lived. But a year later came the typhoid and it was gone."

"Boy or girl?" Sarah asked.

"Girl," Galen said. "It was a little girl."

Under the shame Galen's mother cracked, began to slip sideways. "Mama," says Galen, "was never what you'd call strong." Then came the days when she wouldn't go out of her room, days of nibbling from full trays of food that were then sent back to the kitchen. And finally, a note left in the empty space in her husband's medicine chest where the laudanum bottle had been: *Now, darling, don't be angry*, it began.

"I burned it," Galen said. "That's all I remember. I was so angry I burned it. Went to the medical college so—"

"It would be different," Sarah finished, and Galen nodded, just one jerk of his head. "It will be different," she'd told him. "We can make it be."

Sarah is strong; she uses this knowledge to beat back the fear of what will happen if she tosses on that mattress and the baby grips her and grips her but can't be born, and Galen can't bring his child out of her. She is strong, she will live, hasn't that been proven already? Hasn't she made the trip here to Iowa, cleaned and gardened and washed and assisted her husband in his office without flinching? Can't she speak with some confidence of her own survival?

Her husband is not his father. She will not let him be. She will keep him here, with her.

And once this winter is over, with its deepening snow and its fading light that leaves them sitting around the lamp to read at six o'clock, then to bed at eight—with its uncrossable silent plains— well, everything will be different.

❧

Something inside her floats between brain and heart, churns like the child pressing against her stomach and her bladder, treading its feet against the floor of her hips. It is pushing her toward something she cannot see. It is pushing, all of it.

Will the baby feel like when Marie's colt was born?

"Stay out of there, all of you," Mama had warned her and Jane and Rosa Lee and Seth, carefully turning the bolt to Marie's stall door. "Too many things can go wrong."

But Marie was a special horse. She wouldn't hurt me, Sarah thought. She knows me. The early summer afternoons, wandering out in the big pasture under the pecan trees among the horses: all the other horses, even Speedwell, drifted close to her and then away again, while only Marie remained, soft tail switching, browsing in the grass at Sarah's feet. She had decided she would go in and sit with Marie, just hunker down in the corner of the stall and be quiet. Nobody could find her. Nobody would scold her if they couldn't see her. Only Marie would know she was here, the only person who cared. But Mama had checked on Marie just that morning, rubbing her long forehead, holding out a palmful of sugar for Marie to lick. The softness in Mama's voice—"good girl"—made Sarah jealous. But maybe if she was here, and the foal started to come, she could run and get Mama before anyone. She could be a heroine. And Mama would be proud.

In her big box stall Marie grew restless. She paced, her distended belly scraping the walls. A ridge of muscle tightened below her ribs, released, and tightened again. She raised her head and lowered it with a sudden huff of breath, swung her head back to nip her own flanks. Sarah huddled in the corner of the stall. The impatient hooves, churning the straw, pacing and pacing, seemed large and dangerous all of a sudden. But she couldn't stop looking. Marie was being taken over by something from inside. This was how the baby would come.

But then Marie slowed and stopped. She tilted her head just a little, like a wondering dog. And then she lowered her nose to Sarah's face and began to lick her. Astonishing—the wide slobbery tongue roughing up Sarah's cheeks, her hair, her dress—but she was held by it like a kitten is held, given over to the rough businesslike touch. Maybe the foal inside Marie, nudging his way up and up, was making her think Sarah was her foal already. Little whickers of breath, came from the mare's nose, happy murmurings in some horse language. Marie was just practicing. It couldn't mean anything. But Sarah shut her eyes and leaned into the horse's strange care, wondering at the feeling of being taken for another creature entirely.

Even more than the moment when Mama arrived and sent Sarah to fetch the water, even more than the moment Marie flopped into the straw and stretched out all four legs, even more than the first sight of the long pointy feet with their seaweedy cartilage feathers on the bottom (so they wouldn't tear Marie's insides), even more than the forward gush of the foal's long body and the moment when he staggered up at last and butted his head up against Marie and drank, this was the moment Sarah would remember.

And suddenly today, there is also the memory of Mama cradling the colt's body in her arms. "You have to teach him to accept a human touch," Mama explained, "teach him to be still." He jerked back and forth, his legs scrabbling in the straw on the floor of the stall, but Mama held on. And the colt quieted, with his nose against Marie's flank and Mama's arms encircling him from his narrow chest to the floppy carpet-strip of his tail. Sarah watched them from the door. *Oh, Mama. Hold me. Hold me.*

And she saw it then.

How the untelling of truths—or of anything at all of importance, weight, reality—builds up and becomes its own silent force. Until there is literally nothing to say when your mama asks you, "Sarah, what's wrong?" And because you could not say, then, *you sent Seth away, you thought we were dirty, you thought I was a bad girl, and you never punished Uncle Eugene, you never said how Father really died*—because you couldn't say all that, or any of that, you never said anything. Because there was no way, either, to ask Mama your real question: *Why wouldn't you let yourself be real, Mama? Let yourself be true? Or let me?*

And this leads you to your present instance. Alone in the black grainy loneliness because your husband sleeps right next to you and your friend downstairs. Hollowed out most by the letters from your mama signed *love* although you wonder more and more if either of you have ever meant it. Although you wonder, now, if either of you have ever—*ever*—known what the other really means. Or wanted to know. Wanted, genuinely, to listen, and to hear.

Oh, Mama.

Isn't it from you I am supposed to learn what is real? To be born full and real into the world and keep seeing it—real—as it is?

Why can we never speak the truth?

What happened? What went wrong?

What happened.

This is the only way to be real: to keep asking. And to do it yourself.

Nobody else can do it. Mama cannot. And that fact is not always her fault.

Oh, Mama. How I loved you. Love.

✤

Even before Sarah hears all their words, she knows that Oyvind has confessed his feelings. "How can you say that?" hisses Rosa Lee from the porch, in the stomping and sliding of snow-covered boots. "How can you even dare?"

"But he told me," says Oyvind, "he told me he—" There's a hard note of pain in his voice that pins Sarah to the floor where she stands, in the hall, passing the door. In his front parlor office, the rustle of Galen's working noises has paused too.

"Your brother," snaps Rosa Lee. "Lyin there and you come courtin me."

"But listen," pleads Oyvind, "just let me tell you—"

"I won't hear it." Rosa Lee's voice rises in a low harsh shriek.

"You know I always, you know I—" Oyvind's voice rises too, reckless.

"Turn loose of me," says Rosa Lee. The door opens and bangs shut again and Rosa Lee stands in the hall, whirled about by a cold wind that's come in with her, the smell of the cold still on her dress and hair. She drops her cloak neatly on the hall rack and hurries back to her room. "Wait," calls Sarah, but Rosa Lee's door closes. Behind it her feet still move back and forth, back and forth.

❧

It would be so much harder with us, Sarah thinks, if we weren't teaching. Every morning, she and Rosa Lee wrap up and trudge down to the schoolhouse to help Nils Erickson give lessons. Many of the mothers help him; with the deep snow, there's little else to do. With ten children and five women, plus Nils, each child now has his or her own teacher, or close to it. Sometimes all the children sit together, while Mrs. Preus, the Reverend's wife, teaches French or Mrs. Johnson teaches arithmetic or Sarah leads a song. Nils paces from group to group, smiling and encouraging, his coat sleeve slipping back to show the blue tattoo at his wrist. They've talked optimistically about bringing the piano over from the church, but the snow might damage it. "See the little squirrel in the hickory tree," Sarah sings, "looking down at you, looking down at me." She reads them stories from Mrs. Wollstonecraft—*Do you know the meaning of the word Goodness? I will tell you. It is, first, to avoid hurting any thing*—and tries not to remember Seth's hands shaping the mockingbird nest back together around the fallen chicks. Sometimes with the children watching, Sarah and Rosa Lee and Mrs. Preus and Mrs. Johnson act out scenes from Shakespeare, with Mrs. Johnson's oldest girl Jenny to fill in if there are too many parts. "What light through yonder window breaks?" Mrs. Johnson declaims theatrically. "It is the east, and Juliet is the sun!" Mrs. Preus, standing behind the teacher's desk, rolls her eyes and clutches her shawl tighter around her head, and the children giggle.

"Cuh, at, cat," recites Jimmy Johnson to Rosa Lee. "Cat," and Rosa Lee smiles. "Take your time," she says, "just take your time." On their slates, the children scrawl cursive script, French verbs, simple division. Sarah sits next to Clara Preus, eight years old, but small enough to be five, and watches her draw elaborately costumed queens on sheets of paper. Mrs. Preus always seems to have paper; someone must be charged with making sure the minister's family never runs out. Paper is dear. She's lucky. "Who is this?" she asks.

"Eleanor of Aquitaine," Clara says seriously. "She's a very important queen, so I drew her largest." She swirls her pencil in a wide spiral and adds two leaves underneath. "Wars of the Roses, white rose York, red rose Lancaster."

"How are they related to the Plantagenets?" Sarah prods.

"It's complicated," Clara says. "They're all family, but they live in different places. Like we have family back in Norway. And they got to be so far away from each other they forgot they were family and started fighting. Mama told me kings and queens don't think about family like we do."

"They can't afford to," Sarah confirms. "Because when you want to be queen bad enough, or king, you can't let anything get in your way." She dredges her brain for scraps from Miss Spofford's school: *all the money I pay to send you girls,* Mama's voice sighs, *and you can't recall any more than this?* "Next week," she promises, "we'll read about Henry the Eighth and his six wives and Queen Elizabeth. Their name was Tudor."

Across the room, Rosa Lee is sitting with Clara's brother Samuel, who is reading aloud to her from a novel propped open on his lap. "The perfidy of the evil Count was not to be thought of, much less to be described," Samuel intones. "What's 'perfidy?'"

"It's when—" Rosa Lee pauses. "Someone is disloyal, does something to hurt you." She pauses again. "A friend, in particular."

"Like Count Renaldo," Samuel adds, "when he stole the maiden Lilla."

"Just like that," Rosa Lee agrees. Sarah fights the clutch of shame in her throat, the heat in her cheeks. No one is looking at her.

"Matthew did some perfidy to me," Samuel says, "when he took the last popover when Mama said I could have it."

"She said I could have it," Matthew calls from the back of the room, where he is working sums with his mother. "Didn't you, Mama."

"This hurlyburly is too utterly trivial," observes Jenny, who is fifteen now and literary. She is memorizing Lady Macbeth's soliloquy to perform for all of them at the end of the week.

"Nobody asked you," Samuel says.

"Why can't you all be like Clara?" Mrs. Preus pleads. "Look how quiet she is, just sitting there drawing." In unison, Samuel and Matthew turn their eyelids inside out, scornfully. Clara, absorbed in the fur trim of Eleanor's robe, doesn't notice.

"Come on, y'all," Rosa Lee says. "Back to work. Samuel, you keep reading. We need to find out whether that Count ever gets out of his dungeon, remember?"

At three o'clock, Rosa Lee and Sarah help the children bundle into their coats and scarves and boots and wave goodbye to Mrs. Preus and Mrs. Johnson at the schoolhouse door. The trampled path through the snow from the schoolhouse to the main street is just wide enough for them to walk side by side. "'Perfidy,'" Sarah says, experimentally. Rosa Lee walks on in silence, with only a flick of her eyes at Sarah to indicate she's heard.

"Rosa Lee," says Sarah, taking her friend's arm, "I'm sorry I went in your desk that day."

"I know," says Rosa Lee. Her face doesn't change.

But Sarah, embarrassed, committed, presses on. "You seem so quiet." She pauses. "Are you all right—I mean—"

Rosa Lee sighs. Something in her stiff shoulders and her averted eyes hovers on the edge of silence, but tilts back the other way. "I go see Trygve and he's there in that bed," she says finally. "And he's lookin at me, still, like—" She stops. "I can't," she says. "I can't think of Oyvind, with his own brother layin there. But Oyvind wants to court me, he told me—" She swallows. "He says Trygve told him not to be leavin me alone. He is a good man, I can see that. But

I ain't just to be handed off, one brother to the next." Behind the welcome bolster of anger in these words, her eyes film with tears. "And Trygve—he's the first man I ever even kissed." She pauses. "He's not going to get well. I know it. But I can't just—"

Sarah knows what the women in Eldorado, like Mrs. Preus, would say. What her mother would say. What Alvah would likely say, too: *Girl—honey, I know it's hard, but—you got to be realistic. That poor boy's gonna pass on before too much longer, and here's his brother who loves you, wants to marry you. Here's another good man, fit for this territory. How else you gonna live out here on your own? How much longer you want to keep livin in somebody else's house? Honey, you got to be realistic.* And Sarah thinks, again, of what she could say: *Rosa Lee, you think Trygve doesn't know what's happening to him? He cares for you, he doesn't want you to just live on by yourself, unhappy, with his brother so unhappy too. He knows that Oyvind cares for you.* But there's no way to say any of this. She flinches from the biblical sternness of this logic: Ruth is left a widow, so the town decrees that Ruth must marry again, no matter how much she loved her husband. A woman can't roam loose in the world, mad with mourning and grief, determined to cut herself off. The people around her won't allow it. She has to marry again, and she's lucky if the new man's a good one. This doesn't feel like the right way to look at things. But it's the only available one, even in Eldorado. *Whither thou goest, I will go. Whither thou lodgest, I will lodge.* Women's lives are set in front of them in a series of stories, a set of paths down which they might or might not turn. There are women in other times and places—like Mrs. Wollstonecraft, like the three Bronte sisters—who have cut paths of their own. But that is only in the world of books. Not in a frontier town at the edge of winter. The edge of the whole known world.

Rosa Lee tucks Sarah's arm against herself and sighs. The two of them lower their heads against the wind and make their way home.

✲

On Friday night, it begins to snow again and continues all day Saturday. By Sunday morning Sarah, Galen, and Rosa Lee are so desperate to leave the house that they bundle up and walk the hundred yards to church. Reverend Preus greets them at the door. "Welcome," he says, just as if there were nothing at all unusual about their being here all together for the first time in nearly eight months.

Linka Thorson sits next to Oyvind in a pew halfway to the altar; she waves and so there is nothing for it but to wave back and file into the pew right in front of her. Linka stands and leans over the pew and hugs each of them in turn, smiling. Sarah is shocked by how old Linka looks, suddenly. The gray in her drawn-back hair is deeper now, frizzly, her cheeks hollow, her nose sharp as a crow's beak. Oyvind shakes her hand, Galen's, Rosa Lee's, and sits quietly next to his mother, not looking any of them in the eye. "Trygve seems a bit better this morning," Linka whispers as Reverend Preus steps to the pulpit and clears his throat. "I think it must be the light. We're lucky to get such good sunlight in the winter, even when it snows. Better than Norway."

Indeed, the light through the windows is so bright they don't need lamps or candles. The children sit in a row in the front pew, swinging their legs; Clara's head is bent, drawing in the margins of her little prayer book. Mrs. Preus plays a hymn on the scratchy piano. The wood stove glows. The service progresses, and despite herself Sarah relaxes. She still doesn't know what to say to God, how to untangle the fear and anger and boredom of these days into anything like a prayer, or a plea, or an argument. But it feels good to be here, back in the familiar church smell of old paper and Sunday-best wool and dust. Like the little church near Fairibault. How is it that churches everywhere smell the same?

Reverend Preus begins his sermon. "We know how the nation of Israel got its start," he says conversationally, "from a man and a woman who thought they were too old to be blessed, that God would never bless them with a child. The Bible tells us, even, that Sarah laughed, because she thought—makes sense, I guess—that she was too old to have this promised child. Not like our Sarah, here." He nods to her and Sarah sits straight, blushing, suddenly baffled. "Sarah laughed. But the child Isaac was born, in what must surely have been a wilderness like this. A place of wandering, where it seemed there never would be any rest. That God would never make good on his promises. That there would be no end, no good, that the people could ever see."

Galen shifts in his seat. "I don't like him pointing you out from the pulpit like that," he mutters. Sarah pats him. "Just wait," she whispers back. "It's all right."

And then Reverend Preus begins to tell the story of Isaac, of the child God ordered his father to sacrifice. "I'm not sure I would have obeyed, to be honest," he says, looking at the row of children in front of him. "I would have found a way not to listen. I would have found a way to hide from His word. Because I am a man, I am a father, I love my children and my wife with whom God has blessed me. And there is no way for us to see, when faced with such a voice, what God could possibly want with our child." He pauses, for the barest second. "For Abraham to see what God could have wanted with his boy."

Behind Sarah Linka sniffles. Oyvind shifts to put his arm around her. Sarah feels Linka's tears coming, pressing into her back like a wall of cool air before a coming thunderstorm. But in the corner of her eye she can see Linka nodding. "Yes," she is murmuring, almost too low to hear. "Yes."

"Because we are just humans," Reverend Preus continues, "our vision limited by our lives on earth, even by those we love, sometimes we just can't see what He—"

Galen makes a harsh noise in his throat and rises and snatches his coat and scarf from the heap beside Rosa Lee. "Fatuous," he mutters. "Naïve." He edges out of the pew and strides down the aisle and out the door. It slams behind him and he is gone.

Reverend Preus pauses. Everyone in church turns to look at the door, then at Sarah and Rosa Lee, then back at him. "But . . . because . . . ." He wavers and then catches himself. "Because we are human. As wonderful as that is to be, made in God's image. Because we are humans, we cannot know His plan." He looks at Linka and sets down his page. "I don't understand it all myself. I never will. But I know He sees our trouble. He sees it and he is here with us in the midst of it. Here in our hurting world, with the people we love and who love us in return." He blinks and Sarah is astonished to see that he is on the edge of tears. "We live in faith that this is true."

Sarah and Rosa Lee sit through the rest of the service and shake hands with everyone at the end. No one refers to Galen. "It's nice to see you here," says Reverend Preus, "I do hope you can come back again." When they get home, the door to Galen's office is shut on the angry rustle of pages, the impatient thump and squeak of him rocking back in his chair and letting the legs slam down.

Linka turns Trygve from side to side in his bed. "Rest that back," she croons, "just a little rest, and then Rosa Lee can read to you for a while."

"No," Trygve says against her chest. "Not now."

Linka lifts her son with one arm under his shoulders and one arm under his ribs and cradles him against her chest. With both hands, she rubs his back. The skin is purple from the settled blood. Despite Linka's efforts, there will be sores before long.

Curled on his side, Trygve sleeps; Galen gives him laudanum, more and more. It's best that way. Sometimes Oyvind holds his brother, cradles him upright, while Linka shaves his face carefully, stroke after stroke and swish of the razor, or trims his dark red hair. They swab a rag on a stick over his teeth—the mix of baking soda and mint Linka favors, from Norway—and give him a mouthful of water afterwards: "rinse," Oyvind says, and Trygve spits obediently into the basin. But mostly he sleeps. Each week his legs are drawn tighter, his knees closer to his chest, his feet limp.

Oyvind walks Rosa Lee between the doctor's house and the inn. Sarah stays home more and more. The baby treads the floor of her womb. She is freighted, the child dangling in her like a ripe pear. Sometimes at odd moments Galen floods her, full and sad as a memory. At the thought of his wry upturned smile, his warm roughened hand, his body against her body—the deepening in his eyes, the intention, as he moves to her—an airy white heat bursts in her, floods her, so intensely she slumps against the back of her chair, closing her eyes. Scratchy insistent chemise, prickling. Secret swelling, plumping, secret, freighting each cell of her flesh: *To set to budding. To fill all fruit with ripeness to the core.* To feel him close his mouth upon her, here, and here—

But he does not touch her now, except when he huddles against her, helpless, in a dream too dark for her to find him in.

Rosa Lee stands on the porch with Oyvind in the evening light. Their voices are low. "It's no kind of life," Oyvind murmurs, as if to himself. "Can't hardly call it life, even." His voice cracks and Sarah flees from the parlor to the kitchen, where she cannot hear their words. Back in the Fairibault days the Sawyers' second son fell off a bad half-broken colt and spent his last days in a bed, just like Trygve. She remembers Johnny at the dinner table, shaking his head soberly: "If I ever end up like that poor son of a bitch, you better shoot me in the head. Dear God." In his voice Sarah heard the rueful, wordless understandings by which men steered through the world of other men like bats flickering in an evening sky. Honor. Bravery. A hard and clear-edged kind of mercy. That world would say a man bound to a bed was not a man, even when the woman who loved him tried to tell him otherwise. But men did things out of love, too, that women never saw.

Eventually, Rosa Lee comes in the house, her face thoughtful. She sits with Sarah in the kitchen, sipping tea, as the snow comes down outside with its million tiny voices. "I don't guess I was ever as mad at Oyvind as I told him I was," Rosa Lee says finally. "Not really. I was just—I was scared. Easier to be mad than—"

Sarah nods. Easier to be mad than to think about how Trygve's going to die.

⁂

Two days before Christmas, Linka finds Trygve's body cold and still. The bottle of laudanum on the bedside table is empty, sparkling in the first light. Trygve's sharp face is upturned, his eyes closed. No one, not even Linka, asks how a paralyzed boy could empty the bottle of laudanum into his own mouth. And how he could be sure, even then, that it would stop his breathing.

Oyvind comes to take Rosa Lee for walks in the snow. Beyond the house Sarah sees them paused, their bodies tense. They stand and face each other, and then turn to walk away, together.

One night they come back well after dark; Sarah is sitting at the window, which is open a crack. The baby's pressing; she can't sleep, she can't breathe. "He didn't want to stay on like he was," comes Oyvind's voice from the front steps. "You'd've been the only thing keeping him here. And even for that, well . . . He knew he wasn't going to get well, he knew it."

From Rosa Lee, silence.

"He told me," Oyvind says. His voice trembles. "He told me it was what he wanted." There is another silence, and a scuffle of boots in the snow, then Oyvind's sobs, muffled. Against his own sleeve. Against Rosa Lee's shoulder. Against the hood of her cloak, as he holds her, and she holds him, and he cries.

Sarah shuts the window and crawls under the quilts next to her husband and sleeps. Slowly she becomes tangled in dreams that wrap around her and hold her deep into themselves. She is dancing. She is dancing with Trygve as Galen watches, as Seth and Rosa Lee come and go through a door in the far wall. The light is troubled and bright, like gas jets turned up just one notch too high. She is caught in something moving on without her, something that nevertheless has to move and has to be.

And a week later, just before the New Year, Rosa Lee comes in from walking with Oyvind, again, and catches Sarah's questioning eye. She smiles, shrugs her shoulders just slightly, smiles a bit deeper, and moves on through the kitchen to her room. Sarah follows her and finds her sitting at her small desk, writing a letter. Rosa Lee turns and stands, flipping the letter over in one smooth motion, and her eyes are bright. "He aims to marry me," she says. "And I've said yes."

Sarah embraces her and Rosa Lee hugs back. They stand in Rosa Lee's small room without moving. There's nothing more to say.

❧

There is a memory of the summer moving in her, nudging her toward the surface of her sleep, where dream becomes the waking world. What is it?

She is walking with Rosa Lee and Mrs. Preus, the minister's wife, along the wide plain near the river. They're farther than they've ever been from town, but Mrs. Preus is intent. "It's just ahead, girls," she says. "The seeds. Still here. It's a marvel. Nobody knows why." And around the bend of the wide shallow river they are upon it: a round depression in the ground, centered on a ring of stones where someone, once, had built a fire. Mrs. Preus looks left and right toward the line of trees, centers herself directionally, walks seven careful steps to the east. Sarah follows her and looks down. She's standing in the ghost of a garden now, a squash patch where vines tangle and sprawl in the grass. Animals have nibbled the hearts of the great fruits, which are faded orange in the sun, exposing a palmful of seeds. "The . . . natives." Mrs. Preus's voice is rueful. "They were . . . moved on from here. 1861, it was." *The start of the war.* Sarah feels this recognition on her own face, sees it on Rosa Lee's. The war wouldn't have touched this frontier town, so far from anywhere. "Chief Wa-kon De-ko-rah. And his people. Moved on by the soldiers." Sarah waits, but Mrs. Preus's face is turned away. "And they left this here."

Like the Indian camp in the woods in Alabama. And then the memory is there in Sarah's mind. It nudges through the surface of the dream and wakes her. A grave, a freshly churned rectangle of earth, two feet by a little more than five. She saw it, walking one day all by herself. There was a grave up there in the clearing in the woods where no one but Alvah and Rosa Lee and Sarah and Jane had ever gone, or ever would go, since the land had passed into Father's hands. Already the surface was settling, the black dirt pitted with rain. Morning-glory vines tangled toward it through the grass. In six months no one would ever know it was there.

That night at Fairibault, Mr. Wainwright had got up from Mama's dinner table and smiled and helped Uncle Eugene out the door and onto old Job the mule's back. He had ridden away on patchwork Jim with Job following, with Uncle Eugene reeling in the saddle. The next morning, Job had been back at home. Except he was in the wrong place. He was in the sandy pen Mama had put the colt in to recover after he got cut, not his usual pasture with the big pecan tree he loved to scratch himself against. He'd been put back by Mr. Wainwright, not by Uncle Eugene. Because Uncle Eugene was in that grave up by the Indian camp.

Mama had never forgotten Sarah's panicked flight up out of that creek, her hand clutched in Jane's. She had never forgotten it at all.

After Father died, she had asked Mr. Wainwright to keep Uncle Eugene away from them for good. And Mr. Wainwright—*your servant, Livia*—had obliged.

&

The next morning, Bessy McElvain finds her father dead. Galen climbs the stairs in Bessy's house to set his fingers against the old man's throat, and nods. Sarah helps Bessy wash her father's body and dress him in his rusty black suit. Bessy smoothes the long curling hair at his temples with a comb, then takes the comb away and sets her fingers there.

Mr. Gabrielson the blacksmith—who's also the undertaker—helps Galen and Reverend Preus and Nils Erickson carry the long body downstairs and lay him out in his coffin. He's as light as a dragonfly. Bessy settles his head on the pillow, straightens his somber black tie, and kisses him on the forehead. "Papa," she murmurs. Her long hands soothe down his last flying wisps of white hair. And she shuts the lid, and Mr. McElvain, the first mayor of Eldorado, is gone.

The snow is too deep, the ground frozen too hard, to dig a hole in the cemetery now. The men carry the coffin outside and load it into the sleigh, where it will ride to Mr. Gabrielson's shed to wait, alongside Trygve's body, for the thaw.

Sarah leans against Bessy and puts her arms around her. "Oh, wait," Bessy murmurs, "just a minute." She draws away, goes into the kitchen, and returns with a lumpy, clinking flour sack, full of little bottles. "Been meaning to give these back to you, surely you can use them for more 'medicine.'" She quirks her eyebrows at Sarah and smiles, but then her chin trembles, and Sarah holds her tighter. Bessy cries. "Oh, oh my," she sobs. "My father."

"You loved him," Sarah says. "He loved you." In her hand, the tiny bottles shiver in their sack. She remembers the old man in his stained waistcoat, slipping one of these bottles proudly into his pocket. She remembers his wind-teary eyes as he perched on the cemetery wall, staring up the hill toward his daughter. *I remember a girl. Maybe she was real.*

"I always wonder if I could have done more," Bessy murmurs, close to tears.

"What more could you possibly have done?" Sarah asks. "You gave up—I mean, you let Nils have the school so you could take care of your father." It has not escaped her, even at such a time, that Nils has come to help Bessy, that he's watching her with a look of quiet, firm concern that seems deeper, rarer, than just sympathy. He's younger than Bessy. But with all he's done, with all he's seen as a sailor and a minister-in-training, he carries years inside him that will make him an understanding man for her. Someone to take her long, still-lovely hands in his own. Someone who can let her rest, at last.

Their house is quiet when they return from laying Mr. McElvain's coffin in the shed. Galen listens for a moment, then turns to latch the door, tightly. "Come with me," he murmurs, and Sarah reaches for his hand and they climb the stairs, side by side.

Their bed is deep and still, fresh with sheets that Sarah has just laundered and ironed and changed herself, and chilly with the cold of the upstairs, far from the wood-stove fire. Their hands are chilly too despite the thick mittens they wore as they kept a swift homeward pace through the cold. They twitch and flinch like nervous horses at each others' touches, giggling as they unbutton their funeral clothes and slide their hands into the warm spaces next to skin. Galen's ribs, his fine long muscles, sinew and bone. Sarah's breasts freed from the Motherhood Corset with a hiss of strings and canvas, lifted and cradled from the wide swell of her belly, prickling, in his fingers, so that she leans against him, closes her eyes, and moans. With his lips on her neck, she settles carefully with her husband into their bed. No one else is home, yet, to hear.

"I don't want to hurt—" Galen murmurs, but she shakes her head, clasps his narrow face in both her hands, and lets the kiss dissolve her in the way she remembers from their very first days. With their legs tangling, his arms arching over her shoulders, her hair, her great belly, he is suddenly gentle, slow. "You won't hurt me," she murmurs. "Oh, God—" She shudders, straining to reach him.

In the blue winter dark, there's a voice that belongs to them both.

And as they curl deeper into their bed, drowsy, warm, one of them says, *Look. It's snowing.*

Galen huddles lower to rest his lips against her belly as he falls asleep. And Sarah falls asleep, eventually, watching her husband's face slacken and ease into a dream, watching the snow swirl and fall into the windowpanes, glowing with a soft moony light of its own.

Unto us, a child is born.

Oyvind comes to call the following week. Rosa Lee and Sarah are in the parlor, knitting and stitching to finish the baby's capelet and socks. Galen is reading. "I'd like to speak to you," Oyvind says formally. He wants to do this right, although Rosa Lee's father and mother are dead and her brother in the gold fields and Sarah and

Galen are the closest thing to family he has ever known her to have. He clears his throat, and Sarah and Rosa Lee set their needles down. "I would like to propose matrimony to Miss Rosa Lee Lincoln," says Oyvind formally, "if she's agreeable."

"Congratulations," Galen says, and smiles. Rosa Lee's eyes are on Oyvind, approving, Everyone is thinking of Trygve, and everyone knows it. "Your mother," Galen says, "she's willing?"

"She is," says Oyvind, "for Miss Rosa Lee and Trygve she was willing, and for Miss Rosa Lee and me. Some wouldn't be. But it ain't like that here, and it don't matter none to us. And not to me. I've never known to be feeling such a way. I think—" he paused. He looks at Rosa Lee, his eyes luminous. "I think she's beautiful. And everything a man could want a wife to be."

Sarah reaches for Rosa Lee's hand and squeezes it, and Rosa Lee squeezes back. Her brown eyes fill with tears. She rises and goes to Oyvind, who wraps his arms around her and kisses her, holding her close. A bright sphere of happiness floats around them, light and sturdy as a soap bubble blown through a hoop. To be loved. It's a chancy thing. But it's real.

Sarah realizes it, then. You think you will find some mythical place up ahead in the future where you will understand everything, and then one day you look and realize you may already be standing in that place, in the life no one but yourself can make real.

Sarah sits, shivering, in a bath of hot water in the kitchen. She's filled the tub herself, shooed Galen out, and drawn all the curtains shut. The soap and water feel so good on her skin, despite the cold. Her breasts are sore: "raw cabbage leaves in your dress are good for that, Mama always said," Rosa Lee remarks, "but where we gonna get cabbage leaves in all this snow?" Once a week is the most any of them can manage a bath now. How she would have laughed, disbelieving, three years ago at the thought that a once-a-week bath would be a luxury.

She swirls her hands slowly through the suds over her belly. The child is turning in her now, head downward, nudging toward the world. Seeking and seeking, like a key into a lock, just the right angle to twist, and nudge, and open.

I know you. I'll see you, honey. Very, very soon.

Lift the sponge and squeeze and let the water trickle down, trapping bubbles like seed pearls against your skin. This human skin that is mystery and fact, shared and touched in the hundred ways one person tries to reach beyond it, toward somebody else.

That night Sarah dreams that she is following her mother up a wide sunny hill, a prairie hill with high grass streaming backwards in the wind. On top of the hill is a piano: farmers have stacked hay on top of it, and birds have built nests inside, but when her mother sits and places both hands on the keys, it answers her, singing. And Mama plays, and Sarah dances. The bright notes of Chopin's *Polonaise* in A-flat minor—so clear in the dream Sarah can identify it on waking, *polonaise,* just the word is a bright flag—fling outward in the wind just like her skirts blowing and tossing as she spins and laughs, bending back like a flower, flinging both arms high. Mama looks at her, laughing too. The notes flutter like gypsy scarves, red and yellow. And at the bottom of the hill a figure catches Sarah's eye: sturdy, dark face revealed to the sun as he takes off his hat and peers at her. It's Seth, on his way somewhere. Sarah waves at him. He hesitates and waves back. And then he's gone.

Sarah wakes with the bright notes rippling in her still, above the single word: *Forgive.*

I sent him away for you. And she remembers how Mr. Wainwright set his hand just above Uncle Eugene's elbow, turned to Mama, and nodded his head. How their eyes locked.

Forgive. The envelope with the letter from Mama is still at the bottom of her trunk, unopened.

Forgive Mama for withholding the truth. Forgive herself for believing Mama had intended Mr. Wainwright to take Seth. It was Uncle Eugene Mama had summoned him for, all along. It was Uncle Eugene who lay in that grave in the woods, dead by Mr. Wainwright's hand and Mama's will. Sarah had not seen that, or believed it, until now.

Seth had fled for nothing. No, not nothing. Because a world in which such fear could banish him was not a world in which he could have—would have—wanted to remain.

Galen's thin body sinks into the mattress next to her, unmoving, snores rattling his ribs. She can't risk waking him, disrupting his precious sleep. But she must know what Mama has written, now, in the still-unopened letter in her trunk. She edges out of bed and shuffles to the corner. The pop of the latches is loud and Galen stirs but doesn't wake. Carefully Sarah opens the trunk's big domed lid and lets it rear back against the wall. There are the layers of summer work dresses and the worn-out chemises she can't bring herself to throw away: so much wear left in them, and who knows when she'll get any more of them, out here in Iowa? She plunges her hand down through the layers. The thick soft edge of paper meets her fingers, right where she left it.

Out in the hallway she stands at the top of the stairs, ripping the envelope open. No need for a candle. The moon spreads a bar of white light across the page and she can see it plain.

My girl, I can't think what has laid it on my heart to write to you this way. I must be an old woman and getting sentimental now as a soldier's daughter is taught she has no room to be. But I am awake alone here in Aunt Maude's house at night (Jane and Felix were by earlier; even with the coming child she's strong as an ox, always was such a resilient girl) and thinking of you and your baby away off in that Godforsaken place and I will write. I will write and put it in an envelope and mail it without looking in the morning so I will not stop myself.

Somehow I feel I should tell you that I know those years of whis-pers hurt you and I know you did nothing to deserve them. Feelings, those cannot be helped. But you did nothing to deserve such talk. You and Seth did nothing wrong. I see it now. If I knew where he had gone I would tell him so.

He thought Tom Wainwright was after him but he was not.

A pause. A musing line unspools across the center of the page.

Tom Wainwright would have done anything I asked. Even after he married that poor inbred milktoast Catholic girl. I told him what your father's degenerate brother did to you in the creek that day and I expressed myself quite plainly. And I was understood.

If I had been as brave a woman as I should be I'd have done the job myself.

Another pause, and when her mother's writing resumes it is upright, composed. *I trust that you will burn this although I have said nothing that could compromise me. But I do not like the thought of these words lingering. I need to know that I have written them. I need to know that you have read them. That you have received these lines.*

A mother needs to know that she is understood.

Sarah stands in the moonlight at the top of her stairs for a long time. And then she slips back into her bedroom and gathers all the clothes she has left lying across the chair and bed-foot, hauling them back out onto the landing to dress by moonlight. She eases downstairs and takes a piece of paper and an envelope out of the secretary and uncaps the ink-bottle. She too will write. *Mama. I got your letter. I understand. I love you, Mama.* She waves the letter in the air and folds and seals it and scribbles Mama's name and address on the front—she'll mail it tomorrow. Then she pulls on Galen's boots and walks out into the night.

The snow glitters, and the world is dark and silver and white. Far off on the bluff a coyote yaps and another howls to join it. No other sound comes to Sarah's ears but the crunch of her own feet in the snow and the creak of the wind-vane on the roof, the bronze angel with his trumpet swinging north, then south. She passes the back of the Gundersons' barn; behind the wall, their big Belgian stirs in his sleep, dreaming heavy, satisfying horse dreams of a good day's work. A scatter of cat tracks, or maybe fox, threads around the foundation of the general store and out of sight. Mice are moving now, emboldened by the night. Sarah passes the red brick seminary and heads for the church. She knows it will be open. God's house, Reverend Preus always says, is never locked.

The heavy door latch opens with a clunk that echoes through the dim cold dark, startling the ranks of obedient pews from their sleep. The wooden candlesticks shiver upright on the altar: no money for gold here, and no need. Against the wall stands the upright piano, carted here in who knows what wagon from who knows how far. Sarah sits down on the hard bench and she plays, with greater and greater fluency and speed. She lets the notes tip her from side to side, billowing out around her like air. She plays Bach's *Aria from Goldberg Variations*, again and again, and at some point she realizes she's crying, although not from any feeling she can identify. And then she plays the *Polonaise*. In the dream, Mama had been smiling so bright, so warm and real. She had been touching Sarah, holding her close. Sarah runs the picture in her mind backwards and then forwards to examine it again. It is an image of her mama loving her, in a way neither of them had ever been able to say. Its warmth is inside her, now, in the way that love must surely be between even those who should know better: wordless, known and relied upon even in that silence. Being a woman means recognizing you will be alone even among the people you love, and who say they love you. There is something lonesome in that truth, and, because it is the truth, something rare and fine resides in it as well—something that settles in the scale opposite the lonesomeness and holds it in balance, inside your own particular heart.

She plays the *Songs from Childhood* last of all, the song of foreign lands and people. *Come a-way with me, and go wan-dering, come a-way with me, my fair la-dy.*

Seth, she thinks suddenly, sadly. *Seth. You should be here to see us. We're going to be all right, Seth. We're going to be just fine.*

And she knows that wherever he is, Seth has heard.

In St. Paul, Galen bargains with the stonecutter. "My God, he laughs, a rasping bark, "it's hard enough I'm here to buy a gravestone for my wife. You can't concede to even this?"

"I'm sorry for your loss," the man mumbles. He stands like a marble giant, big loose hands at his sides.

"Where she was born and where she died," says Galen. "I want them cut on there. If I've got to leave her in this Godforsaken place, she must be known. Can't you at least—"

"It's twenty extra," says the man.

"Good God," Galen blurts. He crumples, reels, straightens. The weight of all of it is on him now: the trunk into which he had pushed Sarah's things and shut the lid (a letter in Livia's handwriting on top crumpled, heedlessly, under the weight of the green dress, the narrow boots, the tiny sweater softened by her fingers in the yarn each day), the intimate heft of the whiskey bottle, swinging in the pocket of his coat, the worried faces of Rosa Lee and Oyvind, the doctor's house from which he had now simply walked away.

The big man watches him. "It's twenty extra for those lines," he repeats, uncertainly. "It's extra, mister."

"Franz," says his wife, touching his arm.

"Can't help it's extra," says the giant. "We got to eat."

Galen slaps the flat top of the stone nearest him. "That's right," he hisses. "Right. How bout—" He looks at the young woman, then looks closer. "You and your wife will need a doctor soon, I see."

The girl blushes, smiles.

"How bout if we exchange—"

"We got a doctor here," the giant interrupts. "We got to eat."

"Franz," says the girl.

"Go in the house, now, liebchen," says the man. "Go on."

She wanders toward the back door, but she doesn't go inside. She stands at the pump. As Sarah used to stand. The girl's hair is golden, too. The same round swelling underneath her apron.

Oh, where melancholy leads those who let it in. That's what Sarah's mother, that Roman matron Livia, would say. *But there's no way to hold yourself up, Livia, against such grief as I feel right now.* He would say this to her if she were here and not back in Mobile, locked in her bed like old Aunt Maude, raging, dying, inflamed by the injustice of that final thing.

"All right," he snaps. "Just this, then. Sarah Fairibault Archer. Born 1846. Died 1876."

The giant nods, pulls a notebook from his pocket, grips a pencil in his stubby fingers, scribbles.

"Now the child," Galen snaps, as if he's in an operating theatre, extending a hand for an instrument to be slapped into his palm. "Clear. He must be clear."

"Baby girl—" He pauses. "Baby girl—"

They never knew her name. They never decided. His brain roots desperately in Sarah's books, in Sarah's voice reading to him and Rosa Lee and Oyvind in the lamplight. Those wild aching novels of Currer and Ellis Bell. Dickens and Milton. Keats and Whitman. Shakespeare.

A lost daughter, dead in her father's helpless arms.

"Cordelia," he says. "February 2, 1876."

The giant nods. "I'll have them ready," he says, "when you come back. Two weeks. I'll hurry."

Galen nods back and slaps the money—all the money in his pocket—onto the stone. He will not touch the giant's puffy rough palm, even though it's reaching now for his, to shake his hand—

"Sorry, mister, but we got to eat."

He strides to his wagon, reels against the horse's neck. When has he eaten last? He can't remember. He swallows hard, tears knotted in his throat. Pictures cluster around the names beating in his brain like two chambers of a heart. Cordelia. And Sarah.

"Mister." There's the young wife's voice behind him, and he turns. So bright is the sun on her hair, so similar the shape, he has to grip the bridle with both his hands to hold himself upright. "Mister. Your wife, your Sarah. Was born where?"

"Alabama," he says. His voice rattles. If he says any more, he'll cry. "She was born in Alabama." He nods to the girl, clambers onto the wagon seat, slaps the reins against the horse's back, and drives away.

The girl stands in the sunlight, her lips moving. Then she turns and bears the quick weight of her belly through the bright winter sun, over the ice and mud, into the dark door of her husband's workshop, her hands already reaching for a pencil. For a scrap of paper big enough for just one word.

ENDNOTES

1. Thanks to Nick Flynn, from *The Ticking Is the Bomb* (New York: W. W. Norton, 2010).

2. From the diary of nineteen-year-old Anne Eliza Pleasants Gordon, quoted in Anya Jabour, *Scarlett's Sisters: Young Women in the Old South* (Chapel Hill: University of North Carolina Press, 2007), 184.

3. "She says that . . . she cannot say that . . . she will not say that . . . " Thanks to Anne-Marine Feat for the translation.

4. Charles Bell (1824), quoted in Charles H. Tator and Edward C. Benzel, eds., *Contemporary Management of Spinal Cord Injury: From Impact to Rehabilitation* (Park Ridge, IL: American Association of Neurological Surgeons, 2000). Wallerian degeneration from Michael E. Selzer and Bruce H. Dobkin, *Spinal Cord Injury: A Guide for Patients and Families* (New York: Demos Medical Publishing, 2008).

Among so many others, I found these books helpful: Eugene Genovese, *Roll, Jordan, Roll: The World the Slaves Made* (New York: Vintage, 2011); Elizabeth Fox-Genovese, *Within the Plantation Household: Black and White Women of the Old South* (Chapel Hill: University of North Carolina Press, 1988); James Marten, *The Children's Civil War* (Chapel Hill: University of North Carolina Press, 2000); and Jennifer Ritterhouse, *Growing Up Jim Crow: How Black and White Southern Children Learned Race* (Chapel Hill: University of North Carolina Press, 2006).

CPSIA information can be obtained
at www.ICGtesting.com
Printed in the USA
LVHW111235160619
621371LV00002B/520/P

9 780999 472965